D0982828

IN THE SHADOW OF EVIL

IN THE SHADOW OF EVIL

A DCI Neil Paget Mystery

Frank Smith

severn House

This first world edition published 2012
in Great Britain and in the USA by
SEVERN HOUSE PUBLISHERS LTD of
9–15 High Street, Sutton, Surrey, England, SM1 1DF.

British Library Cataloguing in Publication Data

Smith, Frank, 1927–
  In the shadow of evil.
  1. Paget, Neil (Fictitious character) – Fiction.
  2. Police – Great Britain – Fiction. 3. Detective and
  mystery stories.
  I. Title
  813.5'4-dc23

ISBN-13: 978-0-7278-8152-6 (cased)

Severn House Publishers support The Forest Stewardship Council [FSC],
the leading international forest certification organisation. All our titles that
are printed on Greenpeace-approved FSC-certified paper carry the FSC logo.

Typeset by Palimpsest Book Production Ltd.,
Falkirk, Stirlingshire, Scotland.
Printed and bound in Great Britain by
MPG Books Ltd., Bodmin, Cornwall.

ONE

Thursday, September 8th

Antonia Halliday pushed the rolled-up paper serviette across the table, then withdrew her hand quickly and dropped it into her lap as if to distance herself from the action. 'I know it's only a ring,' she said defensively, 'but honestly, Simon, it's the best I could do. I mean, she does have a lot of jewellery, and she's careless with it, but she's bound to realize that some of it is missing sooner or later. And those *are* diamonds.'

Simon Conroy's dark eyes continued to hold her own as he palmed the serviette and put it in his pocket. 'And stop looking at me like that,' she said petulantly. 'You've no idea what it's like to be stuck out there in that God-forsaken place. It's been eight boring weeks, and—'

'Seven.'

'And five days,' she shot back. Tears of frustration glistened in the corners of her eyes. 'And I'm bloody well fed up with it. It isn't working and I want to go back to London.'

'And live on what?' he asked mildly. 'Remember what it was like before? Remember how you were living? That money belongs to you, Toni. It's yours, you deserve it. A few more weeks and I'm sure your mother will—'

'A few more *weeks*?' The very thought chilled her. 'Impossible!' she said. 'I've tried everything, but every time I think I have her convinced, she starts talking about my settling down with them out there and becoming a real family. God! If she only knew how much I hate that place, and how much I despise her. And then there's Charles. He's always there, hovering in the background like some sort of guardian angel, and I know he's not buying it. It just might work if he weren't there, but he isn't going to budge.'

'I know it's hard, love,' he said soothingly, 'but we knew it would take time. And if it's happy families she wants, then give it to her. You won't have to put up with it for long, and once she loosens the purse strings, you can do what the hell you like.'

Conroy reached across the table, his hand palm upward in a silent invitation for her to put her hand in his. Almost against her will, she slid her hand across the polished wood; their fingers touched. His hand was warm. She looked into his eyes, and suddenly everything she had planned to say melted away. She squeezed her eyes shut. It wasn't fair, but she knew what his response would be, and she couldn't risk losing him. He was her lifeline, and she needed him more than she had ever needed anyone before. She sucked in her breath. Thank God she hadn't told him . . .

She felt the tug of his hand. 'Toni . . .? Are you listening to me?' His voice was sharp. Like that of a teacher she'd once had. Sharp, with a hint of warning.

She opened her eyes. 'Yes, yes, of course, Simon. Sorry. I was just—'

'You've been drinking,' he accused.

'Just one before lunch,' she lied. 'Honestly, Simon, it was just one. You were late and I was afraid you weren't coming . . .' She shrugged an apology.

Conroy released her hand and sat back in his chair. 'Oh, Toni,' he said despairingly. 'I am so disappointed in you. Do you really want to throw everything away for the sake of a few drinks when you know what they do to you? Well, do you?' he prompted harshly when she didn't answer.

Toni bit her lip. If only she could make him understand how hard it was. She shook her head. 'I am trying,' she whispered, 'I really am. It's just . . .'

He sighed heavily. 'I had such faith in you,' he said sorrowfully, 'but perhaps it was too much to ask. I've tried my best to help you, I really have, love, but if you simply can't do it, then there's not much point in carrying on, is there?' He dropped his crumpled serviette on his plate and started to rise.

'No! Don't go, Simon. *Please* don't go.' Panic gripped her. She could hardly breathe. 'I *can* do it, Simon. Honestly, I won't let you down. Please, Simon?'

He pursed his lips, eyes narrowed as he studied her. She forced herself to hold his gaze, afraid that if she so much as blinked he might leave.

'Well,' he said diffidently, settling back in his chair. 'If you *really* think you can; if you're sure . . .?'

She nodded vigorously and allowed herself to breathe again. 'I am, Simon, I am sure. I won't let you down. I swear. It's just that it's taking so long and I feel so alone out there.' She knew she was babbling but she couldn't seem to stop. 'If it wasn't for our time together I don't know what – are you sure you couldn't make it *every* week? Two weeks is such a long time, and I do miss you, Simon. It would mean so much to me if—' She stopped. The lines around his eyes and mouth were beginning to set in a mould she'd seen before. 'Sorry,' she said hastily. 'I know you're busy; I didn't mean to upset . . . I shouldn't have asked. Let's just enjoy the afternoon.'

'Not today, I'm afraid,' he said perfunctorily. 'I can't stay. I have other commitments, so I'll give you this now.' He took a slim brown envelope from his jacket pocket and slid it across the table. 'But remember,' he warned. 'It has to last you for two weeks, so use it sparingly.'

Toni picked up the envelope. Her eyes widened in alarm. 'You can't be serious,' she breathed. 'There's hardly anything in here. I can't . . .' Her eyes filled with tears. 'For God's sake, Simon,' she pleaded. 'The ring is worth a lot more than that! I *need* it!'

He shook his head. 'Think of it as a reminder,' he said as he pushed his chair back and stood up. 'A reminder of what it will be like if you can't afford it. It will help you focus.' He looked at his watch. 'Now, I do have to go.'

'But what about this afternoon?'

'Sorry, love, I told you, I have commitments here until the evening, and I have to get back to London tonight.'

'But . . .' she swallowed hard, 'I've booked the room.'

'Then you'll just have to unbook it, won't you, love?' He took out his wallet and laid several notes beside his plate, then came around the table to put his hands on her shoulders. She reached up to clutch them tightly, bending her head back to look up at him. 'Please, Simon,' she whispered, 'if it's only for an hour I'll understand.'

'There's nothing I'd like better, love, you know that,' he said, withdrawing his hands. 'But I have to go.' He bent to brush her hair with his lips. 'I'll ring you tomorrow.'

Toni pushed back her chair. 'At least I can come with you to the . . .' she began, only to see he was already halfway to the door.

She sank back in her seat. There were tears in her eyes as she watched him go. Perhaps she should have told him. It might have made a difference. But deep down she had the feeling that it would only have made matters worse. You never knew with Simon. Toni brushed the tears from her eyes and sighed heavily as she slipped the envelope into her handbag, along with the two peppermints that came with the bill. She looked at the bill, then counted the money he'd left behind. It was too much. She took out five pounds and put the rest back beside his plate. It wouldn't leave much of a tip, but why should the waitress have it anyway? The service hadn't been that good.

Toni looked at her watch. So what to do for the rest of the afternoon? There was nothing she wanted to do in town, so she might as well go back home. 'Home,' she mouthed bitterly as she pushed her chair back and stood up. 'Not for long if I have anything to do with it.'

She started toward the door, then stopped. On the other hand, why should she go back before she had to? The bar was open, and she needed to try to relax. Just one, she told herself, mindful of Simon's warning. She'd sit in the lounge and make it last. Just one wouldn't hurt.

Dead Man's Hill the locals called it, and with good reason, although in fact two of the people who had died there in recent times were women. Steep and narrow as it wound its tortuous way from the top of the escarpment into the valley below, Dead Man's Hill had killed five people in recent times. At least, that was the way the residents of Clunbridge saw it, but police and coroners' reports were more pragmatic, referring to the events leading to the tragic deaths as driving without due care and attention, failure to take road conditions into account, and, in one case, involving an ancient lorry stacked high with bales of hay, overloading, and faulty brakes.

But the locals still blamed the hill.

Toni Halliday rarely mixed with the locals, so she wasn't aware

of the hill's reputation when she started down on Thursday afternoon. Not that she would have paid any attention to warnings in
any case. To her it was just another silly little country road built
for wagons, not for cars. Grassy, bramble-covered banks rose
high on both sides. Visibility was limited to the next sharp bend,
but that didn't slow her down. Tyres screamed in protest as she
flung the car around each corner, scraping against the bank before
hitting the next curve and scraping the other side. So who cared?
It wasn't her car, and it wasn't as if her mother couldn't afford
to have the damned thing repainted. White was such a sick colour
anyway.

The car shot round the last bend and Toni hunched down
behind the wheel as if taking aim at the narrow bridge that would
take her into Clunbridge. She grinned as a man scuttled to safety
as she thundered through. She laughed out loud and turned to
wave as she went by . . .

'Oh, Christ!'

She grabbed the wheel and swung it hard, jabbing at the brake
pedal as she tried to make the right-angled turn into Silver Street.
The car jumped the kerb, trailing lines of smoking rubber down
the pavement beside the high brick wall. Sparks flew as the car
bounced off the wall and straightened out and began to slow.
Toni threw back her head and breathed a sigh of relief. 'Made
it!' she whispered shakily.

Which may have been why she didn't see the child come out
of the gate and stop, eyes wide with dawning terror as the car
bore down on her.

Charles Bromley, MB, ChB, FRCS, and local Justice of the Peace,
rolled out another blueprint on the desk and put paperweights
on each corner. Tom Houghton would be coming in a week
tomorrow to shore up the kitchen garden wall and put new foot-
ings in where it joined the house. 'Underground stream, that's
what it'll be,' Houghton had declared, but Charles had scoffed
at the idea, pointing out that the manor had been there for close
to four hundred years, and if there had been any underground
streams, they would have known long before now.

Houghton hadn't argued, but had set his son to digging. He
found water four feet down.

'We've seen a lot of that round here,' Houghton told him. 'Started with that earthquake at Bishop's Castle back in nineteen ninety. Shifted some of the underground streams, it did, but the only time you find out is when something like this wall starts leaning. And I don't suppose that jolt they had in Melton Mowbray in two thousand and one did us a lot of good either. Mind you, it wasn't as big, but they're funny things, earthquakes. No telling what's going on right under your feet.'

No telling indeed, and the idea that there could be more structural damage to the manor had worried Charles. But Houghton had brought in a water diviner, and it seemed that the stream had merely looped beneath the wall, and posed no threat to the house or the rest of the outbuildings. 'It'll take a bit of work,' Houghton told him, 'but it can be diverted, and we'll see if we can straighten that wall up at the same time.'

'And thank God for that,' Charles muttered as he continued to look at the blueprint. But at what cost? It seemed there was always something to get in the way of completing the work that still needed to be done on the chapel. It was taking so much longer than he'd thought it would because of things like this, and there were days when he felt like giving up, abandoning the whole project. But then, as always, he reminded himself that he'd made a solemn promise, and he intended to carry it out, no matter how long it might take or how much it might cost.

The crunch of tyres on the gravelled driveway leading to the stables behind the house drew him to the window. A car he didn't recognize, sporty with lots of chrome, slid past his line of vision and stopped just past the side door. The driver clambered out.

Charles didn't recognize the man at first. With his head down and holding a broad-brimmed hat in place against a sudden squall of wind-driven rain, it was only when he seemed to sense he was being watched that he looked up and waved.

Paul? What the devil was he doing here? Charles watched with narrowed eyes as his brother made a dash for the side door. He crossed the room to the door and went out into the hall to wait for his brother to appear.

The door at the end of the hall opened, and a somewhat dishevelled Paul Bromley, minus hat and coat, came through. Younger than Charles by four years, he was a slimmer version of his brother. Tall, lean, dark-haired – compared to Charles, who was heavy set and grey – Paul, at forty-seven still had those boyish looks that seemed to attract women of all ages, and Charles couldn't help wondering if this unexpected visit had anything to do with yet another of his brother's disastrous flirtations.

'Damned strange weather for September,' Paul said as he ran his fingers through his hair. 'Cold and wet when I left London, and then the sun came out somewhere around Oxford, and it was as hot as blazes until I hit this lot a couple of miles back. Anyway, enough of that. How are you Charles? Good to see you again. You're looking chipper.'

'I'm well enough,' said Charles cautiously as he turned to lead the way into the study. 'How are things in London? You should be doing all right with the price property is fetching there these days. Care for a sherry after your long drive?'

'I'd prefer some of that twelve-year-old Glenlossie you keep tucked away at the back of the cabinet,' Paul said as he bent to study the blueprints spread out on the desk. 'Still at it, then?' he observed as Charles took out a bottle and a single glass. 'Still bent on rebuilding the chapel? Why don't you pull the damned thing down and be done with it? It never did look right when it was first built, and it's not as if you'll ever use it if you do get it done. In fact, the thing's a bloody great waste of time and money if you ask me.'

The lines around his brother's mouth tightened as he poured the whisky and handed the glass to Paul. 'I don't recall asking you,' he said. 'You've never understood, have you, Paul? I don't have a choice; I made a promise to our grandmother, and I intend to keep it. The work has to be done.'

Paul made a face as he turned away. There was nothing to be gained by going over old ground again. Charles had his own agenda, and there was nothing he could say that would change his brother's mind. He raised his glass against the light from the window. 'Lovely colour,' he said appreciatively, and downed half of it in one gulp. He grinned as he saw his brother wince. 'Good stuff, Charles,' he said. 'Gets the old blood circulating. Why don't you have some yourself?'

'I try to keep it for special occasions,' Charles said tersely, 'so go easy on it, will you? He waved a hand in the general direction of the two leather chairs beside the window. 'So, what brings you down here at this time of year? I would have thought this would be a busy season for you.'

'It is,' said Paul absently as he twirled the glass in his fingers. His face became serious. 'The fact is, I need a loan,' he said baldly, then held up his hand as he saw the look on his brother's face. 'I know what you're going to say, but just hear me out, Charles. It's not like the other times. This really is a loan. I'll be able to pay you back in a few weeks, a couple of months at the outside, but I do need it now to tide me over. As I said, it will only be for a short time, I promise. I'll pay you back.'

Charles let out a long sigh and shook his head. 'The same way you've paid me back before?' he said. 'Oh, no, Paul, I don't think so. I'm not lending you a penny. The well's gone dry as far as you're concerned.'

Paul eyed his brother stonily over the top of his glass. 'I could go to prison if I don't have the money by mid-week,' he said tightly. 'Is that what you want?' He swallowed the rest of his drink.

Charles shook his head. 'You can cut the dramatics, Paul. You seem to forget we've been through this many times, and I'm not falling for yet another of your stories.'

'I mean it, Charles.' Paul leaned forward and spoke earnestly. 'Look, I know I've been a damned fool before, and I don't blame you for not trusting me, but it *is* serious this time, and it's not my fault.' He hesitated for a moment, then drew a deep breath and plunged ahead. 'There was this opportunity to go into a joint venture with a friend – well, a friend of a friend, actually – and it was just too good an opportunity to miss. But I didn't have quite enough money, so I – well I borrowed it from the firm.' He hurried on as he saw the look on his brother's face. 'Believe me, Charles, it *is* going to pay off. It's just that it's taking longer than expected. A few more weeks, perhaps, but it *will* pay off, and when it does you'll get your money back with interest, and we'll both be laughing. In fact it's more of an investment than a loan.'

Charles eyed his brother coldly. 'You *borrowed* money from the firm you work for?' he said icily. 'I don't believe that story for a minute.'

'It's true! The point is, I thought I had plenty of time to put it back and no one would have been the wiser, but I just found out we're to have an audit next week. We had one less than a year ago so that was the last thing I expected when I took the money, but we've changed accounting firms, and they insist on doing a complete audit before they take over.'

'As they should,' Charles said coldly, 'assuming that what you say is true. But it isn't, is it, Paul? You don't take a large sum of money out of a firm such as the one you work for, then casually slip it back again, so I'm assuming it's gambling again, and they want their money. But this time you are on your own, Paul. I mean it. You got yourself into this mess and you can dig yourself out or take the consequences.' He rose to his feet. 'You're welcome to stay on for the weekend, of course, but I mean what I say. You will get no more money from me, and that's final.'

Paul scrambled to his feet. 'Take the consequences?' he exclaimed. 'That's all very well for you to say, but I'm telling the truth; I *did* borrow it from the firm and I *could* go to prison. Is that what you want? The Bromley name dragged through the mud . . . again?'

Charles eyed his brother coldly. 'Don't you *dare* try using that argument to cover your own folly,' he said. 'I don't believe your story, and I'm not going to lend you any money, and there is nothing you can do or say that will change my mind. So find another way. You could start by selling that fancy car out there.'

Paul shook his head impatiently. 'It's not mine. It belongs to a friend. I sold mine last week, so you have to help me, Charles. I need at least twenty thousand pounds by next Tuesday.'

Charles stared at his brother. 'At *least* twenty thousand pounds?' he challenged. 'For God's sake, Paul, how much is this debt of yours?'

Paul grimaced guiltily. 'Close to forty grand,' he muttered almost inaudibly. 'But I have managed to raise roughly half of it, so all I need from you is twenty, although, to be honest, twenty-five would be better.'

'To be *honest?*' Charles echoed contemptuously. 'I don't think you know the meaning of that word, Paul, and I meant what I said. You're wasting your breath, because I couldn't lend you the money even if I wanted to. I don't have it. In fact it looks as if

I will have to sell the land next to top farm if I'm to keep things going, so don't come asking me for money.'

'You're selling . . .?' Paul rolled his eyes heavenward and shook his head in despair. 'To pour more money into this place,' he said scathingly. 'More good money after bad.' He looked around. 'It's a bloody mausoleum, for Christ's sake. It's a bottom-less pit and it isn't worth it. The maintenance alone . . . the heating . . . Where has all the money gone, Charles? You got God knows how much money when Helen died. Are you telling me that's gone as well?' His eyes narrowed. 'Don't tell me that you're going through Margaret's money as well?'

'Of course not, and I wouldn't take it if she offered it. This house, this estate is my responsibility and mine alone, as you well know. As far as your problems are concerned, it might be better if you did spend some time in jail. It might jolt a little sense into your head.'

'But—'

The sound of the telephone on the desk interrupted whatever Paul was about to say, but when Charles moved to pick it up, Paul grabbed his arm. 'Never mind the bloody phone,' he grated. 'I'm telling you, Charles, I have to have that money.'

Charles shook his brother's hand off and picked up the phone.

Paul stalked to the cabinet, grabbed the bottle and poured himself another drink. Grim-faced, he turned to renew the argument as Charles put the phone down, but something in his brother's eyes stopped him.

'I have to go,' Charles said. 'That was Sergeant Maddox in Clunbridge. He says Toni was involved in an accident. She'd been drinking, lost control of the car and hit a child. The child has been taken to hospital in serious condition and may not live. Maddox says Toni will be charged, but she refuses to talk to anyone unless I'm there with her.'

'Toni? She's here?'

'She's been living here for the past few weeks,' Charles said as he moved toward the door.

'Good God! And she actually asked for you? Not Margaret? And you're going?'

'I don't think I have much choice, under the circumstances,

but I suspect the only reason she is asking for me is because she thinks I may have some influence with the police.'

Paul gave a grudging nod. 'I suppose you must,' he said, 'but we do have to talk about this as soon as you get back, because I must have—'

Charles swung round to face his brother. 'You still don't understand, do you, Paul?' he said harshly. 'This conversation is over. You are on your own. You are not getting any more money from me, not now, not ever. Understand? And if you intend to stay, you'd better tell Mrs Lodge, so she knows how many there will be for dinner.'

Paul Bromley's eyes were like stones as they followed his brother's retreating figure down the hall. He could feel a cold, hard knot forming in the pit of his stomach. He'd been so sure that Charles would cave; he'd always come through before, but there was something different about his brother this time. Something . . . He raised the glass to his lips, then tipped his head back and drained it.

Neither of them spoke as they made their way to the car. Toni shrugged off Charles's guiding hand as she got in and slumped down in her seat. He closed the door, then walked around and got in the other side.

'All right, Toni, you're out, at least for tonight,' he said quietly. 'Though why Sergeant Maddox agreed to release you into my custody, considering your condition and your performance in there, I don't know. Do you have *any* idea how much trouble you're in? Tracy Nash may die because of your stupidity. Don't you have *any* feelings for her? Or for her parents?'

Toni shivered and wrapped her arms around herself. 'Of course I do,' she said sulkily. 'But it was an accident. The accelerator jammed.'

It was all he could do to hold his anger in. 'Accident?' he said thinly. 'With a blood-alcohol level more than three times the legal limit? The police have an eye-witness who is prepared to swear that you were going far too fast when you came across the bridge and tried to make the turn into Silver Street, and the damage to your mother's car will bear that out. Do you realize that you could be charged under Section Three A of the Road

Traffic Act Nineteen Ninety-Eight? Causing death by careless driving while under the influence of drink or drugs?'

Toni rolled her eyes as she looked away. Trust Charles to quote chapter and verse, but that was the least of her worries right now, because all she could think about was the loss of the envelope Simon had given her. She'd had the presence of mind to take it from her handbag and slide it under the seat before the police arrived on the scene, but it hadn't occurred to her that they would impound the car. She couldn't go on, not after this. She would have to ring Simon. Business or not, he would have to help her.

'Are you listening to me, Toni?'

'I *said* I was sorry,' she said truculently. 'What else can I say, for Christ's sake! You make it sound as if I hit the kid deliberately. All right, so maybe I was going a bit too fast; maybe I did have a bit too much to drink, but with good reason after . . .'

She stopped herself just in time.

'After what?' Charles demanded as he started the car. 'Because somehow I don't think saying you're sorry will satisfy the child's parents. And I don't know how I'm going to break this to your mother. As for your hopes of persuading her to release the money your father left in trust for you, I think you can kiss that goodbye – unless it's used for your defence.'

'*You* don't have to tell my mother anything,' the girl shot back. 'That's between me and her. And as for the trust, it's none of your business.'

Charles bit back the reply that rose to his lips. There was no point in arguing with Toni. There never had been. As for how Margaret would feel about all this, he hated to think. She still clung to the illusion that her daughter was trying hard to change and was truly sorry for the damage she'd done to both their lives.

Charles had never believed in Toni's supposed change of heart. Admittedly, she'd put on quite a show at the beginning, and Margaret so desperately wanted to believe that her daughter had come to her senses and wanted to make amends for what she'd done, but he wasn't convinced. He'd been tempted to speak out many times, but remained silent, because he knew that Toni would be quick to point out that he was trying to drive a wedge between her and her mother, and it proved that she'd been right about his motives all along.

He cast a sidelong a glance at her. She was a pretty girl – or she would be if she would wipe that sullen look off her face. Twenty-three years old. Good features framed by auburn hair, wide-set eyes, straight nose. Took after her mother there, but the stubborn set of the jaw must come from her father's side, as did her mercurial disposition.

Toni sensed his eyes on her and turned to face him. 'I meant it when I said I'll tell mother,' she said sharply. 'I don't want you to tell her. Just leave me alone when we get there and let me clean up first. Then I'll tell her. OK?'

Charles drew in a long breath and let it out again. 'Very well,' he said, 'but just be careful how you—'

'I don't need any lessons from you about how to talk to my own mother, thank you very much,' she cut in sharply. 'So you can forget the lecture, Charles.'

Grim-faced, he concentrated on his driving. There were days when he could have cheerfully strangled Toni Halliday, and this was definitely one of them.

They continued the drive in silence. A blustery wind and dark, fast-moving clouds threatened more rain, but the sun broke through just as they reached the manor. Charles had intended to drive around the side of the house to let Toni out at the side door so she could go up to her room by the back stairs, but when he saw the black BMW sitting beside the front door, he changed his mind.

'I hope this doesn't mean your mother has had another of her bad turns,' he said anxiously as he pulled in beside the other car.

Toni gave a derisive snort. 'If she ever had one at all,' she said callously. 'More likely it's one of Dr Lockwood's "just popped in to see how you are" visits. A very attentive chap is Dr Lockwood, especially to my mother. Or perhaps you hadn't noticed, Charles?' She cast a sly glance in his direction. 'Funny, but I can't think of any other doctor who makes house calls without actually being called, can you?'

'You don't know what you're talking about,' he said brusquely. 'Steven Lockwood is a dedicated doctor, as was his father before him, and I value his opinion. He is very concerned about your mother, as am I. As you should be, if you actually cared,' he added savagely.

'Oh, but I do care, Charles,' she said as they got out of the car. 'And I don't doubt for a minute that he's dedicated. In fact, I'm told that all his women patients really like him, and I must admit he's not bad looking for a man in his forties. Considering what else is on offer around here, he can take my temperature anytime.'

'Now you are being ridiculous,' he said. 'The Lockwoods have been friends of the family for years, and Steven is . . .' He stopped in mid-sentence. Toni had walked away and was halfway up the steps to the front door.

Charles stood there for a moment, breathing deeply. Something was going to have to be done about that girl, because they couldn't go on like this. She would appear in court tomorrow, but he didn't doubt for a moment that she'd be bailed, and that could mean they would be stuck with her for months before her case came to trial. He brushed past Lockwood's car, then stopped to look at it. Steven was dedicated; he cared for his patients – and not just the female ones as Toni had implied. That was ridiculous. Even so, Toni's words lingered inside his head as he made his way up the steps and entered the house.

TWO

B ob Thorsen rose stiffly from his chair and switched off the television set. He tamped fresh tobacco into the bowl of his pipe and tried to tell himself again that there was nothing to be concerned about, but the sound of rain beating hard against the window did nothing to allay his fears. It wasn't like the major to be this late, no matter what the weather, and he'd never keep old Toby out in weather like this if he could help it.

On the other hand, he was more than likely tucked up nice and snug with that woman in her caravan at the top end of the lane, while he waited out the storm. But he might at least have phoned. Thorsen would have phoned himself, but her number was ex-directory. A tight smile flickered across his craggy features. Be a bit of a shock for the major if he did get through, because he was quite sure that the man thought no one knew about his visits to the caravan.

He returned to his chair and picked up the paper and tried to read, but he couldn't settle. Almost ten thirty. The major would know that he'd be worried about Toby, so why hadn't he rung? Besides, he was never this late on a Thursday.

The telephone rang. Ah! That would be him now. Thorsen heaved himself out of the chair and picked up the phone.

'Mr Thorsen?'

He recognized the voice immediately. The high, querulous tones, reflecting pain rather than age, belonged to Harriett Farnsworth, the major's wife.

'That's right, Mrs Farnsworth.'

'I'm sorry to trouble you, but I wondered if the major is with you?'

She always called him that. Never by his name. 'Sorry, Mrs Farnsworth,' he replied, 'but I haven't seen him since he left here with Toby just after seven.'

'He's terribly late, don't you think, Mr Thorsen?'

'I was just thinking the same thing myself, Mrs Farnsworth. But I'm sure he's all right. He's probably taken shelter somewhere and he'll be along as soon as the rain eases off.'

'There's only the manor, Mr Thorsen, but I doubt if he'd have stopped there. Besides, it's Thursday, and he never misses *Days of Glory*. It's not like him at all, is it, Mr Thorsen?'

She was expressing nothing more than his own uneasy feelings. The major was a man of rigid habits.

'They said on the wireless that the storm had brought trees down,' she went on. 'They didn't say where, but . . .'

Thorsen sighed. 'Perhaps I should take a walk up the hill,' he said grudgingly. 'I suppose he could have taken shelter in the stables behind the manor.'

'Oh, would you, Mr Thorsen?' There was a world of relief in her voice. 'I'd be terribly grateful.'

Thorsen hung up the phone and began to don his rain gear. He poked a blackened finger into the bowl of his pipe to make sure that it was out before laying it aside, then picked up a heavy torch and opened the door. The wind tugged at it as he pulled it closed before making his way down the short path, where he stopped to make sure the wooden gate was firmly latched before setting off up Manor Lane.

Thorsen had walked the lane so often that he hardly needed a torch to tell him where he was. Even so, it was reassuring to see the beam pick out the rear entrance to the stable yard behind the manor. He plodded on until he came abreast of a wooden door set in the wall. On the other side of the wall, across the gravelled drive that led to the stables, was the side entrance to the manor.

A light over the door came on as he approached. It was operated by a sensor that detected movement, and the pool of light was just enough to illuminate the wooden gateposts marking the beginning of the gravelled track on the far side of the lane. But the moment he moved toward them and started up the track, the light went out, and he was left in total darkness.

The old man paused, waiting for his eyes to adjust to the less powerful beam of the torch before moving on. Originally, the short track had led only as far as the old hay barn, but it had been widened and extended by some two hundred yards five years ago, with the intention of turning the top end of the field into a caravan site.

But it had proved to be too isolated, and the only caravan up there now was that of Vanessa King, an artist and free spirit, who seemed to enjoy the solitude, although Thorsen had noticed that she did have a number of male friends, who visited her from time to time.

He paused to brush the rain from his face, and was about to move forward when he heard a sound. He stopped, cupping his ear against the wind. The sound came again, soft, then suddenly sharp and unmistakable. 'Toby?' The beam of the torch probed the darkness. He called again, and the dog answered with a short, sharp bark.

'Come on, then, boy,' he coaxed as he made his way forward, swinging the beam from side to side. 'Toby!' he called again impatiently. 'Stop messing me about. Where are you, boy?'

Toby barked again, then suddenly Thorsen saw the flash of white on Toby's face as the dog came rushing at him. 'Toby? What . . .?' he began, but the dog dashed around his legs, then shot off into the darkness. 'Toby!' he called, angry now as he lumbered after the dog. 'What do you think you're doing? Where's the maj . . .? Oh, Jesus Murphy!'

Major Farnsworth, splattered with mud and gravel, lay on his side next to a rusted water tank half-buried in the weeds. There were deep gouges in the mud beside him where a car or truck had spun its wheels before snaking into the rutted track. Thorsen knelt in the mud, feeling for a pulse in the side of the neck as he'd seen them do on television, but his fingers were cold and wet and he couldn't feel a thing. He fumbled for the major's wrist to try again, then shone the light on the major's face and called loudly to him several times, but there was no response.

He clambered to his feet. He needed help. He hoped that Mr Bromley hadn't gone to bed. He turned to go, but Toby ran ahead, then turned to face him crouching low, teeth bared, barring his way. Thorsen started forward, but Toby was there before him, growling.

'Toby! Don't be so bloody daft,' the old man scolded as he attempted to go round the dog, but Toby circled his feet so closely that Thorsen was forced to stop.

'For God's sake, what's got into you?' he demanded. 'I'm going for help, so get out of the way.' But every time Thorsen moved, the dog was there in front of him. The old man had watched Toby do the same thing hundreds of times before, but that was out there on the hillside when the dog was herding sheep.

He stood still. 'What is it, boy?' he asked in a gentler tone, knowing that something must be wrong for the dog to be acting the way he was. Perhaps Toby had been hurt as well. 'Come here, boy,' he said softly, stretching out his hand, but Toby jumped away and ran toward the barn. When Thorsen didn't follow, the dog returned, barking even more shrilly than before, then ran off in the same direction. Shaking his head, Thorsen followed the dog by the light of the torch, and saw that the small door in the side of the barn was open. Torn between the need to get help for the major as soon as possible, but curious about Toby's strange behaviour, Thorsen moved toward the dog.

Toby stood beside the door until Thorsen reached down to take his collar, then ducked away and disappeared inside the barn. 'For pity's sake, Toby!' Thorsen grumbled as he pushed the door wider and went inside. Toby stood facing him in the middle of the floor, head up, tail wagging in much the same stance as when he was waiting for someone to throw his ball. But there was something behind him. A shadow beyond the beam of the torch? No, not a shadow, something more substantial.

Thorsen reached along the wall and found the light switch. Toby settled on the floor as if to say he'd done his job and now it was up to Thorsen to take over.

The body, shapeless in dishevelled clothing, lay on its side in a pool of blood, congealed, and looking almost black beneath the dust-encrusted bulb dangling on a length of flex directly overhead. The head was facing him, the eyes wide open, staring, but the features were distorted by dried rivulets of blood and matted hair. Even so, there was no doubt in Thorsen's mind as to who it was. There was only one person around these parts who had auburn hair like that.

THREE

Detective Chief Inspector Neil Paget was awake when the bedside phone rang. He snatched it up, hoping to keep it from waking Grace, but she stirred beside him and said, 'It's all right. I'm not asleep.'

Paget put the phone to his ear and said, 'Hello?'

'Paget?'

'Sir . . .? Suddenly he was wide awake.

'I've just had a call from the chief constable,' said Chief Superintendent Morgan Brock. 'We have a suspicious death at Bromley Manor over Clunbridge way. Two people involved, one dead, one seriously injured. The dead woman is Mr Bromley's stepdaughter. The other, a Major somebody-or-other, is badly injured. Better get over there right away. I had Control call DS Tregalles, and SOCO, so there's no need to waste time ringing them. And I'm sure I don't need to tell you to tread carefully on this one, Paget, because the chief constable will be monitoring the investigation personally.'

Paget slid out of bed. 'Is there something I should . . .?' he began, only to find that Brock was gone and he was talking into a dead phone.

'Trouble?' asked Grace as she raised herself up on one elbow. 'Where do you have to go?'

'A girl's been killed at a place called Bromley Manor near Clunbridge. Sounds as if someone out there must have some clout if they called the chief constable directly. You ever heard of it?'

'The name sounds familiar, but I can't think why, exactly. But do be careful, Neil. It's a rotten night, and you'll be driving across country.'

'Good thing you're not on call this week,' he said as he began to dress. 'Brock's called your lot out already.'

Grace pulled the covers up around her, and smiled wickedly as she blew him a kiss. 'I'll think of you out there as I snuggle down in this nice warm bed,' she said. 'Just turn off the alarm before you go.'

Paget waited until he was on the road before calling Control for directions to Bromley Manor. 'It's a big old place off to the right about a mile and a half out of Clunbridge on the road to Selbury Cross,' Control told him. 'PC Hurley will meet you there. He says to go past the entrance to the manor, then turn sharp right down Manor Lane. He'll have his flashers on, so you shouldn't have any trouble.'

In the event, not only was the police car there, but the ambulance and several other cars and vans were clogging the lane, and he only just managed to squeeze his car in behind the police car. A uniformed constable got out of one of the cars to greet him. 'PC Hurley, sir,' he said. 'DS Tregalles is inside with Doctor Starkie, and SOCO should be here any minute now.'

'Right. So, what have we got, then, Constable?'

'Best get in the car, if you don't mind, sir,' Hurley suggested, opening the door. 'It's a bugger trying to keep the notebook dry.'

The two men got in and Hurley switched on the overhead light. 'There are two victims,' he said. 'One is a young woman, a Miss Antonia Halliday, twenty-three years old. She's in the barn, and she was dead when we arrived. Not much doubt about that. Killed with a sickle, she was. I didn't touch it; it's still there

on the floor. All but took her head clean off.' He took a deep
breath. 'Believe me, sir, it is not a pretty sight, as you'll see for
yourself.'

'A sickle?' Paget echoed. 'Who uses a sickle these days?'

'It's an old one,' Hurley told him. 'Thorsen, the man who
found her, told me it's been hanging on the wall for years. It's
a rusty old thing, but the edge of the blade is still very sharp by
the look of it.'

'And the other victim?'

'Major Farnsworth – fiftyish I should think, but that's just a
guess. He was unconscious and bleeding from the head when
we arrived. He suffered other injuries; nothing broken as far as
the medics could tell, but they reckoned he'd been lying there
for some time, and his breathing wasn't all that good. One of
them said it looked as if he'd been hit by a car.'

'Who is this man who found them?'

'A chap named Thorsen, sir. He's the gardener and general
handyman from the manor. Lives in one of the cottages just down
the lane. Pretty shaken up, he was, too, poor old chap. Says he
was out looking for the major. The major's wife became worried
when he didn't come home after taking Thorsen's dog for a walk
earlier in the evening, so Thorsen came up the lane to look for
him.' Hurley pointed to a gravelled track that was barely visible
in the headlights through the rain. 'That's it over there, sir. Seems
like the dog stayed with the major after he was knocked down,
and it was the sound of the dog barking that led Thorsen to him.
I've put markers round the spot.'

'But the young woman is in the barn, you say, so what prompted
Thorsen to go inside?'

'He says it was the dog again. Thorsen says he was about to
go to the manor for help when the dog more or less herded him
back to the barn. He says the door was open, and he followed
the dog inside and found Miss Halliday. That's when he went
up to the house and got Mr Bromley.'

'Bromley,' Paget repeated. 'Should I know that name?' he
asked Hurley. 'It sounds familiar.'

'Probably because he's a local magistrate, as well as being a
brain surgeon, sir. Well, he was when he was in London – come
to that, I suppose he still is, except he doesn't operate in London

anymore. And he wants to talk to you as soon as possible. Says he has information regarding who might have done this.'

'Does he? In that case we'd better get on with it. Where is he now? And where is this man, Thorsen?'

'They're both up at the house. My partner, PC Renshaw, is with them. Quite a shock for the old man, finding a body like that, and for Mr Bromley, 'specially as it's his stepdaughter, so I thought it best to get them back inside.'

'Good idea,' Paget agreed. 'So let's take a look before we go up to the house.'

He suited up in the car. It was no easy task, even when Hurley got out to give him more room, but it was better than getting soaked in the process.

Even if they'd had more light, there was little to be seen where the major had been found, but the area had been marked off and would be examined thoroughly by SOCO later on.

They moved on to the barn and went inside.

DS Tregalles, who had been talking to Reg Starkie, the pathologist, came to greet Paget. 'Nasty one, boss,' he said quietly. 'The victim lost a lot of blood, but Starkie says it could still have taken the girl several minutes to die. Come and take a look for yourself, but watch your step. Looks like the killer was looking for something in her suitcase and carryall.'

The lights were on but they were no match for the sheer size of the cavernous building, and Paget found himself having to pick his way gingerly through clothing and shoes and jars of cosmetics littering the floor to where Starkie was packing instruments away.

'Paget,' Starkie greeted him tersely. 'Or should I be addressing you as "Superintendent" Paget now? I hear you've taken over from Alcott.'

'Acting unpaid until they find a replacement,' Paget told him.

Starkie grunted. 'They shouldn't have to look far,' he growled. 'So good luck to you.'

'Well, thank you for the vote of confidence, Reg,' Paget said. 'I appreciate it.' He took a deep breath to calm the tremors in his stomach as he bent to examine the body at his feet. 'Meanwhile, what can you tell me about this young woman?'

'Not much you can't see for yourself,' the doctor told him. 'She was attacked from behind and to one side. There is no indication that she tried to defend herself. The blade entered just below her right ear, clipping the jawbone and severing the carotid artery, the external jugular, and the tip of her chin. And she was finished off with a blow to the head with the same sharp-pointed instrument.' He pointed to the sickle beside the body.

Antonia Halliday lay partly on her left side. One arm lay straight out as if pointing to something in the distance, while the other was tucked beneath her. She wore a light jacket over a denim shirt, jeans, and trainers, and every pocket was turned inside out.

'Thorsen told me they were like that when he found her,' Tregalles said. 'Obviously, the killer was looking for something, but I don't think he found it, because every single thing has been taken out of the suitcase and the carryall. Even the lining's been pulled out, and every jar has been opened, so whatever he was looking for was small. So, the questions I have are: Why was she here in the barn? Where was she going? Why was she killed, and what was her killer looking for?'

'All very good questions,' Paget agreed as he looked around. Whatever the original purpose of the barn had been, it now seemed to be a catch-all for everything from an assortment of rusting farm machinery – including a tractor that looked as if it hadn't moved from that spot in years – to odd bits and pieces of furniture, an upright piano missing a top, canvas awnings, lawn chairs, assorted bits of wood and metal, and several tyres.

Paget turned to Starkie. 'What can you tell me about the time of death?' he asked.

'She's not been dead long. Two to four hours ago at most. You won't go far wrong if you assume she died between eight and ten this evening.'

They heard the sound of several vehicles arriving. 'That'll be SOCO,' said Hurley, and went out to meet them. Paget moved to the door to watch as the forensic team, led by the Scenes-of-Crime Officer, Inspector Charlie Dobbs, began setting up portable lights in the lane to illuminate the area where Farnsworth had been found. Dobbs, a tall, thin, gaunt-looking man, saw Paget standing in the doorway and came over to look inside. 'Don't know that we can do much outside in all this rain,' he said dolefully. 'So I think I'll tell them to start in here.' He sneezed. 'Summer cold,' he explained, and sneezed again. 'Tried everything, but the bloody thing won't shift.' He pulled out a large handkerchief and blew his nose. 'And the first thing we're going to need is a lot more light than this,' he continued as he looked around. 'Good job we have our own generator.'

Hurley appeared at Paget's elbow. 'Chief Super's here, sir,' he said in a hoarse whisper. It was more of a question than a statement, as if he couldn't quite believe what he was saying. Paget found it hard to believe as well. He'd never known Brock to visit a crime scene before. In fact he had never seen Brock anywhere except in his office surrounded by his beloved charts and graphs.

Both Hurley and Tregalles melted into the background as Brock appeared. The chief superintendent was holding an umbrella above his head with one hand, while the other was waving about in an attempt to maintain his balance as he picked his way fussily across the rain-soaked grass. 'Well, Paget?' he said sharply as he shook out his umbrella and joined the DCI in the shelter of the doorway. 'What are you doing out here? Mr Bromley tells me you haven't been in to see him yet, and he distinctly told one of the constables to tell you that that he knows who killed his stepdaughter. Some fellow by the name of Nash, who broke into the house and threatened Miss Holliday while they were at dinner.'

'Halliday,' Paget corrected gently. 'And Constable Hurley did relay the message, but I'm sure you will appreciate that I can hardly talk to Mr Bromley before I've looked at the crime scene and discussed the manner of death with the pathologist. In fact, sir, now that you're here, I'd like you to see the body for yourself. The manner of death is somewhat unusual, and I'm sure Dr Starkie would be pleased to explain . . .'

But Brock was shaking his head and grimacing as he looked toward the body on the floor. 'No, no, that won't be necessary,' he said quickly. 'Time is getting on and the chief constable will be awaiting my report, so I must get back. And, as I said, Mr Bromley is expecting you, so I won't take up any more of your time, Chief Inspector. I've assured him that, once he's given you the information on this fellow, Nash, you will be taking action immediately to bring him in. So the sooner you get over there the better, and I can tell Sir Robert that you have things well in hand.'

Brock moved to the open door and was about to open his umbrella, when he paused. 'You *do* realize who you're dealing with, don't you, Paget?' he asked. 'I mean you do *know* who Charles Bromley is?'

'I'm told he's a surgeon and a local magistrate,' Paget replied, 'but I don't think our paths have ever crossed.'

Brock eyed Paget suspiciously as if he thought the chief inspector was being deliberately obtuse. 'For your information,' he said coldly, 'Mr Charles Bromley is one of this country's top neuro-surgeons. At least he was before he retired after that unfortunate business with Halliday in London a few years ago, as I'm sure you will remember, being on the scene at the time, as it were. The Bromley name is highly respected in this part of the world, and you would do well to bear that in mind.'

'Indeed, I will, sir,' Paget replied. 'And would I be correct in assuming that Mr Bromley is also a personal friend of the chief constable, since it was Sir Robert he rang to report the murder of Miss Halliday?'

'They've been friends for many years,' Brock conceded, 'which is why Sir Robert is taking such a keen interest in the result. But if you are implying that this investigation should be treated any differently from any other, Chief Inspector, I can assure you that is not the case. Is that understood?'

'Understood, sir,' said Paget.

'Right.' Brock eyed Paget narrowly for a long moment. 'Right,' he said again. 'In that case I'll leave you to get on with it, and I shall look forward to your progress report first thing tomorrow morning.' With a brisk, dismissive jerk of the head, Brock opened the umbrella and stepped out into the night.

Tregalles appeared as if by magic at Paget's side. 'Never known the chief super to come out to a crime scene before,' he observed mildly. 'Especially on a night like this. Sort of gives you a warm glow all over, knowing that he cares, doesn't it, boss?'

Paget suppressed a smile. 'I'm surprised you could feel it from wherever you were while he was here,' he said. 'So tell me, what were you doing?'

'Checking out the rest of the barn,' Tregalles told him. 'This place is bigger than it looks, and you wouldn't believe all the things they've got stored here. And there's a room that looks like it might have been some sort of farm office at one time, but I think it's been used for other things more recently. I think you should take a look for yourself.'

'Later,' Paget told him. 'I'm told Mr Bromley is waiting for us, so let's go and see what he has to say.'

FOUR

H aving stripped off their protective clothing and donned their coats again, they followed Hurley to the end of the track, where he pointed his torch at the door in the wall on the other side of Manor Lane. 'Go through there, sir,' he told Paget, 'and you'll see the back door to the manor on the other side of the driveway down the side of the house. Renshaw will meet you there.'

PC Renshaw was waiting to let them in. He led them into a tiled passageway where the smell of freshly painted walls was almost overpowering, and there were drop-cloths neatly folded on the floor. One side of the passage was lined with wooden coat pegs, but they were bare and empty now.

'Paint's still a bit wet,' Renshaw explained as the two men shrugged out of their coats. 'So I'll just take them along to the kitchen before I take you through.' He took their wet macs from them and disappeared through a doorway farther down the hall.

'Didn't think anyone still used oil-based paints,' Tregalles muttered, rubbing his eyes. 'Place stinks to high heaven.'

'Makes my eyes water and gets me in the throat,' Renshaw said as he rejoined them. 'But Mr Bromley said it's better in the long run, because it lasts something like five times longer, when I asked him why they used it. It's not as bad in the rest of the house, so if you'd like to follow me I'll take you to him now.'

Their footsteps echoed hollowly on the tiled floor as they followed Renshaw down the long corridor. He took them past the foot of narrow service stairs leading to the upper floors, then abruptly turned a corner where they found themselves facing a set of padded double doors. Renshaw shouldered one aside and held it as they stepped through into a wider hallway . . . and another world.

The hallway was carpeted, and the wainscoting gleamed softly in the subdued light of wall-mounted lamps. They had, it seemed, crossed a demarcation line dividing those who served from those they served; a sort of lateral version of *Upstairs, Downstairs,* thought Paget.

'This is Mr Bromley's study,' Renshaw told them in hushed tones as he came to a halt before a recessed door. 'Thorsen's in there with him. Mr Bromley thought it best not to disturb the others in the house for the time being. Except for Mrs Bromley, of course. She had to be told as it was her daughter who was killed. See, before she married Mr Bromley, she was Mrs Halliday, so the girl who was killed . . .'

'I think we understand,' said Paget. 'Where is Mrs Bromley now?'

'In her room upstairs, sir. Naturally, she was very upset. Mr Bromley was with her for a while, but he's given her something to make her sleep, and the housekeeper is with her now.'

'Have either of the two men in here said anything to you about what happened out there tonight?'

'No, not really, sir, but Mr Bromley is most anxious to talk to you. He says he has important information for you.'

As if on cue, the door of the study opened and a tall but slightly stooped grey-haired man, whom Paget judged to be in his fifties, came out and shut the door behind him. He looked drawn and very tired, but he made a visible effort to overcome it as introductions were made.

'I'm sorry we have to trouble you at a time like this, sir . . .' Paget began, but Bromley brushed his words aside.

'I quite understand what you have to do, Chief Inspector,' he said, 'so the sooner we get on with it the better. I assume Chief Superintendent Brock told you about what happened here tonight? This man, Nash . . .?' Bromley frowned and shook his head as if deeply puzzled. 'He's normally such a mild-mannered man, and I was sure he had gone away, but it seems I was wrong.'

'Perhaps we could go inside,' Paget suggested, indicating the closed door, but Bromley shook his head. 'Thorsen's in there,' he said tersely, 'and there's no need for him to hear this.'

'Is there somewhere else we can talk?'

'The library. It's just down the hall.' Bromley turned to lead the way.

'In a moment, sir.' Paget turned to Tregalles. 'Take Mr Thorsen's statement while I see what Mr Bromley has to say, then come along to the library when you've finished.' He turned to Renshaw. 'And make sure Mr Thorsen gets home safely, then come back here and stand by in case we need you.'

'Right, sir.'

For a man who had been so anxious to tell his story, Charles Bromley seemed reluctant to begin once they reached the library. He walked to the window and stood there in silence, hands thrust deep inside his jacket pockets as he stared into the darkness.

He was younger than Paget had perceived him to be in the soft light of the hallway. Late forties or early fifties might be closer to the mark. 'When you're ready, sir,' he prompted.

Bromley turned to face him. 'I'm sorry, Chief Inspector, but as I said, I'm still finding it very hard to believe. I should have listened to . . . Sorry. I'm not being very clear, am I?' He took a deep breath and let it out again. 'I believe the man you want is George Nash. He's a plumber; he's done a lot of work for me over the years. He has a shop and yard in Silver Street in Clunbridge and he lives behind the shop. Earlier this evening –' he paused to look at the clock on the mantelpiece – 'or I should say *last* evening, Nash burst in on us while we were at dinner, and he threatened to kill Toni for injuring his young daughter. There were half a dozen witnesses.'

'I think you'd better sit down and begin at the beginning,' Paget said quietly. He took out his notebook and sat down himself.

Bromley brushed a weary hand across his face. 'Yes, yes, of course,' he said testily. 'Must get things in the right order, mustn't we?' He lowered himself into an armchair and sat hunched forward, elbows on his knees, hands clasped in front of him.

'I suppose it all really began yesterday afternoon,' he said, and went on to tell Paget what had happened when Toni Halliday had lost control of the car and hit a child. 'Her name is Tracy Nash,' he said. 'She's the five-year-old daughter of George and Sheila Nash, and she's in critical condition in hospital in Broadminster. Toni was arrested at the scene, but was released into my custody overnight, and she was supposed to appear in court later today.

'We had just sat down to dinner last evening,' he continued, 'when George Nash burst into the room and started shouting at Toni. He was angry because she was here and not in jail, while his young daughter was in hospital fighting for her life. And then he threatened her, saying he would kill her if Tracy died.'

'Did Nash actually approach her or make an attempt to attack her physically?'

'No. In fact he stopped just inside the door. He was distraught, shouting and crying at the same time. To be honest, I felt sorry for the man.'

'But he did say he would kill her. Can you remember exactly what he said? His exact words?'

Bromley made a face. 'As I said, the man was in a terrible state, so it was a bit of a jumble, but I do remember one thing he said very clearly, and those words have been playing over and over again in my mind this past hour. He said, "I'm telling you, if our Tracy dies, she won't be the only one, because you'll be next!" And he pointed straight at Toni.'

'Tell me about Nash,' said Paget. 'How did he get into the house?'

Before he could answer, there was a light tap on the door and Tregalles entered the room. 'Sorry to interrupt,' he said, 'but I thought you'd like to know that Thorsen's statement was pretty straightforward, and Renshaw is seeing him home. He lives just down the lane.'

'Thank you, Sergeant. Mr Bromley was about to tell me about a man who threatened Miss Halliday last night,' Paget said, then went on to tell Tregalles what he had learned so far as the sergeant sat down and took out his own notebook.

Paget turned to Bromley and repeated the question.

'He came to the front door and rang the bell,' Bromley said. 'When Gwyneth opened the door, he pushed his way inside and demanded to know where Toni was. When she told him we were all at dinner, he forced her to lead him to us. Gwyneth is our maid.'

'I see. And when he came into the dining room, what happened?'

'As I said, he just stood there at the door. I recognized him at once, of course, and I tried to tell him how sorry we all were, but I'm afraid that just set him off.'

'And that was when he made that specific threat?' said Paget. '"If our Tracy dies, she won't be the only one!" Right?'

'Yes. In fact those words came back to me very clearly when I saw Toni lying there in the barn. Believe me, Chief Inspector, you don't forget words like that.'

'Is Tracy Nash dead?'

Bromley's face clouded. 'I don't know,' he said slowly. 'I do know she was alive about nine o'clock last night because Dr Price rang me. He's Tracy's doctor, and I'd asked him to keep me informed. I felt it was the least I could do under the circumstances.'

'And what time was it when Nash came into the room?'

Bromley thought for a moment. 'It would be shortly after seven,' he said. 'Toni had just dropped her little bombshell, and we were still digesting that when Nash—' He broke off as Paget held up his hand.

'*Bombshell*, Mr Bromley? I don't recall your mentioning this before, sir. What was that all about?'

Bromley sucked in his breath and rubbed his face vigorously with both hands. 'Sorry, Chief Inspector,' he apologized. 'I'm afraid I'm not thinking too clearly right now. Toni had just finished telling us that the reason she'd been drinking was because she'd been in to see a doctor in Worcester that day, and he had told her she was pregnant. She was trying to justify her actions to her mother, and as I said, we were still digesting that little gem when Nash came through the door.'

Paget turned to Tregalles. 'Ring the hospital and find out how Tracy Nash is doing,' he instructed with a nod toward the door. 'And you might find out if Nash is there or has been there. If the girl's condition is that critical, I'm wondering why her father would come all the way back here to threaten Miss Halliday, when one would expect him to be at his daughter's bedside.'

He turned his attention to Bromley. 'What was Miss Halliday's reaction to the threat?' he asked as Tregalles left the room.

'I think she was more stunned than alarmed. Now I come to think of it, I don't think she said anything at all while Nash was here.'

'Who else was in the room at the time, sir?'

Bromley made a mental count. 'There were eight of us, apart from Nash. As I said, Gwyneth was there, then there was my wife, Margaret, my brother, Paul, who is down here for the weekend, my son, Julian, Beth, or I should say, Elizabeth Etherton – she's my first wife's sister – then Toni, me, and Dr Lockwood. He's our local GP. He was here to see Margaret and I invited him to stay for dinner, so that makes eight.'

'Is everyone you mentioned, other than Dr Lockwood, still in the house?

'And Gwyneth. She lives in the village, Hallows End. She comes in daily.'

'Constable Renshaw mentioned a housekeeper.'

'Mrs Lodge. Yes, but she wasn't in the room at the time. She was probably in the kitchen.'

'Any other staff?'

Bromley shook his head. 'There is a woman who comes in to help with the cooking for a few hours each day, but she's usually gone by about four in the afternoon.'

'I see. Please go on. What happened then?'

Bromley hesitated. 'It was odd, really, because once he'd made his threat, the man just stood there leaning against the wall. It was all he could do to stand up. He looked utterly exhausted. I couldn't bring myself to believe that he'd really meant what he'd said, so I left the table and went to him. I tried to tell him again how sorry we were, and gradually persuaded him that he should be with his wife and son at his daughter's bedside. Lockwood joined me, and offered to take Nash to the hospital in his car. But Nash refused, shrugged us off and said he didn't need any help from us, then left the house.'

'He left the house?' said Paget. 'No more threats? Do you know if he'd been drinking?'

Bromley shook his head. 'As far as I could tell, he was perfectly sober,' he said. 'It was really strange. It was as if he'd done what he'd set out to do, and that was it. Lockwood and I followed him out; he got into his van and drove off, and that's the last we saw of him.'

Paget sat back in his chair and said, 'Tell me about Miss Halliday. You say she was to appear in court today, but judging by what I saw out there in the barn, it suggests to me that she was running away and was waiting there for someone to pick her up. Did she not have a car of her own?'

Bromley shook his head. 'She did when she first came down here,' he said, 'but she'd only been here about three weeks when she sold it. At least that's what she told us, but judging by the way she was acting, I suspect it was repossessed. Toni told us a lot of things that turned out to be false, and she could go through money faster than anyone I know.

'As for her running away, I suppose I should have anticipated it,' he said wearily. 'God knows she could never admit her mistakes, never own up to anything, and perhaps Nash's appearance here made her realize how serious the charges were, and what could happen in court today. So she decided to make a run for it rather than face the consequences. As you say, she must have arranged for someone to pick her up at the barn, but what really puzzles me is how Nash could have known she'd be coming out of the house at all.'

'Do you know if she had a mobile phone?' Paget asked. 'I didn't see one out there.'

'Yes, she did,' Bromley told him. 'She was always calling someone on it or texting messages.'

'Do you have any idea who her friends were or where she might have been going?'

Again, Bromley shook his head. 'She said she'd been living with a friend in London, but she didn't elaborate.'

'Why did she move down here?'

Bromley sighed. 'It's a long story,' he said wearily, 'but I'll try to make it brief. Toni *claimed* it was to make amends for all the things she'd said about us to the Press five years ago – I'm sure you'll remember. She said she realized how wrong she'd been, and she hoped her mother and I could forgive her. It was all claptrap, of course, but Margaret wanted so desperately to believe that Toni had finally come to her senses, that I didn't

have the heart to argue with her. After all, Toni is her – *was* her
only child. But people like Toni never change, and I was suspicious of her motives from the very beginning.'

Charles Bromley looked off into the distance, eyes narrowed
as if reliving a memory. 'And I was right,' he said, 'because it
soon became clear that Toni's real purpose was to persuade her
mother to loosen the purse-strings on the trust set up by Toni's
father. He left money to be held in trust until her twenty-fifth
birthday, but Toni wanted the money now. Margaret didn't have
the power to break the trust ahead of time, but Toni wanted her
mother to advance her an equivalent amount from Margaret's
own holdings, which would be paid back when the trust is opened
in two years' time.'

'How much money are we talking about?' asked Paget. 'In
the trust, I mean.'

'For Toni, roughly six million pounds. Her father, Bernard
Halliday, was a wealthy man. The bulk of the estate went to
Margaret, and Toni gets a generous allowance until she's twenty-
five, but I think Halliday knew his daughter well enough to make
her wait until she was older before inheriting the rest of the money.'

'Six million!' echoed Paget softly. 'I take it she didn't
succeed?'

'She tried,' Bromley said. 'In fact, she put on quite a show
for her mother. Did her best to be the loving daughter that
Margaret so badly wanted her to be. She even tried to be nice
to me for the first few weeks, but she couldn't keep it up. She
never did have any use for me, especially after I married her
mother, so that didn't surprise me, but I thought it best to let
things run their course. Toni was Margaret's daughter after all,
and I felt sure that Margaret would come to realize the truth
herself.'

'Do you know what will happen to that money now? The
money held in trust for Miss Halliday.'

'Yes, I do. It reverts to Margaret.'

'No strings attached?'

'None that I know of.'

Tregalles re-entered the room, and both men looked up expect-
antly. 'I've just had a word with Tracy Nash's doctor,' he began,
but Bromley cut him off before he could continue.

'You spoke to *Price*?' he said. 'What is he doing at the hospital at this time of night?'

'It seems the night nurse became worried when Tracy's blood pressure suddenly dropped, so she rang Dr Price at home and he came in to see to her. He went home again at ten, but he was called back again about half an hour ago when it dropped again. I'm afraid it doesn't look too good. According to Dr Price, it could go either way for young Tracy, so he's going to remain at the hospital for the next few hours. But here's the interesting part. He told me that both Nash and his wife have been at the hospital since before eight o'clock last evening. He says Nash was there when he signed in at two minutes to eight. I had the night nurse check the book, and she confirmed the time. Mrs Nash is still there, although Nash left the hospital about half an hour ago. Apparently Nash's son rang the hospital to say there was some sort of emergency at home. So I got the doctor to put Mrs Nash on, and she told me that the family dog had gone into labour earlier than expected, and the son was in a bit of a panic about it. She said the dog and Tracy are virtually inseparable, so the last thing they wanted was for something to happen to the dog as well.'

'Could Nash have left the hospital after Price saw him, I wonder?' asked Paget, but Tregalles shook his head.

'Dr Price said Nash was there all evening. He said the man was pestering him for news about Tracy every few minutes. Nash never left the ward, let alone the hospital until just before I rang.'

Paget turned to Bromley. 'What time would it have been when he left here?' he asked. Charles thought for a moment. 'It must have been getting on for half past seven by the time he left,' he said slowly. 'Which means . . .'

'That he must have gone straight from here to the hospital,' Paget finished for him. 'And he couldn't do that in much less than half an hour if you take into account the time it takes to park and get up to the ward. So, unless Dr Starkie's estimated time of death is out by a country mile, there is no way that Nash could have killed Miss Halliday.'

Charles Bromley nodded slowly. 'To be honest,' he said, 'I think I'm as much relieved as I am perplexed by this turn of events, because I've known George Nash for years, and he's always struck me as a very level-headed man.' He shot a quiz-zical glance at Paget. 'But, then, if not Nash, who?' he asked softly.

'Who, indeed?' said Paget. 'Tell me what happened after Nash left the house? What did the others do while you and Dr Lockwood were dealing with Nash?'

Bromley frowned. 'I don't know, exactly. I think Toni and Beth both went upstairs. Paul simply disappeared, and once we'd seen Nash off the premises, Lockwood and I came back to find Margaret about to go upstairs. She said she was going up to talk to Toni, but Lockwood and I advised her against it.'

'Oh? Why was that, sir?'

Bromley hesitated. 'My wife has had trouble sleeping,' he said. 'Terrible nightmares brought on, or at least made worse, Lockwood and I suspect, by Toni's behaviour these past weeks. The last thing she needed was a confrontation with Toni, which would lead to even more stress. I wanted her to get some rest and wait till morning before trying to talk to Toni. But Margaret insisted that Toni had to be suffering from delayed shock after the accident, and said she was going up to see what she could do for her. That was nonsense, of course, but I realized that there was nothing I could say to change her mind, so I let her go. Later, when I asked how she'd got on, she refused to talk about it, but I gathered from her expression that it did not go well.'

'And your son, Julian?'

'No idea. Probably went up to his room.'

'And what of Dr Lockwood? Did he stay or leave?'

'He left. He said he was going into Hallows End to see a patient there.'

'He was making a house call at that time of night?'

'It's not something he would normally do, but I think this was an emergency, and since he was so close, he decided to go himself rather than call for an ambulance.'

'And you, sir? What did you do?'

'I came along to the study. I had intended to report the matter to the police, but I finally decided that Nash had more than enough on his plate as it was. I couldn't see the point of making even more trouble for him, so I didn't call.'

'And then?'

'I had some work to do, so I got on with it. I spent something like an hour at it, then went along to the kitchen in search of a cup of tea. We had the painters in this week. I had asked them to use oil-based paint, because it lasts longer, but I'd quite forgotten how noxious and pervasive the smell could be, and you could smell it all through the house. Still can for that matter, as I'm sure you are aware. Mrs Lodge very kindly made a fresh pot, and I spent a few minutes in the kitchen talking to her and Beth. She and Mrs Lodge were making up a tray for Beth to take up to her room.'

'So that would be about eight thirty or quarter to nine?'

Bromley nodded. 'Something like that, yes.'

'And you were alone all the time you were in your study?'

'Yes. Well, Margaret popped her head in somewhere around eight fifteen or eight thirty to ask if I'd seen Paul, but I was alone the rest of the time.'

'Did she say why she was looking for your brother?'

'No. I was a bit preoccupied at the time,' he said, 'and I didn't ask. But later, when I was in the kitchen, Mrs Lodge said that Paul had gone out and Margaret had gone looking for him. A short time later, Margaret came hobbling in with a sprained ankle, and looking like a drowned rat after being caught in the rain. I helped her upstairs and made up a cold pack for her ankle with a packet of peas from the freezer, and got her to bed. I went back downstairs, and that was when Paul came in, and he was soaking wet as well.'

'And that would be what . . .? Nine thirty or so?' Paget asked.

Charles shrugged. 'Probably, but I really don't know.'

'Did your brother say where he'd been?'

'No, but he had a cut on his face, quite a deep one, and when I asked him what had happened, he said he'd run into a door.' Charles grimaced. 'Hardly an imaginative explanation, but then that was Paul. He can be quite surly at times, so I didn't bother to pursue it. I told him he should have a couple of stitches in it, but he ignored my advice and went on up the back stairs to his room. I went in to check on Margaret, then returned to the study.'

'Did you see or talk to anyone after that?'

Charles shook his head. 'Not until Thorsen came to the door.'

'Did Miss Halliday and Major Farnsworth know each other?'

'I don't think she ever met the man,' Bromley said. 'And if you're thinking there was some connection between the two, you're barking up the wrong tree. However, from what I could see of his injuries, I did wonder if the major had been run down by whoever killed Toni.'

'That is certainly a possibility,' Paget agreed as he rose to his feet. 'Sorry to have kept you up so late, sir,' he said, stifling a yawn himself, 'but you've been a great help and I do appreciate it.'

'Only too happy to help under the circumstances,' Bromley said as he, too, got to his feet. 'What happens now?'

'I would like to take a look at Miss Halliday's room before I leave. Our people will be in to do a thorough search later on today, but I would like to have a quick look round now if I may. We will leave someone on duty here in the house overnight, and Sergeant Tregalles and I will be back first thing in the morning to talk to the rest of the members of the household.'

Bromley frowned. 'I'm not at all sure that my wife will be up to it,' he said. 'This has come as a terrible shock to her.'

'I do understand, sir, and we are not insensitive to the feelings of members of the family, but I'm sure you realize how important it is that we talk to everyone while events are still fresh in their minds.'

'I'll talk to Margaret in the morning,' Bromley said, 'but I don't know what you hope to gain from her at this stage. In any case, whether she feels up to talking to you or not will have to be her decision.'

'Of course.'

On their way up to Toni Halliday's room, Bromley warned Paget that the room might be in a bit of a mess, and he was right. The bed was made but it looked as if it had been slept on, and there was a pillow on the floor. A glass and a half-empty whiskey bottle were on the bedside table, and several items of clothing were draped haphazardly over the back of a chair. A pair of shoes looked as if they had been kicked off and left where they'd landed; a dresser drawer was partly open, as was the door to the wardrobe, and there were signs everywhere of a hasty departure. Even the dressing table had been cleared of all but an empty face cream jar, an eyeliner pencil, and a box of tissues.

Tregalles sniffed the air. 'Is that what I think it is, sir?' he asked innocently. The question was directed at Paget, but it was Bromley who answered.

'It is, Sergeant,' he said. 'Marijuana. I tried my best to get Toni to stop smoking it, but I might as well have saved my breath.'

'Tell me,' said Paget, 'how would Miss Halliday get downstairs and out to the barn without being seen?'

'It wouldn't be difficult if she was careful and chose her time,' Bromley told him. 'There are two sets of back stairs, one at each end of the house, and both go down to the passageway where you came in tonight. She *could* have gone out through the chapel at the other end of the house, but that would have meant a long trek around the stables to get to Manor Lane and the barn, so, I suspect she simply waited until the coast was clear, then left by the same door you used. From there, as you know, it's only a short distance to the barn.'

Paget nodded. 'You mentioned a chapel. Is that part of the house?'

'Yes. It's a small, private chapel. My grandmother became quite religious toward the end of her life, and she had it built as an addition to the house in the sixties. Unfortunately, one of the roof beams collapsed when a tree came down on it during a storm some years ago, resulting in a great deal of damage to the interior. I've been working with architects and builders on the restoration ever since, but it's a slow business.'

Bromley smothered a yawn. 'So, if you've finished here, Chief Inspector, I'd like to look in on Margaret and then get some sleep myself.'

'Of course, and thank you again, sir. Just once more question. It appears that Miss Halliday's person and her belongings were searched after she was killed. Do you have any idea what the killer might have been looking for?'

'I noticed that myself,' Bromley told him, 'but I have no idea what it could have been.' He led them down the back stairs where they were met by Renshaw, who must have heard them coming, because their coats were draped over his arm.

'I'd like PC Renshaw to remain here for the rest of the night, if that's all right with you, Mr Bromley?' Paget said as he shrugged into his coat. 'And a policewoman will be here first thing tomorrow morning as well.'

'Of course. And if you become hungry,' said Bromley, turning to Renshaw, 'there's plenty to eat in the kitchen, and I'm sure you can make yourself a cup of tea.'

'Very kind of you, sir,' said Renshaw. 'Thank you.'

'I know this means a double shift, for you,' Paget told the constable, 'but I'll arrange for someone on the early shift to relieve you at six. Meanwhile, I don't want anyone to leave the house. Understood?'

'Understood, sir.'

Bromley opened the door. 'I suppose it's too much to hope that the media won't connect this to what happened five years ago,' he said with a weary sigh, 'but I imagine they'll catch on soon enough and they'll dredge it all up again. But then, that's hardly your problem, is it, Chief Inspector?'

Paget was about to move on, but Bromley wasn't finished. 'I would appreciate it if you would keep that in mind when talking to the Press,' he said. 'I did mention my concern to Chief Superintendent Brock earlier tonight, and he assured me that the investigation would be kept "low-key", as it were, and nothing would be given out to the media without his personal sanction. Has he mentioned this to you?'

'No, he hasn't,' said Paget, 'but no doubt he will. Good night sir.'

The door closed behind them, followed by the metallic click of the lock.

The wind had dropped, but leaves and twigs littered the ground, and a pallid moon cast ghostly shadows on the wall. The light over the door set in the wall came on as they approached. The sergeant lifted the latch and pulled, but he had to tug hard before it would open, and the hinges groaned in protest.

'Wood's probably swollen with the rain,' he said as he pulled it to.

'Doesn't sound as if the hinges have been oiled for a while, either,' Paget said, and wondered if anyone in the house had heard the sound when Toni Halliday slipped through.

FIVE

There was a second police car parked at the end of the track, and two more uniformed men had joined Hurley at the barn, but there was no sign of Charlie Dobbs or any of his people. PC Hurley told them that Inspector Dobbs had decided that, as everything around the crime scene where the major was found had been trampled into the mud, there wasn't much point in staying. As for the crime scene inside the barn, he said it could wait till morning as well, so he had sent everybody home.

'Might as well be on our way, then,' Tregalles said, and was about to walk away when Paget stopped him.

'Tell me,' he said, 'when Mr Bromley talked about the media raking everything up again, I had no idea what he was talking about, but you looked as if you did, so what was that about? Some sort of local scandal?'

Tregalles shook his head. 'I suppose he assumed that you'd remember it. It was in all the papers. The Halliday affair four, maybe five years ago?

Paget shook his head. 'Don't recall it,' he said. 'Enlighten me.'

'I'd almost forgotten about it myself, until I heard the name, Toni Halliday, when I got the call to come out here,' Tregalles said. 'It was when Bernard Halliday died. He was the archaeologist who used to do those shows on TV where they'd take you on a tour of some old city they'd dug up, then recreate the way people lived back then. He did a series, *Journey into the Past*, or some such thing. The wife and I enjoyed it. Anyway, Halliday got this tumour on the brain, and Mr Bromley was the surgeon who operated on him. He was one of the top Harley Street men at the time, according to the papers, but when Halliday died on the operating table, his daughter accused Bromley of killing him so he could marry her mother. Made a proper meal of it, the papers did. Knocked Tony Blair, the Euro, David Beckham and the Spice Girls right off the front pages for days. There was an enquiry, Bromley was cleared, but Toni Halliday wouldn't shut up about it. The media kept egging her on, of course, and it got so bad that Bromley finally got fed up with it and packed it in and came back down here. I think he's a sort of consultant now, although I've heard he still operates every now and then.'

'It doesn't seem to have done him much harm locally,' Paget observed. 'Magistrate and friend of the chief constable.'

'True, but Toni Halliday was right in one respect. Whether he had anything to do with her husband's death or not, Mr Bromley did marry Margaret Halliday a year later. Not that anyone should have been surprised, when you think about it. Mrs Bromley was a Chadwick, originally, and the two families, the Chadwicks and the Bromleys, go back a long way. Both made their money from coal, in fact I think they were in business together many years ago.'

Tregalles pursed his lips. 'Come to think of it, she could be the last Chadwick. Her parents are dead, and there was a brother, but he was quite a bit older and I think something happened to him. Don't remember what, exactly, but Audrey would know. I'll have to ask her.'

'I'm impressed,' said Paget. 'And surprised. I had no idea you were so well informed about the local gentry.'

Tregalles chuckled. 'I'm not,' he said, 'but the Bromleys and the Chadwicks have lived here since God was a boy, and there was a lot in the papers at the time. Besides, there was a feature article about the chapel Mr Bromley's restoring in the *Star* a year or so back. And when Audrey went with the WI on a tour of old churches, they stopped in there for a look, and she said Mr Bromley himself came out to talk to them and tell them about it.'

'Interesting. Anything else?'

'Can't think of anything else at the moment.'

'All right. Now, what about Thorsen. What did he have to say for himself?'

'Not much we didn't know already. Turns out the dog, Toby, actually belongs to the major, but since Mrs Farnsworth became allergic to the animal, Toby stays with Thorsen. The major picks him up each evening and takes him with him on his walks across the heath and along the river path above the river. Thorsen said he usually picked up Toby just after seven, and he was usually back by nine or nine thirty. Last night, when Farnsworth hadn't returned by ten thirty, Mrs Farnsworth telephoned Thorsen to see if the major was there, and when he said he wasn't, she persuaded him to go out and look for him. The rest we know.'

'How old is Thorsen?'

'Didn't ask him, but I should think he's seventyish or there-abouts. Hard to tell, because he's a bit bent over and he walks sort of stiff legged. Rheumatism or arthritis or some such thing, I shouldn't wonder.'

'And yet this old man sets out to look for someone, when it's pitch dark, blowing hard and pouring rain? The major could have been anywhere out there on that stretch of land between here and the river. Unless, of course, Thorsen knew exactly where to look.'

Tregalles chuckled. 'Tell you the truth, I think he was more concerned about the dog than he was the major. I got the impression he didn't like Major Farnsworth very much.'

'Anything else?'

'I asked him if he knew Toni Halliday, or if he'd had had any dealings with her. He said he knew who she was, but he'd made a point of staying clear of her, because kitchen gossip had it she was a trouble-maker.'

'Interesting,' Paget observed, then abruptly changed the subject. 'When you spoke to Mrs Nash on the phone, you said she told you that her husband had gone home to see to the whelping of their dog. Which means that he will probably still be up. We have to go through Clunbridge on the way home, so why don't we stop and have a word with him?'

Tregalles, already looking forward to spending what was left of the night in a nice warm bed, made a face. 'It *is* the middle of the night,' he reminded his boss. 'Can't it wait till morning?'

'I think we'll have more than enough to do at the manor in the morning,' Paget replied, 'and the sooner we talk to Nash, the better. Silver Street, wasn't it? I'll meet you there; it shouldn't take long.'

Fifteen minutes later, Paget was already out of the car and examining the gouges in the wall adjoining the shop by the light from

his own headlights when Tregalles joined him. 'Careful where
you put your feet,' he warned the sergeant. 'Whoever cleaned up
didn't make a very good job of it. There are still bits of glass
around.'

The lettering on the window of the shop said, *G. L. NASH –
Plumbing and Heating Supplies. Installation – Repair –
Maintenance,* and there was a similar sign on the double wooden
gates leading to the yard next to the shop. The shop itself was
in darkness, and a CLOSED sign hung crookedly in the window
in the door. Tregalles stepped back into the street and looked up.
'No lights on,' he said, preparing to return to his car and head
for home and bed. 'Gone back to the hospital, I expect. We can
catch him in the morning.'

'Then, why are the gates unlocked?' Paget asked, pushing one
of them open. 'His van is here and the bonnet's still warm. And
there's a light on over the door to the house at the back of the
shop.'

Tregalles sighed as he followed his boss into the yard. He
stumbled in the dark and banged his knee against the bumper of
the van. Muttering beneath his breath, he limped after Paget, who
was already knocking on the door. He knocked again as Tregalles
caught up with him.

The door opened, and a pale, stocky young man, dressed only
in cut-off shorts and sandals, eyed Paget suspiciously. 'Yeah?'
he said cautiously.

'Police.' Paget held up his warrant card. 'I'm Detective Chief
Inspector Paget, and this is Detective Sergeant Tregalles, and
we'd like to talk to George Nash. Is he here?'

'Dad!' the boy called without taking his eyes off Paget. 'Dad!'
he called louder. 'It's the police. They want to talk to you.'

A sinewy, gaunt-looking man appeared beside his son. Dressed
in work clothes and a long plastic apron, he was wiping his
hands on a towel streaked with what looked like blood. His face
was pale, his eyes deep-set and dark, and he looked exhausted.
'Police . . .?' he said, looking from one to the other.

Paget repeated the introduction.

'Bloody hell!' Nash said softly. 'A chief inspector *and* a
sergeant in the middle of the night? Old Bromley must have
really thrown his weight about. I suppose the lord of the manor

wants you to throw me in jail for disturbing his dinner, does he?'
He seemed to be trying to make light of it, but there was an
undercurrent of unease in his voice.

'May we come in?' asked Paget.

Nash hesitated, then turned to his son. 'You go back and see
to Ginger,' he said. 'I think she'll be all right now, but best stay
with her for a while.'

The boy hesitated, but a look from his father sent him off
down the corridor. 'It's our dog, Ginger,' Nash explained. 'She's
just given birth to eight pups. The first one died. Head got stuck
and Mickey was here on his own and he couldn't get it out.
Fortunately, I was able to get back here in time to save the rest.'

He opened the door wider and stood back. 'You'd best come
in, then, and get it over with,' he said with weary resignation.
'The wife rang from the hospital to say the police had been
asking about me, but I hardly expected you to come round in
the middle of the night.' He shut the door, then led the way into
an old-fashioned kitchen.

'Sit yourselves down, then,' he said, 'but if you think I'm
going to say I'm sorry for what I did, you can think again. When
one of your lot at the hospital told me that bitch had been let
go, I couldn't believe it. But that's the way it is, isn't it? They
all stick together, that lot. So what sort of story did they give
you up at the manor? I'll bet it was a good one.'

'I'm more interested in what you have to say about it,' Paget
told him as he opened his coat and sat down. Tregalles pulled a
chair away from the table and followed suit.

Nash eyed Paget warily for a long moment before settling into
a chair at the end of the table himself. 'I don't know what they
told you up there,' he said, 'but that woman ran our Tracy down.
Came right up on the pavement and . . .' Nash swallowed hard.
His voice disappeared into the back of his throat, and he had to
swallow several more times before he was able to continue.

'Driving like a madwoman, she was. She wasn't just drunk,
she was way over the top. Your own blokes told me. They tested
her. There were witnesses who said she was going like the clap-
pers when she tried to make that turn. She hit the wall, and
Tracy . . .'

Nash lowered his head. 'She could die!' he said huskily, 'but does that bitch up at the manor care? Not her! Sitting there stuffing her face while Tracy . . .' His voice broke and he blinked back tears.

He looked up to meet Paget's eyes. 'Oh, yes,' he said, 'I went up there and told her. I told them all what I'd do if anything happens to Tracy, and, by God, I meant it at the time. Is that what you came to hear, Detective Chief Inspector whatever-your-name-is?'

'What I came to hear,' said Paget patiently, 'is your side of the story. I'm well aware of how painful and difficult this must be for you, but it is important that you answer my questions. So tell me, what prompted you to leave the bedside of your critically injured daughter to drive all the way out to the manor to threaten Miss Halliday?'

Nash eyed him stonily for a long moment, then looked away and shook his head. 'It was a stupid thing to do,' he said tightly. 'The wife begged me not to go, but when I heard that the woman who'd run our Tracy down had been let go, I wanted to see her pay for what she'd done. I really did want to see her dead!' He looked away. His eyes were moist. 'Except I lost my nerve when I got there,' he ended bitterly.

'So you didn't kill her?'

'Kill her? Nash stared. 'Don't be daft. Of course I didn't kill her – not that I didn't want to, mind, but I think I knew all along that wasn't going to happen. What I *did* want was for her to be as shit-scared for her life as I was about our Tracy's.' He lowered his head to stare at the floor. 'I must have looked a right fool to them up there,' he muttered as much to himself as to the two detectives.

'Tell me where you went when you left the manor.'

'Where do you think I went?' Nash demanded, clearly both puzzled and annoyed by Paget's question. 'I went straight back to the hospital, *and* I went over the speed limit, so you can have me for that as well while you're at it.'

'Are you quite sure you didn't stop anywhere?'

Nash sighed heavily. 'I don't know what it is you're after,' he said, 'but like I told you, all I wanted to do when I left the manor was to get back to see how Tracy was doing.' He glanced at the kitchen clock. 'Like I should be doing now.'

'Do you remember what time it was when you got to the hospital?'

'Oh, for Christ's sake! How the hell should I know what time it was?' Nash snapped. 'Why do you want to know that?'

'Because Miss Halliday was found dead last night,' Paget said quietly. 'Slashed and cut down not long after you threatened to kill her. So you see, Mr Nash, it is important that we establish where you were and what you did after you left the manor.'

Nash eyed Paget suspiciously. 'Slashed?' he repeated. 'I don't believe you. I don't know what your game is, but—'

'It's no game, Mr Nash. Antonia Halliday was murdered after you had threatened her in front of witnesses.'

Nash continued to stare at him. 'You're serious?' he said at last.

'Extremely serious,' Paget told him.

Nash sucked in his breath. 'Well, it wasn't me,' he said flatly, 'and you can check all you like, but I went straight back to the hospital when I left the manor, and I never left there until I had to come back to see to Ginger. They'll tell you; just ask them.'

'Oh, I will,' Paget assured him as he rose to his feet. 'Tell me, do you have another vehicle other than your van?'

'There's the wife's car,' Nash said cautiously. 'Why?'

'Just wanted to make sure we didn't leave you without trans-portation,' Paget told him, 'because I'm afraid you're going to have to do without the van for a day or two while our forensic people have a look at it.'

'But you can't,' Nash said desperately. 'I *need* the van for business. I don't see the point to any of this.'

'The point,' Paget said, 'is that, not only was Miss Halliday killed, but a man was struck down by a car, or possibly a van, very close to where Miss Halliday was killed, and he is now in hospital.' He held out his hand. 'So, the keys, if you please, Mr Nash. Oh, yes, and please leave the gates unlocked until someone can come out to collect it. I should be able to get someone here within the hour. In the meantime, Sergeant Tregalles will remain here until they arrive.'

SIX

With less than three hours sleep behind him, Paget was in the office by eight o'clock. Even so, there was a message waiting for him on voice mail to call Chief Superintendent Brock ASAP. He picked up the phone.

'But if Nash couldn't have done it, then who?' Brock demanded when Paget finished his verbal report. 'You said yourself the man admits to going out there with the intention of killing the girl, so he could be lying about where he was, and if this Dr Price was busy, he may not have realized that Nash was missing. It has to be him.'

'It is still possible,' Paget agreed, 'and we'll be following that up with Dr Price and the hospital staff, but it's also possible that Antonia Halliday was killed by whoever was going to pick her up, or even by Major Farnsworth, for that matter. Unfortunately, he can't be questioned yet, but there are things we can do on site, so I'd like to get an incident room set up as close to the crime scene as soon as possible.'

'You're not suggesting the manor?' Brock said sharply. 'That's out of the question.'

Paget smiled to himself. 'No, sir, not the manor. Sergeant Ormside tells me there's a church hall we can use in Hallows End at the bottom of Manor Lane. He's looking into it now.'

'How are you doing with OSPRE?' asked Paget as he settled into the passenger's seat and snapped his seatbelt on. He was referring to the Objective Structured Performance-Related Examination programme, or OSPRE for short, which he was encouraging Tregalles to take.

'I know you say you're happy in your present job,' he'd told the sergeant when he'd first suggested it, 'and I'd be sorry to lose you, but perhaps it's time to move on. If you leave it too late you could find yourself overtaken by some of these youngsters with a fistful of degrees who are being fast-tracked these days.'

That might be, but it seemed like only yesterday that Tregalles had spent countless hours studying for the sergeant's exam, and the prospect of buckling down to more months of hard studying didn't appeal to him at all. 'I am giving it some thought,' he'd hedged, 'but what with the workload the way it is, this may not be the best time.'

'There may never be a "best time",' Paget countered, 'and the sooner you start . . .' He'd left the rest unsaid, but as far as Tregalles was concerned it was more than a suggestion, and he didn't like to be pushed.

Deep down, he knew Paget was right; he wasn't getting any younger, and already there were a couple of inspectors in the division who were younger than he was by several years. But it would mean months of hard slogging on his own time, learning and memorizing things he would have to know for the exam but would probably never use on the job. And with the way things were at work, he could see himself spending almost every waking hour away from the job, either on the computer or with his head stuck in a book, and he just wasn't ready for it. He was seeing little enough of his family as it was. Olivia and Brian were growing up fast, and as for Audrey . . . it seemed they hadn't had time for a decent conversation in months.

He wished Paget wouldn't keep asking. It was almost as though his boss wanted to be rid of him, and with Molly Forsythe well on her way to becoming a sergeant, he couldn't help wondering if Paget was looking for a change himself. Certainly he'd been using Molly more and more on jobs Tregalles felt should have been his. He liked Molly; she was sharp, and they'd worked well together in the past. But she was ambitious, and he knew Paget thought highly of her, so perhaps she saw herself as his successor.

But when he voiced his suspicions to Audrey, she'd scoffed at the idea. 'Now you are being silly,' she told him flatly. 'You know as well as I do that Molly Forsythe is as straight as they come. She's a bright girl; you've said so yourself, and it's only natural she wants to get on, but she isn't the sort to go behind your back. And as for Mr Paget wanting to be rid of you, that's ridiculous. What he's telling you is that he thinks you are ready for promotion, and like he said, you don't want to leave it too late. So you can get those conspiracy ideas out of your head for a start and think about what he's saying.' Audrey had put her arms around him. 'I'm not saying you *ought* to do it just because he suggested it, love, nor should you do it if you really don't want to, but if Mr Paget moves into Mr Alcott's old job, who will you be stuck with then? Could be Parsons or someone like that, and you know what he's like. But if you became an inspector, there's a good chance you'd still be working for Mr Paget.' She sighed. 'But no matter what he says or what I say, you must do what's right for you.'

And that was the trouble – he didn't know what was right for him, and he still hadn't done anything about it. And now, just as they were setting out for Bromley Manor on a bright and sunny September morning, Paget had to spoil things by bringing it up again.

He tried to keep his voice light. 'Schedule's been a bit tight, lately, I'm afraid, boss,' he said. 'What with the way things have been at work, and with the kids home for the summer holidays, and Audrey's part-time job at the book shop, it's been a bit hectic around the place. Still, now the kids are back at school, I'll be taking another run at it.'

They drove in silence for the rest of the journey. Both men were tired after a night of little sleep, and with the warm sun in his face, Paget found himself fighting hard to stop himself from drifting off.

'Gates to the manor are open,' Tregalles observed. He slowed to a crawl and turned in. 'Let's see what the place looks like in daylight, shall we?'

The lawns on either side were neat enough, as were the flower-beds, but tufts of grass and weeds were poking through the gravelled surface of the driveway, and the edges needed trimming. Not neglected, exactly, but it would soon look that way if not attended to.

But the manor itself was a different story, thought Paget as it came into sight. No sign of neglect there. Built of local stone and timber, it looked fresh and clean after the rain, with its long mullioned windows gleaming brightly in the morning light.

'Nice looking place,' Tregalles observed, breaking into Paget's thoughts, 'but I bet it's a bugger to heat in the winter. And that's the chapel I was telling you about last night.' He pointed to the west side of the house, where a small, church-like building was all but concealed behind scaffolding draped in a dull green mesh and topped by heavy blue tarps.

'Doesn't look like they've made much progress, does it?' he commented. 'It must be three or four years since the tree came down on it. I should have thought they'd have had it done by now. Can't say it does much for the look of the rest of the place.'

'There are twelve bedrooms,' Charles Bromley had told them on their way to Toni's room earlier that morning. 'Six at the front of the house, and six at the back. Then there are the servants' rooms of course – or what used to be the servants' rooms – in the attic, but they haven't been used for years.'

A grey-haired woman, dressed only in a nightgown, stood framed in the open window of the corner bedroom at the east end of the house. Her face was lifted to the morning sun, and she seemed unaware of their approach until she heard the crunch of gravel beneath the tyres. She looked down, then drew back and closed the window. Mrs Bromley, Paget wondered?

They continued on, following the narrow driveway between the house and the high stone wall separating house and grounds from Manor Lane, to the stables behind the manor. They were stables in name only now, the stalls having been replaced by a row of blank-faced garages.

'At least they don't have to be shovelled out,' Tregalles observed, 'but they don't really go with the rest of the place, do they? Out of sight, out of mind? A bit of penny-pinching there, I'd say.'

A gate between the yard and Manor Lane was open, tied back with rusted wire that looked as if it had been in place for years. Tregalles drove through, turning back up Manor Lane to park next to one of SOCO's white vans.

'You might as well go in and get things organized for the interviews,' Paget told Tregalles as they got out of the car. 'I'll be along after I've had a word with Charlie.'

Charlie wasn't there, but one of his men helped Paget into a coverall before allowing him to proceed. Two more of Charlie's people were inside; one, a man named Felix, was sitting cross-legged on the floor, filling in some sort of form, while the other was Grace.

'Charlie phoned to say he was taking to his bed with a bottle of rum,' she told him. 'And knowing Charlie, he's probably done exactly that. What would you like to know, Neil?'

'Everything,' he said. 'As I told you this morning, with this man Nash pretty well ruled out, we're back to square one, so what do you have?'

'Not much, I'm afraid. Couldn't find any prints on the weapon. It's gone to the lab for further examination, but I doubt if they'll get much off it. I don't know if the killer wore gloves or wrapped the handle in something like a cloth, but there was a smear of what looks like fresh green paint on the handle, and that might tell us something.'

Green? Paget's thoughts flashed to the house. 'That's interesting,' he said. 'You might try taking a sample from the hallway between the side door of the manor and the kitchen. The paint was still a bit wet when we were there last night, and if it does match, it could suggest that our killer came from *inside* the house rather than outside. Anything else? What about the suitcase and the carryall? Anything there?'

'Everything was pulled out and scattered around, as you probably saw last night,' Grace said, 'but I don't think the killer found what he was looking for, although he didn't spend much time on her bag of dirty laundry.' Grace pointed to a large evidence bag containing a smaller plastic bag. 'It was open and he probably looked inside, but when he realized it was underwear that needed washing, he left it alone.

'But I didn't,' she said smugly, 'and I found these.' She plunged a hand in one of the pockets in her white suit, and pulled out a glassine envelope and held it up. 'Take a look at these little beauties. They were tied up in her tights and knickers. Two rings, a chain bracelet, a necklace and two pairs of earrings. You might want to ask them at the manor if they can identify them, because judging by what you told me this morning about the girl, I doubt if they belonged to her.'

Paget held the bag up to the light and whistled softly. 'I think you're right,' he said. He started to slip it into his pocket, but Grace's hand shot out to grasp his arm.

'Not so fast,' she told him. 'You're not leaving here without signing on the dotted line for that lot.'

'Don't you trust me?'

'Don't trust anyone when it comes to evidence,' she said with a grin, 'especially coppers, and that's a direct quote from Charlie.' Grace produced a receipt book. 'So let's have your autograph, Chief Inspector. And remember, they have been recorded and photographed.'

'Was there anything else?' he asked when Grace had finished listing the items on the receipt.

'About the only other thing of interest was a minute quantity of a white powder, wrapped in a twist of paper at the bottom of her handbag, which I'm pretty sure will turn out to be cocaine,' she said as he scribbled his name and handed the book back to her.

Paget wasn't surprised, considering the picture of Antonia Halliday that had begun to form in his mind, and it might go a long way to explaining her behaviour. 'What about the scene outside the barn? Anything there, yet?'

'Several things,' Grace told him. 'We found shards of glass from a car's back-up light next to the rusty old water tank out there, which is where Major Farnsworth was found. We found paint from the car on one of the pipes as well as on the side of the tank itself, so between that and the glass, we're hoping that Forensic can come up with a make and model of the car. It looks as if the car backed into the water tank and the major at the same time, then spun its wheels before taking off down the track. There is one identifiable tyre impression close to the barn, where it was sheltered from the rain, but there is no way of knowing when it was made or if it has anything to do with the crime. Just about everything else was destroyed by the rain.'

'Have you checked the tyre impression you do have with any of the cars belonging to the manor?'

'Yes. The housekeeper gave us the key to the garages, but none of the tyres match our impression. Mrs Bromley's car is normally garaged here, but I was told it was impounded in Clunbridge yesterday after it was involved in an accident. So, assuming Miss Halliday was waiting here to be picked up by car, the tyre impression and the glass could have come from the car that came to pick her up. We didn't find a mobile phone amongst her belongings, but if she had one, she may have used it to arrange for transportation, and if she did . . .'

'We can go to the source for her phone records,' Paget finished for her. 'And we know she did have one because Mr Bromley told me she was always using it.' He smothered a yawn, and rubbed his face vigorously to stave off a sudden urge to close his eyes. 'Anything else?'

'Just one thing,' Grace said, 'but you may know about it already. The small office at the back?' She flicked her head toward the back of the barn. 'By the look of some of the furniture, it was probably used at some time in the past as an office for the farm manager or some such person, but the lights and some of the fixtures have been upgraded, and it's clear that it's been used for other purposes quite recently.'

'*Other* purposes?' he asked quizzically. 'Such as . . .?'

Grace frowned. 'Can't say for sure,' she said slowly, 'because I've led a very sheltered life. But you're the detective, so you tell me. Would a blow-up mattress and a packet of condoms give you a clue . . .?'

SEVEN

Paget found Tregalles and Charles Bromley in the study. They were standing facing each other in the middle of the room, and Paget sensed tension between them.

'Good morning, sir,' he said cautiously. Charles responded with a curt 'Good morning' of his own, but managed to make it clear by his tone that the 'good' part of his greeting was in serious doubt. There were dark circles beneath his eyes, but the eyes themselves were clear and sharp beneath their bushy brows.

'Is there a problem?' asked Paget, looking from one to the other.

'I'm afraid there is, sir,' Tregalles said. 'It seems that Mr Bromley's brother, Paul, has disappeared. His bed's not been slept in; his clothes and bag have gone, and so has his car. As far as I can tell, he may have left the house last night before we arrived.'

'I see.' Paget turned to Charles. 'And you weren't aware that your brother had left the house when we were here earlier?' he said.

'Absolutely not, and I've been trying to explain to your sergeant that Paul's departure can have nothing to do with Toni's death. He couldn't have even known about it, but Sergeant Tregalles seems to think otherwise.'

Charles Bromley was not a simple-minded man. He must realize the implications of his brother's disappearance. 'When did you last see your brother?' Paget asked.

'I told you last night – or rather earlier this morning, I suppose it was – I saw Paul around nine o'clock last evening, and I haven't seen him since. I assumed he was upstairs in his room.'

'Do you know if anyone else was aware that he'd left?'

'I've asked everyone, and no one knew he'd gone.'

'Where did your brother leave his car?'

Charles frowned. 'He parked it here beside the house when he first arrived, but after we had seen Nash off, Paul asked if he could put his car in Margaret's garage, since she wasn't using it.'

'So you would have heard his car if he had come back up the drive on his way out before you left your study at eleven?'

'Of course. He would have driven right past my window. But it would be quicker to drive directly out of the stable yard into Manor Lane, and I imagine that's what he did.'

'Can you normally hear cars going by in Manor Lane?'

'You can, but that wall out there acts as a pretty good sound barrier, and unless it's something like a tractor going by, it doesn't even register.'

'Which means he could have left at any time after you saw him.'

'Which is exactly what I've been trying to tell your sergeant.'

'But that still leaves us with a problem, doesn't it, Mr Bromley? Are you quite sure there isn't something you haven't told us? Something you may have forgotten or overlooked, perhaps?'

Charles shook his head impatiently. 'Paul can be unpredictable at times, and he may have decided, for whatever reason, to return to London. I don't see anything particularly significant in that. You surely can't suspect him of having anything to do with this terrible business?'

Paget remained silent, but his expression spoke for him.

Charles sighed. 'This is ridiculous,' he said, struggling to contain his exasperation. 'Paul hardly knew Toni. Last night at dinner was the first time he'd seen her in several years. The very idea that he might have had something to do with her death is ludicrous.'

'Is it, sir? You told us that your brother came down here for the weekend. Now he's gone within hours of his arrival, apparently without a word of explanation to anyone. You also told us that he was out of the house during the time when we believe Miss Halliday was killed. You said you saw him returning to the house about nine, and when you asked him about a cut on his face he said he'd run into a door, an explanation you doubted yourself, so I don't call that ridiculous, Mr Bromley. I think it is behaviour that calls for an explanation. Which means I shall need your brother's address, and a description of both him and the car he was driving. A photograph would be helpful if you have one.'

Charles eyed Paget stonily for several seconds, then made a face. 'I suppose I do owe you an apology,' he said grudgingly. 'I'm afraid I wasn't quite straightforward with you when I told you that Paul was down for the weekend. He came down yesterday for a reason. It has nothing to do with Toni, I assure you. It was a private matter, a bit embarrassing, actually, and I saw no reason to mention it at the time, but now it seems I must.

'The truth is, Paul and I had a bit of a row. He came down to try to borrow money to cover some . . . business losses. This wasn't the first time he'd come down here expecting me to bail him out of some hare-brained scheme or other, you understand, and, quite frankly, I'd had enough. And when he told me the amount and said he needed it immediately, I'm afraid I lost my temper and told him he would have to look elsewhere for his money. I suppose, in the light of my refusal to help him, he decided he was wasting his time here and returned to London to look for help there.'

'I see. We will still need his address,' said Paget. 'You may be right about why he left, but he was here last night and we shall need a statement from him.'

Charles moved to the desk and took an address book out of a drawer. He opened it and handed it to Paget, who copied the address. 'Is there a business address where he might be reached if he's not at home?' he asked.

'I'm sure there is, but I don't have one. He didn't say, but I'm assuming he's still with Bainbridge-Grayson.'

Paget knew the name. Property developers specialising in industrial development, with offices throughout south-east England and the Home Counties. Not a small company by any means.

'Do you know what his position is there, by any chance?'

'Sorry, no.'

Paget closed the book and handed it back. 'When, exactly, did you have this argument with your brother?'

'Somewhere around three o'clock yesterday afternoon, as near as I can remember.'

'And you had made it quite clear that you wouldn't change your mind regarding his request for money?'

'Quite clear.'

'I see. Then, doesn't it strike you as strange, given the urgency of the matter, that your brother would wait until late last night before seeking help elsewhere?'

Charles Bromley had offered Paget a choice when the Chief Inspector asked for a room in which he could conduct interviews. 'There's this room,' he said. 'I shan't be using it this morning, and I can clear the desk. Or you can use the library if you prefer.'

Although the study was ideal for interviews in many ways, it was the presence of the desk that put Paget off and made him choose the library. It was a magnificent piece of craftsmanship, but it was so large that it dominated the room. He wanted the interviews to be as low-key and informal as possible, and he couldn't see himself conducting them from behind such a massive piece of furniture. It was far too intimidating.

The same desk appeared in an oil painting on the wall behind it. A grey-haired woman, head bent and eyes fixed in studied concentration on a leather-bound ledger, was seated at the desk.

It was hard to tell her age. Her features were strong yet finely drawn and unblemished. A handsome woman rather than a beautiful one, and there was a sense of purpose in every line.

'My grandmother, Ellen Bromley,' Bromley told him with almost reverential pride. 'I had that painting commissioned as a gift to her on the occasion of her seventy-fifth birthday. I spent hours in this room when I was a youngster, watching her work, and playing quietly so as not to disturb her. And that's the way I remember her,' he said with a nod toward the painting. 'It's funny, but even though she's been gone for more than twenty years, I still think of it as her desk. She raised us, you know. I was nine and Paul was five when our parents died. Killed in an avalanche while skiing in the Dolomites in nineteen sixty-eight.' Charles had spoken of his parents in a flat, unemotional voice as if speaking of strangers.

The opening of the library door broke into Paget's thoughts. He stood to greet Mrs Bromley as Tregalles, together with a uniformed WPC by the name of Maitland, ushered her inside and guided her to a seat. Slighter build, finer features, younger, and darker hair, this was not the same woman they had seen at the bedroom window when they arrived. Her right ankle was bandaged, and although she masked her discomfort well, she sank into the chair with obvious relief.

Paget pulled up a chair and sat down facing her. The young WPC retired discreetly to sit by the door, while Tregalles settled himself comfortably in a leather chair next to the window, and took out his notebook.

At forty-five, and despite her obvious grief, Margaret Bromley was an attractive woman with dark, expressive eyes. She wore a grey, long-sleeved dress with charcoal-coloured collar and cuffs. Made of a fine knitted material, and belted at the waist, it moulded to her body, a fact that did not go unnoticed by Tregalles, who remarked upon it later. Her short, dark hair was cut in a casual style that suited her, but nothing could conceal the pain and sadness in her eyes as she sat, hands folded in her lap, waiting for Paget to begin.

He said, 'I know how difficult this must be for you, Mrs Bromley, so I'll try to be as brief as possible. Your husband told us of the events leading up to dinner last night, and about what happened there, but I understand you went to see Miss Halliday in her room after Mr Nash had gone. Would you tell me about that, please? What did you talk about?'

'Toni,' she said quietly. 'Please call her Toni. "Miss Halliday" sounds so cold.'

'Of course. What did you and Toni talk about?'

Margaret Bromley closed her eyes for a moment, perhaps recalling the scene in her mind. 'I went along to ask her if what she'd said at dinner was true. About being pregnant, I mean, because I thought she'd made it up on the spur of the moment as an excuse for her drinking and the accident.' She looked down at her hands. 'I don't like saying this about my own daughter, Chief Inspector, but I'm afraid Toni was like that, even as a small child. She could never bring herself to admit that she was responsible when she did something wrong.'

She fell silent, and Paget waited. 'This is very hard for me,' she said at last, 'because I know the sort of things you will hear about Toni from other people, and I don't deny that she could be difficult at times, but no matter what she may have done, she didn't deserve to die like that.'

'Can you think of *anything* she might have done, either recently or in the past, that might lead to such an attack?'

Margaret Bromley shook her head, unable to bring herself to speak. Tears were very near the surface. Paget allowed her time to regain her composure before he spoke again. 'You were going to tell me about your conversation with Toni,' he prompted.

'Yes. Well . . .' Mrs Bromley took a deep breath to control the tremor in her voice when she continued. 'As I said, I was hoping she would tell me the truth. I tried to make her understand that I wanted to help her, but I had to know the truth. But she wouldn't listen to anything I had to say. She wouldn't even stand still. She kept pacing back and forth, muttering to herself as if I wasn't even there. When she did finally stop and face me, it was to repeat all the old accusations, and blame me for everything that was wrong in her life. I tried to reason with her, but it was no good, and we ended up having the most fearful row. In the end, I couldn't take it any more, and I literally ran from the room and nearly knocked poor Julian down on the way. I was so upset I didn't even see him standing there.'

'Where was this?'

'Outside Toni's room. I ran right into him.'

'Was he at the door or just passing?'

'I think he may have been about to knock, although he must have heard us screaming at each other inside. I'm really not sure.'

'You went from there directly to your room?'

'Yes.'

'What time would that be?'

She shook her head. 'I'm sorry; I have no idea.'

'Can you recall roughly how long you were in Toni's room?'

'Just a few minutes. Perhaps ten. No more, I'm sure.'

'Did you leave your room again after that? Talk to anyone?'

'Mrs Lodge came up shortly afterwards. Something about the meals. We'd never finished dinner, you see, but I'm afraid I wasn't much help to her. I was still very upset. She wasn't there long.'

'Mr Bromley said you looked in the study somewhere between eight fifteen and eight thirty.'

Margaret Bromley stared at him blankly, eyes unfocussed, vacant as if she had drifted off into a realm of her own, and Paget had an almost irresistible urge to snap his fingers to bring her out of it. Her eyes closed, then opened again, and she shook her head as if to clear it. She looked confused. 'I'm sorry,' she said huskily. 'What did you say, Chief Inspector?'

Paget repeated the question. 'Mr Bromley said you were looking for his brother, Paul.'

Mrs Bromley looked away, frowning slightly as if trying to remember. 'Yes. Yes, that's right,' she said vaguely. 'And then I went into the kitchen to ask Mrs Lodge if she had seen Paul. She said she thought he had gone down to the village.'

Margaret Bromley stopped speaking. The silence between them lengthened.

Concerned, Paget leaned forward. 'Mrs Bromley . . .? Are you all right?'

His words seemed to bring her back. 'Yes, yes, of course I'm all right,' she said sharply, then shrugged guiltily and said, 'I'm sorry, I didn't mean it to sound that way. I really am all right, so there's no need to look so worried. It's just that I haven't been sleeping very well lately, and now, with this happening . . .

Charles says it's stress. He didn't want me to talk to you this morning, but I wanted to do it if it will help you find who did this terrible thing.' She lifted her eyes to meet those of Paget. 'So,' she said firmly, 'where were we, Chief Inspector?'

'You said Mrs Lodge told you she thought your brother-in-law had gone to the village,' he said. 'What did you do then?'

'I went outside to see if his car was there. The garage door was up and the car was there, but Paul wasn't, so I thought he might have decided to walk to the village. It was a nice evening, so I decided to walk down there myself.'

'It wasn't raining then?'

'No. Clouds were gathering, and there was some rumbling in the distance, but I thought the storm was still a long way off, so it took me by surprise when it started to rain.'

'Even so, it must have been getting dark by then. May I ask why it was so important for you to find your brother-in-law?'

A hint of colour crept into her face as she shook her head. 'I wanted to talk to him about a business matter before he returned to London.'

'You knew he intended to return to London last night?'

'Not last night, no, but I thought he might be planning to leave early this morning.'

'Did you find him?'

'No. I had just started down the long hill when I turned my ankle and I had to turn back. It was my own fault. I should have known better than to go down Manor Lane in high heels, and to make matters worse, that was when it started to rain. I couldn't hurry because the ankle was so painful, so I was completely drenched by the time I reached the house.'

'Did you meet anyone, either on the way down or on the way back?'

Margaret Bromley shook her head.

'I was thinking in particular of Major Farnsworth,' Paget said. 'I assume you do know the major?'

A flicker of distaste crossed her face. 'Not really. That is to say I met him once, briefly. It was shortly after he and his wife moved into Lower Farm, and I have seen him go by in the evening with the dog, but I didn't see him last night. The only one I saw was Julian.'

Her voice faded, as did the light in Margaret Bromley's eyes, and Paget had the eerie feeling once again that there was no one there.

'Mrs Bromley?' he prompted. There was no response. Paget exchanged glances with Tregalles, and was halfway out of his chair when she blinked and said, 'I'm sorry, Chief Inspector. What did you say?'

'Perhaps you would prefer to finish this later?' he suggested.

'I am rather tired,' she admitted, 'but I would like to get this over with now that I'm here. Is there much more?'

Wherever Margaret Bromley had been a few moments ago, she seemed to be in full control of herself now. 'You were saying that you saw Julian when you were on your way back to the house.'

'That's right. He came through the gate from Manor Lane as I reached the door. We came into the house together.'

'Did he say where he'd been?'

'No. We were both soaking wet and cold, so we were more interested in getting out of our wet clothes. Julian dashed upstairs, and I went into the kitchen to sit down, and found Charles there. He took a look at the ankle, then helped me up the stairs. I had a warm bath, then laid on the bed with a packet of frozen peas and a bandage on the ankle.'

As if reminded of her injury, Margaret Bromley drew her outstretched leg closer in an attempt to find a more comfortable position for her foot.

'I won't keep you much longer,' Paget assured her, 'but there is just one more question before you go, if you don't mind. Did you by any chance see Paul Bromley later in the evening?'

'Yes, as a matter of fact, I did,' she said. He knocked on my door and said Charles had told him I was looking for him.'

'Do you remember what time that was? Approximately?'

'Around ten, I think it was. I remember I was hanging my clothes up to dry before turning in for the night, when Paul knocked on the door. I'd left them on the floor when I stripped off, and they were still wet,' she explained.

'Did he say where he'd been?'

'No.'

'Did he mention anything then about leaving for London?'

Margaret Bromley pulled herself forward, placing both hands on the arms of the chair, testing her foot against the floor. 'No,' she said vaguely as if thinking of something else, 'and I think I would like to lie down, now.' She stretched out her hand. 'Would you mind, Chief Inspector?'

'Of course, and thank you for being so patient, Mrs Bromley.' He stood up to help her to her feet.

They made their way to the door where WPC Maitland stood waiting to take Mrs Bromley's arm and escort her back to her room. But before they could leave, Paget took out the glassine envelope Grace had given him, and held it up for Mrs Bromley to see. 'Tell me,' he said, 'do you recognize these pieces of jewellery, Mrs Bromley?'

She stared. 'I most certainly do!' she said. 'They're mine! What are you doing with them?'

'You didn't give them to anyone?'

'Give them to anyone? Of course I didn't give then to anyone. Where did you get them?'

'They were found among your daughter's belongings in the barn,' he said gently.

'Oh!' Margaret Bromley's eyes expressed such a mixture of emotions that Paget couldn't tell what was going through her mind. She held out her hand. 'May I have them?' she asked huskily.

'I'm afraid not,' he said. 'They are part of the evidence recovered at the crime scene, but they will be returned to you as soon as possible. Sergeant Tregalles will give you a receipt to show that we have them in our possession. Could you give me some idea of their value?'

'I really don't know what they would be worth now,' she said as she continued to stare at them as if hypnotised, 'but I believe it would be safe to say the figure would be in excess of six or seven thousand pounds. Charles could tell you. He will have the insurance policy filed away somewhere.'

EIGHT

Before going in search of the next person on his list, Tregalles took time to catch up on his notes. 'She *seems* like a very nice woman,' he observed as he flipped through the pages, 'but I don't think she was being quite straight with us.'

Paget walked over to the window and stood looking out. 'Not that I disagree with you,' he said, 'but why do you say that?'

'Well, for starters, she was so upset with her daughter that she stormed out of the room and almost knocked Julian down, then she couldn't even talk straight to her housekeeper, but then things suddenly change.'

'Go on.'

Tregalles tapped his notebook. 'I don't know what happened, but something must have, because suddenly the only thing she's interested in is finding this brother-in-law of hers. Asks her husband if he's seen him; asks the housekeeper, then goes tearing off down the road in her high heels to find him, even though it's beginning to get dark and a storm's in the offing, and I can't help wondering why?'

'She said it had to do with a business deal,' Paget said.

'I know what she *said*, but it must have been one hell of a deal to make her go tearing off like that. Didn't even stop to change her shoes? And we've only got her word for it that that was where she went. She said she twisted her ankle when she was part way down the long hill, and that has to be at least a quarter of a mile from here. So, if that ankle is as bad as it appeared to be this morning, I don't see how she managed to get back here in the pouring rain without help.'

'So, what are you suggesting?'

'I think something happened between the time she saw Mrs Lodge and the time she started to look for Paul,' Tregalles said slowly. 'Something that scared the hell out of her, maybe?'

'Such as?'

'Don't know,' Tregalles admitted. 'Maybe she found out that Paul was going to kill Toni? That would explain her trying to find him. She tried to stop him but she was too late, because he hadn't gone to the village at all, but to the barn.'

Paget turned to face him. 'If that was the case, why didn't she enlist the aid of others to stop him? Why didn't she raise the alarm or call the police? And why didn't she tell us just now?'

'Well, put that way, that might not have been the reason,' Tregalles admitted, 'but you know what I mean. It's just that it must have been something out of the ordinary to make her go dashing off like that. And was it my imagination, or did she go blank on you a couple of times? Or was that some sort of act?'

'I don't think it was an act,' said Paget slowly. 'She seemed to be genuinely out of it for several seconds each time. Mr Bromley said she was suffering from stress, but that looked like something more than stress to me.'

'Drugs?' the sergeant suggested. 'Seems like Toni was into drugs as well as drink, so maybe mummy's into them as well.'

'Or a side effect from medication,' Paget said. 'But both her husband and her doctor would have picked up on something like that.'

'Unless Bromley is just saying it's stress so he won't have to admit his wife's an addict.'

'And Lockwood?'

Tregalles shrugged. 'We don't know what he has to say yet, do we? Family doctor to the Bromleys . . . He might just go along with it if Bromley asked him to. In fact,' he added darkly, 'it may be Lockwood who's keeping her supplied.'

'I think that may be a bit of a stretch,' Paget said drily, 'but I'll keep it in mind. Anything else?'

'Just one thing. If Mrs Bromley still had any illusions about her daughter, I think they were knocked sideways when you showed her the jewellery.'

Paget nodded. 'I think you're right,' he said soberly. He moved back to his seat and sat down. 'So, who's next?'

Julian Bromley's name was next on the list, but Paget decided to rearrange the order. 'Let's have Gwyneth Jones in,' he said.

'So far, everything we've heard has come from the family. We might get a different view of things from the maid.'

Gwyneth Jones looked more than a little apprehensive when Maitland ushered her in. 'Nervous' was the note Tregalles put down beside her name, then added 'Why?'

She sat down on the edge of the chair, hands clasped tightly together, knuckles white and rigid. She was a pretty girl, but her dark-blue eyes were rimmed with red, and it was clear that she'd been crying.

'Do you mind if I call you Gwyneth?' Paget asked by way of opening the conversation.

The question seemed to surprise her. 'No, sir. Everybody does.'

'Good. And there is no need to feel nervous, Gwyneth. All we are trying to do is find out as much as possible about Toni Halliday's movements prior to her going to the barn last night, so we will be talking to everyone in the house.'

'Yes, sir.' It was as if she had brushed his words aside and was bracing herself for what was to come.

'I'd like you to begin by telling me what happened at dinner last night. Just take your time and tell me how you remember it.'

'You mean about Mr Nash coming in, sir?'

'Let's start before that. What time did dinner begin?'

'Seven o'clock on the dot, like always,' Gwyneth told him. 'Mr Bromley is very particular about that. But Miss Halliday came in a few minutes later, after I'd served the soup.'

'You seem quite sure of the time.'

'Yes, sir. Mr Bromley doesn't like people to be late, and I kept looking at the time and wondering where Miss Halliday had got to.'

'Did she offer any explanation for her late arrival?'

'No, sir.'

'How would you describe Miss Halliday's condition?'

Gwyneth frowned. 'I'm not sure what you mean,' she said hesitantly.

'Well, was there any indication that she'd been drinking, for example?'

The girl looked at Paget as if trying to judge what he might want her to say. 'I think she might have, sir,' she said cautiously.

'Might have . . .?' Paget probed gently.

'Well, it's just that she wasn't too steady on her feet, and she knocked her knife off the table when she sat down, and I had to get her another one.'

'Was that normal? Would you say she was in the habit of drinking?'

Gwyneth considered the question. 'Not really,' she said slowly. 'More fits and starts, if you know what I mean, sir. I never actually saw her take a drink, except for wine at dinner. But there were times when she acted like she'd a had a drink or two too many, but different somehow.'

'Different in what way?'

'It's sort of hard to explain, sir.' Gwyneth sat frowning down at her hands in her lap. 'It was like she was – well, off in a world of her own, sort of.' She looked up at Paget. 'She could be quite nice, then.'

'So there were times when she wasn't very nice. Is that right, Gwyneth?'

The girl shifted uncomfortably in her chair. 'It's just that she could be a bit sharp sometimes, if you know what I mean.'

'Can you give me an example?'

Gwyneth squirmed. 'If you don't mind, sir, I don't think it's for me to say.'

'But I do mind, Gwyneth. You see, if we are to find out who killed Toni Halliday, we have to know as much as possible about her, so all we want is the truth, good or bad. And what you tell us here remains here, if that's what you're worried about. Now, I get the feeling that you and Miss Halliday didn't get along very well, and if that is the case, I'd like to know why.'

'Well . . . it's just that there was no pleasing her some days. It used to be nice working here, but everything changed when she came. It was like walking on eggs being around her, because you never knew what sort of mood she was in.' Gwyneth rolled her eyes. 'And the way she spoke to her mother—'

She stopped dead. Colour flooded into her face. 'Sorry, sir,' she said in a small voice. 'I didn't mean . . .' The colour deepened.

'No need to apologize, Gwyneth,' Paget said. 'How did Miss Halliday speak to her mother?'

Gwyneth tilted her chin and looked squarely at Paget. 'It's just that I didn't think it was very nice, that's all, sir,' she said, ''specially with her mum being ill and all. It was like Miss Toni was always trying to put her mum in the wrong and make her feel guilty so she'd give in to her.'

'I'm afraid you're going to have to explain that for me, Gwyneth,' Paget said. 'Making Mrs Bromley feel guilty? About what?'

'About everything. It was the *way* she said things. I know if I spoke to my mum like that I'd get a clip round the ear. It didn't matter how nice Mrs B was to her, Miss Toni always managed to twist it around somehow to put her mum in the wrong. And it wasn't only her mum; she did it with everybody.'

'Again, can you give me an example?'

Gwyneth eyed him uncertainly. 'Well, like yesterday morning. I was upstairs doing the rooms when she came along the corridor. Mrs B was just coming out of her room, and Miss Toni says, "I have to go into Worcester, so I'll need the keys to the car." Just like that! No "please" or anything like that. More like they were *her* keys. You'd have thought it was *her* car, not her mother's.'

'How did Mrs Bromley react?'

'She said she wouldn't mind a day out herself, and it would be nice to have lunch out for a change, just the two of them. But Miss Toni went right off the deep end. She said if her mother didn't want to let her have the car, then why didn't she say so straight out. She went on and on about her mother not trusting her with anything of her own. Got into a proper old snit about it, she did.'

'What did her mother have to say?'

'She gave in to her, sir,' Gwyneth said with a puzzled frown. 'She said if Miss Toni needed the car that badly, she could have it, then she went into her room to get the keys, and that was when Miss Toni spotted me tidying up in her bedroom. The door was wide open, so I couldn't help but see and hear what was going on. I mean it wasn't as if I was *trying* to listen; I was just there doing what I was supposed to, but she came to the door and told me to stop sneaking around and spying on her.'

'What did she say, exactly, Gwyneth? Her words as near as you can remember them.'

'Like I said, sir, she told me to stop spying on—'

'Her actual words, if you don't mind, Gwyneth,' Paget said firmly.

The girl glanced around the room as if afraid of being overheard and lowered her voice. 'It's just that I wouldn't want Mrs B to know I told you,' she said, 'specially now her daughter's dead.'

'She won't hear it from us,' Paget assured her, 'so, please, Gwyneth, tell me what Miss Halliday said.'

Gwyneth drew a deep breath. 'She said, "And you can keep your shitty little snout out of my business, Miss Nosey Parker. Creeping around, spying on me so you can tattle-tale to the lord of the manor." She meant Mr Bromley,' Gwyneth explained. 'She'd say things like that when Mr B wasn't around. Sort of sneering, like, if you know what I mean. I told her I was just making the beds like I was supposed to, but she wouldn't have it. She said, "Just remember your place here. One word from me and you'll be out on your arse, and then where will you be? There's not much call for *scullery* maids around here, is there?"'

Gwyneth's eyes flashed angrily. '*And* she meant it!' she concluded heatedly. 'She was the sort who would do it out of sheer spite.' There was a hard edge to the words that hadn't been there before, making Paget wonder if there might be more to Gwyneth Jones than they'd seen so far.

'Did you tell anyone about this?'

Gwyneth shrugged. 'Wouldn't be much point, would there, sir?' she said. 'If I told Mr B it would be like telling tales, and I didn't want that. And Mrs B wouldn't have believed me, because she wouldn't hear anything bad said about her daughter, and Miss Toni would have denied it anyway, and then she'd have seen me sacked for sure, and I need this job.'

Paget was about to ask another question, but Gwyneth continued on. 'She wasn't like that when she first came here,' she said. 'She was all charm and friendly then, and I quite liked her. But then she changed. Like with Julian. She and him were as thick as thieves at first; took to one another straight off. But it didn't last more than a couple of weeks before she went off him. I felt sorry for him, actually, because he didn't go off her, you could tell. Not even when she treated him the way she did.

Proper misery, he was, moping about the place, but she didn't care. I think she enjoyed it.'

'You say they were as thick as thieves. Do you mean romantically?'

Gwyneth became still, as if realizing that perhaps she had said too much. Colour crept into her cheeks once again. 'You could say that, sir,' she said cautiously.

'Were they sleeping together?'

'Some nights, yes sir. That is,' she added quickly, 'like I said, just at first.'

'When did that relationship come to an end?'

'Couldn't have been more than a couple of weeks after she came. I mean that's more or less when she cut him off, as you might say, but he kept after her for weeks after that.'

'Do you know why it ended?'

Gwyneth shook her head.

'Did you ever see Miss Halliday with anyone else – either here or outside the manor?'

'You mean another man? No, sir.'

'Did Miss Halliday go into town very often?'

'She did at first. Almost every day when she had her own car, but not so often since she's been without it. But when she does, it's usually on a Thursday, like yesterday.'

'Do you know where she goes? And what's so special about Thursdays?'

Gwyneth shrugged. 'She told her mum she was going into Worcester yesterday, but I don't know if that's where she always went.'

Paget decided to leave that line of questioning for the moment, and asked Gwyneth what she had done after Nash left.

'I cleared up,' she said. 'Nobody came back to the dining room, and the dinner had gone cold anyway, so Mrs Lodge told me to clear up. So I did.'

'And then?'

'I put everything in the dishwasher, and went home.'

'What time did you leave?'

There was a slight hesitation before Gwyneth said, 'I get off at eight.'

'That's not exactly what I asked, is it, Gwyneth?' Paget said.

'So, what time did you actually leave? And can Mrs Lodge confirm that?'

Gwyneth looked guilty. 'Well, no, not really. I mean she wasn't there when I left, and to be honest, sir, I did leave just a *few* minutes early, and she must have come in just after I'd gone, because she gave me a proper ticking off this morning. I don't think she would have minded so much if I hadn't forgotten to do the broth before I went, but she was none too pleased about that, I can tell you.'

'Broth?' Paget queried.

'It's for soups and things. Cook left it simmering. I was supposed to take it into the wash-house to cool before I left, but I forgot. Mrs Lodge came back just after I'd gone and saw it was still there on the cooker, so she had to do it. It's very heavy, and Mrs Lodge isn't too steady on her feet, so I usually do it. It's not that I mind doing it; I just forgot last night, that's all. I told her I was sorry.'

'And you went straight home?'

Gwyneth's eyes shifted away. 'That's right.' she said. Her voice sounded strained.

'You live in Hallows End?'

'Yes.'

'Which way did you go? Down Manor Lane or round by the main road?'

'Manor Lane,' she said promptly. Her hands were clasped again.

'Did you see anyone or anything unusual along the way? Did you speak to anyone?'

The girl shook her head. 'No.'

'Do you know the man who was injured last night? Major Farnsworth?'

'No, sir,' she said quickly.

Paget looked puzzled. 'But surely you must,' he said. 'He lives at Lower Farm, and you must pass it on your way back and forth to work.'

'Oh, well, yes, if that's what you mean,' she said hastily. 'I've *seen* him out walking with the dog, but I don't *know* him, if you see what I mean?'

'But you didn't see him last night?'

'No, sir.'

Paget eyed Gwyneth thoughtfully. He felt sure that she was holding something back, but it might not have anything to do with the investigation. 'Thank you, Gwyneth,' he said as he got to his feet, 'you've been very helpful.'

Her relief was evident as she scrambled to her feet. 'Just one question before you go,' he said as she reached the door. 'It looked to me as if you'd been crying when you came in. Is there something wrong? Something you would like to tell me?'

'Crying, sir?' The words caught in her throat. She forced a small laugh. 'Oh, no, sir. I wasn't crying. I got something in my eyes coming to work on the bike. It made my eyes run, that's all. May I go now, sir? Mrs Lodge will be needing me.'

NINE

Margaret Bromley sat on the floor in her room, legs drawn up, hands clasped around her knees. Every drawer in her desk, the dressing table, even the small drawers in the bedside tables had been pulled out, some of them overturned on the floor, their contents scattered across the carpet as her search had become more frantic. It was her own fault for being so careless about where she left her jewels, she told herself, because those stored in the wall safe were untouched as far as she could tell. Thank God she hadn't shared the combination with Toni, as she had shared so many other things these past few weeks.

More than half the pieces she had left so thoughtlessly in drawers were gone. Toni must have been stealing things bit by bit ever since she'd arrived, then scooped up whatever she could find before leaving the manor for the last time. Margaret felt the anger rising; anger at herself for being such a fool. Anger for allowing herself to believe that Toni had changed, when it was clear that she would never change.

How foolish and pathetic she must have looked to Charles,

she thought bitterly. And how Toni must have despised her for her weakness.

And now she was dead. Her only child was dead, but she felt nothing. There was no sense of loss, no pain, just emptiness and . . . relief? Shocked and shaken to the core when Charles had told her what had happened the night before, she had broken down and wept. But there were no tears now. Just images of years gone by, flickering like old movies inside her head. Images so real and vivid she could hear the nurse's voice saying, in her lovely Irish brogue, 'It's a girl, a lovely baby girl. You have a daughter, Mrs Halliday.'

Margaret opened her eyes, half expecting to see the nurse standing there in mask and gown. Just as well, she thought sadly, because she would have had to tell her that she'd been wrong. Toni, difficult from the very beginning, had never been 'her daughter'. Even feeding had been hard. Nothing seemed to suit, nor would she settle, which led to sleepless nights and ragged nerves. Toni had fought her every inch of the way, and Margaret had been driven to despair in those first few years with no one to turn to for help. Bernard was away for months at a time, and when he did return he blamed her for Toni's bad behaviour. Then, when Toni was five, and he realized how photogenic she was, he began to use her as a prop in photo ops with the Press and on TV.

Only five years old, but Toni had known instinctively how to play up to him. For his part, Bernard had used her shamelessly and catered to her every whim. From that point on, Toni was his . . . for life!

Margaret pulled herself to her feet. It was over she told herself. She'd wasted enough of her life on dreams and false hopes. She looked around the room. Time to pick up the pieces and move on. She smiled wryly at the unintended metaphor as she picked up a drawer and slid it back in place.

Julian Bromley, a self-styled actor who was 'resting' at the moment, slouched inelegantly in the chair, his long, thin legs stretched out before him, crossed at the ankles. He was taller than his father, slim, dark-haired, and deeply tanned. His face was long and lean – a bit too narrow to be really handsome, but striking nevertheless, and no doubt there would be women who would find the wolfish look attractive. His blow-dried hair was practically a work of art, and whether consciously or unconsciously, he kept drawing attention to it by stroking it with his fingertips throughout the interview.

He wore a deep magenta shirt, and jeans so faded and threadbare that they looked as if they'd lost an argument with a rock crusher, but expensive if the label on his backside was to be believed, as were the heavy sandals that completed the ensemble.

Paget began the questioning by asking him when he had last see Toni Halliday.

Julian frowned in studied concentration. 'It was just after dinner last night,' he said.

'Can you give me a time? It's important.'

'Half past seven, more or less,' he said. 'We sat down at seven as usual. Toni came waltzing in a few minutes later, then this plumber chap came crashing into the room, waving his arms about and threatening Toni. Near hysterics all round. I'm sure you can imagine, but to tell you the truth, Chief Inspector, I thought the whole thing was a bit of a farce. Over-acting in the theatrical sense, if you will. Not that I was unsympathetic to what had happened to his daughter, of course, but it really was a bit over the top. But then, considering what happened later . . . Terrible,' he concluded, pursing his lips and composing his features into a sorrowful frown.

'So the last time you saw Miss Halliday was around seven thirty,' said Paget, bringing him back to the original question. 'Where were you in the house at the time?'

'At the bottom of the main stairs. Charles and Lockwood were outside seeing the plumber chap off, and no one seemed interested in finishing dinner, so we all went our separate ways.'

Tregalles spoke up for the first time, pen poised over his notebook. 'You're quite sure about that, are you sir?' he asked. 'You didn't see her leave the house, for example?'

'Quite sure, Sergeant,' said Julian sharply. 'Did you not hear me?'

'Just making sure I've got it right for the record, sir,' Tregalles told him blandly.

'But that's *not* quite right, is it, Mr Bromley?' Paget said. 'Or did you simply forget about your meeting with Miss Halliday later that evening? The one in Miss Halliday's room?' He knew he was taking a chance, but from what both Margaret Bromley and Gwyneth had told them, he thought it a risk worth taking.

Julian wrinkled his nose in distaste and rolled his eyes. 'I suppose it was dear Margaret who told you that,' he said acerbically. 'Not that it's any of her business. What did she do? Listen through the wall? Her room is right next door, you know.'

Paget didn't answer. Julian Bromley would hang himself, given enough rope.

'I'll bet she didn't tell you what *she* said when she came charging out of Toni's room like a mad cow, did she?' Julian threw a questioning glance at Paget. 'No, I thought not. She didn't tell you *she* threatened to kill Toni, did she?' Clearly disappointed at the lack of reaction, he plunged on. 'She was in such a blind rage that she ran right into me. She said, "I swear I would have strangled that girl if I'd stayed in there one more minute," or words to that effect. Then she pushed me out of the way and went storming off to her room and slammed the door so hard it's a wonder it didn't come off its hinges.'

'Did Mrs Bromley say anything else?'

'Isn't that enough?' Julian heaved himself out of the chair and crossed the room to stand in front of the fireplace. 'Well, isn't it?' he repeated.

Paget ignored the question. 'Right now, I'm more interested in *your* movements last evening,' he said. 'So, tell me, how long were you in Miss Halliday's room?'

Julian eyed him stonily, then grimaced as if remembering something unpleasant. 'No more than a few minutes,' he said. 'I wouldn't have been there that long if Toni had had her way. Spent half the time trying to shove me out of the door. She wouldn't take anything I said seriously. There was no reasoning with her at all.'

'What was she being unreasonable about, Mr Bromley?'

'I don't think that is any of your business,' Julian said loftily.

'You talked about the child, didn't you?' Paget prompted. It was a guess, but once again a fairly safe one. 'You wanted to know if Toni intended naming you as the father.'

The expression on Julian's face told him he had scored a direct hit. Suddenly the arrogance was gone, and he looked at Paget with troubled eyes. 'I had nothing to do with her death, if that's what you think,' he protested. 'We had a row, yes, but . . . She was killed in the barn, for God's sake. I left her in her room.'

'You could have followed her there.'

'But I didn't!' His voice was beginning to rise.

'Then, let's go back to the beginning. Tell me what happened when you went into the room after Mrs Bromley left.'

Julian shook his head. 'I didn't go in right away,' he said. 'I'd heard Toni and her mother shouting at each other, so I decided to let Toni cool off before tackling her myself. I was going to wait for half an hour or so before going back upstairs, but I couldn't wait; I had to know what she was going to do.'

'Time?' Paget said.

'Eh?'

'What time was it when you went back up to see Toni?'

'Who knows?' Julian snapped irritably, but stopped when he saw the expression on Paget's face. 'Eight, eight fifteen, something like that,' he said sullenly. 'I was hoping Toni would have cooled down by then, but she'd been drinking, her eyes were red, and by the way she kept snuffling I'm sure she'd been snorting cocaine as well. But she wouldn't even listen to me. Just kept telling me to get out. Even tried to push me out the door physically. When that didn't work she went on charging around the room, pulling clothes out of drawers, throwing them on the bed.'

Julian sighed and shook his head. 'It was useless,' he said bitterly. 'There was no reasoning with her at all, so I left. I thought I might stand a better chance in the morning when she'd slept it off.'

'You say she was pulling things out of drawers and throwing them on the bed,' said Paget. 'Did it not occur to you that the reason she wanted you out of there was because she was getting ready to leave?'

Julian shook his head impatiently. 'No it didn't,' he said huffily, 'but then I'm not a detective and I had other things on my mind.'

'Let's go back to *why* you went to see her in the first place. It was to talk about the child, wasn't it?'

Julian gave a grudging nod. 'I wanted to find out if she really was pregnant, and if she was, whether it was mine. And if it was, I wanted her to promise not to tell anyone, least of all my father. I didn't want him to know that we'd been sleeping together.'

'What did you do after you left?' asked Paget.

'I went out. Went for a walk along the path above the river, trying to think about what I was going to say to Charles if Toni did tell him. She would have, you know. She was like that.'

'Did you meet anyone while you were out?'

'No, except for some kids on bikes some distance off. Not that I was out there for very long, because the storm came up and I had to leg it for home. Even so, it was blowing gale-force winds and the rain was coming down in sheets by the time I got back.'

'You went straight up Manor Lane, across the road and out onto the heath when you left the house? Is that right?'

'Yes.'

'Major Farnsworth was out walking with his dog around that time,' said Paget. 'Did you happen to see him?'

'No. I told you, I didn't see anyone . . . well, except for the two cars on my way back. I didn't get much of a look at the first, although I'm pretty sure it was a light-coloured Jag. But I did recognize the second car. It was Lockwood's. Then, when I went through the gate, Margaret was coming up from the stables, hobbling and moaning about her ankle, and we went inside together. I didn't think about it at the time, but I wonder . . .?' Julian pursed his lips and screwed up his face as if in deep thought.

'Exactly what do you wonder?' Paget prompted.

Julian shrugged. 'Oh, Charles doesn't see anything wrong with it, but one can't help wondering, can one? I mean, considering the number of times Lockwood pops in to see how Margaret is getting on, it just struck me as a bit of a coincidence that she was coming up to the house from the stables, while Lockwood was coming up the lane on the other side of the wall.' He flicked his fingers through his hair. 'But then, Charles is always accusing me of having an over-active imagination.'

Paget decided it was time to bring Julian down to earth. 'So,' he said coldly, 'let's leave that for the moment and look at what you've told us so far. You were scared to death for fear that Toni Halliday would name you as the father of the child she claimed to be carrying, but when she refused to talk to you, and pushed you out of the room, you simply left it at that and went for a walk. And shortly after that, Miss Halliday turns up dead. As I see it, you realized that she was preparing to leave the manor; you followed her, confronted her in the barn, and when she refused to listen to you, you grabbed the closest thing to hand and killed her. You had motive, means, opportunity, and by your own admission, no alibi. And to top it off, considering that you and she were sleeping together only a few weeks ago, you don't appear to be very troubled by her death. In fact, I suspect that you're relieved.'

Julian stared at him. 'You can't be *serious* . . .? Oh, for Christ's sake, man . . .' Words failed him.

'Oh, but I am very serious, Mr Bromley,' said Paget. 'So, unless you can produce a witness, someone who can confirm where you were and what you were doing during the time you claim to have been out walking, then I'm very much afraid you are the prime suspect. Is there anything you wish to tell me?'

Julian swallowed hard. 'I didn't,' he said hoarsely. 'I *couldn't*! I swear, Chief Inspector, I had nothing to do with it. I was out walking where—'

'Where no one saw you,' Paget broke in.

'There was Lockwood. He must have seen me in the headlights. And Margaret. You can ask them.'

'Mere yards from the barn where Toni Halliday lay dead?' Paget countered. 'Hardly a cast-iron alibi, is it, Mr Bromley?'

'But I couldn't!' Suddenly, Julian Bromley looked more like a frightened schoolboy about to burst into tears. 'Honest to God, I swear the last time I saw Toni was when I left her room.'

Tregalles looked up. 'You also told us that the last time you saw her was at the bottom of the stairs just after dinner,' he said. 'And that was a lie, wasn't it, sir?'

'Yes, but that was before . . .' Julian sucked in his breath. 'What I'm telling you now is the truth, I swear to God!'

Paget and Tregalles exchanged glances. Tregalles shook his head.

'We'll see about that,' Paget said. 'Meanwhile, please don't leave the area without speaking to me first, and do let us know if you remember seeing anyone else while you were out . . . walking.'

The look on Julian's face was almost comical. 'You mean I can go?'

'For now,' Paget told him as he got to his feet. 'Has anyone taken your fingerprints this morning?'

Julian shook his head.

'They will,' Paget assured him, 'so please stay close to home until they have.'

Before Paget had a chance to call the next person on his list, there was a light tap on the door, and Gwyneth entered the room.

'Excuse me, sir, but a Chief Superintendent Brock would like you to ring him at this number.' She handed him a slip of paper, then scuttled out of the room as if afraid he might start to ask her more questions.

'Ah, Paget,' Brock said when he rang. 'I need you back here straightaway. I have a meeting with my opposite number in the West Mercia Force at two thirty this afternoon. It's regarding this combined training schedule and exchange of junior officers starting next year. Alcott used to take care of all that, but I know you were involved as well, so I need you back here so we can go over some of the details before the meeting. In fact, since there can't be much more for you to do out there, you might as well sit in on the meeting with me this afternoon as well. I'm sure DS Ormside and DS Tregalles can run things from the incident room in Hallows End once everything is set up.'

'We are in the middle of taking statements,' Paget pointed out, 'so—'

'Statements?' Brock asked sharply. 'From whom?'

'Family members and . . .'

Something like a heavy sigh came down the line before Brock spoke again. 'I thought I had made myself clear last night,' he said. 'This is a very difficult time for the family, and I don't want you making things even harder for them by intruding on their grief. After all, it's not as if you're going to find the girl's killer there, is it? So, the sooner you and DS Tregalles are out of there the better. DS Ormside can run things from Hallows End, and he can start with this man, Nash. I'm not entirely satisfied that he's in the clear, despite what you told me this morning. He did threaten the girl in front of witnesses, so I want his alibi checked again.'

'With all due respect, sir, I'm afraid it's not *quite* as simple as that . . .' Paget began, only to find himself speaking into a dead phone. Brock had hung up.

'Problems?' Tregalles asked.

'Mr Brock seems to think that our presence here might upset the family, and we are wasting our time and theirs, so he wants us to start looking elsewhere for our killer.'

Tregalles made a face. 'Pity he wasn't here to listen to some of the rubbish we've been listening to this morning,' he said. 'So, what do we do now?'

'We carry on here and treat them the same as anyone else,' Paget told him. 'At least you do. Mr Brock wants me back in the office, and it looks as if I'll be gone for the rest of the day. But I think we should go down to the village and find out how Ormside is getting on and bring him up to date before I go back to town. After that I want you to come back here and finish the interviews, regardless of what Mr Brock seems to think.'

TEN

They found Len Ormside in the parish hall surrounded by boxes, desks, filing cabinets, computers, trays, chalkboards and easels, and all the paraphernalia needed to support the team who would spearhead the investigation into the death of Toni Halliday.

Stepping over cables, Ormside led them to a corner of the room where he'd set up his own desk, then dragged up a couple of metal chairs for Paget and Tregalles to sit on before settling comfortably into the padded swivel chair that always managed to accompany him no matter where he was asked to set up shop.

'We'll have things organized by the end of the day,' he said with the quiet assurance of one who had been through this many times before, and Paget didn't doubt it, despite the seeming chaos. Sergeant Leonard Ormside, grey-haired, long, lean, and sharp-featured, had been on the force for almost thirty years, and Paget had come to rely on the man and trust his judgement.

Bctween them, Paget and Tregalles spent the next half hour bringing the grizzled sergeant up to date. Chair tipped back, Ormside sat with his eyes half closed while he listened. From time to time he would lean forward to make a note, then resume his position once again.

'I can add one bit of information to that,' he told them when they'd finished. 'I've had Molly Forsythe at the hospital chasing down the evening and night staff and getting their statements, and unless they're all lying, this man, Nash, is in the clear.'

'Good,' said Paget. 'Nice to have that out of the way, although I doubt if Mr Brock will be any too pleased.' He glanced at the time. 'And he won't be too pleased with me if I hang about here much longer, so I'll be on my way. Has there been any word on Farnsworth's condition?'

'Last report was that he is recovering,' Ormside said. 'His injuries aren't as bad as they first thought. The doctor said he'll take another look at him this afternoon, and let us know if he thinks Farnsworth is up to talking to us today. Otherwise it will be sometime tomorrow.'

'Right,' said Paget, 'but whenever it is, I want to be informed immediately. And let's get Forsythe back out here to assist Tregalles with the interviews with Mrs Etherton and Mrs Lodge. Oh, yes, and I want someone to follow up on Paul Bromley. His brother seems to think he's gone back to London, but we can't be sure of that. We have his address.'

'I'll get someone on it,' Ormside promised. 'What was he driving?'

'According to Mr Bromley, it's a white or possibly cream sports car, and Paul Bromley claims he borrowed it from a friend,' Tregalles said.

'That's it?'

'That's it, I'm afraid,' Tregalles told him.

The phone on Ormside's desk rang. He picked it up, then shot a warning glance at Paget. 'Yes, Chief Superintendent,' he said as Paget rose quickly and made for the door. 'Yes, sir, he's on his way. Yes, sir, that's right, he left some time ago . . .'

With introductions made, Mrs Etherton sat facing Tregalles, hands lying loosely in her lap as she waited for him to begin. She reminded Molly of an aunt of hers, who lived on a farm. Same straight back, same weathered features, and the same no-nonsense set to the mouth, but younger by about ten years.

'Just to keep things straight in my mind,' Tregalles said, 'do you live here at the manor, Mrs Etherton?'

'Yes, I do.' Her voice was clear, precise, and pleasant to the ear. 'Bromley Manor has been my home for the past twelve years. After my husband died, Charles and Helen – Helen was my younger sister and Charles's first wife – invited me to stay here for a while. It was to be a temporary arrangement to give me time to sort things out, which was extremely kind of them under the circumstances, because it was only after Lionel died that I discovered he'd gambled away virtually everything we owned, leaving me with nothing but debts. I say "gambled" because that was more or less what it was. He was an investment broker, and a very bad one as it turned out, and what was worse, he took his own advice. I quite literally had no home, and only a small income of my own.'

'I see,' Tregalles said, 'so—'

But Mrs Etherton wasn't finished. 'As I was about to explain,' she continued firmly, 'with Charles away so much of the time, working in London, and only coming home on weekends, Helen was left here on her own throughout the week. Julian was away all day at school, so Helen and I were company for one another, so she asked me to stay on. Charles didn't mind. In fact I think he was rather pleased that he wouldn't have to feel guilty about leaving Helen by herself so much, and since I had started to do a bit of secretarial work for him while he was away during the week, it meant he wouldn't have to ask Helen to do it.' Mrs Etherton leaned forward and lowered her voice. 'You see, Helen didn't really like the manor all that much, and she thought Charles was wasting his time and money on trying to maintain what she called "a great barn of a place" that would bankrupt him in the end. Helen had money of her own, of course, and I think she might have let Charles have some of it in a pinch, but Charles is a very proud man, and knowing how she felt about it, he wouldn't take a penny from her.

'So it was something of a relief to both Helen and to Charles when I offered to take on the job of dealing with the steady flow of jobbers and tradesmen coming through the place almost every week, and keeping a record of everything that had gone on during the week, so it would be available to Charles when he came home on the weekend.

'Of course, things changed a bit when he gave up his practice and wasn't going up to London every week, but by then I was so used to dealing with the local people, that I continued on, which allowed him time to do some consulting work at the hospital, and to take on the job of local magistrate.'

Quickly, before she could say any more, Tregalles asked her to take him through the events of the previous evening, and, as expected, Mrs Etherton's version differed little from those he'd heard before. 'And when I last saw Toni,' she concluded, 'she was going up the stairs ahead of me. She went to her room and I went to mine.'

'Did she say anything to you?'

'No. She went straight to her room. She'd been very vocal at dinner before Mr Nash came in, but I don't think she said a single word while he was there or after he left.'

'What did you do then?'

'I went to my room for a while, then, at about half past eight, I went down to the kitchen to look for something to eat. We'd only had soup at dinner before Mr Nash came in, so I was getting a bit hungry.'

'Did you meet anyone while you were out of your room?'

'Mrs Lodge was in the kitchen. Then Charles came in looking for something to drink. He said he was dry because of the smell of the paint.'

'How long were you in the kitchen?'

'Perhaps fifteen or twenty minutes. Mrs Lodge helped me make up a tray, and I took it back to my room.'

'I'd like to talk about Miss Halliday,' Tregalles said. 'We get the impression that she was not very well liked, but can you think of anyone who might have hated her enough to kill her?'

Mrs Etherton shook her head. 'Toni took pleasure

in antagonizing people, but I can't think of anyone who would actually want to *kill* her. Except George Nash, of course, but since you're still here asking questions, I have to assume you are not convinced that he did it. Sensible of you, too. The man wouldn't hurt a fly, though Lord knows he had reason enough to hate Toni.'

'Do you know where Miss Halliday lived, and what she did for a living before she came down here?' Tregalles asked.

'No. She never talked about where she'd been or what she had been doing before coming here. At least not to me. The only reason she was here was to try to persuade Margaret to give her more money.'

'Do you know if she succeeded?

'I know Margaret was tempted at first, but I don't think she gave in. I hope not. I know I wouldn't have if I were in Margaret's position.'

Molly looked up. 'Why was that, Mrs Etherton?' she asked.

'Because it would be throwing good money after bad,' Mrs Etherton said. 'You see, Toni literally wasted her life. She had the best education, and she was clever in many ways, but she frittered everything away. She was a professional dabbler. She would flit from one thing to another, and never stick to anything. She spent six months in Paris, where she was supposed to be studying art. Then it was Spanish – she was going to be an interpreter at the UN or some such thing, but that didn't work out. Then it was dance and then acting, all pie in the sky. She couldn't stick to anything for more than five minutes. Then she disappeared for several months, and Margaret was convinced that something terrible had happened to her. Then she turned up here.

'She talked a lot of rubbish about having taken courses in self-analysis or self-awareness, or whatever, and said she'd come to realize how wrong she had been in the past, and she wanted to make amends.

'The girl was as transparent as that window. It was obvious to me what her game was, but Margaret bought her story, at least at first, because she so wanted it to be true.' Mrs Etherton wrinkled her nose. 'To give the girl her due, Toni did manage to play the part *fairly* successfully for the first couple of weeks, but she couldn't keep it up, and I think even Margaret realized in the end that Toni was never going to change.'

'Do you know if Toni had any friends? Did anyone ever come here to the manor?'

'If she did, I never saw them, but I know she used to talk or text a lot to someone on that phone of hers.'

'Just one more question, then,' Tregalles said when Molly remained silent. 'Did you know that Paul Bromley planned to leave here last night? Did you see him, perhaps talk to him at any time after dinner?'

'We exchanged a few words about what had happened at dinner, but he didn't say anything to me about leaving. And I heard his voice in the corridor later on when I was getting ready for bed, but that's all.'

'Do you remember what time that was?'

'Ten or thereabouts. I like to retire early and read,' she explained, 'and I was just settling down with a new book from the library when I heard him.'

'Do you know who he was talking to, or hear what was said?'

Once again, Mrs Etherton shook her head. 'I'm afraid not, Sergeant. It was just a few words, and I didn't hear anyone else speak.'

ELEVEN

Mary Lodge sat up ramrod straight on the very edge of her chair as she faced Tregalles. Her sharp, bird-like eyes followed his every move, and her slight figure remained poised as if ready to dart away at any moment.

To put her at ease, Tregalles began by asking her about herself. She told him she had come to the manor almost forty years ago when she married Sid Lodge, the Bromleys' butler at the time. They'd met, she said, in hospital when he was a patient and she was a nurse.

'I hated to give up nursing when I got married,' she confided, 'but you didn't have any choice in those days. Then, when Mrs Inkster broke her hip – she was the housekeeper before me – I filled in for her. Then, later, when she had to give up the job altogether, I took over and I've been here ever since.'

It took Tregalles several tries before he managed to steer the conversation to the events of the previous evening, but it soon became clear that the housekeeper knew nothing of what had happened in the dining room beyond what she had learned from Gwyneth. She confirmed the stories of those who said they had visited the kitchen throughout the evening, but she was hazy about the times.

He tried another tack. 'I believe you went upstairs to see Mrs Bromley after dinner,' he said. 'What time was that?'

'That's right, I did. I wanted to know what Mrs Bromley wanted me to do about dinner. I thought she might want me to put out a bit of a buffet supper, because all they'd had was some soup, so . . .'

'It would help us a great deal if we knew *when* you went upstairs,' Tregalles said gently.

'It must have been shortly before eight,' she said, 'because when I got back, young Gwyneth had gone off without taking the broth out to the wash-house like I'd asked her to. Young devil! Had a date, I'll be bound. Oh, I know, she can deny it all she likes, but I know the signs. Couldn't wait to be off. Been wool-gathering these past few weeks, she has.'

Her voice softened. 'Not that I minded, really. She's a good girl, is Gwyneth. Does her work and doesn't have to be told twice. It was just the broth. It's my back, you see. It's always been a bit weak, and that big bowl is heavy. Had to carry it to the wash-house myself, and then it was all for nothing.'

Tregalles was about to go on, but Molly spoke up before he could ask the next question. 'You say it was all for nothing, Mrs Lodge. Why was that?'

'Well, somebody had been in and slopped it all over the table, and the cloth I'd put over it had fallen in,' the housekeeper said indignantly. 'Found it first thing this morning. And water on the floor as well. I could have slipped and killed myself on those wet tiles.'

'What you call the wash-house is that small room off the passageway leading to the back door, isn't it?' asked Molly.

'That's right.'

'And you say there was water on the floor there this morning? Where did it come from?'

'From somebody's wet mac, I should think,' Mrs Lodge said

promptly. 'Must have hung it there last night when they came in and it dripped on the floor. It was gone this morning – the mac, I mean – but that's a damp old place, and water stays on those tiles for days if you don't mop it up. Wouldn't have happened if it wasn't for the painters.'

Mrs Lodge went on to explain. 'You see, when the painters came in, we moved all the hats and coats and boots into the wash-house while they painted the back passage. There aren't as many pegs in the wash-house as there are in the passage, so we had to hang them all on top of one another, all higgledy-piggledy like. When I took the broth in last night, I had to squeeze between the coats and the table to set it down. But somebody must have come in later and hung their wet mac on the peg. That's when they slopped the bowl and knocked the cloth in.'

It was probably Charles Bromley's mac, Tregalles thought. It would have been soaked after his visit to the barn with Thorsen, but Mrs Lodge shook her head when he voiced the thought.

'No, it wasn't Mr Charles's,' she said. 'His was on the clothes-horse all spread out to dry like always. Very particular about his clothes, is Mr Charles. He always puts his coat to dry when it gets wet.'

And Thorsen's cape, together with Renshaw's coat, had been draped over chairs in the kitchen by PC Renshaw, Tregalles recalled. 'What time was it when you went into the wash-house this morning?' he asked the housekeeper.

Mrs Lodge thought about that. 'It was before I started break-fast,' she said slowly, 'so it must have been around seven or just after. Set me back a bit, it did, what with mopping up the floor, tipping all that good broth away and washing out the bowl.'

Tregalles winced. If the wet mac didn't belong to Charles Bromley, and none of the others, who had been outside, had been wearing coats, then it was just possible that the wet mac belonged to the murderer. And if he or she realized that they'd nudged the bowl, they might have grabbed it to steady it, leaving fingerprints behind. But Mrs Lodge had washed it out.

The sharp eyes of the housekeeper caught the expression on his face. 'Well, what was I to do?' she said defensively. 'What with the cloth being in there and all, I didn't know what else might have gone in as well, did I?'

'I understand,' Tregalles told her, 'and it may not be important at all, but perhaps we should take a look for ourselves, just to be sure.'

Halfway between the kitchen and the side entrance to the manor was a door to the room still called the wash-house where, years ago, all the household washing was done in the copper boiler. It was a small room, and the old bricked-in copper took up one corner of it, while next to it, in sharp contrast to the monument to the past, stood a washer and drier of more recent vintage. And next to them was a stainless-steel sink.

The room contained only two other items of consequence: a large folding clothes-horse with a man's mackintosh draped over it, and a wooden table whose top had been scrubbed white. As Mrs Lodge had said, the floor was tiled, its smooth surface worn hollow in places by the passage of many feet.

'There, see, just like I told you,' the housekeeper said. 'You can still see the wet patch on the table where I mopped up the broth. And that's where the water was on the floor.'

The peg above the spot to which she pointed was empty. All the rest had two or three coats and jackets on them, while below them were several pairs of shoes and a pair of wellingtons. 'They're the outside shoes,' she explained, 'and boots for the garden. Mr Charles insists that we change shoes when we come in from outside since he had the new carpets put down in the halls upstairs and down. Not that I blame him after what they must have cost. Those belong to Gwyneth,' she said, pointing, 'and those and the wellingtons belong to Mrs Etherton – she loves gardening, does Mrs Etherton; she's always out there helping Thorsen. And these tatty old things are mine,' she said disparagingly. 'Mind you, I only use these when the garden's wet; I keep my shopping shoes upstairs.' She came to the last in line. 'And these boots belong to Mr Bromley,' she concluded.

Tregalles examined them all, but the only ones that showed any signs of having been exposed to rain were those belonging to Gwyneth and Charles Bromley. 'I don't see Mrs Bromley's shoes,' Molly said.

'Nor Julian's,' Tregalles added. 'Yet they both say they were caught in the storm last night.'

'Mrs Bromley never leaves her shoes down here,' the

housekeeper said. 'Always takes them off and carries them upstairs when she's been out in the rain, As for young Julian, he takes his off *if* he remembers, but that's not often. There was mud all the way up the back stairs this morning. That'll be his, I'll be bound.'

'Are there any coats missing?' Paget asked.

The housekeeper's eyes ranged back and forth across the coats, lifting one or two to look underneath. 'Just Miss Toni's,' she said. 'But then, it would be, wouldn't it?' She stepped back and folded her arms. 'And if it's all right with you, Sergeant,' she continued, 'I'd like to get back to the kitchen, because I've got work to do.'

'In that case,' Tregalles said amiably, 'let's all go into the kitchen, because I do still have a few questions, Mrs Lodge, and to tell the truth, I wouldn't say no to a cup of tea.'

Seated at the big wooden table while the housekeeper filled an old-fashioned kettle, the sergeant continued to question her. 'When you went upstairs to speak to Mrs Bromley after dinner, how did she seem to you? Was she calm, upset, angry?'

The housekeeper frowned. 'Funny you should ask that,' she said, pausing in what she was doing, 'because I thought she looked sort of troubled, like.'

'Troubled, Mrs Lodge . . .?'

'It was like something was bothering her,' the housekeeper said slowly. 'Like she was trying to work something out, if you know what I mean. I don't think she heard a word I said.'

'Mrs Bromley told us that she came into the kitchen later in the evening to ask if you had seen Paul Bromley,' Tregalles said. 'How did she seem then?'

Mrs Lodge cocked her head on one side. 'That was different,' she said. 'More like she'd decided what to do. She was looking for Mr Paul. Asked me if I'd seen him. I told her I thought he'd gone down to the village.'

'How did you know that?'

'Well, he told me, didn't he? Well, more or less.'

'When was this?'

'When I went up to see Mrs Bromley. Come round the corner at the top of the stairs as if the Devil was after him. Ran right into me, he did. Almost knocked me down, so I asked him where he thought he was going in such a hurry.'

'And he told you he was going to the village?'

'Yes . . . well, not in so many words, but as good as.'

'What, *exactly,* did he say, Mrs Lodge?'

The housekeeper sighed. 'When I asked him where he thought he was going in such a hurry, he said, "Anywhere away from this damned house where I can get a drink!" And the only place he could do that around here is in Hallows End.'

'Thank you, Mrs Lodge. You say he came round the corner fast? Was he running?'

'No. Just walking too fast and not looking where he was going. He was just the same when he was a boy. Never looked where he was going, always into scrapes, that one. Ran into a door, indeed! A likely story.'

'I don't understand. What door, Mrs Lodge?'

The housekeeper looked at Tregalles as if she thought him particularly thick. 'He was holding this handkerchief to his eye, and when I asked him what had happened, he said he'd run into a door.' She sniffed. 'Not that I believed him, of course, but that's what he said.'

'Did you see a bruise? A swelling or a cut?'

'I told you, he had a handkerchief over it. But there was blood on the handkerchief. Quite a lot of blood, and you don't get that from running into a door, now do you, Sergeant?'

'Did you happen to see where he came from?' Tregalles persisted. 'Which room?'

'Now, how could I do that?' Mrs Lodge asked indignantly. 'I was at the top of the stairs, round the corner from the long corridor. Maybe you can see round corners, but I can't.'

Tregalles sighed. 'And neither can I,' he told her. 'But it's a pity you couldn't in this case.'

Tregalles and Molly were comparing notes when Ormside rang. 'Had a call from Farnsworth's doctor,' he told Tregalles. 'He says we can talk to the major as long as we make it short. I've informed DCI Paget, and he reckons he'll be free by four thirty, so he wants you to meet him at the hospital at quarter to five.

'And Reg Starkie rang to say he's finished the autopsy on Toni Halliday, and we can pick up his report if we can get there before five. So perhaps you could drop Molly off, and she could do that while you interview Farnsworth?'

'Can do,' Tregalles said. 'There's not much more we can do here today anyway. No word on Paul Bromley, I suppose?'

'Not so far. But I have put in a request for Toni Halliday's phone records, and I should have something back by tomorrow. And that could lead us to whoever she was waiting for to pick her up last night.'

TWELVE

Major Farnsworth lay back against the pillows, eyes half closed. His rugged face was pale and drawn beneath the bandages that capped his head. The little nurse from Ghana stood on tiptoe to reach across the bed to straighten out the sheet. He felt a thrill of pleasure as her firm young breast put pressure on his arm. Her plump, dark cheek was just inches from his face, and he imagined her silken skin pressed hard against his own white flesh. She smelled of antiseptic, but if anything it intensified the pleasure, and his fingers twitched in anticipation against the counterpane.

'There, now, all nice and neat for your visitors.' The girl's teeth flashed briefly in a bright, professional smile before she turned and left the room. He followed her with his eyes, the pleasure lingering as he watched the small, neat bottom vanish through the door.

'Thank you, Nurse,' Harriett Farnsworth called out belatedly.

She left the corner of the room where she'd been standing while the nurse attended to the major. A little grey ghost of a woman made weary by her lonely vigil. 'Are you sure you feel up to talking to the police, dear?' she asked hesitantly. He didn't like fuss.

'I've had worse to put up with, m'dear, as well you know,' he said stoically. 'Not a patch on the time I had the old leg blown to bits. Not a patch.'

Harriett smiled wanly. She wished he wouldn't keep bringing

that up. She shuddered inwardly at the memory of those two terrible years. The military exercise; the land-mine that shouldn't have been there; the operations, the frustration, the rage and the interminable ranting and cursing that followed.

Only a slight limp remained, but the scars were deep, and having to leave the army had hurt him most of all. He was forty-nine, still vigorous, still handsome in a boyish way, and he could be so charming when he put his mind to it.

'Why don't you go and get something to eat?' he said. 'Get a bit of fresh air. You look tired. There's nothing you can do here, and I'd like to sleep. Come back tomorrow.'

It almost sounded as if he cared, but he probably wanted her out of the room so that he would have time to think and get his story straight before the police talked to him. She didn't believe the explanation he had given her. The part about being run down by a car might be true, but what she didn't understand was why he was where he was at the time of the accident.

There was something he was hiding; something he wasn't telling her.

'Yes, of course,' she said meekly. 'I'll do that and come back tomorrow. I'll bring your shaving things and your pyjamas. Is there anything else . . .?'

'No, no, you go,' he said firmly. 'I'll be fine. You'll have to take a taxi, I suppose, so make sure he doesn't take you round the old road to jack up the fare. And no more than a couple of pounds for the tip, mind.'

'I know you've had a rough time of it, Major,' Paget said once the introductions were over, 'but we would like to ask you a few questions, if you feel up to it.'

'I've been through worse, Chief Inspector,' Farnsworth said stoically. He pushed himself higher against the pillows, and smoothed his clipped moustache. 'Hit my head when I went down, apparently. Have to lie around for a bit until the pressure on the old skull goes down, but it could have been worse.'

'I'm sure it could have been, sir,' said Paget. 'Now, we've spoken to Mr Thorsen, and he told us when you left his cottage last night. Could you pick it up from there? Tell us where you went and what you did?'

Farnsworth nodded, then winced and put a hand to his head. 'Things are still a bit fuzzy, you understand,' he said apologetically, 'but I'll do my best.'

After leaving the cottage, he said he'd taken Toby up Manor Lane and out onto the heath above the river as usual. He couldn't be sure how long they were there, but he thought it must have been about an hour to an hour and a half. 'It was a nice evening – at least it was before the storm came in,' he said. 'Should have started back sooner, though.'

It was raining hard and almost completely dark by the time he reached the top end of Manor Lane, and started down. 'I was hurrying to get home,' he said, 'but suddenly old Toby ran off up the track leading to the barn, and he wouldn't come when I called him. He's a good dog, so I knew something must be wrong, and I went after him. I had a torch, but I could hardly see anything because of the rain.'

The major eased himself up in bed and winced. 'I heard a motor start up, and suddenly I was blinded by the lights. There was a hell of a roar as the driver put his foot down, and the next thing I knew, the car was coming straight at me and I had nowhere to go. That's the last thing I remember until I woke up to find a nurse bending over me.' He smirked. 'Pretty thing she was, too.'

'Is there anything you can remember, other than the lights and the sound of the engine?' Paget asked. 'Did you see any light coming from the barn?'

'No.' Farnsworth looked grave. 'My wife told me about the girl being killed there. Terrible thing. Absolutely terrible.'

'Did you see anyone else while you were out there?' Paget asked. 'In the lane or on the heath?'

'Didn't see anyone in the lane. There were one or two people on the heath earlier on, but none close enough for me to tell you who they were.'

'Was there any activity around the manor as you went by? Either on your way up or on your way back?'

'No.' Farnsworth closed his eyes tightly as if in pain, and said, 'Look, Chief Inspector, I'd like to help, I really would, but that's all I can tell you, and I'm still a bit groggy.' He drew attention to his bandaged head again by touching it with his fingertips.

'Mild concussion, according to the MO. Left arm and ribs took a bit of a beating, but thank God the bastard who ran me down didn't run over the leg again. Now that was painful, I can tell you. Blown to bits by a land mine three years ago. Took the medics a couple of years and half-a-dozen operations to put it together again.'

Paget took out his card case. 'We'll leave you to get some rest,' he said, 'but should you think of anything else, please call that number, day or night.' He set the card on the bedside table. 'And thank you, Major. I hope you make a speedy recovery.'

Major Farnsworth lay back on his pillows and allowed himself to relax. Not a hint of suspicion about his story. But then, why should there have been? It wasn't hard for someone like him to fool the police. They were an unimaginative lot, by and large, and the old reflexes were still as good as ever. And speaking of reflexes . . .

He moved his head experimentally. Not bad. Not bad at all. The door opened and a nurse came in. Pasty face and hair turning grey. He grimaced and turned his thoughts to Nurse Adamu. That was the name on the nametag clipped to her lapel. He felt the blood stirring in his loins, the muscles tighten. It had been a long time since he'd been in Africa. He'd hated the place, hated the heat, hated the flies – but there was something about the smell and the feel of young black flesh that excited him. He ran his tongue over his lips and gave himself over to the rush of pleasurable thoughts.

Molly Forsythe was waiting for them in the car park when Paget and Tregalles emerged from the hospital. Standing beside Paget's car, she was deep in conversation with a man who looked to be in his early to mid-thirties. Almost a head taller than Molly, there was more than a touch of the oriental in the chiselled features. Dressed casually in a polo shirt and shorts, his arms and legs were deeply tanned. Clearly a man who liked to keep in shape.

'Sir,' said Molly as the two men approached, 'I'd like you to meet Mr David Chen. He's Dr Starkie's nephew – or rather *Mrs* Starkie's nephew – and he's here on holiday.' Introductions made,

Chen reached over to grasp Paget's hand in a firm handshake. 'It's a pleasure to meet you Chief Inspector. And you, too, Sergeant.' He shook hands with Tregalles.

'Not that it's been much of a holiday for him so far,' Molly broke in as if she felt an explanation was necessary. 'Mr Chen is a surgeon who has been working overseas with Doctors without Borders for the past three years, but he's helping Dr Starkie while his assistant is on holiday. And he's been offered a job here.' Molly sounded pleased about that prospect.

'But *not* in my uncle's line of work,' Chen said with a smile. 'I prefer to see my patients up and about after I've finished with them. It would be quite different from what I have been doing, but I need a change. Reg put in a good word for me here, so I'm giving it serious consideration.' He looked at Molly and smiled. 'And I must say prospects are looking more and more attractive every day.'

Colour rose in Molly's face. Suddenly she remembered a large envelope she'd been holding, and handed it to Paget. 'Dr Starkie's report on Antonia Halliday, sir,' she said stiffly.

'I worked with Reg on that,' Chen said, 'and I doubt if you will find much in there that you didn't know already. In fact I can give you the main points right now in plain English if you wish.'

'By all means, since we are all here,' said Paget, 'but are you sure we're not keeping you from something?'

Chen shook his head. 'As Molly said, I'm on holiday.'

So it's Molly, is it? thought Paget as he studied Chen. There was an air of quiet competence and confidence about the man, and he would have to have both those attributes if he'd been working with Doctors without Borders. But his features . . . Suddenly the light went on. Of course! He was *Ellen* Starkie's nephew, and Ellen was half Chinese herself, having met and married Reg Starkie during a stint in his younger days as a cruise ship's doctor.'

'There were two blows, both delivered from behind the victim,' said Chen, breaking into Paget's thoughts. 'Although "slices" might be a better term in this case. The first came in at close to a forty-five degree angle, entering just below the right ear, slicing into the neck, cutting through the internal jugular and the carotid artery right down to the trachea, cutting across the lower part of the jaw as well.

'The young woman would have died within very short order from that blow alone,' he continued, 'but apparently your killer wasn't satisfied, because he or she finished off with a blow to the back of the skull with the point of the sickle – assuming that was the weapon used, and I don't think there can be much doubt about it – penetrating deep into the parietal lobe. In fact it was delivered with such force that it split the skull. Both Reg and I believe the second blow was administered while the victim was on the floor more or less face down.

'There was extensive bruising on the chest and upper arms, but the bruises were too far advanced to have been inflicted at the time of death.'

'She was involved in a car accident earlier in the day,' Paget said.

Chen nodded. 'That could account for them, then,' he said. 'There was nothing to suggest there had been a struggle,' he continued, 'neither was there any indication of sexual activity or molestation. There were no external indications of drug use – needle tracks on her arms and legs, that sort of thing – but there was damage to the septum and mucous membrane and nasal cavity in general, suggesting that the victim had been using drugs for some time, and I imagine the toxicology report will confirm that. Her blood alcohol level was high – I'm afraid I forget the exact figure – but unless some other factor was involved, she could have been functioning more or less normally. Oh, yes, and she was approximately six weeks pregnant.

'The estimated time of death,' he concluded, 'is between eight and nine last evening.' Chen looked from one to the other. 'Does that help?' he asked.

'It does indeed,' said Paget, 'and thank you very much, Mr Chen. But you'd better be careful or Reg will be wanting to take you on permanently himself.'

'Not a chance,' Chen said firmly. 'Fascinating as it is, I prefer the living to the dead.'

'As do I,' said Paget. 'It was a pleasure meeting you, Mr Chen, but I must be going. Are you waiting for Reg, or do you need a lift anywhere?'

'The pleasure was mine,' said Chen. 'And Reg has already gone. He and Aunt Ellen are off to a friend's anniversary dinner this evening, which is why I was the only one here when Molly arrived to pick up the report. So, thank you very much, but Molly has already offered to give me a lift.'

Has she, now? Tregalles thought, and, catching Molly's eye, grinned and gave her a surreptitious thumbs up sign – and chuckled to himself when he saw colour flare in Molly's face.

THIRTEEN

They were sitting down to dinner when the phone rang. 'I'll get it,' said Grace, 'and if it's work, I'll tell them you've left home.'

But no sooner had Paget picked up his knife and fork than Grace was back. 'It's Andrea McMillan calling from the hospital. She says they have a "situation" there, and she wants to talk to you.'

Regretfully, he put his knife and fork down and went to the phone. 'Andrea,' he said, 'what's the problem?'

Andrea McMillan wasted no time in coming to the point. 'Sorry to trouble you, Neil, but we have a situation here, and I didn't want to call the regular police number until I'd spoken to you. It concerns Major Farnsworth and one of our nurses. I know it's an imposition, but I would really appreciate it if you could come and help me deal with it.'

'If it's that serious, of course I'll come, Andrea,' he said. 'But can you give me some idea about what happened?'

'Major Farnsworth took a fancy to one of our nurses,' she said, 'and she ended up on the floor with a three-inch gash in the side of her face, and she is extremely shaken up.'

'And Farnsworth . . .?'

'Dead,' Andrea said coldly. 'Now do you see why I'm asking you to come?'

'I do indeed,' he said. 'Has Mrs Farnsworth been notified?'

'Not yet, no. But I will do that as soon as—'

'No. Don't do that, Andrea,' he cut in sharply. 'I think it might be best if I have someone go to the house to break the news, and bring her to the hospital. She will want to be there, and I will need to talk to her as well.'

Gwyneth closed the gate behind her, mounted her bicycle, and set off down Manor Lane. She didn't bother with the light. It didn't work properly anyway, and there was hardly ever any traffic in the lane. Besides, it wasn't as if she was unfamiliar with the route, and there was still enough light in the sky to see her home.

She rode blindly, more by instinct than conscious thought, her mind in turmoil. How she had managed to get through the day without doing or saying something really stupid she did not know. Most of it was just a blur, except for all those questions by the police. Those she remembered vividly. If she'd known she would have to answer questions like that, she'd have stayed home this morning and said she was ill.

She'd considered it as she tossed and turned and tried to sleep last night, but something had warned her not to draw attention to herself. Better to go to work as if nothing had happened; after all, what was there to fear? She was just a maid. Nobody paid any attention to maids. It had all seemed so simple then in the quiet of her room.

Her thoughts turned to the young man who had come into the kitchen late in the afternoon. Nice looking, he was, with grey eyes and a gingery moustache. She knew he must be with the police, but he looked so young and inexperienced that she was not unduly worried.

'Sorry I missed you earlier,' he'd apologized. 'I thought I'd got everyone this morning, but then someone mentioned you, so I'm here to take your fingerprints. It will only take a couple of minutes. Have you ever been fingerprinted before?'

She couldn't remember what she'd said to him. She vaguely recalled him explaining the procedure and taking her fingers one by one, rolling each one on the pad and . . .

The glare of headlights hit her squarely in the face as she rounded the bend by Lower Farm. Startled, she wobbled to a stop.

The oncoming car swung into the lane leading to Lower Farm and stopped before the gate, barring the way. A police car. The door opened on the observer's side and a policewoman got out, while the driver remained behind the wheel.

'That's not very clever, Gwyneth,' the policewoman said. 'Riding without lights. You'd better be careful, my girl. You could run into a copper.'

Gwyneth squinted against the light reflected off the gate.

'Val?' she said shakily. 'Val Short? You did give me a start.' Confidence began to return as she recognized the girl she'd chummed around with for a while after leaving school. Val had gone on to university, and neither had made the effort to keep in touch.

'You should be more careful yourself, speeding in a narrow lane like this,' she said. 'You could have had me off.'

'Come off it, Gwyn,' Val said. 'We weren't speeding, as well you know, but you're right about one thing: if we hadn't been stopping here, we might not have seen you until it was too late, coming round the corner without a light on your bike.'

'It was on a minute ago,' Gwyneth said defensively. 'I hadn't noticed it had gone off.'

'Well, you'd better put it back on again, then, hadn't you?' Val didn't sound particularly friendly now.

'You're not going to give me a summons . . .?'

Val moved to the gate and opened it. 'Not this time, Gwyneth,' she said quietly. 'We've got more serious business to attend to here.'

The car moved forward and Val swung the gate to behind it.

'What's that, then?' Gwyneth called.

Val stopped, one hand still on the gate. 'We've come to take Mrs Farnsworth to the hospital. Her husband just died, and we have to break the news. Nice seeing you again, Gwyn. Take care.' She got back in the car and it moved off up the lane.

Gwyneth couldn't breathe. Her mind was numb as she stood there astride her bike, heart pounding painfully as she tried to think. Tears rolled down her cheeks. She had to *talk* to someone. Not the police. Oh, no, not the police. They'd blame her . . . Oh, God! Those fingerprints! Gwyneth squeezed her eyes shut in a futile effort to banish the images inside her head. Perhaps they wouldn't check back there, she thought hopefully, but she knew they would.

It would be no good talking to her mum, because she'd never understand. But if she didn't talk to *someone* soon, Gwyneth felt that she would burst.

Driving into Broadminster, Paget's thoughts turned to Andrea McMillan. There had been a time when he'd thought that Andrea might be the one for him, but to have carried their relationship further would have been a mistake. There had been a strong mutual attraction, but having been burned badly by one disastrous marriage, Andrea was not ready to make any long-term commitments, while Paget couldn't shake the feeling of guilt for even thinking of another woman in those terms after losing Jill.

But time had healed. Now Andrea was married to Sten Wallen, a man she'd known since childhood, and Paget had met Grace. Deep in his heart he kept the memory of Jill alive, and he always would, but Grace had changed his life, and he still found it hard to believe that he could be so lucky twice.

Visiting hours. Paget had to circle the car park several times before he managed to squeeze in between two oversized SUVs, and once inside the hospital and he saw the number of people waiting for the lifts, he decided to take the stairs.

He was puffing hard by the time he reached the fourth floor, where Andrea met him at the desk.

'It might be best if you had a look at Major Farnsworth's room before we do anything else,' she said, leading the way along the corridor. 'And thanks very much for coming. I really do appreciate it, Neil.'

A student nurse stood beside the closed door. 'Just a precaution in case one of the cleaners decided to go in,' she explained, then told the girl she could go. She opened the door and Paget followed her into the room.

Andrea pulled back the curtain screening the bed. 'I asked them to leave everything as it was so you could see it for yourself,' she said. 'It's a bit of a mess as you can see.'

And something of an understatement, thought Paget. Bedclothes and pillows, soaking wet from the contents of an overturned water jug, were strewn about the floor. The remains of a meal – the major's dinner, presumably – were trodden into the sodden sheets, and a metal tray and overturned chair completed the picture.

There were bloodstains on the floor and wall.

A single sheet covered the body on the bed. Andrea removed it, then stood back.

The major lay on his back. The hospital gown left his legs exposed, and Paget could see the jagged scars where surgeons had rebuilt the shattered leg. The head lolled to one side, slack-jawed in death. With cheeks collapsed and a haze of stubble white against the grey pallor of his skin, Major Farnsworth looked much older than he had when Paget had seen him last.

His attention was caught and held by four deep and ragged, blood-encrusted gouges that ran from the hairline to the chin.

Paget looked at Andrea. 'Fingernails?' he said. It was more a statement than a question.

She nodded, then moved forward to lift the major's head. The hair was matted with blood not yet crusted. She let it down gently. 'He hit it on that when he fell out of bed,' she said, pointing to the corner of the bedside table. 'His heart had stopped. They got him back on the bed and used the paddles on him, but there was no bringing him back after that.' Andrea drew a deep breath and let it out again. 'So,' she concluded, 'if you've seen enough, I'll take you along to the staff room, and you can hear the rest of the story.'

They walked the length of the corridor to the staff room. Two people sat close together on an old vinyl-covered couch that sagged in the middle, and Paget recognized one of them from his time in hospital the previous year. Grey-haired, she was the oldest nurse on the ward. Her name was Madge, and she was talking in low tones to a much younger nurse beside her.

The girl was small and pretty, and very, very black. Paget remembered seeing her earlier in the day in the corridor outside Farnsworth's room. She'd been smiling, he recalled, but she wasn't smiling now. Her head was bowed, and she was shivering despite a heavy blanket wrapped around her shoulders. Her hair was in disarray, and the front of her uniform looked as if it had been torn away. It covered her now only because her folded arms were holding it in place. There was a dressing on the right side of her face.

'I believe you know Nurse Fallowfield,' said Andrea, indicating the woman Paget knew as Madge. 'And this is Nurse Adamu. She was in the room when Major Farnsworth died.'

The older woman looked up and smiled briefly at Paget, but the girl kept her head down.

'Is she in shock?' Paget asked quietly.

'Badly shaken,' Andrea said, 'but not technically in shock. You can certainly talk to her.'

Madge looked up. 'She's scared,' she said softly. 'She's afraid that she'll be blamed for what happened. I've told her she has nothing to be afraid of, that it was not her fault, but . . .' She shrugged and turned back to the girl.

'This is Chief Inspector Paget,' she said, 'and I want you to tell him what happened. There's nothing to be scared of; no one's blaming you, but you must tell him everything. Understand?'

The young nurse lifted a tear-stained face and looked up at Paget, then at the woman beside her. 'Will you stay?' she whispered.

'I'm not going anywhere until I can take you out of here with me,' Madge assured her.

Paget pulled up a chair and sat facing the girl. 'Just tell me what happened,' he said gently. 'Take your time.'

The girl nodded but she wouldn't look at him. Then, very softly, she began to speak.

'Major Farnsworth rang the bell, so I went to his room to see what he wanted. He said his pillows weren't right, and he wasn't comfortable, and asked me to help him.' She glanced at Andrea. 'I knew I had to watch his hands,' she said plaintively, 'but I didn't expect anything like that.'

Paget threw a questioning glance at Andrea.

'The girls have to put up with a lot of that from the male patients,' Andrea explained. 'The gropers and feelers are the ones who let their hands drop casually over the bedside when a nurse is leaning over, to "accidentally" stroke her thigh or perhaps her breast. Then there are the bolder ones – we get them all. The girls can usually take care of themselves, but some, like the major, are very persistent.'

'So, how do you deal with it?'

'As best we can. Sometimes it's as simple as adding more

adhesive than necessary to a dressing, then yanking it off when they're not prepared for it. And there's always the next injection. Done properly, it can hurt like hell. They usually get the message.'

Paget turned back to the girl. 'Please go on, Nurse Adamu,' he said.

'I began to straighten out his bed, but as soon as I leaned over I knew what he was up to. Like Doctor McMillan said, he had his hand down between my legs. I moved back and pretended I thought it was an accident, but . . .' Her eyes filled with tears, and her voice rose to a squeak. 'But he didn't stop.'

She brushed the tears from her eyes. 'He grabbed my uniform and pulled me down on top of him. He kept talking to me, low, like just above a whisper, saying things, saying what he wanted to do to me . . .' She bit her lip, and for a moment anger flared in her eyes.

'I'm sorry to have to ask you this, Nurse Adamu, but I must. Did you call out? Scream or call for help?'

'I couldn't. He had his arm around my neck, forcing my face into the covers. I couldn't get my breath. He was trying to drag me into the bed, and he was very strong. I was suffocating, and all the time he was talking, groping. He kept telling me to be quiet.

'I fought. I got one arm free and hit him on the side of the head and dug my nails in as hard as I could, but he wouldn't let go even when I started to fall off the bed. I kept struggling, but I couldn't get free. Then I did fall off the bed, but he still wouldn't let go, and he fell out on top of me. He screamed and sort of reared up then fell back, and that was when Dave, the orderly, ran in and pulled him off me.'

The young nurse dropped her head in her hands. 'I didn't do anything wrong,' she sobbed. 'Honestly, I didn't, I didn't.'

Behind him, Paget was aware that the door had opened and someone had entered the room. He'd assumed it was another nurse or a doctor, but it was only when Nurse Adamu raised her head to look past him, and he saw her eye grow round with fear, that he turned to look for himself.

A uniformed policewoman stood in the doorway, and beside her was a small, grey, rather sad-looking woman. They had never met, but Paget knew instinctively that this was Major Farnsworth's wife.

How much she had heard, he didn't know, but to have her walk in at a time like this . . . He started to get up, but Harriett Farnsworth moved first. She plodded purposefully across the scuffed lino of the staff room with the awkward gait of one who lives constantly with pain, and came to a halt in front of Nurse Adamu.

The girl rose to her feet. It was clear she knew who Harriett Farnsworth was. 'I'm so sorry,' she began as tears rolled down her cheeks. She couldn't go on. The blanket fell from her shoulders, and the torn uniform dropped away to reveal deep scratches and bruises from her neck to her breast.

Harriett Farnsworth reached out and put her arms around the girl and pulled her to her. 'I know,' she whispered softly. 'I know it wasn't your fault, my dear, and I'm so sorry this had to happen to you, so terribly, terribly sorry.'

They stood there, locked in an embrace. Tears continued to roll down the young nurse's face, but Harriett Farnsworth's eyes were dry.

FOURTEEN

Saturday, September 10th

The church clock in Hallows End was striking nine when Molly Forsythe arrived on the doorstep of Number 42 Claremont Road in Hallows End. She lifted the doorknocker and gave three sharp raps, then stepped back a pace. Within seconds, her keen eyes detected movement behind lace curtains next door, but there was no response from Number 42. It took several more heavy knocks before the door was suddenly flung open.

The woman who stood before her looked as if she'd just tumbled out of bed. She was small and plump, and her hair was in curlers. A faded woollen dressing gown was tied tightly at the waist, and her feet were bare.

'Yes?' she said suspiciously as she leaned out to look up and down the street as if to make sure that Molly was alone.

'Mrs Jones?'

'That's right.'

Molly identified herself and held up her warrant card for Mrs Jones to see. Alarm flared in the woman's eyes. 'It's Gwyneth, isn't it?' she said hoarsely.

'That's right. I'd like to ask you a few questions. May I come in?'

'Never mind the questions. What's happened?'

'Happened? I'm sorry Mrs Jones, but I'm just here to—'

'Something's happened to her, hasn't it?' Mrs Jones broke in. 'Where is she? Is she going to be all right?' Her eyes searched Molly's face for answers.

'Are you saying that Gwyneth is not at home, Mrs Jones?'

'Of course she's not at home,' the woman snapped impatiently. 'Why would you be here, else? She's not been home all night. I just went up to call her and her bed's not been slept in and I don't know where she is. So don't just stand there. I want to know. Just tell me what's happened to my Gwyneth?'

'Mrs Jones said she was feeling tired, so she went to bed early last night. She assumed that Gwyneth was working late again, as she has been recently, and she'd be in later. But when she went in to wake Gwyneth this morning, there was no sign of the girl ever having been home. When I asked if Gwyneth could have come home late last night, then gone out early this morning, Mrs Jones said that she would never have stopped to make her bed, and she wouldn't have gone out again without at least leaving a note.'

They were in the parish hall. It might be the weekend for some, but it was just another working day for Paget, Tregalles, Ormside and Molly.

'I rang Mrs Lodge straightaway, of course,' Molly continued, 'and she told me that Gwyneth left the manor on the stroke of eight last night. But she did say that Gwyneth hadn't been herself. She said she'd found the girl in tears a couple of times, yesterday. At first, she put it down to the fact that everyone was upset about the murder, but she couldn't see why Gwyneth would be crying over the death of a woman who had made her life miserable, and she wondered whether Gwyneth had had a fight with her new boyfriend.'

Paget looked up sharply. 'New boyfriend? Does Mrs Lodge know who he is?'

Molly shook her head. 'In fact, from what she told me, it's by no means certain that there *is* a boyfriend, new or otherwise. Mrs Lodge only thinks there is because, as she put it, "the girl's been acting giddy lately". Also, she says Gwyneth has been wearing a new perfume for the past couple of weeks, and Mrs Lodge is pretty sure she didn't buy it herself.

'There is one thing that suggests Mrs Lodge may be right,' Molly continued. 'Mrs Jones told me that Gwyneth had worked late several times during the past few weeks, but when I asked Mrs Lodge about that, she said Gwyneth only worked late if the Bromleys were entertaining in the evening, but that doesn't happen very often during the summer months, and Gwyneth hadn't been asked to work late for at least the past two months.'

'It may or may not have anything to do with the killing of Toni Halliday,' said Paget, 'but I don't like the sound of it, so you'd better get on it, Len.' He turned to Molly to ask if she'd looked at Gwyneth's room.

'I did,' Molly replied. 'It was a bit of a jumble, so I just had a quick look round to see if there were any obvious clues to where she might have gone, but it will take some time to do a proper job.'

'Someone else can do that,' said Paget, 'but I'd like you to start checking with Gwyneth's friends to see if they know who her boyfriend is. She may have been more forthcoming with someone her own age than she was with her mother.' He turned back to Ormside. 'And let's get some people out knocking on doors of the cottages along Manor Lane to find out if anyone saw Gwyneth after she left the manor last night.'

Ormside made a face. 'Not many doors to knock on in that lane,' he reminded Paget, 'and it would be getting dark by the time Gwyneth left the manor.'

'As for friends,' said Molly, 'Mrs Jones gave me a few names, but there aren't very many. She said with the split shifts Gwyneth was working, from nine till two, and six till eight in the evening, she doesn't have much time to have any close friends.

'Did you get a picture of Gwyneth?' Ormside asked.

'I did, and it's quite a good one,' Molly told him. 'Taken last year, and it should enlarge nicely.'

A uniformed policewoman approached Ormside's desk. 'This fax just came in, Sergeant,' she said, handing him several sheets of paper. 'It's a prelim from Forensic.'

Ormside looked surprised. 'On a Saturday?' he said. 'That's got to be a first for Forensic. Somebody must have got the whip out.'

'I had a quiet word with Peter Dexter yesterday,' Paget told him. Dexter was a senior crime lab technician whom Paget had met during a conference at Hindlip Hall the year before. 'He's doing this as a favour, but I suspect it's going to cost me dearly somewhere down the road.' He spread the sheets on the desk for all to see.

It was, as the policewoman had said, a preliminary report, and it was sketchy, but almost anything was welcome at this stage of the investigation, and Paget gave a grunt of satisfaction when he read the first item on the list.

The green paint on the handle of the sickle matched the sample taken from the newly painted wall in the manor, which meant that the killer had been inside the manor while the paint was still drying. It confirmed Paget's suspicions, but he knew it would not sit well with Morgan Brock, who was doing his level best to point the finger away from the family. Nor could anyone be excluded, because, according to Dr Starkie's report, the sickle was extremely sharp, and the blows that killed Toni Halliday could have been delivered by a man or a woman.

Toxicology testing still had to be done, but there was a lengthy sub-section on what had been found in the farm manager's office at the back of the barn.

In addition to the air mattress and the condoms Grace had mentioned, there was a sleeping bag, a blanket, a foot pump, several candles, a torch, and a small lantern.

'A foot pump, no less,' Tregalles exclaimed. 'Probably wanted to save their breath for the main event.'

The vinyl-covered, blow-up mattress was the sort normally found in backyard swimming pools. Cheaply made, it was available in any one of hundreds of shops throughout the country, as was the sleeping bag. The blanket was no longer manufactured, but it had been a standard issue to Britain's Armed Forces prior to 1998.

There was hair in abundance on the blanket and in the sleeping bag, including that of a dog. There were traces of face powder, lipstick, saliva, semen stains, and a variety of fibres on both as well, all of which had yet to be identified. But the two sets of fingerprints found on the torch, the candles and the lamp belonged to Gwyneth Jones and Major Farnsworth.

'Farnsworth?' Tregalles exclaimed. 'When were his prints taken?'

'They weren't,' Paget told him, 'but they'd be on file with the military.'

'But *Farnsworth?* And *Gwyneth?*' The sergeant shook his head in disbelief. 'I don't understand it,' he said. 'Why would a nice kid like her take up with a randy old sod like Farnsworth? He must have been at least twice her age. What would she see in him?'

'Could be he was different,' Ormside said. 'There's not much to choose from among the local lads in these small villages, especially for a girl like Gwyneth Jones, who's stuck in a dead-end job, and probably never ventured far from home. So when someone like the major comes along with his air of worldliness and sophistication, and starts chatting her up and making a fuss of her, she'd be easy prey. Age wouldn't even come into it.'

'Still . . .'

'Well, whatever the reason,' Paget said, 'my main concern is to find the girl, and the sooner the better. If she was in the barn the night Toni Halliday was killed, that would explain a lot of things. Her tears weren't for Toni Halliday, they were for the major. And if she *was* out there, she may have seen the killer.'

'Or she could be the killer,' Ormside said.

'Gwyneth . . .?' Tregalles scoffed. 'You must be joking.'

'You never know,' Ormside said stubbornly. 'If the Halliday woman caught her there in the barn, and there was a confront-ation, Gwyneth could have grabbed the sickle and killed her. She may not have meant to, but all I'm saying is we shouldn't rule her out.'

'Fair enough,' said Paget, 'but I'm inclined to agree with

Tregalles. I can't quite see Gwyneth as a killer, and I certainly can't see her coming to work next morning and sitting through an interview without going to pieces.' He paused, eyes thoughtfully on Ormside as he said, 'When I was checking the records of calls on Thursday evening, there was a phone call logged in shortly after nine o'clock. It came from the phone box in Hallows End. The caller was a woman, who said something terrible had happened "in the lane behind the house", but she rang off when Control asked for details and asked for her name. Now I'm wondering if that woman could have been Gwyneth.'

'Was there any follow up, do you know?' Ormside asked.

Paget shook his head. 'They didn't have enough to go on, so it was shelved pending further information. We can check the phone box for prints, and see if we can recognize the voice on the tape.'

The phone on Ormside's desk rang. He answered it, spoke briefly, then handed the phone to Paget, mouthing 'Bromley' as he did so.

The conversation was short, ending by Paget saying, 'We'll be there shortly, Mr Bromley, and thanks for letting me know.' He hung up the phone.

'Mr Bromley's brother, Paul, turned up at the manor late last night,' he said. 'He claims he knew nothing about Toni Halliday's death until he heard it on the news yesterday afternoon. Personally, I find that very hard to believe, but there's only one way to find out, so let's go, Tregalles.'

Margaret Bromley was alone when Paul entered the dining room. She glared at him. 'You've got your nerve, coming back here,' she said scathingly. 'I couldn't believe it when Charles told me you were back.'

Paul closed the door behind him and leaned against it. 'Don't be that way, Mags,' he said. 'I knew how you must be feeling, and regardless of our differences, I thought I should be here, so I came back as soon as I heard about Toni.' He spread his hands. 'It was the least I could do.'

Margaret's lip curled. 'The least you could do, Paul? Oh, yes, you're very good at that, aren't you? Doing the least.' She walked toward him until they were almost touching. 'Now tell me what *really* happened out there in the barn. You told her, didn't you? You bastard! And then what happened? She turned on you, did she? Toni may have been many things, but she had spirit, which is more than I can say for you! Now look me in the eye and tell me that you didn't kill her, Paul . . . if you dare!'

'Kill her?' he echoed. 'Oh, for Christ's sake, Mags, don't be ridiculous. I told you what I was—'

'I know what you *told* me, you lying bastard,' she broke in, thrusting her face so close to his own that spittle flecked his face. 'Some cock and bull story about falling asleep in your car, and I, like a fool, believed you.'

'But it's true. Honest to God, I swear, that's what happened. I was never anywhere near the barn. The last time I saw Toni was when she went upstairs after dinner.' Paul grasped her shoulders with both hands, and took a deep breath. 'Please, Mags, think about it. I know I *threatened* to tell her, but I just said that to shake you up because you were being so bloody obstinate about the money. Honest to God, I never intended to carry it out. I knew she wouldn't believe me if I did, so I went down to the car to get some tablets for my headache, and I sat there thinking about what to do and I fell asleep. Later, after I left you, there was no reason to stay any longer, so I left and drove straight back to London. For God's sake, *think,* Margaret. I didn't like her; she could be a nasty little bitch – and you should know that better than anyone, but you'll never admit it, will you? But I had no reason to *kill* her.'

His voice changed. 'But I will admit I wasn't in the car *all* the time. I stood in the doorway waiting for the rain to ease up before making a dash for the house, and there was more going on out there than I've told that chief inspector. But I'm saving that for later.'

Margaret Bromley's suspicious eyes never left his face as she shook herself free and stepped back. 'You . . .' she began, but whatever she was about to say was interrupted by a sharp rapping on the door behind Paul, and a voice they both recognized as that of Elizabeth Etherton.

'Paul? Paul, is that you?' she called. 'This door seems to be stuck. Could you try it from your side, please?'

FIFTEEN

The past few days had been unseasonably warm, but today there was a welcome lightness to the air, and a thin band of feathered clouds drifted lazily across the sky as the two detectives drove the short distance up the hill to Bromley Manor.

Mrs Lodge let them in, and Paget questioned her again about Gwyneth, but she could add nothing to what she had told Molly on the phone. 'I just hope she hasn't gone and done something foolish, that's all,' the housekeeper said over her shoulder as she left the kitchen to find Mr Bromley for them.

The smell of paint still lingered in the passageway. Green paint – except for a patch of yellow down in the corner by the door – where Grace had taken a small sample for forensic examination. Paget examined the wall beneath the clothes hooks, and saw marks where something had rubbed against the paint while it was still wet.

Mrs Lodge returned, followed by a concerned Charles Bromley.

'What's this I hear about Gwyneth?' he asked Paget. 'Mrs Lodge tells me she's missing.'

'She is,' Paget said, 'and I'm wondering if she said anything to you about going away?'

Charles shook his head. 'I'm afraid I can't help you, Chief Inspector,' he said. 'Are you sure she didn't say anything to you, Mrs Lodge?'

'Quite sure,' the housekeeper said firmly, 'and she would have done if she'd known ahead of time. It's not like her to go off without telling me.'

'Can you think of *anywhere* she might have gone? Has she spoken of any friends or relatives . . .?'

'Don't think she has any apart from her mum,' said Mrs Lodge. 'The two of them are more like sisters; they go around everywhere together when she's not working.'

Charles looked at his watch. 'I'm afraid you'll have to excuse me,' he said, 'but I have an appointment in town within the hour. The funeral arrangements for Toni.' He started to turn away, then paused. 'I suppose I should tell you,' he said grudgingly, 'that the jewels you found among Toni's things were not the only ones she stole. Margaret told me last night that Toni must have been stealing from her all the time she was here, so I'm preparing a list for the insurance people. It's quite a lengthy one. Bernard Halliday used to bring Margaret jewellery every time he came home from one of his trips. He'd make a big fuss about giving it to her, then he'd ignore her for the rest of the time he was there. I expect you would like a copy of the missing pieces as well? I could fax it to you.'

'Please do,' Paget said. 'The sooner we can circulate the descriptions, the better. Do you have pictures of each piece?'

'No, but I'm sure the insurance company will have, and I can give you their name.'

Paget wrote the name down.

Charles looked at his watch. 'Now I really must go,' he said briskly, 'so unless there is anything more . . .?'

'Just one thing,' Paget said. 'Do you mind if we use your study while you're gone?'

'Ah, yes, of course, you'll want to see Paul?' said Charles. 'And if there is anything you need, just ask Mrs Lodge. I'm sure she will be happy to oblige.'

Paul Bromley was thinner and less robust than his brother. At least, that was Paget's first impression of the man as he faced him across the desk. There was a superficial similarity in build and facial characteristics, but Paul's features seemed to lack the definition and strength so marked in his brother.

And his eyes were shifty, according to Tregalles, who took an immediate dislike to him.

Paget led Paul through the events of Thursday afternoon and early evening, and found nothing in his story that conflicted with what he'd heard before. Paul admitted that his reason for coming down from London was to try to borrow money from his brother, but dug his heels in when Paget asked what the money was for.

'It has absolutely nothing to do with this investigation,' he insisted. 'And, with all due respect, Chief inspector, I don't think it is any of your business.'

Paget didn't press the point. Time enough for that later if it appeared to be relevant.

When asked about his movements after Nash had gone, Paul said he'd gone up to his room. 'I had a headache,' he said. 'I get them when I'm over-tired.' He went on to explain that he'd taken a couple of tablets during his drive down the day before, and he'd left the rest of them in the glove box. So when he felt another headache coming on, he said, rather than go down for them, he went along to Margaret Bromley's room to ask if she would let him have a couple of paracetamol tablets, because he knew she suffered from headaches herself.

'Unfortunately, she didn't have any,' he said. 'She said she'd been meaning to get some, but it had slipped her mind, so I went down to get them from the car.'

Paget asked him about his encounter with Mrs Lodge at the top of the stairs. 'Why were you in such a hurry, Mr Bromley? Mrs Lodge says you almost knocked her down.'

Paul smiled. 'Mrs Lodge does tend to exaggerate,' he said, 'although I suppose I did startle her. But I didn't actually bump into her.'

'Did you tell her you were going to the village?'

Paul thought for a moment. 'I think she asked if I wanted anything to eat,' he said, 'and I said I'd get something later if I needed it.'

'She also said you were holding a handkerchief to your face, and she saw blood.' Paget pointed to the jagged scar on Paul's face. 'How did you get that cut, Mr Bromley?'

Paul grimaced. 'I stepped inside Margaret's room while she looked for her tablets,' he said. 'The door must have swung partly shut behind me, because when I turned to go I ran right into the edge of it. Didn't do the headache any good either, I can tell you.'

'I see,' said Paget neutrally. 'Please go on.'

Paul said he had gone down to his car, found the tablets, and taken two of them, washing them down with water from a flask he always carried when driving. He went on to say he'd remained in the car while he tried to decide what to do about the money he needed, since Charles had refused to help him.

'I was very tired,' Paul explained. 'I'd been up half the night

before, then driven down from London in all that heat. The head
was still aching, so I put the seat back to rest it, and I fell asleep.'

Paget looked sceptical. 'And how long do you estimate you
were asleep?' he asked.

'Three quarters of an hour, give or take. I looked at the time
when I woke up, and it was ten to nine, and it was raining hard,
so I decided to wait for it to let up. But when I realized it wasn't
going to, I made a dash for the house.

'Charles saw me come in,' he said. 'I'm sure he'll remember.'

'And you left for London shortly after that?' Paget said.

'Yes. About an hour later. My head was feeling better, and
there didn't seem to be much point in hanging about until
morning, so I left. It was still raining, of course, but I ran out of
the storm after about an hour, and it was clear sailing after that,
no traffic to speak of, and I got home shortly after two o'clock.'

'And after that . . .?'

Paul said he'd gone to bed for a few hours, then made the
rounds of his friends later in the morning.

'Trying to raise the money you needed?'

'Yes.'

'Were you successful?'

'I was, yes.'

When Paget asked him how he'd spent the rest of the day,
Paul said he'd gone into the office to pick up some papers relating
to a property in which a client was interested.

'It's a commercial property,' he explained, 'and my client had
rung up to ask if I'd go over it with him. I was on my way to
see him when I heard the news on the car radio. I couldn't believe
it at first, but then I heard it again. It was a terrible shock, I can
tell you. I met with the client, concluded our business, then came
straight on down here.'

'From . . .?'

'Oxford. That's where the property is.'

'What time did you leave Oxford?'

Paul sat forward in his chair. 'Look, Chief inspector,' he said
in a let's-be-reasonable-about-this tone of voice, 'isn't this
becoming a bit ridiculous? All this business about times and
trivial details . . .'

'Do you find murder trivial, Mr Bromley?'

Paul flushed. 'No, of course not. That's not what I—'

'Good. So what time did you leave Oxford?'

'Oh, for God's sake!' Paul flared. 'I don't know what time it was when I left bloody Oxford. If I'd known there was going to be an inquisition, I'd have looked at the clock.'

Paget ignored the outburst. 'Let's try it another way. What time was it when you arrived here last night?'

Paul sighed heavily. 'I don't know – it must have been about eleven. Charles was still up. I'm sure he'll remember.'

'Why did you come?'

'Why?' The question took Paul by surprise. 'I don't understand what you mean.'

'I mean why this sudden dash across the country when you heard the news? I gather you didn't know Miss Halliday particularly well.'

'Well, I . . .' Paul fumbled for words. 'It just seemed the right thing to do,' he said at last. 'I mean, I'd been here the night before, sitting next to Toni at dinner, and now she was dead. She was more or less my niece – well, in a way, through Charles, if you see what I mean?' He stumbled to a halt.

'No, I'm afraid I don't see what you mean,' Paget said. 'Because if that was the only reason, why not wait and come down first thing this morning. Surely that would have done just as well?'

'No, it wouldn't,' Paul said stiffly, 'because I knew Margaret would be in a state of shock and I felt I needed to be here if only to offer moral support, so to speak.'

'Very commendable, I'm sure,' said Paget drily. He looked at Tregalles. 'Do you have any questions, Sergeant?'

'As a matter of fact, I do,' said Tregalles. 'I would like to know more about this money you say you needed, and why you would come all the way down here to ask your brother for it, rather than ask these friends of yours in London for it in the first place? Especially since they seemed to be quite prepared to give it to you within hours of your return to London.'

'It was a matter of pride, if you must know,' Paul said loftily. 'It's not the sort of thing one likes to ask of friends, and Charles had always come through in the past. But not this time. In fact, he *claims* to be strapped for cash himself.' He made a face. 'I suppose he *could* be telling the truth, when you consider how much it costs to keep this place up. God knows how much he's poured into it over the years.

'But, no, Granny Bromley made him promise to keep the manor in the family, no matter what, and she could always count on Charles to do anything she wanted. But times change. The local developers have been trying to get him to sell off some of the land for years, and if he had any sense he'd take the money and run. Instead, he's selling it off bit by bit to the local farmers on the understanding that they will keep it as farmland, then sinking the proceeds into this old place.' Paul glowered. 'And I wouldn't have had to go begging to friends,' he concluded sullenly.

'So why didn't you return to London straight away?' Tregalles asked. 'You say this argument with your brother took place in the middle of the afternoon, yet you waited until something like ten o'clock to leave.'

Paul shrugged. 'Don't know, really,' he said. 'I suppose I thought if I stayed over, I might get him in a better mood next morning, and he'd change his mind. Charles has come around before. But the more I thought about it, the less I thought it likely, so I left.'

'And your friends came up with the money in a matter of hours,' Tregalles observed drily. 'I wish I had friends like that.'

Paget stirred in his seat. 'Thank you, Mr Bromley,' he said. 'We won't detain you any longer, but I would like your business address, if you don't mind.'

Paul took out a business card and handed it to Paget.

'And your client's name, address, and telephone number, if you have it,' Paget said. 'The client you went to see in Oxford.'

'You can't be serious?' Paul turned to face Paget. 'My client has nothing to do with your investigation, and I refuse to drag him into it.'

'Nevertheless, Mr Bromley, I would like the name and address,' Paget said. 'You have told us you were in Oxford yesterday, and we may wish to verify that.'

Paul's answer was to turn and walk to the door.

'Would you prefer that I get the information from your employer?'

Paul stopped. Grim-faced, he took out a notebook and gave Paget the information.

'Thank you, Mr Bromley. Just one more question, sir, before you go. I understand that you and Mrs Bromley are engaged in some sort of business venture. Would you mind telling me what it is?'

Paul's eyes narrowed suspiciously as if suspecting some sort of trap. 'Sorry . . .?' he said.

The silence between them lengthened. 'Perhaps I misunderstood,' Paget said. 'Can I take it, then, that you are *not* engaged in a business deal of some sort with Mrs Bromley?'

'You can take it any way you please,' Paul snapped, 'because I don't know what the hell you are talking about.'

'In that case, thank you, Mr Bromley,' Paget said pleasantly. 'I trust you will let us know if or when you plan to leave, because I'm sure we will need to talk again before you go.'

'I think we'd better have another chat with Mrs Bromley,' he said when Paul had gone. 'So let's go and find her before Paul has a chance to talk to her and they sort out their stories.'

Directed by Mrs Lodge, they found Margaret Bromley in the summer house on the west side of the house. Set in a semi-circle of Katsura trees, their leaves already tinged with autumn colours, it was a pleasant, warm and restful spot. And Margaret Bromley, sitting in a cushioned rattan chair, with a book in her lap, had fallen asleep. She looked so relaxed and peaceful that it seemed a shame to wake her.

Paget coughed discreetly, then louder. Mrs Bromley opened her eyes and tilted her head to squint at them against the sun, and sighed. 'There's no escape from you, is there, Chief Inspector?' she said as she pulled herself upright in the chair. Her words were delivered lightly, but Paget sensed annoyance there as well.

'I do apologize for disturbing you again, Mrs Bromley,' he said. 'Unfortunately, we don't have much choice, and I'm hoping you can help us. You see, Gwyneth Jones didn't come home last night. She seems to have disappeared.'

'Gwyneth? Disappeared? That's not like her at all. Are you quite sure there isn't some mistake?'

Paget shook his head. 'I'm afraid not, Mrs Bromley,' he said gravely. 'Her mother told us much the same thing, so we are taking her disappearance very seriously.'

'You don't think anything has happened to her, do you? One hears such dreadful things these days.'

'We don't know,' Paget told her candidly. 'Can you think of anywhere she might have gone? Anything she may have said to you that might suggest where she's gone?'

Mrs Bromley shook her head. 'Sorry, but nothing comes to mind,' she said. 'Her mother has no idea?'

'I'm afraid not. Sorry to have troubled you again, Mrs Bromley.' He made as if to turn away, then paused. 'But perhaps you can help me with another matter?'

'If I can,' she said cautiously.

'It's a matter of clarification, really. Tell me, when you went out the other night to try to find your brother-in-law, did you actually look *in* his car?'

'No. When I saw it sitting there in the garage, I assumed he had walked to the village. It never occurred to me that he might be in the car. It might have saved me a lot of trouble if I had,' she concluded with a nod toward her swollen ankle.

'How is it today?'

'Somewhat better, thank you. The swelling is going down, but I still have to be careful. Perhaps if I hadn't been in such a hurry and I'd looked where I was going . . .'

Tregalles spoke up. 'Like Mr Bromley's accident,' he said. 'Your brother-in-law running into the door.'

Mrs Bromley looked puzzled. 'The door . . .?' she said hesitantly. 'Sorry, Sergeant, but I'm afraid you've quite lost me.'

'Oh, I'm sorry, Mrs Bromley,' he said contritely, 'but I thought he said it was your door he ran into on Thursday evening?' She still looked mystified. 'The cut on his face?'

Unaccountably, colour rushed into Margaret Bromley's face. 'Oh, yes. Yes, of course,' she said. 'The door. Yes, I'm sorry, I'm afraid I'd quite forgotten. It was . . .' She stopped speaking. The light in her eyes died. It was as if a shutter had dropped down behind them, leaving her face blank and featureless.

It was happening again.

Paget bent and waved a hand in front of her eyes. Nothing.

No response. He touched Margaret Bromley's shoulder. 'Mrs Bromley?' he said quietly. 'Can you hear me?

No response. 'Mrs Bromley?' he said louder. Suddenly, she shivered and shrank back in her chair. 'Chief Inspector . . .?' She seemed surprised to find him standing there. 'I'm sorry, I'm afraid I was . . .' She sighed heavily. 'It happened again, didn't it?' she said with weary resignation. It wasn't a question. 'Sorry, Chief Inspector. I'm all right now. You were saying . . .?'

'Perhaps it would be best if we go back to the house,' Paget suggested solicitously. 'I'm sorry if my question upset you.'

'Yes, perhaps we should.' Margaret Bromley picked up her walking stick and eased herself forward in her chair. Paget offered his hand, and was somewhat surprised when she grasped it tightly and allowed him to help her out of the chair. He was even more surprised when she said, 'I'll take your arm, if you would be so kind. I'm afraid the ankle isn't healing quite as quickly as I'd hoped.'

She leaned heavily against him as they made their way across the lawn. He felt sure that what he and Tregalles had just witnessed had not been faked, but it had occurred immediately following a question about Paul's alleged encounter with a door. And it was clear she had not known what Tregalles was talking about.

Walking beside her, Tregalles asked another question. 'It's about something Julian said. He told us that, when he was on his way down from the top end of Manor Lane, Dr Lockwood's car was coming up. He said it passed him just before he reached the gate. Yet you made no mention of seeing the doctor on your way back to the house. Did you not see him go by?'

Paget felt Margaret Bromley stiffen, but she answered readily enough. 'You're quite right, Sergeant,' she said. 'I did see Dr Lockwood – at least I saw his car. He passed me in the lane, but I'd quite forgotten it until you reminded me. Sorry, but I really don't see—'

'He *passed* you, Mrs Bromley? He must have seen that you were having difficulty walking, to say nothing of getting soaking wet. Didn't he stop and offer you a lift?'

'I . . . I was at the entrance to the stable yard . . . well, inside it by that time, actually, so he wouldn't have seen me.'

'Too bad he didn't come by sooner,' Tregalles said. 'It would have saved you from having to walk all that way back.'

They continued on to the house in silence and went inside. Paget offered to escort Mrs Bromley up to her room, but she declined, saying she preferred to tackle the stairs on her own because it was easier that way.

It was clearly a lie, and they both knew it, but lie or not, it was also clear that they were being dismissed.

SIXTEEN

'Lies,' Paget muttered softly when Margaret Bromley had gone. 'I don't know how Paul came by that cut on his face, but I'm sure it had nothing to do with a door, and Mrs Bromley knows it. The question is: why is she going along with his story? And you certainly hit a nerve when you asked her about seeing Dr Lockwood.'

'I couldn't see how she could get all the way back to the manor without help,' Tregalles said. 'Maybe she didn't go down the lane at all. Maybe there's something going on between her and Lockwood. Julian as good as suggested there was. But whether there is or not, she was certainly evasive.'

'Evasive? That's putting it mildly,' Paget declared. 'As far as I'm concerned, we've heard precious little in the way of truth from any of them.' He looked at his watch. 'I'm afraid I'm going to have to leave you to it,' he told the sergeant. 'I have at least half a week's work sitting on my desk, and if I don't get it done over the weekend, I'll have Mr Brock on my back, and that is something I can do without. And since I'm taking the car, have Len send someone up for you when you're finished here. In the meantime, see if Julian's about and, if he is, have another go at him. Find out if he knows anything about Gwyneth. She's a good-looking girl, and I wouldn't be surprised to find that he's tried it on with her at some time or other. And see if you can shake his story about where he went and what he did the night Toni died. After that, go and see Dr Lockwood.

I doubt if he can help us in the search for Gwyneth, but let's see if his story matches that of Mrs Bromley and Julian.'

Julian was not being particularly helpful. He claimed to know nothing about Gwyneth's private life, and said he resented the suggestion that he might. 'I mean she's all right, but she *is* just the maid,' he said disdainfully. 'Although one would hardly know it by the way Charles treats her.'

'And how is that, Mr Bromley?' Tregalles asked.

Julian made a face. 'He treats her as if she were one of the family,' he said. 'If one didn't know better one might wonder . . .' He broke off in mid-sentence to wave a dismissive hand. 'There's no need to put *that* in your notes, Sergeant,' he said airily 'That was meant to be a joke. I mean we are talking about my father, brilliant surgeon, magistrate, pillar of the community, and all-round good fellow.'

'So why suggest it if you don't think it's true? I seem to remember you suggesting much the same thing when you were talking about your stepmother and Dr Lockwood. Was that meant to be a joke as well?'

'Oh, for God's sake!' Julian said irritably. 'There's no need to take something like that literally. It was just one of those off-the-cuff remarks one makes.'

'Then I suggest you consider your answers more carefully in future,' Tregalles said bluntly. 'We do tend to take things seriously in a murder investigation. Now, when was the last time you saw Gwyneth Jones?'

Julian gazed upward, appearing to concentrate. The pose might have worked on stage, but it wasn't doing much for Tregalles's patience. 'Difficult question, is it sir?' he asked with barely concealed sarcasm.

'I'm trying to comply with your obsession with time,' Julian shot back. 'It was at dinner last night.'

'Do you have *any* information that could help us find her?'

'No, I do not! So can I go now, Sergeant?'

Julian Bromley had gone, and Tregalles was glad to see the back of him. 'What that lad needs is a swift boot up the backside!' he muttered savagely as he stuffed his notebook into his pocket.

The boy – hell, he must be twenty-five or -six, but he was acting more like a spoiled teenager – seemed to lack all feeling other than for his own wellbeing. He'd displayed no emotion over the death of Toni Halliday. Nor had he shown any concern or even interest in the disappearance of Gwyneth Jones.

Was it a pose? Was it possible that there was more to Julian Bromley than the seemingly uncaring layabout who had just left the room? Was it possible that *Julian* had killed Toni? Certainly he'd been worried about what she might say. He could have followed her to the barn, perhaps pleaded with her not to name him as the father, then struck her down when she refused to listen.

Reluctantly, Tregalles shook his head. Julian was not that good an actor. But he had said one thing that intrigued the sergeant, and that was the throwaway remark about Charles Bromley's treatment of Gwyneth, and the veiled suggestion that there could be more to it than that. He'd insisted he'd been joking, but why mention it even as a joke unless there was something behind it? Worth keeping in mind, anyway, Tregalles thought as he left the room.

On his way out, Tregalles met Mrs Lodge in the hall, and stopped to ask her if she knew Dr Steven Lockwood's telephone number. 'It's on the pad beside the kitchen phone,' she told him. 'Had one of her funny turns again, then, has she?' she asked archly. 'That man must spend more time here than he does with the rest of his patients put together. Not that he seems to mind, and he is a very good doctor; I go to him myself. Still, you can't help but wonder, can you?'

'Wonder, Mrs Lodge? Tregalles asked innocently.

The housekeeper glanced up and down the deserted hall as if fearful of being overheard, then lowered her voice. 'Not that it's any of my business, of course,' she said, distancing herself from what she was about to say, 'but I think it's all in her head, and I don't like to see poor Mr Charles getting so upset about it. In fact,' she added boldly, 'I think she's putting it on. All those blank stares of hers. I mean, I ask you! Worrying Mr Charles like that. The poor man's got enough on his plate as it is.'

'But why, Mrs Lodge? Why would Mrs Bromley do such a thing?

The housekeeper drew back. 'All I'm saying is that every time she has one of her bad turns, Dr Lockwood is here within the hour, day or night.'

Tregalles did his best to look mystified. 'I don't understand,' he said. 'Why would he have to come every time Mrs Bromley has a short lapse of memory?'

'Oh, it's not just those,' the housekeeper said disdainfully. 'It's the fits and the nightmares that has poor Mr Charles up half the night calming her down.'

'Really?' Tregalles said. 'How long has this been going on?'

'Two or three months, must be,' the housekeeper said. 'He'd like her to go into hospital for observation, but she won't go. Says she can't stand hospitals, and Mr Charles says he won't force her to go.'

Mrs Lodge leaned closer. 'If you ask me, I think it's because she's afraid they'll find out it is all in her head.' She lowered her voice even further. 'Or she's putting it on a bit, and she's afraid they'll find that out.' The housekeeper stepped back. 'But like I said, it's none of my business, Sergeant, and since Mr Charles isn't here, I'd best go up and see what I can do. And you'd best get on and ring Dr Lockwood.'

'Oh, there's nothing wrong with Mrs Bromley,' Tregalles told her. 'At least she was fine when I left her a short time ago. She's just gone up to rest. I need to ring Dr Lockwood to make an appointment to see him myself.'

Having copied Lockwood's number down, Tregalles made his way outside before calling it and reaching the doctor's answering service.

Tregalles left a message, then made his way down the side of the house to the row of garages. Paul's car was parked in the end garage, and at least he'd been right about one thing: anyone sitting in the driver's seat would be completely hidden from the view of someone glancing in as they went by. But that still didn't mean he was actually sitting there when Mrs Bromley looked in. Nor, for that matter, did it prove that Mrs Bromley's story was true. They had both lied about other things, and it was quite possible that they were lying about where they were as well. Never mind Mrs Lodge's suspicions about Margaret Bromley's relationship with Lockwood; what about her relationship with Paul? After all, she was a very attractive woman, and life here at the manor must be pretty dull for her, especially after being married to a man like Bernard Halliday. Charles seemed like a decent enough man, and he did seem to be genuinely concerned about his wife's health, but he hadn't struck Tregalles as the most exciting man he'd ever met.

It was such a pleasant day that he decided to walk down to the village, and call in on Thorsen on the way. But there was no answer to his repeated knock on the cottage door, and the lady next door came out to tell him that Thorsen had gone into Clunbridge, and she didn't know when he would be back. In answer to Tregalles's question about Gwyneth, she said she knew Gwyneth Jones, but she hadn't seen her go by the previous evening. 'But I would have been doing the ironing about that time,' she explained, 'so I wouldn't, would I? But you might try Mr Evans down at the end,' she said after a moment's thought. 'He works in the garden most evenings. He might have seen her.'

Mr Evans turned out to be a robust man of eighty whose life now centred on his garden, and it was with some difficulty that Tregalles managed to turn him from his favourite subject.

Oh, yes, he said, he'd seen Gwyneth go by last night. He said she often waved and had a word as she rode past. But not last night. 'Went right past without a word,' he said. 'In a hurry to get home, I shouldn't wonder. It was getting dark and she had no lights, so I expect she wanted to get on. I called out, but she went right on by without saying a word. Funny, that. She always waves.'

SEVENTEEN

D r Lockwood called back while Tregalles was having lunch at the Cobbler's Last in Hallows End, and they arranged to meet later in the afternoon. 'Let's say three o'clock, shall we? I should be free by then,' he told Tregalles. 'I'm on duty at the Cleebury Hill Climb until two, so I'll meet you in the Cross Keys in Clunbridge? That's assuming no one here breaks their neck before then and I'm held up. But if they do I'll let you know,' he added cheerfully. 'It's blazing hot out here, and I'll be needing a drink by then.'

Tregalles finished his ham and cheese baguette, washed down with a pint of Theakstons Best, then made his way to the parish hall, where he found Ormside and Molly in a sombre mood.

'Not a thing,' Molly told him when Tregalles asked if there was any word on Gwyneth. 'The trouble is, she doesn't have any close friends. Almost everyone in Hallows End knows her, but she didn't have much of a social life. Hardly surprising, when you consider the odd hours she worked. When she did have time off, she spent most of it reading, according to her mother, and judging by the number of Mills & Boon romance novels I found in Gwyneth's room, I suspect she's an incurable romantic.'

'And probably a bit naïve when it comes to men,' Tregalles suggested. 'So she'd be easy prey for someone who could string a good line, like the major, even though he was more than twice her age.'

'I suppose,' said Molly doubtfully, 'but then I never met him, so I can't really say. What was he like?'

'Superior, snobby. Thought a lot of himself. Very much the old-school military man. Good looking in a flash sort of way. I couldn't take to him.'

Molly smiled. 'But then, you're not a young girl with a head full of romantic ideas, are you, Sergeant?' she said. 'And I very much doubt if you have ever read a bodice ripper in your life. Right?'

'Bodice ripper, eh?' Tregalles eyed Molly as if seeing her in a new light. 'Sounds as if I might have been missing something. Is that what you read?'

'*Used* to read when I was very much younger,' she admitted. 'But then I joined the police, and reality set in.'

'Speaking of which,' Tregalles said, 'how did last night go with your Chinese doctor? What was his name?'

'He's a *surgeon*, so it's *Mr* David Chen to you, Sergeant,' Molly said, sounding more defensive than she'd intended. 'And he is *not* Chinese. His grandparents were Chinese, but he's second-generation British, born and bred.'

Tregalles grinned. 'Well, whatever he is, he certainly took a shine to you, didn't he? And I bet it didn't end with just giving him a lift home did it? Take you out last night, did he?'

Molly could feel her face becoming warm. 'Well, the man is down here on his own,' she said stiffly, 'and with the Starkies away for the evening, he asked if I could recommend a good restaurant, then asked me to join him, because he didn't like to eat alone.'

'In other words, a date. Nice going Molly. Where did you go?'

'The Tudor, but it wasn't really a date as such, it was—'

'Sounds like a date to me,' Tregalles interrupted. 'Take you home, did he? I mean he could hardly take you back to the Starkies' could he? Invite him in, did you? You know, a nightcap to finish things off, and then—'

'And then nothing!' Molly said firmly. 'We had a very pleasant dinner, coffee in the lounge afterwards, and then he took me home. End of story.'

Tregalles chuckled. 'But you're seeing him again, aren't you? Did you ask him if he's married? Good looking chap, a doctor – oops! Pardon *me!* I mean a *surgeon* – it would be surprising if he isn't. And if he isn't, why not, eh?'

'If you're that interested, perhaps you should bring him in for questioning,' Molly replied in an attempt to make light of the matter, but Tregalles wasn't to be put off.

His grin grew wider. 'Must be serious for you to get so het up about it,' he said. 'I haven't seen your face that colour since you walked into the men's by mistake.' His expression changed to one of mock concern. 'But I must say I am relieved. To tell the truth, Molly, with you being without a boyfriend for so long, I was beginning to wonder about you. If you know what I mean?'

'Oh, I know *exactly* what you mean,' Molly said tartly as she turned away. She'd had a lovely time last night, and she didn't want anything or anyone to spoil it. She'd felt very comfortable with David Chen, and she was looking forward to seeing him again.

'*If* you don't mind, Tregalles,' Ormside broke in heavily, 'some of us have other things on our minds beside Forsythe's love life, so can we please get on? What did Paul Bromley have to say for himself?'

Tregalles and Ormside were working together transcribing key points of information to the whiteboards, when the door opened and Paget walked in.

'Didn't expect to see you out here again today,' Tregalles greeted him. 'Has something happened?'

'The hospital administrator rang me and we discussed the circumstances surrounding the death of Major Farnsworth,' Paget told him, 'so I thought it best to come out and explain things to Mrs Farnsworth myself. Anything new on Gwyneth Jones?'

Tregalles shook his head. 'Haven't talked to Mrs Etherton, yet,' he said, 'but I doubt if she knows any more than the rest of them up there. Mr Evans, who lives in the same row of cottages as Thorsen, says he saw Gwyneth go by on her way home last night. He said she usually waves, but she didn't last night. Just went sailing straight past without a word.'

Paget shot a questioning look at Ormside, who shook his head. 'Nothing,' he said. 'We still have one or two people to talk to in the village, lads and girls around her own age, but none of them are considered to be more than acquaintances, so I'm not holding my breath. We've spoken to the bus driver who was on the local run last night – the last one left Hallows End at ten past nine; the one before that left around seven, so she couldn't have been on that – and he said there were only five people on the bus, and none of them came close to matching Gwyneth's description.'

The sergeant drew in a long breath. 'I could be wrong,' he said in a way that said he didn't think so, 'and I know she's only been missing for a few hours, but I have a bad feeling about this. According to her mother, Gwyneth has no money to speak of, and she's never done anything like this before. I know it's early days, but I think we should go to the media now and get her picture out there.'

Paget nodded agreement. 'As a matter of fact I had a word with the press officer this afternoon,' he said, 'but I told her to hold off until I'd spoken to you again. So, give her a call, send her a copy of the picture of Gwyneth, and tell her I'd like to see it on the news tonight if at all possible. She has the details.'

Lower Farm was a farm in name only. It consisted of the house itself, a rambling two-storey place built of local stone, and a farmyard now seeded entirely to grass. The house and the land around it was owned by Ewan Davies at Top Farm, high up on the brow of the hill. He'd bought the hillside farm, known locally as Lower Farm, some years ago, but, not needing a second house, he'd been letting it out ever since. The major and Mrs Farnsworth had been there just over six months.

All this Paget learned while Mrs Farnsworth made tea. Now, seated in comfortable armchairs on either side of the open fireplace, an awkward silence fell between them.

'You may find some of the questions I have to ask distasteful,' Paget warned, 'but I'm afraid they have to be asked.'

Mrs Farnsworth set her cup aside. 'I quite understand,' she said. 'And I don't think there is anything you can tell me that will shock me, so please, don't feel embarrassed on my account. I expect it will all have to come out at the inquest anyway?'

'You're thinking now of an inquest into your husband's death?' he said.

'Why, yes, of course.'

Paget shook his head. 'That's not the main reason for my being here,' he said. 'But since we're on the subject, I should tell you that Nurse Adamu has no intention of causing any trouble. As far as she and the hospital are concerned, the major was hallucinating, probably due to the injuries he received the night before, and the injuries to his face occurred when she tried to hold him down. But she couldn't hold him, and he struck his head when he fell out of bed – which, in the broad sense at least, is quite true. When I spoke to her late last night, she said she'd suffered no serious harm or injury, and all she wanted to do was forget about it.'

'But you . . . the police . . .?'

Paget shook his head. 'I've had a word with my chief superintendent, and he feels there is nothing to be gained by pursuing the matter further.' In fact, Morgan Brock had been more than thankful to see the incident swept well and truly under the rug. The last thing he wanted was to have the details of the major's untimely death linked in any way to the Bromley investigation.

Mrs Farnsworth picked up her cup again and looked at Paget over the rim. Her hand shook as she sipped her tea. 'If you should see Nurse Adamu again,' she said softly, 'I'd appreciate it very much if you would tell her how much I appreciate what she's doing. I'm very grateful.'

'I shall,' Paget promised her. 'But, while I'm here, I would like to ask you about the events of Thursday evening; when Toni Halliday was killed.'

Harriett Farnsworth became very still. 'You believe that Adrian killed that girl, don't you?' she said softly. 'But you're wrong, you know. He isn't . . . wasn't a bad man. It's just that, after the accident, it was as if he had to prove that he could still . . . That he was still a man.'

She sighed. 'He had a temper, I won't deny that. And it became worse after his accident. He would get so frustrated. But he would never *kill* anyone. Not like that . . .' Her voice trailed off raggedly.

Paget had considered the possibility that Farnsworth had killed Toni, and had then been struck down himself by some third person, but it seemed an unlikely theory. Now, however, faced with the evidence of his association with Gwyneth, and his attack on Nurse Adamu, it might be time to reconsider. Given the major's proclivity toward young women, it was just possible that he had made advances towards Toni.

'Have there been other cases such as occurred in the hospital last night, Mrs Farnsworth?'

'Oh, no!' She seemed shocked by the suggestion.

'But there have been other women?'

'Yes.' Mrs Farnsworth struggled to her feet to busy herself with the teapot, refilling first his cup and then her own. It was a familiar routine and it gave her time to think and compose herself before settling back in her chair.

'I don't know how I can explain this, to you,' she said at last, 'but Adrian needed . . . reassurance. He needed other women, Chief Inspector, and, terrible as it may sound, I had come to accept that. We never spoke of it, you understand. In fact in his own way he tried to be discreet about it.'

Harriett Farnsworth smiled sadly.

'He wasn't very good at it. I had thought – hoped, perhaps is a better word – it might end when we came down here to live. Living in the country; not knowing anyone. It's different when you're in the army. It can be a dreadfully dull existence for wives, and there are always some who . . . Well, I'm sure I don't have to tell you what it's like.'

Harriett Farnsworth sighed wearily. 'But it didn't end, you

see. When he started going for these two-, three-, and four-hour walks in the evenings, I knew it was all a nonsense, and nothing had changed. Walking the dog was just an excuse.'

'Did you ever actually see him with any of these young women?' Paget asked.

'No. But I didn't have to see them. Adrian was not a clever man; not really. It never seemed to occur to him that I would notice the smell of cheap perfume on his clothes – he always bought them perfume; always the same cheap brand, and lipstick.'

She shuddered. 'I hated doing his laundry. In fact I didn't in the end. I sent it out. Told him I couldn't do it because of my arthritis.' Tears glistened in her eyes.

'You don't know who your husband was seeing that night?' Paget said.

'No. I knew he was seeing someone because of the way he got himself up. It was a sort of ritual with him. I could always tell.'

'Do you know Gwyneth Jones? She's a maid up at the manor.'

Mrs Farnsworth frowned at the question. 'Yes, I think I know the girl you mean. She lives in the village. I've seen her riding her bike back and forth to work.'

'Did you happen to see her last night, say just after eight o'clock?'

'No, that would be about the time the car came for me . . .' She stopped, her eyes suddenly focussed intently on his face. 'Are you saying that *she* was the one he was seeing? That young girl?'

'We believe so, based on the evidence we have so far,' Paget said. 'We think that Gwyneth Jones and the major were in the barn when Toni Halliday was murdered.'

'But they said he was hit by a car outside on the track. I saw him there myself.'

'That's right, he was,' Paget agreed, 'and we're not quite sure why, unless he ran out and tried to stop the person from getting away.'

'I doubt if he'd do that,' Mrs Farnsworth said, 'not if he was with a young woman. He'd try to stay out of it. What does the girl have to say?'

'That's the problem I'm afraid,' said Paget. 'Gwyneth Jones has disappeared.'

'Disappeared? You mean she's run away?'

'We don't know, Mrs Farnsworth. That's what we're trying to find out. We know she left the manor about eight last night. One of the cottagers up the lane saw her go by, but she never arrived home.'

'Oh, dear. I am sorry, but I'm afraid I can't help you. I think I've told you everything I know.'

He rose to his feet and thanked her. 'If you should think of anything else, you will let me know?'

'Of course. I shall be gone for a few days next week,' she said. 'Adrian's parents live in Worthing and he will be buried there, but I'll be back by the end of the week.'

Paget felt uncomfortable about leaving her. 'Are you sure you'll be all right?'

Mrs Farnsworth smiled. 'You're very kind,' she said, 'but I shall be all right here by myself. I'm quite used to it.'

Having no transport of his own, Tregalles asked Molly for a lift into Clunbridge for his appointment with Dr Lockwood. 'In fact, you might as well sit in,' he told her, 'and you can give me a ride home when we're finished.'

Dressed in a white shirt, baggy shorts and trainers, Dr Steven Lockwood was not quite what Tregalles had expected. He'd pictured a bigger man, tall, good looking, dark hair, a ladies' man, but Lockwood couldn't have been more than five seven or eight. Sandy hair, thinning slightly, pale skin and faintly freckled face, in appearance he was a lightweight. But there was a vibrancy and quiet confidence about the man that went beyond his otherwise rather ordinary appearance.

'Playing mixed doubles at four, so I am a bit pressed for time,' he explained after introductions had been made and they had their drinks in front of them. A pint of Wood's Special Bitter for Tregalles, a lager for Lockwood, and an orange juice for Molly, the designated driver. 'So how can I help?'

Tregalles took the doctor through the events of Thursday evening at the manor. There were no surprises; Lockwood's account tallied closely with that of Charles Bromley and the others. 'So what did you do once Nash was off the premises?' he asked.

'I went to see a patient in the village,' Lockwood said.

'A bit unusual, wasn't it?' Tregalles asked. 'I mean, it was in the middle of the evening.'

Lockwood shook his head. 'Not really,' he said. 'At least not for me. Mary Catchpole is ninety-three and dying. She should really be in care, but she refuses to leave her cottage, and she still manages to take care of herself with the help of a very good neighbour. It was the neighbour who rang to tell me that Mary had cut herself on the door latch when she was letting the cat out, and she asked me to come. Mary's on blood thinners, you see, and the cut was rather a bad one and wouldn't stop bleeding.'

'So what time did you leave there?' Tregalles asked.

Lockwood thought. 'Must have been close to nine,' he said.

'And Mrs Catchpole will be able to verify that, will she?'

The corners of Lockwood's mouth twisted into a wry smile. 'Probably not,' he said. 'She was asleep when I left her.'

'You came back up Manor Lane, did you?'

'That's right.'

'Did you see anyone or anything out of the ordinary along the way?'

Lockwood shook his head, then stopped. 'I saw young Julian just before I got to the Clunbridge road. He was coming down while I was going up. At least, I'm pretty sure it was Julian. He was running, trying to get out of the rain I expect.'

'Are you *quite* sure you didn't see or meet anyone else, Doctor?' Molly asked gently, speaking up for the first time.

Lockwood eyed her speculatively as if trying to decide how much she might know, then sighed. 'I assume you are asking if I saw Margaret,' he said, 'and the answer is yes, I did. As I'm sure you know, she'd sprained her ankle, she was soaking wet and hobbling, so I stopped and gave her a lift. I offered to come in with her and attend to the ankle when we got to the manor, but she insisted that I drop her at the entrance to the stables. She said she could manage that short stretch on her own, and Charles would take care of it. I didn't like to do that, because she was clearly in pain, but she insisted. Does that answer your question, Detective?'

'Yes, it does . . . but why didn't you mention it when Sergeant Tregalles asked if you had seen anyone on your way up Manor Lane?'

'I think you will agree,' Tregalles cut in before Lockwood could frame a reply, 'that it does seem a bit of a coincidence that you and Mrs Bromley just *happened* to be in Manor Lane at the same time. And, despite a severely sprained ankle, she was prepared to hobble from the stables to the house rather than risk the chance of being seen getting out of your car.'

Lockwood sighed. 'I can see now why Margaret insisted on getting out of the car when she did,' he said. 'It doesn't take much to set tongues wagging around here, and it sounds to me as if you've bought into the local gossip, so I doubt if anything I have to say will make any difference.' He drained his glass and put both hands on the table as if about to rise.

'Try me,' Tregalles said. 'How *would* you describe your relationship with Mrs Bromley?'

Lockwood started to shake his head, then changed his mind. 'All right,' he said, settling back into his seat. 'First and foremost, Margaret Bromley is a patient I am trying to help under somewhat difficult circumstances. She is also a friend, as is Charles, so I am more than willing to spend as much time as it takes to find the cause of her problem.'

The doctor eyed them both for several seconds before leaning forward and lowering his voice. 'Look,' he said earnestly, 'I'm not in the habit of discussing my patients' problems with others, but I want you to understand why I spend as much time as possible at the manor. Margaret suffers from severe headaches, and brief lapses of memory, which I'm sure you will have observed if you've spent any time with her. When she appeared to have suffered a mild stroke six months ago, we got her into the Brideshill Clinic immediately. They did all the tests, but found nothing to confirm that, nor could they find anything physically wrong with her, so they sent her home, and Charles and I have been working together ever since, trying to find an answer to these odd symptoms.'

'But there must be more tests that can be done,' said Molly. 'Aren't there specialists Mrs Bromley could go to?'

Lockwood nodded. 'There are,' he said. 'In fact, there are several options, but Margaret refuses to have anything to do with any of them.'

'Why not?' Tregalles asked bluntly.

Lockwood hesitated. 'I think it's because she's afraid of what they might find,' he said, 'and if you want to know any more I suggest you ask Mrs Bromley. However, I should warn you that it is a very touchy subject with her, so unless it is *really* relevant to your investigation, I suggest you avoid it.'

'And this has been going on for six months?'

'The first occurrence, attack, or whatever it was happened then,' Lockwood said, 'but then there was a lull. In fact we thought it was just a one-off aberration. But then it started up again a couple of months ago, and it's been happening on and off ever since. It's erratic. Sometimes Margaret will go days at a time and feel perfectly fine, then suddenly it's back again.' Lockwood looked at his watch and got to his feet. 'And now I'm afraid I really must be off,' he said. 'I hope I've been of some help'.

EIGHTEEN

Monday, September 12th

The day did not start well for Paget. He spent the morning in court waiting to give evidence in a particularly brutal grievous bodily harm case that had taken more than six months to come to trial, only to see the case dismissed on a legal technicality. Hundreds of hours of police work down the drain because of a series of mistakes that, individually, wouldn't have mattered very much, but, collectively, they were enough for the defence to argue successfully for dismissal.

Which was why he was not in the best of moods when he returned to the office to find a fax from Morgan Brock on his desk, telling him that a meeting, which had been scheduled for later in the week, had been brought forward to this afternoon. The subject – the examination of the new rules proposed by the Home Office on the treatment of members of identifiable ethnic and/or religious groups before, during, and after arrest – did nothing to improve his sour mood.

Muttering beneath his breath, he crumpled the message and tossed it in the bin beside his desk, then looked up to see a young policewoman standing in the doorway.

'Yes?' he said curtly.

The WPC hesitated, momentarily put off by his abrupt manner.

'Well, Constable . . .?' he prompted.

'WPC Short,' she said crisply. 'I have information regarding the bulletin on Gwyneth Jones, sir.'

Paget looked at her blankly for a second, then, as what she'd said sank in, his face relaxed and he motioned her to come in. 'Sorry,' he apologized, 'but it's been one of those days. What's this about Gwyneth?'

'It's just that I saw her on Friday night while we were on our way to pick up Mrs Farnsworth. Gwyneth was in the lane outside Mrs Farnsworth's house.'

'On *Friday* . . .?'

The girl caught the implied criticism in his voice. 'I was away camping on the weekend,' she said. 'I didn't know Gwyneth was missing until I saw the bulletin just now. I came over straightaway, sir.'

'Are you a friend of Gwyneth's?'

'We used to knock about together after we left school,' she told him. 'Then I moved away and we lost touch. Friday was the first time I'd seen her in several years.'

'I see. Right. Tell me everything from the beginning.'

'There isn't much to tell, really, sir,' Valerie said, and went on to describe her brief encounter with Gwyneth in Manor Lane.

'Did she give you any idea – any indication at all as to where she was going?'

Valerie shook he head. 'I'm sorry, sir, but I've told you everything she said.'

Paget tried not to look disappointed. 'You say she was coming from the direction of the manor when you saw her? What time was that?'

Valerie Short already had her notebook out. 'We arrived at the house at twenty fourteen,' she said, 'so it was two or three minutes before that.'

'Did you see her leave?'

'No, sir. She was still standing there when I got back in the car. It's funny, though; she seemed quite shaken when I told her why we were there. She never used to be like that. Took everything in her stride. Funny how people change.'

It made perfect sense, though, if Gwyneth and the major had been lovers, Paget thought. He questioned Valerie Short closely, asking about mutual friends, places they might have visited together in the past, in fact anything at all that might give him a clue to Gwyneth's present whereabouts, but she could add nothing of value to what she had already told him.

He looked at the time, then at the mound of paper awaiting his attention. 'I want you to call Sergeant Ormside at the incident room in Hallows End,' he said, 'and tell him exactly what you've told me. And if there is anything, and I do mean *anything* you think of later, make sure you let him know. All right?'

'Right, sir.'

'Good. And thank you, Constable.'

In his mind's eye he could see the entrance to Lower Farm, picture Gwyneth standing there, shaken by the news of Farnsworth's death. God knows what thoughts were tumbling through her head as the police car disappeared from view. But what would she have done?

The answer most likely hinged on the answer to other questions, such as: had she been in the barn when Toni Halliday was murdered? If so, had she seen the killer? Because if she had, and the killer realized it . . .

He would have dearly loved to go out to Hallows End to look for the answer himself, but one look at the stack of papers awaiting his attention served as a sharp reminder that he no longer had that choice. It was a sobering thought, and one to consider seriously if he was to consider taking on Alcott's old job.

After hearing from Valerie Short, Ormside and Tregalles were asking themselves the same questions, because they, too, thought it more than likely that Gwyneth Jones had been in the barn at the time of the murder.

'So why didn't Gwyneth simply tell us and save us all a lot of trouble?' Tregalles grumbled.

'And let everybody know she was having it off with a married man old enough to be her father?' Ormside said. 'To say nothing of becoming a suspect herself, since Toni Halliday had threatened to have her sacked.'

'We didn't know that until she told us herself though, did we?' Tregalles objected.

'On the other hand, she didn't exactly volunteer the information, did she?' Ormside countered. 'According to what you told me, it was more or less dragged out of her. And if she was in the barn when Toni Halliday was killed, and the killer knows it, I hope we find her before he does.'

Paget had just finished lunch at his desk, a ham-and-cheese sandwich from the cafeteria downstairs, when Ormside rang to say he'd received records of Toni Halliday's mobile phone calls, and the last call she'd made before she died was to another mobile number registered to a man by the name of Simon Conroy, who lived in London. 'In fact,' Ormside said, 'most of the calls she made while she was at the manor were to the same number. The Lambeth Borough Police say he has no form, but he is known to them. He first came to their notice when his name appeared on a licence for a casino called The Deep Six in Kennington. I spoke to a DS McLean in the Kennington nick, who told me that Conroy is acting for a man by the name of Aaron Webb, who is *very* well known to them. He said they've never been able to pin anything on Webb, but they're sure he's involved in smuggling and human trafficking, and if they could get something worthwhile on Conroy, they might be in with a chance on Webb. So McLean says they would be only too happy to work with us.

'Toni Halliday also made a call every other Wednesday, to an inn called The Latch on the outskirts of Worcester, so I rang the manager there. He told me that she'd called to reserve a table for two in the dining room for Thursday lunchtime, and a room for two the same night.'

'She stayed there overnight?'

'Apparently not, because Mrs Lodge tells me that Toni always came back the same day, usually in time for dinner at seven.'

'So the room was for . . .?'

'Your guess is as good as mine,' Ormside said, 'but I wouldn't mind betting we come up with the same answer.'

'Did the manager know who the second person was?' asked Paget.

'Her husband,' Ormside said drily. 'He says she always booked in the name of Mr and Mrs Halliday and paid by credit card.'

'Any description of the man?'

'Pretty vague. Tallish, dark hair, that sort of thing,' Ormside said, 'but Lambeth is faxing us a picture of Conroy, so I'll have someone show the pictures to the manager and staff of The Latch to see if we can jog a few memories. But the manager did remember one thing. He said the man drives a silver-coloured Jag, and I seem to remember Julian Bromley telling you that he was passed by a Jag in Manor Lane on his way back to the house the night the Halliday girl was killed.'

'You might check with Lambeth to see what this man, Conroy, drives,' Paget suggested.

'Thought you'd never get round to it,' Ormside said, sounding smug. 'Conroy drives – or *used* to drive – a two-year-old silver Jag, but he reported it stolen last Friday. He said he wasn't exactly sure when it went missing, but it could have been the night before. Bit of a coincidence, don't you think?'

'Coincidence indeed,' Paget agreed. 'I suppose it's too soon to expect anything back from Forensic on the paint the car left on the water tank?'

'Nothing yet, no, but I'll keep after them. But there is one other thing before you go. I don't know if you've been up the track beyond the barn where Toni Halliday was found, but there's a caravan in a field up there. It's owned by a woman by the name of Vanessa King. Makes pottery and jewellery and stuff like that and sells it at the local markets. Mid-thirties or thereabouts, and a bit of a free spirit, according to local gossip, if you know what I mean. Seems to have a few men friends who stop by fairly regularly.

'Anyway, when one of my men stopped in there to ask if she knew anything that might help us find Gwyneth Jones, she happened to mention that Farnsworth had been with her the evening of the murder. Seems he was a regular, but she didn't like him very much. She said he was a cocky bastard, boasting about going to meet his new "little beauty" when he left her that night, but he wouldn't tell her who she was. Miss King said he told her he'd arranged to meet the girl at eight, but he deliberately stayed on until after half past, saying that she'd be all the more ready for it if he kept her waiting.'

'Charming fellow,' Paget observed, 'but true to form by the sound of it.'

'So,' Ormside continued, 'I reckon he must have been on his way down to the barn when he was hit by a car backing into the lane from the barn, which would explain why he was found where he was.'

'Good work, Len,' said Paget, and was about to hang up when he paused. 'I was going to wait for the results from Forensic before sending someone up to London, but if they're that keen to help us, perhaps we should get someone up there straightaway. So I'd like you to set something up with this DS McLean, then have Tregalles call me. You can tell him he's won a free trip to London, all expenses paid . . . within reason, of course.'

'Let's leave the washing up and take our wine outside and watch the sun go down,' Grace suggested when they'd finished dinner. 'The nights are pulling in so fast, I don't know where the summer's gone.'

The sun was warm on their faces as they settled into lawn chairs, content to enjoy the quiet of the evening while they watched shadows deepen in the valleys and hilltops turn to gold.

'You were very quiet during dinner,' said Grace. 'I take it you still don't know what's happened to Gwyneth Jones?'

Paget shook his head. 'We've had any number of so-called sightings,' he said, 'but nothing solid, I'm afraid.'

'You don't think she's run away, do you?'

'I keep trying to convince myself that she has, but from what we know of her and what her mother tells us, she had nowhere to go. She's always lived at home; never travelled to any degree, and there are no close relatives or special friends she might go to. She has a small savings account, which hasn't been touched; she has two credit cards, neither of which have been used in the past week, and she has little if any money. So, if she *was* in the barn when Toni Halliday was killed, and the killer found out . . .' He didn't finish the sentence, but the bleak look in his eyes more than expressed what he was thinking.

'I should have pushed her harder,' he said tightly, annoyed with himself for not having done so. 'I *knew* she was holding something back; I *knew* she was lying when I asked her why she'd been crying, but I thought it best to come back to that later when we knew more.' He sipped his wine. 'And now it may be too late,' he muttered angrily.

'Or not!' Grace said, 'so don't go blaming yourself for something that isn't your fault. You did what you thought best at the time, and Gwyneth Jones made a conscious decision to withhold vital information.' She left her chair and squatted down beside him to slip an arm around his shoulders. 'I know how you must feel,' she said softly, 'but it really isn't your fault, Neil. We make decisions as best we can with the information we have, but we can't get it right every time. It's a fact of life, love, so stop beating yourself up over it and move on. The girl may be fine – scared, perhaps, but all right.'

But even as she spoke the words of reassurance, Grace couldn't avoid the feeling that Neil might well be right. And if he was . . .? That was something *she* didn't want to think about.

'At least we have a lead to the man Toni Halliday's been meeting each week,' he said, and went on to tell Grace about his conversation with Ormside. 'So I'm sending Tregalles up to London in the morning to talk to this man Conroy,' he concluded.

'You're assuming that since Toni's last call was to Conroy, he was the one she was expecting to pick her up?'

'Right.'

'So the next question is: was she alive or dead when he got there?'

'And if she was alive, did he kill her?'

Grace thought about that. 'I'd be inclined to say no,' she said. 'I think she was dead when he got there, but he may have been the one who searched her things.'

'Reason?' Paget prompted.

'It's just an idea,' Grace hedged, 'but if Toni was stealing her mother's jewellery, she had to be passing it on to someone, and that someone could have been Conroy. And if she'd told him she would be bringing more with her, he wouldn't have wanted to leave without it.'

'But he didn't find it,' Paget pointed out.

'Because he was either fussy about digging into Toni's dirty laundry, or he was frightened off before he found it.'

'Then took off in such a hurry that he ran Farnsworth down.'

Paget supplied. 'But why do you say you don't think Conroy killed Toni?'

'Because of the green paint,' Grace said. 'There was green paint on the handle of the sickle, and that could have only come from inside the house, which is where I believe you will find your killer.'

'I agree,' he said with a sigh, 'but proving it may be difficult. Brock almost has a fit every time I talk to a member of the Bromley family. Between that and our chief constable having friendly chats with Charles Bromley, it won't be easy.

'However, enough of that,' he concluded firmly. 'Take a look at this.' He drew a folded sheet of paper from his pocket and handed it to Grace.

She unfolded it and scanned the contents, then began to read aloud.

'Interviews for the position of Detective Superintendent CID, A Division, Broadminster, will take place Tuesday, thirteenth of September, beginning at ten a.m. in Conference Room Two, Westvale Police Headquarters, Twelve New Street, Broadmins—' She stopped short. 'That's *tomorrow* for heaven's sake!' Frowning, she scanned the page more closely. 'It sounds as if there are other candidates, but it doesn't give any names, except yours, and you're first up at ten tomorrow morning. What's going on, Neil? Who are the other candidates? And when did you get this?'

'No idea,' he said. 'And it came in just before four thirty this afternoon. Faxed over from New Street. In fact if it had come in a few minutes later, Fiona would have been gone and I might not have seen it until tomorrow.'

'So what's Brock playing at?' she asked suspiciously.

'Haven't a clue,' he said. 'As for the other candidates, I expect old Tom Rudd from B Division will have put his name in as he has on just about every other posting, but he's just looking to boost his pension before he goes, and everybody knows it. Apart from that, I've heard nothing.'

'So the job should be yours – assuming you still want it?'

'I've been in two minds about it, as you know,' he said, 'but I've decided to go for it. To be honest, Grace, I'm still not thrilled about some aspects of the job, but at least at that level I would have more authority than I do now, and there are a lot of things I would like to see changed.'

Grace tugged on his hand to pull him to his feet, then held out her glass. 'In that case, good luck to you, love,' she said. 'I think you will make a marvellous superintendent, so let's drink to it.'

NINETEEN

Tuesday, September 13th

Wearing his visitor's badge, Tregalles was escorted through the corridors of the Kennington Police Station to the desk of DS George McLean, a balding, ruddy-faced man, who looked surprised to see him.

'You're an early bird,' he said as he got up to shake hands, then waved Tregalles to a seat. 'I didn't expect to see you until later in the day.'

'I came up last night to give myself more time here,' Tregalles told him. 'Why, is it a problem?'

It had been a spur of the moment decision. Not thrilled about the prospect of having to get up at five in the morning, he'd decided it would be simpler to leave that evening, so he'd driven to Birmingham and caught the 20.10 train out of New Street.

'Not for me,' McLean assured him. He grinned. 'But I doubt if Conroy will be too pleased. He doesn't usually leave the casino till two or three in the morning, and he's rarely up before nine or ten, so perhaps we can catch him off guard.' He leaned back in his chair and joined his hands behind his head. 'Funny how things work out, isn't it?' he said. 'As I told you on the phone yesterday, we don't have anything on Conroy himself, but we do know that it was Aaron Webb who put up the money for the casino. We've wondered how we might get at Webb through Conroy, and now here you are from the back of beyond saying Conroy could be a murderer. This could be just what we're looking for.'

'I'm not sure we can go quite as far as that,' Tregalles said cautiously. 'We think we can put him at the scene, and we think he was at least partly responsible for the death of an ex army officer. But whether he killed Toni Halliday or not is still open to question.'

'But more than enough reason to bring him in for questioning,' McLean said decisively. He got to his feet. 'And there's no time like the present, so let's have him in.'

'I *told* you before, I don't *need* a solicitor, because I haven't done anything wrong,' Conroy said when McLean asked him for a second time.

Slightly taller than Tregalles, Simon Conroy was a slim, lean-bodied man, but judging by his upper arms, he was into lifting weights in a serious way. Tanned and wearing a T-shirt, slacks, and sandals, Conroy looked younger than the thirty-seven years McLean's fact sheet on the man showed him to be.

'And I still don't know why I'm here,' Conroy continued as he took his seat facing the two sergeants across the table. 'I told you, as far as Toni Halliday is concerned, she's past history. Yes, we lived together for a while, but she took off months ago, and that's the last I've seen of her.'

'Or spoken to her?' Tregalles asked.

Conroy hesitated. 'She did ring me once or twice,' he admitted, 'but it was nothing—'

'Why'd she ring you, then, if it was nothing?' McLean broke in quickly. 'There must have been a reason.'

Conroy looked pained. 'She . . . she wanted us to get back together again,' he said, 'but I'd had enough of her tantrums and wild behaviour when we lived together, which is why I finally kicked her out. I couldn't take it any more, so I told her I didn't want to see her again until she was off the drugs and straightened herself out. Why, what's she done, and why are you asking me all these questions?'

'When was the last time she rang you?' Tregalles countered.

'Sometime last week. Wednesday, maybe Thursday, I don't remember exactly. She was rambling; I'm sure she was high, so I cut her off.'

'How long was that before you killed her?' McLean demanded, jumping in ahead of Tregalles once again.

'Killed . . .?' Conroy pulled back, eyes narrowed as he looked at each of them in turn. 'I don't know what you're talking about,' he said, 'but if Toni is dead, this is the first I've heard about it. I told you, I haven't seen her since—'

'Last Thursday when you went to pick her up at Bromley Manor,' Tregalles broke in with a warning glance in McLean's direction. No doubt McLean thought he was being helpful, but he was pushing too hard, and his role was supposed to be that of an observer, even if they were on his patch.

'That's ridiculous!' Conroy scoffed. 'As I've told you several times already, I've had phone calls from her, but I have no idea where she is . . . or *was*, if she really is dead. And if she is, I had nothing to do with it.'

'Then let me show you these,' Tregalles said as he took a couple of pictures from an envelope and held them up. 'Copies of these pictures of you and Toni Halliday are being shown to the manager and staff of The Latch even as we speak. It's an inn just off the Bromyard Road near Worcester,' he explained for McLean's benefit, 'where you and Toni Halliday have been meeting every couple of weeks since she left London. And we know that Toni rang you to ask you to pick her up the night she was killed. So why don't we start again, Mr Conroy? But let's have the truth this time.'

TWENTY

Wednesday, September 14th

Paget had been hard at work for more than an hour, when he looked up to see Tregalles standing in the open doorway. 'Clearing out the desk, then, are we?' the sergeant asked with a nod toward the stack of folders on Paget's desk. 'For the move upstairs,' he elaborated when Paget looked puzzled. 'That is what the interview was about, wasn't it?'

'I thought you were in London all day yesterday,' said Paget, avoiding the question.

'I was, but I don't think I was more than ten feet inside the door this morning before I heard they'd been doing interviews in New Street yesterday for the super's job, and I half expected to find you upstairs this morning – sir!'

Tregalles moved into the office and sat down. 'Seriously though, boss, how did it go?'

Good question, thought Paget. The board had consisted of Chief Constable Sir Robert Wyckham, Deputy Chief Constable Adrian Drummond, and Chief Superintendent Morgan Brock. Ordinarily, the third seat would have been occupied by a super-intendent, but there had been no one available, so Brock was sitting in instead.

At least that was what they had told him.

Sir Robert, a lean, athletic-looking man, whose iron-grey hair and chiselled features always showed well on TV, opened the interview by asking Paget about his experience in the Met before coming to Broadminster, and went on to comment favourably on his clear-up rate since joining the Westvale Regional Constabulary. He'd asked why Paget felt he was qualified for the job, and what he would like to see changed or improved if he were given free rein, and seemed satisfied with Paget's answers.

DCC Drummond had grilled him on everything from the way he'd handled specific cases in the past, and what he might have done differently in retrospect. He'd been asked for his thoughts on police policies and regulations. He and Brock between them had quizzed him on his knowledge of the law; PACE and the rules pertaining to the questioning of suspects and witnesses; rules of evidence, as well as his thoughts on what the relation-ship should be between his department, the public, the media and the CPS. There had even been questions on what his response would be, as Detective Superintendent – Crime, to a variety of situations involving terrorists, ethnic groups, and hostage situations.

Inevitably, Brock had concentrated on the importance of records and documentation; the use of civilian staff to cut costs; minimizing overtime; in fact all things financial so dear to the chief superintendent's heart.

It had been a gruelling morning, and he was glad it was behind him.

'I have no idea,' he said in answer to Tregalles's question. 'I'll just have to wait and see.'

Tregalles frowned. 'I don't get it,' he said. 'I mean, who else is there besides you? Did Rudd go for it again? Not that he'd stand a chance with his record, so was there anyone else?'

'Honestly, Tregalles, I really *don't* know,' Paget told him, 'so let's leave it there. How did you get on in London? Local police helpful, were they?'

'Couldn't have asked for better,' Tregalles told him. 'I don't think I was there more than five minutes before DS McLean had Conroy brought in for questioning, he was that keen.'

'And Conroy?'

'Denied everything at first, then changed his story when he realized we knew about The Latch and his visits there, and the phone calls, but he insisted that the reason he came down here to meet with Toni Halliday was because he felt sorry for her, and he was trying to help her.'

'By keeping her supplied with drugs?'

'Just the opposite, according to him. To hear Conroy tell it, he was there to save her. He said Toni went to stay with her mother to put herself as far away as possible from the temptation of drugs. But she found she couldn't manage it on her own, and she kept calling for him to come and help her through it.'

'How very noble of him,' said Paget. 'What did he have to say about the series of calls Toni made to him right up till the time she died?'

'Oh, he had an answer for that as well. He admitted that she'd called him; he even admitted that she wanted him to come and get her and take her back to London, but when she told him about the accident and the reason she was running away, he told her she would only make matters worse if she ran away, and refused to help her. Besides, he said he was back in London by that time, and his staff at the casino would testify that he was there from seven o'clock on that night. Unfortunately for him, his story fell apart when I told him the record showed that the last calls recorded between him and Toni showed they were both in the same area. That's when he decided not to say any more without his lawyer present.'

'What about his car?'

'Still missing,' Tregalles said. 'He still insists that it was stolen. We know he's lying, but it's impossible to prove.'

'What about the jewellery? Did you get anywhere with that?'

'No.' Tregalles grimaced in disgust. 'In fact,' he said sarcastically, 'Conroy said he was horrified to think that Toni would stoop so low as to steal jewellery from her own mother, probably to be used as payment for drugs, especially when he was doing his best to help her break the habit.'

Tregalles spread his hands in a gesture of apology. 'So I had to leave it there,' he said. 'We didn't have enough evidence to justify a warrant to search Conroy's flat and business premises for stolen jewellery, but if they can find his Jag and we can match the paint on the car to the paint on the water tank, we'd have a better chance. However, McLean promised to keep looking for the car, and he's going to keep in touch.'

'Why is McLean being so helpful?' Paget asked. 'I'm sure they're not short of work in the Borough of Lambeth, unless things have changed a lot since I was in the Met.'

'Oh, he has his own agenda all right,' Tregalles said. 'He made no bones about that. The man they *really* want is Aaron Webb. According to McLean, Webb is into smuggling, human trafficking and prostitution, but they haven't been able to lay a finger on him, and they see this as a chance to get at him through Conroy. They need leverage, and if we're successful in nailing Conroy, they want to make a deal with us to drop the charges if Conroy agrees to become their informant.'

Paget grunted. 'I can't say I'm not sympathetic,' he said, 'but they'll have to sort that one out with the CPS if we ever get to the point where we can charge the man. But don't discourage McLean. We can use all the help we can get.'

He looked at the paperwork piled up on his desk, and sighed. 'Meanwhile, let's concentrate on what we have here,' he said. 'I'd like to go back out there myself, but I can't ignore this lot any longer. So I want you to go out to the manor and have another go at Paul Bromley. Len phoned me last night to say he'd managed to track down this man Williams. Remember him? The client Paul Bromley said he was with last Friday in Oxford?'

Tregalles nodded. 'What about him?'

'Williams says Paul did show him some property, but it wasn't last Friday. It was last Tuesday.'

Tregalles scowled. 'Didn't he think we would check? The man must think we're idiots.' Then, 'Okay,' he said wearily, 'I'll talk to him again. I can hardly wait to hear what his explanation will be this time.'

'Better take someone with you,' Paget told him. 'Mr Brock told me again yesterday that the Bromleys aren't very happy about our continued presence at the manor, and he would prefer that we leave them alone. I told him we would as soon as they stopped lying to us, and I'm convinced that they had nothing to do with the murder of Toni Halliday. There's been no formal complaint from Charles Bromley, but I think it would be best if there were two of you out there in case he does, so take Forsythe with you.

'Just one more thing while you're out there this morning,' he continued as Tregalles got to his feet. 'Grace realized last night that her steel measuring tape is missing from her kit, and she remembers leaving it on the seat of the old tractor in the barn. She was planning on going out to look for it this evening, but since you are going out there, perhaps you could pick it up it and save her a trip?'

'No problem,' Tregalles told him. He paused in the doorway. 'I don't suppose there's been anything new on Gwyneth Jones while I was away?'

'Afraid not,' Paget said soberly. 'We put out another appeal last night, but . . .' He shook his head, stopping short of putting into words what was in both their minds.

Tregalles drove out of Broadminster under lowering skies. It had rained during the night, and the sky couldn't seem to make up its mind whether to clear or not. But it was a relief from the on-again, off-again heat of the past few days, and for that he was grateful. In a strange sort of way it reflected his mood, because he couldn't help thinking about what could happen if Paget did get the super's job. Where would that leave him, he wondered? And who would he find himself working for?

He ran over the possibilities in his mind, but none of them
held much appeal. Come to that, if another DI or DCI came in,
he might bring his own sergeant with him, and where would that
leave him?

He should have listened to Paget when he'd first suggested
that he give some thought to promotion. That was almost a year
ago, he thought guiltily, and things might have been different
now if he had taken Paget's advice seriously. But he'd balked at
the idea of having to devote what could amount to hundreds of
hours of study on his own time, when he was spending little
enough time with Audrey and the kids as it was, and the kids
were growing up fast.

On the other hand, did he really want to remain a sergeant for
the rest of his working life? Because the longer he put it off, the
more likely it was that notes such as 'lacks ambition' would start
showing up in his annual reviews, and he would end up working
for some smart-arsed youngster who had leap-frogged over him
on his way to the top.

Len Ormside had done it. He'd remained a sergeant and was
quite content doing the job he was doing. In fact he'd made a
unique niche for himself, and was respected for it. But Ormside
was an exception, and Tregalles couldn't see himself in that sort
of role. In the end, of course, it was down to him, and the one
thing he couldn't afford to ignore was the effect his decision
would have on his pension. What with the mortgage on the house,
the kids growing up, and probably going on to university, he
wasn't putting much by for the future, and the way David
Cameron was going on, he'd be lucky if there was any old age
pension left by the time he needed it.

Tregalles sighed heavily as he pulled up outside the church
hall in Hallows End. The sun broke through the clouds; the sky
was clearing, but the thoughts inside the sergeant's head were
anything but clear.

Molly Forsythe was waiting for him when Tregalles entered the
church hall. She looked very smart in her plain white blouse, navy
jacket and skirt. He studied her as she slung her handbag over her
shoulder and came forward to meet him, and it struck him that
there was something different about her. It wasn't so much in the
way she was dressed – Molly had always been well groomed and

neatly dressed – as it was in her manner. He couldn't quite put his finger on it, but somehow she was no longer simply DC Molly Forsythe, nice girl, willing worker, dependable, good figure, great legs. The woman walking toward him so confidently was soon-to-be-Detective *Sergeant* Forsythe. Still a nice girl and all those other things, but somehow sharper. In fact, very sharp indeed!

Perhaps a bit *too* sharp, he thought disconsolately. He knew that Paget had had his eye on Molly for some time now, and when he put that together with Paget's 'suggestion' that it might be time for him to tackle the inspectors' exam, he couldn't help wondering what would happen if Paget *didn't* get the superintendent's job. Would Molly Forsythe become Paget's first choice as sergeant?

'Well, Sergeant?' said Molly as she came up to him. 'Why do I have the feeling that I've just been through an airport body scanner and come up short?' She looked down at herself, checking to make sure that everything was as it should be, then cocked a quizzical eye in Tregalles's direction. '*Is* there something wrong?' she asked seriously.

He shook his head. 'Just admiring the outfit,' Tregalles said glibly. 'New, is it? To impress the new boyfriend, the doctor without borders?'

'The answer is no to both questions,' Molly told him. 'And a real detective would have remembered that I've worn this very same combination at least twice in the last few weeks. Anyway,' she continued quickly before he could respond, 'I was told to drop whatever I was doing and wait for you. Is this about Paul Bromley lying about where he was last Friday? Sergeant Ormside said he'd been caught out, but he also said something about my being needed at the manor as a witness? Witness to what? I don't understand? Are you going to arrest Paul Bromley?'

'I'd *like* to arrest the lying bastard,' Tregalles said darkly, 'but it seems the Bromleys are "disturbed" by our continued presence there. We're disrupting their ordered lives, so Paget wants someone else there as a witness so it won't be just their word against mine if they do decide to make a formal complaint.

'And speaking of Paget,' he continued as they got in the car, 'Grace Lovett left her steel measuring tape on the tractor seat in the barn the other day, and he wants us to pick it up for her. So

I'll drop you off at the entrance to the stable yard and you can nip over to the barn to look for it. But don't waste time looking for it if it isn't where she thinks she left it, because I want you with me when I talk to Paul.'

The smell of freshly turned earth hung in the air as Molly walked up the lane. She paused at the beginning of the track leading to the barn where Toni Halliday had been killed. She had not visited the crime scene itself before, although she'd driven past the track leading to it several times in the past few days. With the sound of birds chunnering softly in the background, and the distant thrum of a tractor going about its work, the place was so peaceful and serene, it was hard to believe that a cold-blooded murder had taken place in such a beautiful spot. Molly tried to visualise the scene at night in the pouring rain, but it just wouldn't come into focus at all.

Except for patches of trampled grass and weeds around the door of the barn, all signs of a police presence were gone. The door swung open to her touch and she stepped inside, pausing for a moment to give her eyes time to adjust to the dim interior. Gradually, she became aware of light filtering through cracks where time and weather had warped the wooden walls. She wrinkled her nose at the odd, rancid smell of the place. It smelled like wet hay that had been left to rot.

The barn was cavernous, and it took her a moment or two to spot the tractor. It was half buried beneath a jumble of bits and pieces of farm machinery, and as she walked toward it she could see the tape measure on the seat. Molly picked it up and slipped it into her handbag, but as she started to turn away she became aware of a low buzzing sound close to her feet. She stepped back. It seemed to be coming from beneath a rusted sheet of corrugated iron. It sounded like a child's electric toy, but that made no sense. Puzzled, she pulled at the heavy sheet. It didn't budge. She pulled harder and suddenly it came free and she was surrounded by a cloud of flies.

And with the flies came the sickly smell she'd detected when she'd first entered the barn. Except now, it was ten times worse . . .

TWENTY-ONE

The crime-scene tapes were already in place by the time Paget arrived. Tregalles, who had been summoned from the manor by an urgent call from Molly, met Paget as he got out of the car.

'No doubt about it,' he said in answer to the DCI's first question. 'It's Gwyneth Jones all right. Starkie's still with the body. He believes she's been dead for at least four or five days. It looks as if she was killed here in the barn, then dragged over to the side and covered with a sheet of corrugated iron. No sign of a weapon yet, but Starkie reckons she was hit several times by something flat and heavy like a metal bar.'

'And it was Forsythe who found her?' said Paget as they entered the barn.

Tregalles nodded. 'While she was picking up the tape measure,' he said. 'She rang me straightaway and I came over and called you.'

Paget nodded absently as he took in the scene.

Dr Reg Starkie was sitting on the floor, back braced against a piece of farm machinery, while he filled in a form on a clipboard propped against his raised knees. In front of him, just inches from his feet, lay the body of Gwyneth Jones. She lay on her side, her face partly hidden. Blood, dark and crusted, matted her hair, and there were more dark stains on her clothing.

'She was killed over there,' said Starkie, pointing, 'then dragged here. Cause of death, unless the post mortem proves otherwise, was by blunt force trauma, and if it's any consolation, she died quickly. I suspect the first blow killed her, and the rest of the blows were delivered as she lay on the floor. I imagine the killer simply wanted to make sure that she was dead before dragging her over here. As for the weapon,' he continued with a sweeping look around the barn, 'it was a flat metal bar three to four centimetres in width, and judging by the bits and pieces I see lying around here, the killer had plenty of choice.'

Paget continued to stare down at the body. 'Any bruising or signs of a struggle?' he asked.

Starkie shook his head. 'Nothing,' he said. 'I'd say she was taken completely by surprise.'

'The question is,' said Paget slowly, 'how did she get back up here?' It was a rhetorical question, and the others remained silent as he continued the line of thought. 'She was last seen near the bottom of the hill by WPC Short, who told her that Farnsworth was dead, and that must have shaken her up. But why would she come back up here?'

His eyes swept over the jumble of abandoned equipment stacked against the walls. 'And where is her bike?' he asked, turning to Tregalles. 'It may be a long shot, but it might tell us something. If the body was hidden here, why not the bike? And I want you to talk to WPC Short again,' he said as they moved away. 'Find out what Gwyneth was wearing when she saw her on Friday night, and let's see if it matches what she is wearing now.'

Molly lingered behind. She found it hard to tear her gaze away from Gwyneth's face. So young, so . . .

'Would you hand me my case, please, Molly? It is Molly, isn't it?'

It took her a moment for the words to sink in. The pathologist had never called her by her first name before, in fact she couldn't remember him calling her anything at all.

'Yes, that's right,' she said. She handed him the case. Starkie nodded his thanks, and Molly was about to turn away when he spoke again. 'I was wondering,' he said hesitantly, 'if you'd heard anything from David? We haven't, you see, and Ellen, my wife, was wondering this morning if he might have rung or emailed you. He's talked a lot about you these past few days. Mind you, considering he only left yesterday, and between the time difference and jet lag et cetera, I don't suppose he's had much chance to call anyone.'

Time difference? Jet lag? 'I'm sorry, Doctor,' Molly said, 'but I don't know what you're talking about. When I saw David the other night, he didn't say anything about going away. In fact, we'd arranged to go out tomorrow night. You say he left yesterday? And there's a time difference? Where did he go?'

The pathologist grimaced apologetically. 'Sorry,' he said brusquely, 'but since he had mentioned going out with you again this week, I thought he might have let you know. But then, everything was done in such a rush, so he probably didn't have time. He's gone to Hong Kong.'

'Hong Kong?' she repeated dazedly. She couldn't think of anything else to say. Why hadn't David said something? Had he been offered another job? Or called back to his old one? Molly suddenly felt cold. She'd only been out with David Chen a couple of times, but she'd felt a spark there, and she had been almost sure that he'd felt the same. Now she didn't know what to think.

Starkie scrambled to his feet and dusted himself off. 'Sorry,' he said again. 'I should have explained. I don't know how much of his past life David's told you, but it's Meilan, his ex-wife. She lives in Hong Kong. She was cycling to work the other morning when she was knocked down by a van. She's in hospital, and her condition is critical, in fact she's not expected to live. Which is why David left in such a hurry. And if that does prove to be the case, he may be away for some time while he sorts out what is going to happen to their daughter, Lijuan. She's going on fourteen, so it won't be an easy task.'

Molly drew a deep breath and said, 'I see.' But she didn't see at all. Ex-wife? Hong Kong? And a teenage daughter? None of this had come up in conversation, and Molly couldn't help wondering if David had ever intended to tell her about them.

'Is he . . .?' she began, only to be interrupted by Paget raising his voice to say, 'If you're finished over there, Forsythe, you're with me at the manor.'

'Right away, sir,' Molly called back. With an apologetic shrug toward Starkie, she turned to leave, but Starkie stayed her by putting a hand on her arm. 'You will let us know if you hear from him, won't you?' he asked anxiously. 'David has been more like a son than a nephew to us since his parents died, and we've always got on well with Meilan and Lijuan.'

'I will, of course,' Molly assured him, then almost ran across the floor to join Paget and Tregalles.

'You were deep in conversation over there,' Paget observed. 'Did you learn anything new?'

Anything new? Molly had the wild desire to laugh out loud,

but smothered the impulse with a cough before saying, 'No, sir, I'm afraid not.' To cover her confusion, she opened her handbag and handed him the metal tape.

Paget thanked her, but his mind was on other things as he looked around the barn. 'No point in wasting any more time here,' he said, 'so let's move on.' He led the way out of the barn and set off at a brisk pace down the track with Molly and Tregalles trailing along behind. 'What's happening?' Molly asked Tregalles with a nod toward Paget. 'I thought you and I were supposed to be at the manor.'

Tregalles made a face. 'Apparently Mr Brock thinks the Bromleys should be interviewed by someone of a higher rank than a mere detective sergeant, so I'm being sent off to break the news to Gwyneth's mother and talk to WPC Short, while you get to go to the manor with the boss.' He sounded bitter.

They caught up with Paget at the end of the track. 'Take a WPC with you when you go to see Mrs Jones,' he told Tregalles. 'And we'll need her to make a formal identification of the body as soon as possible, so make sure that's laid on for her.'

'Yes, *sir*,' Tregalles said as he ducked under the tape sealing off the crime scene. In other circumstances the words might have been delivered in a jocular manner, but the sergeant's body language said otherwise as he walked up Manor Lane to his car. But if Paget noticed it, he gave no indication.

Paget and Molly ducked under the tape as well, and were about to cross Manor Lane, when Molly noticed a man coming toward them. Head bent, he walked with the measured tread of a countryman. 'That's Thorsen,' Paget said quietly. 'He's the man who found the major and Toni Halliday the other night. He lives just down the lane.'

''Morning, Mr Thorsen,' he said as the man came up to them.

Thorsen acknowledged the greeting with a nod. His deep-set eyes were watchful beneath his shaggy brows. 'So what's all this, then?' he asked. 'Police cars coming and going like they was on the motorway. I thought there must have been an accident, so I came up to see what was going on.' He nodded toward the tape. 'Thought you'd finished up at the barn?'

'This is Detective Constable Forsythe,' Paget said, ignoring the implied question, 'and I'm afraid we have some bad news.

Gwyneth Jones is dead, and we will be trying to trace her movements after she was seen last Friday night near the bottom of
Manor Lane.'

Thorsen didn't actually recoil, but it was as if his whole frame
had become stiff and wooden. The light faded from his eyes.
'Like the other one?' he asked gruffly. 'In the barn?'

Paget nodded. 'I'm afraid so, yes.'

The old man swallowed hard and suddenly there were tears
in his eyes. 'She was a good girl, was Gwyneth,' he said. 'Always
cheerful, always had a word and waved when she went by on
her bike.' He took out a handkerchief and blew his nose, then
cleared his throat noisily and spat into the long grass at his feet.
'I hope the bugger swings for it,' he said with feeling.

'We don't hang people these days,' Paget reminded him.

'More's the pity!' Thorsen growled.

'You say Gwyneth always used to wave when she went by on
her bike,' Paget said. 'You weren't home when Sergeant Tregalles
called round the other day to ask if you had seen Gwyneth go
by last Friday night, but your neighbour, Mr Evans, said he saw
her, but she didn't wave. Were you home that night? Did you
see her go by?'

Thorsen lifted his cap and scratched his head. 'Let's see,' he
said slowly. 'Last Friday. No, I didn't. I took old Toby for a
walk. He misses his walk of a night now the major's gone.'

'What time would that have been?'

'About half seven, near enough. It was getting dark by the
time I got back, say about a quarter past to half past eight. She'd
have gone past by then.'

'Did you see anyone on your walk?'

The old man snorted. 'Just a couple of kids having it off in the
bushes at the top of the lane,' he said. 'Toby flushed them out.'

'Do you know who they are?'

'I didn't get much of a look at the girl, but the boy looked
sort of familiar.'

'Can you describe him? I need to talk to anyone who was
anywhere near here that night.'

'Tallish, sort of skinny, a bit scruffy. I'd know him again if I
saw him, but I don't know what else to tell you.'

'We have people who can help you with that,' said Paget, 'so

I would like you to go with one of our men to work with our
ID man. It shouldn't take long, and you'll be brought back home
when you're finished. Will you do that, Mr Thorsen? It could be
important.'

'I'll have to stop and see to Toby first,' Thorsen said, 'but if
you think it could help to find the bastard who killed young
Gwyneth, then, yes, I'll go.'

TWENTY-TWO

Mrs Lodge took the news of Gwyneth's death extremely
hard. White-faced, she sank into one of the high-backed
kitchen chairs. 'But why?' she kept whispering hoarsely.
'I don't understand. Why would anyone want to kill Gwyneth?'

But Paget wasn't prepared to share that information with the
housekeeper, and once he'd established that she couldn't help,
he was anxious to move on.

Charles Bromley was not at home. 'It's one of his consulting
days at the hospital,' Mrs Lodge explained. 'And Mrs Bromley
is out as well. The vicar rang and said he needed to talk to her
about the hymns and the order of service for the funeral for Miss
Toni on Friday, so Mrs Etherton took her in her van because Mrs
Bromley still hasn't got her car back since it was wrecked last
week. They're stopping for lunch in town, but they should be
back shortly after that.'

Julian, she said, had gone to Birmingham to audition for a
part in a play, but she expected him back in time for dinner. But
Paul was in.

'Do you happen to remember if Julian was here at the manor
last Friday evening?' Paget asked her.

The housekeeper dabbed at her eyes. 'He was here for dinner,'
she said, 'but he left before everyone else was finished. He said
he was meeting friends. I don't know what time he got back –
probably not till well on the next morning, knowing him. Didn't
get up till noon on Saturday, and left me with his bed to do in
the afternoon. Lazy young beggar. He's not a bit like his father.'

They found Paul Bromley in the conservatory. Judging by its heavy, ornate ironwork construction and thick panes of glass, the conservatory was probably as old as the house itself. Braided rugs on the flagstone floor, and colourful, overstuffed cushions on the heavy furniture struggled to make the room look cheerful, but it was a losing battle. The September sun, partially blocked by massive trees that should have been pruned back years ago, tried valiantly to penetrate the moss-stained glass, but the result was a cold and cheerless room.

Paul Bromley was standing at the far end of the room, head down, concentrating on what he was doing as his thumb moved swiftly back and forth across the keypad of his BlackBerry. He looked up, frowned his irritation at the intrusion, and continued texting.

'Mr Bromley . . .?' Paget said. Paul waved an impatient hand. 'What is it now?' he demanded irritably. 'Can't you see I'm busy?'

'I'm afraid this can't wait, sir, *if* you don't mind, sir. This is a murder investigation.'

'Of which I am well aware,' Paul said with exaggerated weariness, 'and I've already told you everything I can.'

'I'm talking about the murder of Gwyneth Jones,' Paget said, 'and I would like to know where you were when she was killed.'

'Gwyneth . . .?' Paul frowned. 'The maid? She's dead? Is that what all the fuss is about in the lane?'

With the image of Gwyneth Jones's battered head still very much in the forefront of his mind, Paget barely managed to keep his temper in check. 'If that's what you call the discovery of the body of a young woman who has been brutally beaten to death, then yes, that *is* what all the fuss is about, Mr Bromley, and I would appreciate it if you would put that BlackBerry away and give us your full attention!'

Paul gave the barest of apologetic shrugs. 'I didn't mean to be disrespectful,' he said, 'but I barely knew the girl, so I don't see what it has to do with me.'

'Then I'll try to make it clear,' Paget said icily. 'You have lied to us consistently, leaving yourself open to a charge of wilfully obstructing the course of justice, and unless you sit down and answer my questions now, I am quite prepared to arrest you and take you in for questioning. Do you understand me, sir?'

Paul eyed him warily, then spread his hands in a gesture of grudging submission and lowered himself gingerly onto the edge of a chair. 'I didn't say I *wouldn't* answer your questions,' he muttered defensively.

'Good,' Paget said, 'so let's begin with why you came back here last Friday evening, and I suggest you tell me the truth this time.'

Paul glanced at Molly, who had settled in a chair and taken out her notebook. 'I did tell you the truth,' he said truculently. 'I heard about Toni on the car radio, and I—'

'That doesn't explain why,' Paget broke in impatiently. 'You told us earlier that you hardly knew Toni Halliday, yet you came dashing down here when you say you heard the news of her death and I keep asking myself why you would do that, Mr Bromley.'

A frown of annoyance crossed Paul's face. 'I didn't *dash* back, as you put it. I simply thought I should come. I knew Margaret would be terribly upset.'

'I see. You also told us that you were on your way to see a client, a Mr Williams, in Oxford when you heard the news, but we've spoken to Mr Williams and that wasn't true, was it, sir? So I want to know exactly where you were and what you were doing last Friday, and believe me, sir, we will be checking your story very thoroughly.'

Paul shrugged. 'All right, so I lied about Williams,' he said airily, 'but I was in Oxford. Well . . . not actually *in* Oxford, since we're being so specific. I was staying at a small hotel just outside Oxford.'

'The name of the hotel, if you don't mind, sir?' Molly broke in, pencil poised above her notebook.

Paul shot her a venomous look. 'The Friedland,' he said tightly. 'It's owned by a German couple.' He turned to appeal to Paget. 'Really, Chief Inspector, is all this necessary? I mean it's a bit delicate and I don't see—'

'More obstruction, sir?' Paget asked quietly. 'As I said, we can do this here or in Charter Lane. It's your choice.'

Paul pushed himself back in his chair and clasped his hands together. 'Oh, what the hell!' he muttered truculently. 'I suppose you'll find out one way or another in the end, so I might as well tell you myself. At least that way you'll get it straight.'

'Assuming you don't try to lie to us again,' Paget warned.

Paul said he and a woman by the name of Marion Maynard, who just happened to be his employer's wife, had planned to spend a weekend together at the Friedland Hotel, while her husband was abroad on a business trip. But when Paul heard about Toni Halliday's death on the car radio, while on their way to Oxford late Friday afternoon, he said he'd left Mrs Maynard at the hotel and driven straight on to the manor.

'*Straight* to the manor, Mr Bromley?' Paget queried.

'That's right.'

'Then how do you account for the fact that you arrived at the manor around eleven o'clock, but say you drove straight here after hearing of Toni's death while on your way to Oxford in the late afternoon?'

Colour flooded into Paul's face. 'So we stopped off at the hotel for a bit before I came on here,' he said sullenly. Molly suppressed an urge to giggle at the Paul's unfortunate choice of words.

'What happened to her? Mrs Maynard?' Molly asked.

'Eh?' Paul looked puzzled.

'What happened to Mrs Maynard? You said you left her there.'

'Oh, I see what you mean. She stayed there overnight, then went back to London by train the next morning, because I was driving her car.'

Molly couldn't help herself. 'This Mrs Maynard must be a *very* understanding woman,' she said, then looked at Paget and shrugged an apology. 'Sorry, sir,' she said, 'but I find Mr Bromley's story somewhat bizarre, to say the least.'

'As do I,' Paget said drily. His voice hardened. 'Do you know what I think, Mr Bromley? I think your actions sound like those of a very frightened man. The actions of a man who has just found out that Gwyneth Jones was in the barn when Toni Halliday met her death, and she might be able to identify the killer. I think someone from this house rang to tell you that, and you came back to silence her before she could tell us what she saw.'

Paul moistened his lips and swallowed. 'Look,' he said earnestly, 'you can't *really* believe that I had anything to do with this girl's death, or Toni's either. I had no *reason* to kill Toni. I mean, why would I? And the same goes for the maid. I was telling you the truth when I said I fell asleep in the car around the time Toni was killed.' He slid forward to the very edge of his chair as he tried to make his point. 'Good God, man, don't you think I'd come up with a better alibi than that if I had killed her?'

Paget shrugged. 'I don't think you had a choice,' he said bluntly. 'You had to account for your absence while you were killing Toni Halliday, which, I suspect, was done on the spur of the moment, and that was the best you could do. Then, when it became necessary for you to kill Gwyneth, you—'

'Oh, for Christ's sake!' Paul burst out. 'I did *not* kill Toni. I could never have killed her, because she was my own flesh and blood. Toni wasn't Halliday's daughter. She was mine!'

After being warned not to leave the area without talking to them first, Paul had been allowed to go. Paget stood by the windows looking out. Low grey clouds had drifted in, obscuring the sun. Leaves rustled softly in a fitful wind.

'What do you think, Forsythe?' he asked quietly. 'Do you think he was telling the truth?'

'When it comes to Paul Bromley, it's hard to know what to believe,' Molly replied, 'but even he must realize by now that we'll check everything he tells us. I do think he was telling the truth when he said he was Toni's father. As for his assertion that he couldn't have killed her because she was his own flesh and blood, I think Paul Bromley would do whatever he thought necessary to protect his own skin.'

According to Paul, Margaret had gone out with Halliday several times before she and Paul got together. Halliday was ten years her senior, and she was flattered by the attentions of the famous man, and she was even more flattered when he asked her to marry him. But she loved Paul, so she turned Halliday down. But when Margaret announced that she was pregnant and suggested they get married, Paul admitted he got cold feet and turned her down.

'It just wasn't my thing,' he explained, 'so I was quite happy when she accepted Halliday's offer. She didn't tell Halliday, of course, but she was six weeks pregnant when she married him.

'She was lucky in a way,' he'd continued blithely, 'because Halliday was about to set off on another of his adventures, so they were married right away. Margaret went with him, but she became ill and had to come home. She went full term, and Toni was born on schedule, but Halliday, who was still away, was told she'd been born prematurely.'

'He never found out?' It was Molly who had put the question.

'Never,' Paul said firmly. 'Margaret went to a *very* private clinic. Private and discreet. I know, because I had money in those days and I arranged it. If he'd even suspected that Toni wasn't his own child, God knows what Halliday would have done. But Toni grew up believing he was the greatest man who ever lived. She idolized him and he doted on her, at least he did when he was home, which wasn't all that often. He'd arrive like a whirlwind; take Toni with him everywhere there was a photo op – Toni was very photogenic as a child, and he'd make a huge fuss of her when the cameras were rolling. Then he'd pop her back home and disappear into some remote part of the world again for months on end.'

When pressed to account for his time the night Toni Halliday was killed, Paul said when Charles refused to lend him the money he so desperately needed, he'd decided to ask Margaret for it. 'She's got pots of it,' he explained. 'Halliday left her very well off indeed.'

He went on to say he'd gone to Margaret's room around eight o'clock to ask her for the money, but all she'd wanted to talk about was Toni. 'Wouldn't listen to me; said she was more concerned about what might happen to Toni, and she didn't give a damn about what might happen to me. I'll admit I became angry and said a few things I shouldn't, but she completely lost her temper. She'd picked up a belt and lashed out at me. I ducked but not soon enough. The buckle caught the side of my head and it bled like hell.'

He said he'd been plagued with a headache all day, and it was getting worse, so he'd gone down to his car to get some Paracetamol tablets from the glove box. He'd taken a couple of tablets, then sat there pressing a wad of Kleenex to his face to stop the bleeding, while he'd tried to think what to do next. 'And I fell asleep,' he ended. 'It's as simple as that.'

'So tell me,' Paget had said, 'why, after virtually driving you out of her room, did Mrs Bromley suddenly go dashing out into the night to try to find you. What had you threatened to do?'

'I didn't intend to actually *do* it,' Paul told him, 'but I did tell Margaret that I would tell Toni she wasn't a Halliday at all, but my daughter, if she didn't come up with the money I needed. As I said, I wouldn't have actually *done* it. Later, when I got back into the house, I realized that I'd been pretty rough on her, so I went along to her room to apologize and tell her that I hadn't told Toni. And then I left. There was no point in staying around, so I decided to return to London then and there. It was a good time to travel; the roads were deserted, so I made it back in record time.'

It was getting on for two o'clock by the time they reached the Cobbler's Last, and the pub was almost deserted. They sat quietly in a corner by the window, each preoccupied with their own thoughts. Molly felt sure that Paget was still thinking about what he'd heard and seen that morning, and although she tried to do the same, her thoughts kept slipping back to her conversation with Starkie.

Would David have told her about his ex-wife and daughter, she wondered? And couldn't he have at least given her a quick phone call? Left a message on her voice mail? Starkie had said it had all been a bit of a rush, and she could understand that, but these days one had to be at airports so far ahead of flight time that there was always a lot of time to kill, so couldn't he have called then?

Or had she misread the signs? After all, they had only spent such a short time together it was silly to start thinking about a long-term relationship, but Molly had felt . . . well, comfortable with David Chen, and she'd hoped that David . . .

'Deep thoughts, Forsythe?' Molly looked up to see Paget regarding her intently. 'You've hardly touched your sandwich. Come to any conclusions?'

Startled, she could feel the sudden rush of colour to her face. 'Afraid not, sir,' she replied. She pushed her plate away. 'I'm just not as hungry as I thought.' She could feel his eyes on her, probing gently, but probing nevertheless.

'Right,' he said abruptly, and shoved his chair back. 'In that case, let's go and see what Sergeant Ormside has for us.'

'Good thing you sent Thorsen down,' Ormside said, 'because we'd no sooner started when he remembered who the boy was.

Name of Ridgeway. He lives on a farm over Sefton way, and
someone is on their way there now to talk to him. And I've just
taken a statement from a man who may have seen Gwyneth on
the night of the Halliday murder. If it was Gwyneth he saw, then
she was lying to you when she said she went home by way of
Manor Lane that night.'

'I did wonder,' Paget said. 'So who is this man and what did
he have to say?'

'His name is Alex Woolgard,' Ormside said. 'He lives across
the border in Newtown. He came in Thursday night to see his
dad, who's got a bit of a farm about a mile up the Clunbridge
Road. He says he'd just turned down the Hallows End road when
a girl dashed across the road in front of him. He said she was
running and pushing a bike.'

Ormside got up and went over to the large-scale map of the
area taped to the wall.

'See, there's this footpath that runs from behind the barn, past
the field where Vanessa King has her caravan, to come out here
on the Hallows End road.' He jabbed a stubby finger at a point on
the map where the path met the road. 'Woolgard says it was
about here when he saw her. He says it was raining hard and
she ran right in front of him. He managed to avoid hitting her,
but she scared the hell out of him. He stopped and got out to
see if she was all right, and to offer her a lift, but she wouldn't
take it. He drives a small truck and he told her he could put her
bike in the back, but she just kept backing away from him and
shaking her head. He said she looked scared to death. Wouldn't
even look at him properly, but he'd seen her face in the headlights when she first dashed out, and when I showed him
Gwyneth's picture, he said it was definitely the same girl. He
said she seemed to be all right, and he was getting soaked, so
he gave up trying to help her and went on his way. Never thought
any more about it until he was talking to his dad on the telephone
last night, and his dad said we'd been round asking
questions.'

'Did he say what time it was when he saw the girl?'

'He reckons it was somewhere between nine and nine thirty.
He says his dad watches the nine o'clock news, and the news
was well on by the time he got there.'

'Well, that certainly fits,' Paget said. 'There was never any doubt in my mind that Gwyneth was there inside the barn at the time of the murder, but whether she actually saw the killer, I don't know. Personally, I'm inclined to doubt it. But the very fact that she was there was enough to make her a threat to the killer, and once he found that out she was finished. The question is, how did the killer find out?'

TWENTY-THREE

E lizabeth Etherton's van was parked in the stable yard, and Paget pulled in beside it. He got out and put his hand on the snub-nosed bonnet. 'Still warm,' he said, 'so let's see if we can get to Mrs Bromley before she and Paul have a chance to talk to each other.'

'If we're to believe the things Paul told us this morning,' said Molly, 'I'd be surprised if he and Mrs Bromley are even on speaking terms by now.'

'*If* we believe what he told us,' Paget cautioned. 'I'm certainly not prepared to take anything that man says at face value until I've checked it up, down, and sideways.'

Mrs Lodge answered the door as usual, and took them along to the kitchen, where they found Mrs Bromley and Mrs Etherton sitting at the kitchen table drinking tea from stoneware mugs. It was a warm day, but Margaret Bromley had her hands wrapped around the mug as if drawing warmth from it. She looked tired and there were deep shadows under her eyes.

She looked up as Paget approached, eyes suddenly bright as they searched his face. 'Mrs Lodge says Gwyneth—' The word caught in her throat. 'Why . . .?' she finally managed after several tries.

'We believe she was in the barn the night your daughter was killed,' said Paget. 'Somehow the killer found out and . . .'

'*In* the barn?' Margaret Bromley stared at him. 'What was she doing there?' The words were sharp and brittle.

'I'm afraid I can't tell you that at the moment,' Paget said.

Her hands slowly tightened into fists. 'But if she saw who did it, why . . .?'

'I don't think she did actually *see*—' Paget began, but Margaret Bromley wasn't listening. 'She *knew!*' she burst out. 'She *saw* him! So why didn't she *do s*omething for Christ's sake? Why didn't she *tell* someone? That stupid, *stupid* girl!' She slumped back in her chair. 'And now she's dead!' She started to cry.

Mrs Etherton came round the table to put her hands on her friend's shoulders. She looked up at Paget and shook her head. 'This is *not* a good time,' she said quietly. 'I'll take her up to her room.'

'I know how hard this must be for everyone,' Paget replied, 'but I'm afraid there are still questions to be answered.'

'But not now,' Mrs Etherton said tightly. 'Margaret has not been well, as I'm sure you know, so—'

'No, Beth,' Margaret said. 'If the chief inspector has more questions, then let's get it over with before someone else is murdered. Though God knows what I can tell him.' She spoke as if Paget wasn't there. She pushed her chair back and stood up.

'I'm sorry,' she said contritely. 'I shouldn't have said that about Gwyneth. I didn't mean it. She was a good girl, and she must have been out of her mind with worry. But, as I've already told you, I know so little about the girl, so I don't know how I can help you.'

'We do have other questions relating to the death of your daughter as well,' Paget said gently, 'and I wouldn't be troubling you at this time if I didn't think it important.'

Margaret Bromley's eyes flicked to Mrs Lodge and back again. 'Then let's go along to Charles's study,' she said. 'He won't be back for a while.'

Paget turned to Mrs Etherton. 'I will need to talk to you as well,' he said. 'Will you be here?'

Mrs Etherton looked at the kitchen clock, and made a face. 'Sorry,' she said, 'but I'm afraid I have to leave in a few minutes. My van is loaded with stuff I've collected around the district, and I promised to get it to the shop this afternoon. In any case, I don't know how much help I can be regarding Gwyneth's death, poor girl. But . . .' She paused, frowning slightly as if trying to decide whether to go on or not.

'Was there something else?' he prompted hopefully.

'There is something I *would* like to talk to you about,' she said hesitantly. 'That is if you are still here when I get back. I shouldn't be gone long.' She looked at the time again, then scooped up her handbag from the table and started for the door. 'I'll be as quick as I can,' she called over her shoulder, and then she was gone.

'Don't know what that was all about,' Margaret Bromley muttered as she made her way out of the kitchen. She was unsteady on her feet, but she wasn't limping as much as she had been before. In fact, it seemed to Molly that she was having more trouble with her balance than with the swollen ankle. She moved up beside Mrs Bromley to offer her arm for support, but Margaret looked straight ahead and pretended not to see it. Even so, it was clear that she was more than happy to sit down when they reached the study.

Paget took the chair facing her, while Molly sat by the window.

Mrs Bromley closed her eyes for a moment, then opened them again and looked around the room almost as if it were the first time she'd been in it. Her eyes settled on Paget. 'I'm terribly sorry,' she said in a thin wisp of a voice, 'but I seem to have forgotten your name.'

Paget and Molly exchanged glances. 'It's Paget, Mrs Bromley,' he said. 'Detective Chief Inspector Paget. And this is Detective Constable Forsythe.'

'Oh, yes, of course. Chief Inspector Paget,' Margaret repeated as if mentally filing it away. 'I remember now; you wanted to ask me some questions about Toni?'

'About her father, actually,' Paget said quietly. 'Your brother-in-law, Paul Bromley tells us that he, not Bernard Halliday, is Toni's real father. Is that true, Mrs Bromley?'

The lines around Margaret Bromley's mouth hardened. 'Yes,' she said tightly, 'that is true, but I fail to see what business it is of yours or what it has to do with the death of my daughter.'

'It might help explain some of the things we've encountered during our investigation.'

'Such as?' she demanded. The words were sharp and brittle once again.

'For one thing, Paul's behaviour last Friday evening when he returned to the manor,' Paget said. 'I take it Toni didn't know that Paul Bromley was her father?'

'Certainly not!'

'Did anyone else know?'

'I never told anyone, and, as far as I know, neither did Paul – at least until now.'

'But he did threaten to tell Toni when he came to see you in your room last Thursday evening?'

'Yes.'

'What was your reaction to that?'

'I told him to get out.'

'He says you struck him with a belt.'

Margaret Bromley said nothing, but her look confirmed his words.

'Tell me what happened after that. Paul says he left your room and went down to his car, and you followed him, but not for something like another fifteen or twenty minutes. What happened during that time, Mrs Bromley? What changed? I need to know because I have the feeling it could be important.'

Margaret eyed him for a long moment. 'I blame myself,' she said abruptly. 'The truth is, I might have saved Toni if I'd acted sooner, but I just sat there in my room and did nothing!' She drew a deep breath, then slowly, quietly, she told them what had happened after Paul had left her room that night. She said she'd felt as if her whole world was collapsing around her. 'Toni's accident; Tracy Nash in hospital; Toni's announcement at dinner; saying she was pregnant, then Tracy's father bursting in, and Toni's refusal to talk to me – I was at my wit's end,' she said. 'And then, to top it all, as if none of that mattered, Paul came along babbling about needing money. He must have it right away, he said. Charles wouldn't give it to him. What was he going to do? My head felt as if it was about to explode!

'Then, when he threatened to tell Toni that Bernard wasn't her father if I didn't lend him the money, I lost my temper. I had the belt in my hand, and I lashed out at him. He was lucky it only caught him on the side of the head. Typical Paul, he hurled some obscenities at me and ran out of the room. It was too much,' she said wearily. 'I couldn't take it any more, so I just sat there, crying and feeling sorry for myself.'

She raised her eyes to meet those of Paget. 'When I finally did pull myself together, I realized that Paul was quite capable of carrying out his threat, even if it meant he would never see the money he so desperately needed. I've known Paul from the time we were children, and charming as he can be when he puts his mind to it, he's quite capable of doing something like that out of sheer spite.

'I couldn't take the chance, so I went after him. I couldn't allow him to do that to Toni. I decided I had to find him, pay him the money and be rid of him. Toni had to believe she was Bernard Halliday's daughter. She adored Bernard. It was the one thing in life she had to hold on to. He meant everything to her. I had to find Paul and stop him at any cost.'

'And did you find him?' Paget asked.

'No, I did not,' she said sharply. 'I told you before what happened. I was part way down the lane when it started to rain and I turned my ankle, so I had to come back.'

'With the help of Dr Lockwood?' Paget said quietly. 'Something you forgot to mention last time we spoke to you. Was there a reason why you didn't tell us?'

Colour rose in Margaret's face, startling in its contrast to her previously colourless skin. 'I didn't consider it any of your business,' she said tartly. 'Dr Lockwood happened to be on his way back from the village when he saw me limping up the lane, so he stopped and gave me a lift. It was kind of him and I was grateful for his help.'

'Dropping you by the entrance leading to the stables,' Paget said, 'rather than taking you to the side gate and much closer to the house. Why was that, Mrs Bromley?'

Her lips tightened into a thin line as if to stop herself from saying something she might regret. 'Because,' she said with deliberate calm, 'I did not want to be seen getting out of Steven's car. And before you ask, no, Steven and I are *not* having an affair or anything close to it. He is a good doctor and a good friend, and that's *all*! I know there have been whispers by some in this house about our relationship, but they are not true.'

'Tell me, Mrs Bromley, what time was it when you next saw Paul?'

'I don't know, exactly,' she said slowly. 'Nine thirty, ten o'clock, perhaps? He came to my room – to apologize, he said, and to ask for the money again, of course. I was so relieved that he hadn't told Toni that I wrote him a cheque and gave it to him on the condition that he leave immediately. I wanted him out of the house and as far away from Toni as possible.'

She took another deep breath to steady her voice. 'You see, I didn't know then that Toni was dead.'

Paget gave her a moment to recover, and to give himself time to think about what she had just told him. Paul had said nothing about her giving him the money. He'd let them continue to think he had found it in London, although, as Tregalles had pointed out at the time, they'd found that hard to believe as well. The man lied even when there seemed to be no need.

'I'd like to ask you now about Friday evening,' he said. 'Do you recall what you were doing, say from seven or seven thirty on, Mrs Bromley?'

She frowned in concentration. 'Friday evening,' she repeated slowly. 'Oh, yes. I had a headache. I'm afraid the stress of the day had been too much for me, and my ankle was playing me up as well, so I didn't go down to dinner. Charles came up with a tray – I have no idea what time that was – but I couldn't eat anything, so he gave me a tablet and stayed with me until I went to sleep.'

'And you didn't leave your room again that night?'

'No. But why are you asking about Friday?'

'Because,' said Paget, 'we believe Gwyneth was killed shortly after she left here that evening.'

'And you think it was . . .?' she began, then stopped. 'I'm tired,' she said abruptly, 'and I would like to go to my room and rest. So if you will excuse me, Chief Inspector . . .?' She didn't wait for an answer, but got to her feet and left the room.

'DS Tregalles told me she was acting strangely,' Molly said quietly, having made sure the door was closed. '"There one minute, and off with the fairies the next", was the way he put it.'

Paget smiled. 'Sounds like Tregalles,' he said, 'but that pretty well sums up her behaviour. I've never seen anything quite like it. Did you notice the way she walked in compared to the way she walked out?'

'I didn't think she would make it on her own coming in,' said Molly, 'and then not remembering your name? It doesn't make sense. Do you think she's putting it on, sir?'

'If so, to what end, Forsythe? That's what I keep asking myself. Of course, she may—'

Whatever he was about to say was cut short by a peremptory knock on the study door before it opened and Mrs Lodge stuck her head inside. 'Excuse me, Chief Inspector,' she said, 'but I think there is something you ought to see.' She opened the door wider and they saw Thorsen standing in the hall behind her. He was holding something up with both hands.

'It's Thorsen, sir. He found it in the garden under some rubbish. You were asking about a mac. He's found one along with a hat.'

The mackintosh was so creased and rumpled it was barely recognizable as a coat at all. Mud and bits of yellowed leaves still clung to it, and it smelled of rotting vegetation.

'It was all wrapped up with the hat inside,' Thorsen explained. 'It's still a bit damp, like.'

The mac was more than a bit damp. It was soaking wet, and the hat was in a sorry state, a shapeless lump, still sodden from the rain of almost a week ago. Wrapped tightly inside the mac, it had had no chance to dry.

Thorsen said he'd found them under a pile of garden refuse piled against the kitchen garden wall. 'Tom Houghton and his boy are coming on Friday to do the wall,' he explained. 'The wet's got in under the foundation, and part of it came down in the storm the other week, so Mr Bromley asked Tom to come and see to it. I reckoned Tom wouldn't be too pleased if he had to shift that pile of rubbish when he got here, so that's what I was doing.'

'I saw him waving it about on the end of his fork from the kitchen window,' Mrs Lodge broke in, 'so I went out to see what it was he'd found. You and the sergeant were asking about a mac, so when I saw what it was, I told him to bring it in and show it to you. It's a good job I did, or he'd've chucked it.' The house-keeper stood back and folded her arms.

Thorsen glared at her.

Paget examined the coat. The inside of the coat was rela-tively dry, but most interesting of all were the streaks of green paint on the lining. He checked the pockets and found them empty.

Paget pushed and pulled the hat into some semblance of its original shape and looked inside. The maker's name had all but worn away, but there were initials imprinted in the leather sweat-band. He pulled it out and turned it toward the light.

'PGB,' he read aloud.

'Paul Grafton Bromley,' said Mrs Lodge. 'Grafton was his mother's name.'

Paget continued to examine the hat. 'Do you have any idea when this might have been put there?' he asked Thorsen.

The old man scratched his head. 'Hard to say,' he said slowly. 'It was sort of stuffed underneath, down near the bottom, but it could've been any time.'

'What would normally happen to the pile if you hadn't had to move it?'

'It'd be burnt come November,' Thorsen told him.

'Good job you were looking at it now, then,' Paget said grate-fully. 'But please don't do any more out there until I can arrange to have someone go through it to see if there is anything else to be found.' He turned to Mrs Lodge. 'Is Paul Bromley still in the house?'

The corners of the housekeeper's mouth turned down. 'I think you might find him using Mr Charles's computer in the library,' she said stiffly.

'You don't approve, Mrs Lodge?'

'That's not for me to say, now is it, Chief Inspector?' the housekeeper replied primly. 'It's just that I know Mr Charles doesn't like him using it when he's not here. I did mention it, but I might as well have saved my breath.' She turned to leave.

'Just one thing before you go, Mrs Lodge,' he said. 'Do you think you could find me a clean bin bag for this hat and coat? I'm afraid the bags I have with me aren't quite big enough.'

Paul Bromley looked up guiltily when Paget opened the library door without knocking, and walked straight in. 'Oh, it's you,' he said. 'I thought it might be Charles back early.' His fingers slid across the keyboard and the screen went blank. 'So what do you want this time? And what's that in the bag? Your laundry?'

'Something belonging to you, I believe,' said Paget. He opened the bag and took out the hat and coat.

'Looks like my hat,' Paul agreed, 'and I suppose it *could* be my coat. Where'd you find them?'

'Under the pile of rubbish in the kitchen garden where you hid them,' Paget told him.

Paul shook his head. 'I didn't hide them anywhere,' he said as he examined the coat more closely. 'I thought I'd lost them. I've been looking everywhere for them.'

'Since when, exactly?'

'Since last Thursday night. I know I had them when I came down here that day, because I had to put them on to come from the car to the house when I arrived. It was a scorching hot day, but just as I arrived this squall came out of nowhere. Charles will tell you.' Paul went on to say he remembered hanging both hat and coat on a peg in the passageway, not realizing at the time that the paint was still wet.

'I wasn't thinking about paint,' he said, visibly annoyed by Paget's open scepticism. 'I had too many other things on my mind.'

He said he couldn't remember seeing his hat and coat after that. He hadn't put them on when he left the house after his argument with his sister-in-law, because it wasn't raining then. Which, he said, was why he'd remained in the car waiting for the rain to ease before returning to the house.

'So they were still there, hanging on the peg when you left the house around eight o'clock that night?' Paget said.

Paul shrugged. 'I suppose so. I can't say I noticed, but I know I didn't take them.'

'What about later when you left for London? Was it still raining then?'

'Not as heavy, but yes it was, and I could have used them. But they weren't there. It was annoying; I couldn't think what I'd done with them, but I was in a hurry, so I carried on without them. The coat wasn't much of a loss, but the hat was expensive. Now, of course, I can see what happened. Someone took them off the peg and used them. Probably the person who killed Toni.'

TWENTY-FOUR

Paget looked at his watch. 'I don't know if there's much point in waiting around for Mrs Etherton,' he said. 'I have things that need attention back at the office, and I would like those shorthand notes of yours transcribed as soon as possible, so they will be ready for tomorrow morning's briefing.'

Molly sneaked a look at her own watch and sighed inwardly as she pictured herself sitting at the computer well after everyone else had gone home.

Pausing only briefly to take a look at the pile of rubbish in the garden, Paget and Molly made their way back to the car just as Charles Bromley drove in and parked beside them.

'Chief Inspector,' he said tersely as he got out of the car. 'So now it's young Gwyneth, is it? Terrible! Poor girl, and all because she was in the wrong place at the wrong time, I'm told.' He shook his head sadly.

'Told by whom, sir?' asked Paget.

'Your chief constable, Bob Wyckham,' said Charles. 'I happened to be talking to him about another matter, and he told me. Why?' he asked sharply when he saw the look on Paget's face. 'Is there any reason why he shouldn't tell me? I have a right to know what's going on when people are getting killed, quite literally on my doorstep. And while we are on the subject, I might as well tell you that I am not altogether happy about the slow pace of the investigation. As I told Wyckham, it seems to me that you are spending far too much time here at the manor, when you have a prime suspect in a friend of Toni's; some casino owner from London, who came out here to pick her up the night she was killed.'

'You did have quite a chat with Sir Robert, didn't you, sir?' Paget said, his voice ominously low. 'Did he also happen to mention that we might have spent far less time out here if some of the members of your household hadn't chosen to waste our time by lying to us? And when challenged, they tried to cover up with more lies? Even Gwyneth would have been alive today if she'd told us the truth. Now, of course, we need to trace her movements from when she left the manor last Friday evening, to when and how she got back here to the barn where she was killed. So, would you mind telling me where you were and what you did that evening, Mr Bromley? As a magistrate, even as a friend of the chief constable, I'm sure you will recognize the need for us to eliminate you as a suspect from our enquiries.'

Charles's eyes were cold as he looked at Paget. He might recognize the truth of what Paget was saying, but it was clear he did not like the chief inspector's tone.

In clipped words, he confirmed what his wife had said about taking a tray up to her room. He said she was completely exhausted, had a terrible headache, so he had given her something to help settle her nerves, and remained with her until about seven thirty when she went to sleep. He went on to say that he had spent the rest of the evening in his study. No, he hadn't seen or spoken to anyone, except Mrs Lodge.

'What time would that be?' Paget asked.

'It must have been shortly after eight. She mentioned that Gwyneth had just gone, and said she was off to her room for an early night. She'd been up half the night before, if you recall.'

'So you didn't go out at all that evening?'

Charles began to shake his head, then paused. 'Yes, as a matter of fact I did,' he said. 'I think it must have been about nine when I heard the side gate banging. The wind was getting up a bit, and I could hear the thing banging away, so I went out and shut it.'

'Do you have any idea how it came to be open, sir? Did you see anyone out there?'

'No. But then, it doesn't always close properly, especially after a rain. It probably didn't latch when Gwyneth left for the night.'

Or someone could have been returning to the manor after killing Gwyneth. Perhaps, in their haste to get back inside undetected, they had failed to make sure the gate was securely latched. But the question still remained: how did Gwyneth get back to the barn from where she was last seen at the bottom end of Manor Lane? And what would draw her back there? Was there something in the barn she needed to retrieve? Something she'd hidden, perhaps?

Paget dismissed that idea. Gwyneth had been on her way home when she met Valerie Short and learned that the major was dead. Which meant that she was on her own, and it would only be a matter of time before the police would match her fingerprints to those in the barn. But returning to the barn would probably be the very last thing she would want to do.

Paget took Paul's hat and coat from the bag and shook them out for Bromley to see. 'Have you ever seen these before?' he asked.

Charles looked down his nose at the rumpled hat and coat as he might have looked upon a dead fish. 'That looks like Paul's hat,' he said. 'What happened to it? It looks as if the dog's been at it.'

Paget explained how Thorsen had come to find it.

'So what has it to do with the murders?'

'I'm hoping that Forensic will be able to tell me that,' Paget said. 'When was the last time you saw them?'

'Paul was wearing a mac and that hat when he arrived last Thursday afternoon,' Charles said. 'It was raining and the wind was blowing hard, and I remember thinking he was going to lose the hat in the wind.'

'What about later? Did you see the hat and coat hanging up in the back passageway?'

Charles shook his head. 'There was nothing hanging there that day as I recall. Everything had been moved into the wash-house because of the painters.'

'Apparently, your brother didn't realize the paint might still be wet, so he hung his coat on a peg when he came in. As you can see, some of the paint stuck to it.'

Charles eyed the coat but remained silent.

'You told me that you saw your brother come in sometime after nine that evening,' Paget went on. 'Do you recall whether he was wearing the hat and coat then?'

'He wasn't wearing the hat,' Charles said promptly. 'I remember his hair was plastered down with the rain. As for the mac . . . no, I'm sure he wasn't.'

The quiet of the afternoon was broken by the sound of an

approaching vehicle, and a moment later Mrs Etherton's white Ford Transit swung into the stable yard and stopped.

'Oh, good, you're still here,' she said to Paget as she got out. 'I came back as fast as I could.' She squinted curiously at the hat and coat in Paget's hands. 'What have you got there?' she asked. 'Looks a bit the worse for wear.'

Once again, Paget explained. Mrs Etherton grimaced. 'I doubt if he'll want them back in that condition,' she observed, referring to Paul.

She spread her arms wide and wrinkled her nose as she looked down at herself. 'God, but it was hot and humid down there in the valley,' she said. 'I was sweating like a pig by the time I'd finished heaving stuff out of the van and carrying it into the shop.' She turned to Paget. 'I hope you don't mind if I clean up a bit before I talk to you,' she said. 'I swear it will only take me ten minutes, so come with me up to my room, and you can have a cup of tea while I take a quick shower, and then we can talk. All right, Chief Inspector?'

Elizabeth Etherton didn't wait for a reply, but set off toward the house, then paused. 'Oh, yes,' she said, 'I almost forgot, Charles. I ran into Bruce Hayden in town. He said he's been trying to reach you. Left several messages. He'd like you to give him a call as soon as possible.' She turned on her heel and strode off.

Bruce Hayden . . . The name was familiar to Paget. It was the name of his bank manager.

Elizabeth Etherton's room was quite large. Situated on the northeast corner of the first floor, the windows at the front of the house looked out over the heath between the road and the river valley a quarter of a mile away. The windows on the east side overlooked the narrow driveway beside the house, and Manor Lane. More like a suite than a bedroom, it had a separate sitting area with comfortable chairs grouped around a small table, a small dressing room, en suite, and an alcove containing a sink, a cupboard, and small table.

'My sister, Helen, bless her, felt I should have something more than a bedroom of my own when it was decided that I would be staying here permanently,' she explained as she ushered them inside. 'She had the wall taken out between this room and what used to be another bedroom next door, and had the whole thing remodelled. Would you like some tea? I can put the kettle on.'

'Thank you, but no,' Paget said quickly. Time was ticking away, and he couldn't rid himself of the image of the pile of work awaiting him back at the office.

'It's stuffy in here,' Mrs Etherton said as she headed for a doorway in the far corner of the room. 'You can open the windows if you like; let some fresh air into the room and enjoy the view. I won't be long.'

The windows were, in fact, double French doors made to look like the original windows from the outside. Molly pulled them open. There was no balcony, but there was a low sill and a waist-high wrought iron railing across the lower half of the opening to prevent anyone from falling out.

Paget crossed the room to join her and watch the people and their dogs out on the heath, no doubt enjoying what could be the last few days of the summer.

'Peaceful, isn't it?' Molly said. She leaned over the railing to look down, then stepped back. 'We're quite a bit higher than I thought,' she said, 'and I'm not sure I would trust that railing very much either.'

'Do heights bother you?' Paget asked.

Molly shook her head. 'Not really, but on the other hand you won't find hang gliding or rock climbing among my hobbies either.'

'Sorry to keep you waiting.' Mrs Etherton re-entered the room, wearing a flowered housecoat and a towel wrapped turban fashion around her head. 'And do sit down.' She waved them to a seat and sat down herself.

'Now,' she said firmly, 'I know you are here to look into the death of poor Gwyneth, and I wish I could help, but I can't. I have been racking my brains all afternoon, but I can't think of anything she said or did that might be of any value to you. But there is something that's been bothering me. It will probably sound silly to you, Chief Inspector. In fact I had almost made up my mind not to say anything, but when you mentioned earlier that Gwyneth might still be alive if she had talked to you, I decided it would be better to speak out and be thought a fool, rather than have something dreadful happen because I'd remained silent.

'It concerns what happened to my sister, Helen, seven years ago. I don't suppose you know this, Chief Inspector, but she died in a fire in the stables. There was a paraffin lamp – the lights in the stables weren't working properly; the wiring was old, they said at the inquest, and the fuses kept blowing, so she was using the lamp. No one knows what happened. It was assumed that either Helen or her horse, Broker, knocked the lamp over and the whole place went up in flames. Helen was trapped. Her death was ruled an accident, mainly, I suppose, because there was no reason to believe otherwise.'

'Are you suggesting that it might *not* have been an accident?' asked Paget.

'Well . . . it was only later that I began to wonder, and even then it was little more than a feeling that something wasn't right. I finally told myself that I was just looking for someone to blame, and I pushed it out of my mind. In fact I'd all but forgotten about it until the other night when Toni was killed, and I suddenly found myself thinking about it again. And now Gwyneth is dead . . .' She stopped. 'I'm sorry,' she said with a shake of the head, 'but I'm beginning to feel a bit foolish for what is probably a waste of your time.'

'No need to be,' Paget told her. 'But now that you have started, perhaps you should let me be the judge of that, so please go on.'

Molly sighed softly as she flipped to a new page.

Except for Lenny Braithwaite, the one-man evening shift, who had his feet up on the desk while he struggled with the Guardian's cryptic crossword, Molly was alone in the church hall in Hallows End. Notebook propped up beside the computer, Molly's fingers had been flying over the keys. She'd finished transcribing the shorthand notes taken earlier in the day, condensing them in the way she knew Paget preferred. But now, pausing to look over the pages of notes she'd taken in Mrs Etherton's room, she couldn't help wondering how much of it was really worth transcribing. Much of what the older woman had had to say was interesting, even informative as background information, but whether it was relevant to the investigation was open to question in Molly's mind. On the other hand, Paget had taken the time to hear Mrs Etherton out, and he'd been quietly thoughtful on the drive back from the manor.

Molly looked at the clock and sighed. DCI Paget had a very good memory, so, condense where possible, but make sure she didn't leave anything out.

Mrs Etherton had begun by explaining the situation leading up to Helen's death. She said Helen was fond of friends and a social life, and had found it difficult to adjust to the comparative isolation of Bromley Manor. She loved Charles, and so she had tried, but with Charles away in London from Sunday evening until Friday afternoon almost every week, it left her alone a lot of the time. And when he was home on the weekends he spent much of the time dealing with things to do with the manor and the estate.

Molly recalled how Mrs Etherton had looked at each of them intently to make sure she had their attention as she said, 'I know Helen would have preferred to live in London, but a place like this needs to be occupied, because there is always *so* much to be done.' Her voice softened. 'Charles loves this place,' she said. 'It's the only home he's ever known, and he's worked very hard to maintain it throughout the years.'

Molly paused to scan the notes ahead. Mrs Etherton had launched into an account of the history of the manor and the estate in general, from the time it was acquired by James Bromley in 1785 to the present day, describing in some detail the fortunes and misfortunes of the manor.

She said that Charles's grandmother, Ellen Schofield as she was then, was just a girl when she first visited Bromley Manor with her parents in the early twenties, and she'd fallen in love with the place. In fact, she said, Charles had once joked that he'd often wondered which had been the greater attraction when his grandfather, Robert Bromley, proposed to Ellen in 1933: being married to Robert or living at the manor?

Molly flipped another page to where Mrs Etherton had gone on to describe the state of the manor after years of neglect in the thirties, followed by its occupation by military personnel during the war. Paget had done his best to get Mrs Etherton to come to the point, but, once started, she was determined to make sure he had the full picture. There was more, but Molly moved on to where Mrs Etherton had finally returned to the events leading up to the death of her sister.

'Julian was away at Cambridge, and Helen was bored stiff,' she said. 'She was looking for something, almost anything to break what she had come to see as the sheer monotony of her life here. I'm sure she never intended to let things get out of hand, but Helen had always been somewhat naïve, and she was certainly far too trusting, especially when it came to Paul. You see, Paul used to spend quite a lot of time down here. Usually it was when he'd run out of money, which was quite frequently. He would come down here, sponge off Charles and Helen for a month or two, then disappear again. He was forever in debt. Gambling has always been his downfall, as it is this time, I'm sure. I certainly don't believe the cock-and-bull story he fed Charles. But then, Paul always did have a flair for making up stories. But, he was Charles's younger brother, and I know Charles used to give Paul money from time to time. Not that he ever mentioned it, of course; that would have been bad form, and Charles has always been a stickler for form. For his part, Paul resented Charles's success, but he was quite willing to profit by it.

'I suppose,' she continued, 'given the circumstances, it was inevitable that Paul should take advantage of the situation. Helen was bored and Paul was attentive, but I don't think the idea of an actual affair ever entered her head. She just wanted someone, *anyone,* to take an interest in her, and Paul happened to be there.'

A wry smile had touched the corners of Mrs Etherton's mouth. 'I was there for her, of course,' she said, 'and we did a number of things together, but it was hardly the same as the attentions of an attentive male. And Paul could be very charming when he wanted something. And believe me, he did want something.

'I tried to warn Helen, but she wouldn't listen. She thought I was much too hard on Paul. She didn't see him for what he was, a schemer with his eye on the main chance. He was after her money, plain and simple, and if, in the process, he could take her away from Charles, so much the better. He and Charles have always been at odds, even as children.

'But Paul was impatient – perhaps his debts were mounting up again; I don't know – and he started pressing Helen for money. I think she gave him some, but he came back for more, and when she balked he threatened to tell Charles that they'd been sleeping together.

'It wasn't true, of course, but Helen came to me in a panic. She said she was sure that Paul would make good his threat if she didn't do as she asked. I told her the only thing she could do was to spike Paul's guns by telling Charles what she had told me. He knew what Paul was like, and if she told him the truth, I felt sure he would believe her. This was on the Thursday, and Charles was coming home for the weekend on the Friday. I suggested that she meet him at the train as one of us usually did, and take him somewhere quiet where they could talk. I didn't say it, of course, but I rather hoped it would make Charles finally realize just how much he'd been neglecting her.'

Pausing, Molly recalled the sadness in Mrs Etherton's eyes as she said, 'But he never had the chance, because Helen died in the fire the following morning.'

Paget had given her a few moments before he'd said, 'I know this must be painful for you, Mrs Etherton, but tell me about the fire.'

'There isn't much to tell,' she said. 'Mrs Lodge was the first one to see the smoke – her room is at the back, you know – and she came along to my room to wake me. I told her to ring for the fire brigade, and she said she'd done that, so I dressed as quickly as I could and ran downstairs. As soon as I stepped outside, I could see the smoke pouring out and drifting across the fields. I ran toward the stables, but the fire literally exploded through the roof just as I got there. It was an inferno. The heat was so intense I couldn't stay there. I knew Helen had probably gone for an early morning ride, and I hoped and prayed that she'd left before the fire started. I knew nothing could survive in there. I ran back to the house and met Mrs Lodge at the back door. She said the fire brigade was on its way.

'It was too late, of course. The Clunbridge men got here first, but the fire was out of control by then. A fire engine came from Broadminster later, but all they could do was to try to stop it from spreading. More than half the stables were destroyed.'

Mrs Etherton took a deep breath. 'They found what was left of Helen and Broker later that day,' she said almost inaudibly.

'You say Mrs Lodge came along to your room to wake you when she saw the fire,' Paget said. 'Did she also wake Paul Bromley? I assume he was still in the house?'

'No. Paul was out riding himself. In fact, he came riding up just as the fire brigade got there. He said he'd seen the smoke from some distance away and he'd come back immediately. I asked him if Helen was with him, and he said no, he hadn't seen her.' Mrs Etherton shuddered. 'That's when I realized she might still be inside.'

'Are you suggesting that Paul had something to do with setting that fire, Mrs Etherton?' Paget asked.

Elizabeth Etherton had met his gaze head on. 'All I'm saying is that I did wonder why Paul had gone out alone that morning,' she said. 'He wasn't all that fond of riding to begin with. He only went because Helen did, so I couldn't see him riding off alone ahead of her that early in the morning. He claimed that he'd gone before she arrived, but it would have still been dark, and even Helen wouldn't have left in the dark. It would be far too dangerous. And it would have been just like Helen to tell Paul that she intended to tell Charles about his threat when he got home, so Paul would know that he could forget about asking Charles for money ever again.'

'Do you have any evidence to support your theory, Mrs Etherton?' Paget had asked.

'Not a scrap, Chief Inspector,' she said, 'and I know I could be wrong, but as I told you, I felt compelled to speak, because I don't want anything to happen to Margaret.'

Paget had looked perplexed. 'I'm afraid I still don't understand the connection,' he said. 'Why does what happened to your sister seven years ago have anything to do with the present Mrs Bromley?'

Mrs Etherton had hesitated at that point, Molly recalled. 'It's just that . . . I heard them talking – Paul and Margaret – in the dining room the other morning. I didn't mean to eavesdrop, but I was about to go into the dining room when I heard them talking on the other side of the door. They were speaking very low, so I stopped, not wanting to interrupt, and that's when I heard

Margaret accuse Paul of killing Toni. He denied it, of course, but I don't think she believed him. Yet she hasn't said anything, and that struck me as strange. It's as if she's protecting him, and I don't understand why, unless he is threatening her with something as he did with Helen.'

'You mean blackmail,' Paget said bluntly.

Mrs Etherton took a deep breath. 'Yes,' she said, 'and I think it is because Margaret is a lot like Helen in many ways, and I'm so afraid that if she gets mixed up with Paul she'll regret it. If Paul did have anything to do with Toni's death, and Margaret knows it, she could be in grave danger.'

Mrs Etherton sat back in her chair and sighed heavily. 'You probably think me very foolish,' she said, 'or worse, a meddler. But I'd rather be thought a meddler, and be proved wrong, than remain silent and be proved right.'

'Have you ever mentioned your suspicions about your sister's death to Charles Bromley, Mrs Etherton?' Paget asked.

'No. I had no proof to offer Charles, and it would have meant telling him the whole story for it to be believable at all. That would have tarnished Helen's memory, so I said nothing.'

'You say he was in London when it happened? The fire, I mean.'

'Yes. As I said, it happened on the Friday morning. Charles used to catch the nine twenty-five out of Paddington each Friday morning, and he got into Broadminster at twelve twenty. Helen and I took it in turns to pick him up at the station each week. Then, on Sunday night, one of us would drive him back to Broadminster to catch the seven twenty. He liked to get back on Sunday night to be ready for what he called his "Monday morning ops".

'But that day, of course, only Paul and I were here, apart from Mrs Lodge and one of the girls who were here before Gwyneth. The police sent someone down to meet Charles off the train in Broadminster. I was prepared to go myself, but the police wouldn't allow it.'

Molly closed her notebook. What Mrs Etherton had told them confirmed some of her own thoughts about Paul, but what Mrs Etherton did not know – at least Molly assumed she didn't know – was that Margaret Bromley knew Paul very well indeed. She would be the last person to be taken in by him unless, as Mrs Etherton had hinted, he was blackmailing her.

The light was fading by the time Molly got home. She set her handbag down on the hall table and wandered into the kitchen. She hadn't eaten since lunchtime, and not very much then, but she didn't feel like preparing a meal. She opened the fridge and stood there, one arm draped over the door as she looked inside.

Meat loaf. Three slices left over from supper on Monday. It had been quite good then but didn't look very appetizing now. She should have put it in the freezer, because if she didn't eat it now it would have to go into the bin. Frowning, she took out a plastic bowl, lifted the lid and wished she hadn't. She snapped the lid back in place. Cauliflower and broccoli soup from . . . was it last week or the week before? She couldn't remember.

A half bowl of custard didn't look too bad, but she would have to make something to go with it, and it didn't appeal anyway. There was all the usual stuff, eggs, butter, cheese and so on . . .

Molly closed the door, and it was only then that she noticed the light blinking on her answering machine. She turned it on and heard David's voice. 'Hi, Molly,' he said, sounding as though he were talking from the bottom of a barrel, with others talking in the background, 'Sorry about our date, but everything happened so fast I didn't have time to call you before I left. And things have been a bit hectic here ever since I arrived. I've only got a minute before I head back to the hospital, so can't stop to explain, but I've asked Reg to fill you in, so please give him a call and he'll give you a full report. Hope to see you soon. 'Bye, Molly.'

Molly pushed the button and listened to the message twice more before shutting it off. Suddenly she was hungry. She picked up the phone and punched in a number. Something with a bit of bite to it. Something to go with that half bottle of Portuguese wine.

'Hello. Pizza Express . . .?'

They'd avoided talking about the case during dinner, but now, as she started rinsing off the plates and Paget was stacking them in the dishwasher, Grace broke the silence. 'Did Charlie tell you

we've searched through everything in the barn, as well as everything in the immediate vicinity, but there's no sign of Gwyneth's
bike?'

Paget nodded. 'He did. And no murder weapon, either.'

'I'm afraid not,' Grace said, 'and believe me, we looked very
hard and we will go on looking tomorrow and the next day if
necessary.'

There was something particularly sad about the death of
Gwyneth Jones, and Paget had found it hard to rid himself of
the image of the young woman sitting in front of him a few short
days ago, so young, so naïve, and so afraid that her guilty secret
would be discovered. Would she still be alive if he had pressed
her harder? He'd sensed that she was holding something back,
but he'd thought there would be time to talk to her again.

How wrong he'd been. Grace had said he'd done what he'd
thought was best at the time, and he shouldn't blame himself,
but that was easier said than done. He changed the subject.

'You've met Mrs Etherton, haven't you?' he said. 'What did
you think of her, Grace?'

'I have, but only briefly when I spoke to her about her car
that first day. She struck me as a very down-to-earth sort of
person, but I really can't say beyond that.'

'But not a fanciful person?'

Grace shrugged. 'I shouldn't think so,' she said cautiously,
'but as I said, my only contact with her was very brief. Why do
you ask?'

'She seems to be convinced that there is some sort of connection between what happened to her sister, the first Mrs Bromley,
seven years ago, with what's been happening recently, and she
sees Paul Bromley as the link between the two.'

'What did happen to her sister?'

'She died in a fire in the stables. It was ruled an accident at
the inquest, and Mrs Etherton said she never questioned it at the
time, but she began to have doubts about the verdict some time
after. Her story is that Paul was trying to get money out of Helen
by threatening to tell Charles that they were having an affair.
Mrs Etherton claims that Helen was going to tell Charles about
his brother's scheme, but she died in the fire before she had a
chance to talk to him.'

'Convenient if nothing else,' Grace observed. 'What evidence does she have?'

'Absolutely none, but it's clear she doesn't like Paul. Not that I blame her for that; I don't like him either, but she only had her sister's word for it that she *wasn't* having an affair with Paul Bromley. And I came away with the impression that, while her sister wasn't happy about Charles spending so much time and money on the house, Mrs Etherton herself rather admires Charles for his dedication to the cause.

'I suppose it's understandable in a way,' he continued. 'I gather she's been working with him now for a good many years, so perhaps she appreciates more than anyone how hard and how costly it is to maintain a place such as Bromley Manor.'

Grace raised a questioning eyebrow. 'She admires him . . .?' she probed gently.

Paget chuckled. 'You and your suspicious mind,' he said. 'No, I said "admired" and I'm sure that's all it is. And why not? He's been very good to her, letting her live there all these years. Hardly surprising, I suppose, considering that the Bromleys, the Ashcrofts, *and,* come to think of it, the Chadwicks have known each other since the year dot. And let's not forget the Wyckhams.'

'Speaking of the Wyckhams,' said Grace, 'how does he feel about all this? Or, more specifically, what does Chief Superintendent Brock *say* Sir Robert thinks about it all? You said you were talking to him this afternoon.'

'The subject never came up,' Paget said innocently as he swilled his hands at the sink and picked up a towel.

'So what were you and he chatting about?' Grace was curious. Neil rarely looked happy after talking to the chief superintendent, but he'd been quite cheerful this evening.

'It wasn't so much a chat as a confrontation when I told him I'd applied for a search warrant for Bromley Manor. You know how pale he is at the best of times; it's as if he's just donated blood and they forgot to turn the tap off, but he actually turned red when I told him, if you can imagine it.'

'I can't,' Grace said, 'but I wish I'd been there. Do you still have a job?'

'I did when I left, but I suspect it may be hanging by a thread.'

'What's the warrant for?'

'We're looking for clothing with green paint on it. Whoever wore that coat after it had been hanging on the peg may have traces of green paint on whatever they were wearing when they put it on. We're probably far too late – whoever hid Paul's hat and coat, whether it was Paul himself or someone else, would be a fool to leave anything with green paint on it lying about – but you never know your luck, they may not have realized it was there, so we'll be out in force first thing tomorrow morning to turn the place over.'

'Is there any chance that Brock might let the Bromleys know ahead of time? You know what he's like.'

'Oh, I don't think so,' Paget said, 'especially after I told him I intended to launch an investigation into who leaked the information about the murder of Gwyneth Jones to Charles Bromley, a potential suspect, within an hour or two of the discovery of Gwyneth Jones's body this morning.'

'But you know who did that,' Grace objected. 'You said Charles Bromley told you it was Sir Robert himself.'

'That's true, but Brock doesn't know that I know who the culprit is, so he went to some lengths to persuade me to let it go, and concentrate on finding the killer – which is how I got my search warrant.'

TWENTY-FIVE

Thursday, September 15th

'Got a message for you from a Mrs Farnsworth,' the duty sergeant told Paget when he came in the following morning. He handed the DCI a page stripped from a memo pad. 'She wants you to give her a ring. Her number's on there, sir.'

'Did she say why?'

'I did ask, but all she would say was she had something she thought you should see.'

Paget glanced at the number. 'Did she say if it was urgent?'

The sergeant shook his head. 'But she did say she thought it might be useful.'

'Right. Thank you, Sergeant.' Paget tucked the memo in his pocket and continued on up the stairs to his office, where he found Tregalles waiting for him, a mug of coffee in his hand. The phone began to ring as he reached his desk. Paget scooped it up. 'Yes, Len?' he said when he heard the sergeant's voice.

'We've identified the two kids Thorsen disturbed on the downs the night Gwyneth went missing,' Ormside said, 'and there's a good chance that they saw Gwyneth in Manor Lane that night. The boy couldn't be absolutely sure it was the same girl when we showed him the photograph of Gwyneth, but he says his girl-friend spoke to her as if she knew her. His name is Cyril Ridgeway, and the girl is Nina Morgan. She lives here in Hallows End.'

'Have you spoken to her?'

'No. She's still at school, but she and her mother are coming in this afternoon. The thing is, Ridgeway says Nina wasn't supposed to be out that night, so she may not want to cooperate if her mother's with her.'

'Tregalles will be out there to give you a hand,' Paget told him. 'I'm sure the two of you will find a way around it. Now, have you had a chance to read the interview with Mrs Etherton?'

'About the fire in the stables seven years ago? Yes, Forsythe left a copy on my desk last night, and I looked at it first thing this morning,' Ormside said. 'Do you think there's anything to it?'

'I don't know,' Paget said, 'but that's what I want you to find out. I want you to look into the investigation that took place at the time, and get back to me as soon as you can. You might start by getting hold of Sergeant Naismith in B Division. He's the one who investigated the fire seven years ago. See if he still has any of his notes left. Find out what his thoughts were about it at the time. Any suspicion of foul play; you know the drill. I've cleared it with his boss.'

'Even if there was, I don't see how it could have anything to do with Toni Halliday's murder,' Ormside said.

'Nor can I,' Paget admitted, 'but I can't help wondering why Mrs Etherton thinks there is.'

* * *

'Please come in, Chief Inspector,' Mrs Farnsworth said. 'It's good of you to come.'

She looked tired but she moved more purposefully, Paget thought, and there was a new assertiveness in the way she spoke. Perhaps a new Harriett Farnsworth was beginning to emerge now that she was no longer in the shadow of the major.

She indicated the same chair he had occupied before, then settled herself comfortably in its twin on the other side of the fireplace

'I know you must be very busy,' she said, 'so I won't keep you very long. But I did think it my duty to ring you. Graham, that is Graham Cairns – he's my nephew – didn't think I should. He said the less said the better, but I didn't take his advice.' She smiled suddenly. It was a funny little smile; a strange mixture of satisfaction and surprise at her own temerity.

'It was Graham who brought me home from Worthing yesterday,' she went on. 'And since I knew he'd always been interested in guns, I asked him to dispose of Adrian's collection for me. It's not much of a collection, really, but I wanted them out of the house.'

Mrs Farnsworth rose and took a cardboard box from the table. She held it in her hands for a long moment as if wondering if she was doing the right thing before thrusting it into Paget's hands and returning to her seat.

'While Graham was going through the gun cabinet, he came across those,' she said quietly. 'They were hidden beneath the ammunition. They're diaries of a sort; diaries Adrian kept of his . . . Well, you'll see for yourself. I suppose he kept them there because he knew it would be the one place I would never go.'

Paget opened the box and removed the contents. 'It's the top one you want,' she said.

There were five books; notebooks rather than actual diaries. Paget opened the top one. It was more than half full of small, neat handwriting, presumably the major's.

The major's affair with Gwyneth took up twelve pages.

It was all there in lurid detail. In such coarse and vulgar detail that even Paget, inured as he was to such things, felt his skin begin to crawl. Farnsworth seemed to have taken special pride in demeaning the women he seduced, and his contempt for them was manifest in every line. Obviously proud of his own prowess, he described each conquest in minute detail, together with his own innermost thoughts at the time.

The last entry was dated the day of Toni Halliday's death. 'Meeting G at 20:00 hours. Try Van before that. Hope she's up for it as well, because I am. Could be a storm. Thank God for the barn.'

He went back through the pages; checked the other books. There were references to other women, many other women, but, with the exception of Gwyneth, Vanessa King, and a brief encounter with a Clunbridge woman he'd met in a pub, the affairs had all occurred prior to the move to Lower Farm.

He looked up to find her eyes upon him. 'Why?' he asked softly. 'Why didn't you just throw these on the fire, Mrs Farnsworth? Don't misunderstand me; I'm very glad you didn't, but the temptation must have been very strong.'

Harriett Farnsworth lifted her head to meet his gaze.

'I was tempted to do exactly that, because that's where they belong. But then I thought about that poor girl who is missing. She must be terribly afraid, and it was Adrian's fault that she was there in the barn, so if there is anything in there that will help . . .'

Paget hardly knew what to say.

'I take it you haven't spoken to anyone or heard any local news since you came back yesterday?' he said.

She shook her head.

'Then, of course, you wouldn't know. I'm afraid Gwyneth is dead. We found her yesterday. Killed, we believe, by the same person who murdered Toni Halliday.'

Mrs Farnsworth stared at him. 'Oh, my God!' she breathed, and a tear rolled down her cheek. 'I'm so sorry. So terribly sorry.'

Later, as he took his leave, Paget thanked her once again. 'I'll make sure these books are returned to you as soon as we have finished with them,' he assured her, but she was shaking her head even before he had finished speaking.

'Burn them,' she told him. 'I never want to see them again!'

'They found Gwyneth Jones's bike,' Ormside said by way of greeting when Paget called in on his way back to town. 'It was round the back of Vanessa King's caravan.'

'Was she the one who found it?'

'No. We did. She says she has no idea how it got there. There's a high grass bank behind the caravan, and if we hadn't found it, it might have stayed there for a long time, because she rarely goes back there.'

'Still . . .' Paget frowned into the distance. 'Perhaps we should be taking a closer look at Ms King,' he suggested. 'From what we know so far, the only connection she has with the events around Toni Halliday's death, is with the major, but perhaps there's more. Where's the bike now?'

'Gone to Forensic,' Ormside told him. 'As for Ms King . . .? I can't see it myself. She seemed straightforward enough when she came in to tell us about the major, but I'll have someone look into it.' He pulled a pad toward him and scribbled a note.

'Now,' he continued, 'I'm still working on the investigation into the death of the first Mrs Bromley, but it's beginning to look like it was a smoke and mirrors job all the way. I spoke to DS Naismith, and he said he was as good as told to make it look good on paper; file his report and forget it.'

'Who gave him those instructions?'

'DI Hawthorne.' Ormside's tone of voice said it all. Hawthorne had been shunted off to one side some years ago to mark time until his retirement – a condition some of his less charitable colleagues maintained he'd been in ever since he'd joined the force.

'Are you saying there never was an investigation?' Paget asked.

'All the right forms were filled in,' Ormside said, 'but some of the stuff Naismith handed in never made it into the final report.'

'Such as?'

'Such as the state of the electrics in the stables. He was told that Mrs Bromley was using a paraffin lamp because the old wiring in the stables kept blowing fuses. But it turned out that the wiring wasn't that old; it had been re-done about ten years before. Mind you, several people said there had been some trouble with the lights down there, including Thorsen, so I suppose there could have been a fault. On the other hand, someone could have been making it look as if the wiring was bad as an excuse to use the paraffin lamps.'

'Who told him that the wiring was old?'

'Paul Bromley. When Naismith found out that it wasn't old, and tackled Paul about it, Paul said it must have been re-wired when he wasn't there – which is possible, I suppose, but that man tells so many lies, everything he says is suspect now.'

'Was arson suspected?'

'Ah, now that's interesting,' Ormside said. 'There was this volunteer fireman by the name of Bright from Clunbridge. He was one of the first on the scene. He said that when he first got there he was able to get inside almost as far as the loose box where Mrs Bromley and the horse were later found. He said there was a timber wedged across both the upper and lower doors of the box. Unfortunately, just as he spotted it, the fire burst through the walls and he had to run for it. Of course, that whole end of the stable was destroyed, and there was nothing left to support his story. But he was so insistent at the inquest that it was given to Hawthorne to look into. He handed it off to Naismith and gave him the nod at the same time.'

'So Naismith did a whitewash job?'

'Not exactly. His original report mentioned all the things he wasn't happy about. He wanted to have an engineer look at the electrics, and he had questions about Paul's story. Paul told him he sometimes went for a ride alone, but Thorsen said he'd never known Paul to go out by himself before. According to him, Paul only went out when Mrs Bromley was riding. And then there was the matter of the paraffin.'

'What about the paraffin?'

'Thorsen told Naismith that the old lamps hadn't been used for years, so he had to buy fresh paraffin when the lights started acting up. He said he bought a couple of four-litre containers. He filled the two lamps and put the rest away – away from the part of the stables destroyed by the fire, that is. But when Naismith had a look, one container was empty and the other had no more than a litre left in it.'

'The inference being that the rest was used to start the fire?'

'Right.'

'Was that ever followed up?'

'No. Hawthorn told Naismith he wanted only facts, not speculation, in the final report. He said that Bright, the fireman, had
admitted at the inquest that he'd only been inside the stables for
a few seconds, and his vision was impaired by smoke, so his
testimony about the doors being barred was worthless. As for
Paul's testimony, Hawthorne said it came down to Paul's word
against Thorsen's, and the old man admitted that he wasn't always
around at that time in the morning. As for the paraffin, he said
Thorsen could have been mistaken. And there was no physical
evidence to suggest that the fire had been anything but a tragic
accident. On top of that, the Chief Fire Officer appeared to be
satisfied.'

'But if paraffin was used as an accelerant, surely that would
have been detected by the investigator?'

'There wasn't one, according to Naismith. Investigator, I mean.
Not necessary, he was told. Sounds to me like the Bromley name
might have had something to do with that,' Ormside said heavily,
'but maybe that's just my suspicious nature.'

'Did Naismith have anything else to say?'

'No, except it just didn't feel right to him. He still thinks that
if he'd been allowed more time he could have found evidence
to support a case for arson – if not for murder.'

'For murder we need a motive,' Paget said. 'Did he have
anything to say about that?'

'Yes, he did,' Ormside said, 'but he was told in no uncertain
terms that he'd exceeded his remit by digging into things that
had nothing to do with the investigation.'

'Namely . . .?'

'The state of the Bromley finances, which were at an all-time
low, according to him. So, as far as motive was concerned, his
first choice was Charles Bromley. But Charles was miles away
at the time, and there were witnesses to prove it, so that information was dismissed as irrelevant.'

The interview was not going well. As Ormside had predicted,
Nina Morgan refused to admit that she had been out that night
as long as her mother was there, so it wasn't until he managed
to separate the two by offering Nina's mother a cup of tea

and biscuits, that Tregalles was able to persuade Nina to talk.

'Now, then,' he said, 'let's cut out the fairy tales, shall we, Nina? Let's have the truth. And I don't mean that load of rubbish you gave us while your mum was here. I haven't mentioned Cyril Ridgeway yet, but I will if I have to, so I suggest you stop lying and talk to me. I don't care what you and Ridgeway were doing, but I am interested in anyone who saw Gwyneth Jones that night in Manor Lane, so let's have it now before your mother comes back or I will drop you in it. Understand?'

Nina glowered. 'My dad always said coppers were cunning bastards,' she said sulkily, 'but you're a first-class shit!'

'Nina knew Gwyneth well,' Tregalles told Molly later, 'and she saw her going into the manor that night. She said she and Ridgeway were at the top end of Manor Lane when they saw Gwyneth coming toward them on her bike. She spoke to Gwyneth as she was opening the side gate, but Gwyneth didn't reply. She pushed her bike through and closed the gate behind her. Nina thought it strange at the time, because Gwyneth was usually quite friendly and chatty.'

'What about the time?'

'She thought it was about quarter to nine when she got home, but she said something else that fixes the time quite accurately. She told me that she was passed by a police car at the bottom of Manor Lane, and that had to be the car that was taking Mrs Farnsworth to the hospital.'

'It always comes back to the manor, doesn't it?'

'Always,' Tregalles agreed.

There was an e-mail from David waiting for Molly when she turned her machine on just after seven that evening. It was actually directed to Reg and Ellen Starkie and several others, whose names Molly didn't recognize, but her name was on the list as well. Meilan, he said, died of her injuries shortly after midnight Friday morning. Conscious of the time difference, Molly looked at the clock. That would have been about three hours ago local time, but it was already Friday in Hong Kong.

He went on to say he didn't know how long he would have to remain in Hong Kong, because Meilan had named him as sole executor of her will, and he would need to familiarize himself with local laws regarding probate. The hospital in Broadminster had agreed to hold the job offer open for thirty days, and he hoped to meet that deadline.

But there was also the future of his daughter, Lijuan, to consider, coping with her loss, her education, and whether she should remain in Hong Kong with her grandmother, or come back to England with him.

Molly read the message several times. Judging by the content, the message was for family members or very close friends, but it pleased her that he had thought to include her, even though they had only known each other for such a short time.

He had closed with, 'Love to all, David.' It was the sort of sign-off anyone might use under such circumstances, but Molly chose to think that, just perhaps, he had been thinking of her when he typed it. She caught a glimpse of herself in the hall mirror and made a face at her image. 'Idiot!' she muttered sternly as she turned away. The man had more on his mind than a woman he'd met only recently.

But it was still a nice thought.

She sent a brief note of condolence, hesitating for some time over how to sign off, then quickly typed, Sincerely, Molly.

TWENTY-SIX

Margaret Bromley entered her room and closed the door behind her. It was only nine o'clock, but she was desperately tired. She felt as if she hadn't slept for weeks. The tablets Steven had given her had helped, but she'd been having such violent dreams – and she'd had another lapse of memory that she felt sure had lasted more than a minute earlier in the evening.

She went to the dressing table and sat down. A crumpled slip lay on the floor beside the chair, but she couldn't be bothered to pick it up. She'd been mending a broken strap earlier in the day, and thread and scissors and needle case from her sewing basket were still there on the dressing table. She pushed them aside, then stared at her image in the mirror as she took off her earrings and necklace. Her hands shook as she set them down, and she had an almost uncontrollable urge to cry. Her reflection stared back at her, pale and hollow-eyed.

'God, but I look a mess!' she said aloud.

'Oh, I wouldn't say it's as bad as all that.'

She whirled to face the speaker. What little colour there was drained from her face, and she felt as if her heart would explode any second. She fought for breath as Paul emerged from the shadows and stood there, smiling down at her.

'Paul! You scared the hell out of me,' she gasped. 'What are you doing in here? Get out!' She turned her back on him and began to comb her hair with shaking hands.

'I've been waiting for you, my love,' he said silkily.

'Get out!' she said again. 'I'm tired, and the last person I want to talk to is you.'

'You used to be very happy talking to me,' he said as he moved closer to stand behind her. He put his hands on her shoulders and rested his chin on the top of her head as he spoke to the image in the mirror. 'And we have so much to talk about, you and I.'

'Such as?' she said icily, but the tremor in her voice betrayed her.

'Such as what you and Steven Lockwood were doing in his car the night Toni was killed.'

Margaret twisted in her chair to face him. 'Who told you that?' she demanded.

'No one *told* me,' he said. 'I was there, waiting for the rain to ease up before returning to the house, and I saw you get out of the car. I saw the way you kissed him. Very tender, very passionate. It brought back memories. But he really should do something about that overhead light when he opens the door. So careless of him. I wonder what Charles would say if—'

'*Kissing* him? Is that the best you can do?' Margaret cut in scornfully. 'I think you need you're eyesight tested, Paul. I leaned back in to say thanks and that's all! So don't think you are going to make Charles believe otherwise. He'd never believe you anyway, because he knows you for what you are. So leave me alone and get out.' She pulled away from him and started to stand up, but Paul's hands circled her throat as he forced her back into her chair.

'Oh, I think he will,' he said quietly. 'You really should be more discreet, my love. You've been lucky so far, but even poor old Charles is going to catch on sometime – with a little help from me, of course. Unless . . .' His hands caressed her shoulders and casually slid down beneath the material of her dress.

Her body shook; her vision blurred, and suddenly a seething rage consumed her as she wrenched herself away. The chair went back so violently that it caught Paul across the knees. Cursing, he staggered back. Margaret's hand swept across the surface of the table; her fingers closed on the first thing she touched, and with a newfound strength born of desperation, she rounded on him and struck! Struck hard!

They stood there, facing each other as if frozen in time. A sluggish bubble of saliva dripped from Paul's open mouth as he pulled back to stare down at the scissors protruding from his stomach. His knees began to buckle; he grabbed at Margaret for support. His clawing fingers caught her shoulder, digging into her flesh as he sank slowly to the floor and pulled her off her feet. She screamed as she went down and fell on top of him.

Paul cursed and gasped obscenities as she tried to pull herself free. His grasping fingers held her tight, her face inches from his own distorted features. Her hands kept slipping as she tried to push herself away. She felt the heat of his blood against her own body and screamed again and again. The room began to spin. Sobbing, gasping for breath, she wrenched herself free to scramble crabwise on all fours across the floor.

The bedroom door banged open. 'Margaret! Oh, my God! What . . .?'

Elizabeth Etherton's words made almost no impression on Margaret's battered senses. Now on hands and knees, and gasping hard for breath, she felt as if the room were spinning out of control. She dug her nails into the carpet with every ounce of strength she had to stop herself from being thrown off into space. The frenzied thumping of her heart pounded in her ears, and the acid taste of bile rose in her throat.

'Margaret! Answer me! Are you hurt?'

She raised her head, her vision blurred. Beth was standing over her, saying something she couldn't hear for the roaring in her ears. 'Not me,' she managed between gasps. 'It's Paul. He . . .'

She vomited.

Beth hesitated only long enough to make sure that the blood on Margaret's clothes was not her own before turning her attention to Paul. He lay with knees half drawn up, moaning and muttering but barely conscious. The scissors protruded from the flesh below the ribs, their handles ringed with blood. Instinctively, Beth reached to pull them out, then paused, afraid of making matters worse; perhaps it would accelerate the bleeding.

Feet pounded down the corridor. 'For Christ's sake, what the hell is all the screaming about?' Julian stopped dead in the open doorway. His face turned pale. 'Bloody hell!' he croaked hoarsely. 'What happened?'

Paul groaned in pain, opened his eyes and tried to speak, gulping, choking on the word. His head fell back, his eyes closed and more saliva dribbled from his mouth.

'Oh, for God's sake, Julian, you can see what happened,' Beth snapped. 'Don't just stand there. Go and get your father up here fast! Then call an ambulance.'

Julian looked at Margaret, then back at Paul. 'Did she . . .?' he began, but stopped when he saw the look on his aunt's face, and set off running down the corridor.

Beth felt Paul's brow. His face was damp with sweat. His lips moved, but there were no words, just muttered sounds. Margaret had managed to prop herself against the bed, where she sat moaning softly and rocking back and forth, head bowed between her bloodied hands.

Beth heard the heavy tread of footsteps in the corridor. Charles. 'Help's on the way, Paul,' she said quietly, but even as she was speaking his body arched in a sudden, violent spasm, then crumpled and fell back. His head lolled to one side and a long, slow sigh drifted into silence.

Charles came through the door, bag in hand. His eyes met those of Beth. Lips compressed and blinking hard, she shook her head. 'I think he's gone,' she said. 'I'm so sorry Charles. There was nothing I could do.'

Charles knelt beside his brother's body. He felt for a pulse, lifted an eyelid, then studied his brother's face for a long moment before turning his attention to the blood-soaked weapon protruding from the body. He opened his bag and took out a pair of thin plastic gloves and put them on. Slowly, carefully, he pulled the scissors out and set them to one side. The bleeding slowed, then stopped.

'Margaret did this?' he asked as if he couldn't quite believe it. Beth nodded silently. He got to his feet. 'Do you know what happened?'

She shook her head. 'I heard her scream and this is what I found when I came in.'

He stood there, looking down on Margaret, who sat rocking back and forth and sobbing quietly. 'What's happening, Beth?' he asked, but it was clear he didn't expect an answer. 'First Toni, then Gwyneth, now this?' He stripped off his gloves and dropped them beside his brother's body. 'God knows what this will do to Margaret.' He sighed. 'But first things first, I suppose. Let's get her out of those clothes, then get her out of here. We'll have to sort out what happened later.'

Julian, panting hard, appeared once more. 'Ambulance is on its way,' he announced. 'Should be here in twenty minutes.'

'Paul's dead,' Charles said cryptically as he got to his feet, 'so call them back and let them know they don't have to hurry.' He helped Beth to her feet, and as she stood there facing him she thought he had never looked so old, so gaunt, and so utterly tired, and her heart went out to him.

'Julian, wait!' he called after his son. 'Better call the police as well,' he said.

'Right, Dad.' Julian set off once more. Funny, Beth thought, but she hadn't heard Julian call his father 'Dad' in years.

For the second time in less than a week, Paget found himself travelling the lanes across country from Ashton Prior to Bromley Manor late at night, but at least the weather was better, and the moon was almost full.

A police car and two white vans bearing the SOCO logo were parked close to the front door of the manor, and, as Paget pulled in beside the police car and got out, Tregalles arrived and parked on the other side of the vans.

'Looks like Charlie's lot got here fast,' the sergeant observed as he joined Paget. 'Is it Charles or Paul?' Tregalles asked. 'The bloke who called me out didn't sound too sure.'

'It's Paul, and the information I have is it was Mrs Bromley who stabbed him – with scissors.'

Tregalles blew out his cheeks. 'You have to give 'em points for being innovative if nothing else,' he said, then shrugged apologetically and said, 'Sorry, boss, but you must admit it is a bit bizarre. First a sickle, then a metal bar, and now a pair of scissors? Does this make Mrs Bromley prime suspect in the other killings? Or is Paul still in the frame?'

'Take your pick at this point,' Paget told him. He led the way up the steps to the front door where a uniformed constable stood guard.

'Top of the stairs, turn right, sir,' the constable said as he opened the door for them. 'Inspector Dobbs' lot just went up.'

'Believe me, Tom, we know the way,' Tregalles said, recognizing the man. 'In fact if this keeps up we're thinking of moving HQ out here.'

Charlie wasn't there himself, but three of his men were already in the room. Geoff Kirkpatrick, a senior member of the scenes-of-crime team greeted them at the door. He eyed the two detectives critically. 'It looks pretty straightforward to me,' he said, 'so you could probably come in as you are, but I'd prefer it if you'd suit up. I have extra suits.'

'Don't worry, we came prepared,' Paget told him. Apart from the fact that it was standard procedure, he knew he'd be in trouble with Grace if he didn't observe procedure. As part of the SOCO team, she taught courses on crime-scene contamination.

Properly attired, the two men entered the room. Paget, as always, had to pause to breathe deeply before looking closely at the body of Paul Bromley, who, in death, seemed smaller than in life. His cheeks were sunken and his mouth was slack, and his face was almost grey.

'Not much doubt about what killed him,' Kirkpatrick observed, pointing to a bloodied pair of scissors on the floor beside the body. 'Or who did it, so this should be an easy one for you. Mr Bromley told us it was his wife. He said she stabbed his brother in self-defence.'

'He actually told you that? Volunteered the information?'

Kirkpatrick shrugged. 'I was surprised myself,' he said, 'but, yes, that's what he told me when we got here.'

'Long, thin, and sharp by the look of them,' Paget observed, pointing to the scissors. 'Not the sort of thing you'd expect to find in the average bedroom.'

'Looks like she might have been mending something,' Kirkpatrick said. 'There's a nightdress or slip or some such thing on the floor, and a sewing basket beside the dressing table.'

'Gutted,' Tregalles said soberly as he bent to take a closer look at the slit in the blood-soaked shirt. 'If he hadn't worn his belt so low, it might have saved his life. Were the scissors there beside him when you got here?'

Kirkpatrick nodded. 'Mr Bromley said he removed them after the victim died.'

'Did he say anything else?' asked Paget.

'Not really, but he said he'd wait for you in –' he pulled a notebook from his pocket and flipped it open – 'a Mrs Etherton's room. It's at the far end of the corridor.'

'We know where it is,' Paget told him. 'And Mrs Bromley . . .?'

'She's there as well. In bed, apparently. Mr Bromley said she was in such a state he had to sedate her, and she'll be out of it at least until tomorrow morning.'

Dr Starkie entered the room. Already suited up, he'd come prepared. 'Ah, there you are, Paget,' he said tersely. 'I knew this would be one of yours. You seem to prefer the nocturnal ones.' He set his bag on the floor. 'The body been photographed yet?'

'We only just got here ourselves,' Kirkpatrick told him, 'so—'

'So what are you waiting for?' Starkie demanded. 'Get on with it man. I don't know about you, but I prefer my bed at this time of night, so the sooner we get this done and I'm on my way, the better. And let's have some light in here!'

It was Charles Bromley himself who came to the door when Paget knocked. He stepped out into the corridor and closed the door behind him.

'It's late and I realize how distressing this must be for you,' said Paget, 'so if you could give me a brief account of what happened here tonight, we can come back in the morning to take more detailed statements.'

Charles gave a curt nod and moved a few steps away down the corridor. 'I appreciate that, Chief Inspector,' he said tiredly, 'but all I can tell you is what I found when I went upstairs. I know nothing about what happened before that. Margaret was in a state of shock, but the only thing she did manage to say before she collapsed was that Paul had attacked her. Beth got there ahead of me, but from what she's said, I don't think she knows what happened any more than I do.'

'I'm told that Mrs Bromley is still here,' Paget said. 'Shouldn't she be in hospital under observation?'

Charles drew back. The muscles around his mouth tightened, and the look he gave Paget bordered on the hostile. 'I appreciate your concern, Chief Inspector,' he said coldly, 'but my wife *is* under observation – by me. She was in a state of considerable agitation and distress, so I gave her something to calm her down and help her to sleep, and I intend to remain with her throughout the night. Strictly speaking, of course, I am not her family doctor; Steven Lockwood is, and I have apprised him of the situation and he will be here first thing tomorrow morning. All right?'

'I wasn't questioning your judgement or capability,' said Paget quietly. 'I was thinking more in terms of the availability of assistance and resources in hospital, should there be a need. You say Paul attacked her. Are any of her injuries serious?'

'Lacerations and bruising around the neck and shoulders for the most part,' Charles said tersely. 'Nothing life-threatening, and nothing that couldn't be attended to here at home.'

'I'm glad to hear it,' Paget told him. 'So, now, if you would tell me what you found when you came upstairs . . .?'

In clipped tones, Charles described the scene, concluding with '. . . and then I had Julian ring you while Beth and I got Margaret out of the room and brought her along here to Beth's room, where she will be staying for the rest of the night.'

'About the scissors, sir,' said Paget. 'You say they were still in the body when you arrived?'

'That's right. Beth was afraid to remove them for fear of accelerating the bleeding, which it would have done.'

'But you removed them. Why was that, sir?'

'Because Paul was dead and I couldn't stand the sight of them sticking out of his stomach, so I pulled the damned things out,' Charles said. '*Carefully*, of course,' he added with just a trace of sarcasm, 'so it won't be a problem for the doctor who performs the autopsy, if that's what you're worried about.' He looked pointedly at his watch, and said, 'So, if that is all, Chief Inspector, I would like to get back to my wife. I'll send Beth out.'

He turned and went back into the room.

'He didn't like that very much, did he?' Tregalles said in hushed tones. 'I wonder why?'

'I don't think he's used to his decisions being questioned,' Paget replied. 'He . . .'

Whatever he's been about to say was kept to himself as Mrs Etherton emerged from her room. She looked extremely tired, so Paget suggested they move to the landing overlooking the front entrance, where she could sit down on an antique wooden bench. The wood was dark and very old and cracked in places, and the padded velvet top was worn and faded. 'They didn't go in for comfort much in the days when this was made,' Mrs Etherton said as she sat down, 'but it's not quite as bad as it looks. It's solidly built.' She patted the seat beside her, but Paget remained standing, and Tregalles propped himself against the wall and flipped to a new page in his notebook.

Paget led Mrs Etherton through the events of the evening. She spoke softly, pausing now and then as if to make sure that what she was about to say was accurate, but all in all, a very credible witness if it should ever come to that.

'Tell me,' he said, 'apart from the trauma and shock of it all, how would you describe Mrs Bromley's physical condition? Did she suffer any serious injuries?'

'She has some bruising and scratches on her neck and shoul-ders, some deep enough to draw blood, but, no, I wouldn't describe her injuries as serious. Charles saw to them and put a couple of dressings on, but I think that was more to keep them from becoming infected than for any other reason. No, I'd say the physical injuries are the least of her problems; it's her mind I'm worried about. She was in a terrible state when I found her.'

'Which is why I can't help wondering why Mr Bromley seems to be so reluctant to get her to the hospital where she can be properly monitored day and night,' Paget said. 'Even before this happened, Mrs Bromley seems to have resisted all attempts to get her into hospital or a clinic for a full range of tests to find the cause of her blackouts, or whatever they are. Do *you* know why that is?'

Elizabeth Etherton's eyes held those of Paget for several seconds before she spoke. 'I can tell you what I *think* is the reason,' she said at last. 'I think it's because of what happened to her mother. You see, when Margaret was about twenty, her mother began to act strangely, forgetting things, wandering off, that sort of thing. Nothing too serious at first, but her condition deteriorated rapidly and when she was arrested for causing a disturbance in the street, she became violent and had to be restrained. In the end she was sectioned, and three weeks later she committed suicide. Margaret is roughly the same age now as her mother was then, and I think she is afraid that if she goes into hospital, they'll put her in the psychiatric ward and she'll end up the same way her mother did.'

'Did Mrs Bromley tell you this?'

'Oh, no. Margaret has never said a word of this to me. In fact, she never talks about her mother at all. No, Charles told me in confidence when I tried to get him to persuade Margaret to go for tests.'

'There must have been an autopsy on her mother,' Paget said. 'Do you know if they established the cause of her illness?'

'According to Charles, that was the troubling part, because nothing abnormal was found. I know he and Steven have tried to point out that diagnostic techniques have advanced a lot in the past twenty-five years, but Margaret refuses to listen.'

'Couldn't she be sectioned under the Mental Health Act?' Tregalles asked. 'I mean it would be for her own good, wouldn't it?'

Mrs Etherton shook her head. 'I think Steven would like to do that if he had Charles's backing,' she said, 'but as Charles says, Margaret isn't acting irrationally, and they can't say in all honesty that she is a danger to herself or other people, besides which, he refuses to force Margaret to do anything against her will.'

'If she won't go to them, what about getting specialists or

whatever to come here?' Tregalles suggested. 'I know they wouldn't do that for you or me under the NHS, but with Mr Bromley in the business, so to speak, he must know some of the top people, and they would probably come if he asked them.'

'I believe something like that has been suggested, Sergeant,' Mrs Etherton said, 'but it's not happening, so I assume Margaret has vetoed that idea as well. She keeps saying, "it will pass, it will pass".'

'Getting back to what happened this evening,' Paget said, 'Did Mrs Bromley say *why* Paul attacked her?'

Mrs Etherton shook her head. 'All she said was, "Paul tried to kill me", and that was it. She could barely talk at all. She was in shock; she was hysterical.'

'You said Paul was trying to speak when you first got there? Were you able to understand anything he said?'

Once again, Mrs Etherton shook her head. 'I'm sorry, but they weren't really words at all, just jumbled sounds. I'm sure he must have been in a lot of pain.'

'Can you think of any reason why he would attack Mrs Bromley in her own room?'

Elizabeth Etherton shook her head. 'Believe me, Chief Inspector, I've been wondering about that myself, and all I can think of is that it must have had something to do with Toni's death. If Paul was the one who killed Toni, he may have thought Margaret had seen him out there, and thought she could be a threat to him.'

'You say Mrs Bromley was still dressed when she was attacked. What happened to her clothes?'

'I put them in a plastic bag and left them beside the laundry hamper in the dressing room. They were covered in blood, so I didn't want them touching anything else. I hope that was all right?'

'Perfectly all right,' Paget assured her. 'Just one more question, and I'll let you go. You must be awfully tired. The scissors: do you happen to know if they are the ones Mrs Bromley normally uses when she is sewing or mending something?'

'Oh, yes. I've seen them many times. Why do you ask?'

'It's just that they seemed somewhat longer and thinner than I would have expected,' said Paget.

'That's because they're actually surgical scissors. Charles was going to throw them away – they don't keep them very long in his line of work – so Margaret took them. She said they were much better than the ones she had.'

It was a very different Julian Bromley who came to the door of his room when Paget knocked. There was little sign of the arrogant young man they'd encountered earlier. Subdued and somewhat shaken, Paget thought, and certainly more cooperative.

'To be honest,' Julian said, 'I was annoyed at first, because I was rehearsing for a part in a play, and I was just getting into it when I heard this scream. I tried to ignore it, but when it kept up, I went down the corridor to see what it was all about. And then I saw my uncle . . .' He paused to catch his breath before continuing. 'He was covered in blood and I could see it sort of bubbling out, and he was trying to talk, but stuff was running out of his mouth. And then there was Margaret being sick and gagging . . .' Julian took a deep breath and blew out his cheeks. He looked as if he might be sick himself at any moment.

'Thank God for Aunt Beth,' he said, shaking his head in silent admiration. 'I don't know how she can cope with that sort of thing, but she was so calm. She told me to go and get Dad, then call an ambulance. So I did that, but when I went back, Dad said Paul was dead, and he told me to call you.'

TWENTY-SEVEN

Friday, September 16th

'**M**rs *Bromley* killed him? Are you sure?' Chief Superintendent Morgan Brock's bulbous eyes stared at Paget in disbelief. Cod's eyes, Paget thought, not for the first time. That was what they used to call them when he was at school. Colourless, fish-like eyes that stared without expression.

'That's what Mr Bromley told me,' said Paget. 'According to

him, Paul attacked her and she stabbed him with scissors in self-defence.'

'He was there?'

'No. He said that was what his wife told him, and Mrs Etherton said the same. They didn't know any more than that, because Mrs Bromley was either hysterical or in shock or both when she said that, but I hope to clear that up when I bring her in for questioning this morning.'

Brock's plump fingers drummed lightly on the arm of his chair. 'For questioning,' he repeated as if mulling the words over.

'And probably charge her,' Paget said. 'There's not much doubt that she killed him. As I said, both Mrs Etherton and Charles Bromley say she admitted that much herself.'

'But it's still hearsay, isn't it?' Brock shot back. 'And there's no telling what people will say when they're in shock, so I suggest you tread very carefully before you prefer charges of any sort.'

'That *is* standard procedure, sir,' said Paget.

Brock scowled. 'Better get out there and get on with it, then,' he said. 'Three murders . . . If the media get on to this, it will be a bloody circus, so tell the press officer that nothing is to be released to the media without my approval, and I want to be informed of any and all developments.'

'Got a surprise for you,' Ormside greeted him when Paget walked through the door. He and Tregalles had stopped in Hallows End on their way to the manor. 'Got a positive result from Forensic on Gwyneth's bike. Two clear prints from a metal piece under the saddle. The rest of the bike had been wiped clean.' Ormside cocked his head on one side and looked at each of them in turn. 'Like to guess whose they were?'

'Paul's,' Tregalles said promptly, but Paget held back. It wasn't like Ormside to play games; there had to be something special about these prints. 'So, whose are they?' he asked.

'Mrs Etherton's,' the sergeant told him. 'I don't know about you, but I wasn't expecting that.'

Tregalles was shaking his head. 'Don't believe it,' he said flatly. 'I can't see her as a killer, can you, boss?'

'Perhaps she's not,' Paget said, 'but we will certainly have to ask her for an explanation.'

'Forsythe couldn't believe it either,' Ormside said. 'She's on her way to the manor now to stir them up about coming in to make their formal statements, and she was all for asking Mrs Etherton herself, but I told her she'd better leave that to you.'

'Glad you did,' said Paget, 'because I'd like to hear the explanation for myself.'

Ormside picked up a slip of paper and handed it to Tregalles. 'Got a phone call this morning from a friend of yours in London,' he said. 'DS McLean rang to say they've been looking into Conroy's credit card transactions, and they came across a payment made last Friday for the rental of a lock-up garage in Hackney. So they went in, and there was the car Conroy claimed had been stolen. One tail light was broken, and there were scratch marks and some damage to the rear bumper. It's been turned over to Forensic, but McLean wants to know how you want to proceed when they've finished with it?'

'Tell him I'll call him back later today,' Tregalles said. 'That is if I get the chance and we don't have any more murders,' he added grimly.

Mary Lodge stood with arms folded at the window, watching the workmen tramp all over the kitchen garden as they set long poles as props against the leaning garden wall. Just one more thing to worry about, she thought disconsolately. Things were going from bad to worse, and she couldn't see them getting any better. Charles – she called everyone in the house by their first names in her thoughts – had worked so hard to keep things going over the years; to get back to the way it used to be when the old lady was alive. But no matter how hard he'd tried, no matter how hard he worked, it was never enough.

'Daydreaming, are we, Mrs Lodge? Nothing better to do?' Startled, the housekeeper turned to face her employer. She hadn't heard him come in. He looked tired and cross, and there was more than a hint of criticism in his voice. 'Has anyone else had breakfast today, or am I the only one left out?' he continued irritably.

The housekeeper bristled. 'I had your breakfast ready for you more than an hour ago,' she said tartly, 'and I looked everywhere for you, but no one knew where you were, so it all went cold.

Charles grunted. 'You couldn't have tried very hard, or you'd have found me,' he countered waspishly. 'And I am very, very hungry, Mrs Lodge.' He walked over to stand in front of the cooker as if expecting it to produce his breakfast.

Suddenly, all the pent up anger and frustration came rushing to the surface and spilled over. 'Then perhaps you should get it yourself for a change,' she snapped. Startled by her own temerity, a tremor of fear ran through her, but she'd started now and there was no going back.

'I know this is a bad time,' she said, trying to calm the tremor in her voice, 'and I shouldn't have said that, and I'm sorry about your brother, but I can't go on like this, Mr Charles. I can't be expected to run this house all by myself. With Gwyneth gone, and the police in the house again, I can't do it. When cook came this morning and saw all the police cars here again, and I told her what had happened, she said she wasn't going to work in a house where people keep getting murdered, and she turned round and went back home. It's the same with everyone in the village. No one's willing to come out here, and as I said, I can't cope on my own, and I don't know where to turn.'

Charles turned to stare at her. He took a step toward her then stopped. He could feel the pressure that had been building ever since last night, pushing its way to the surface, and the house-keeper's words became no more than muffled noises in his head. He wanted to throw back his head and scream at the world; he wanted to scream at the whole damned *universe!* He wanted to lash out at someone, *anyone!* He thrust his hands deep into his pockets for fear he would lash out at the woman in front of him.

He clamped his lips together, willing himself to remain calm. Would there never be an end to it? Never an end to the demands on him? All he'd ever wanted was a peaceful life; to be left alone to get on with what he liked to do, but there was *always* one more problem, *always* another hurdle, *always* another hill to climb, and he was sick of it. Toni was dead; Gwyneth was dead, and now Paul was dead. Police were crawling all over the place, and although it was barely nine o'clock in the morning, he'd just had a phone call from his bank manager, who had insisted – *insisted,* for God's sake – that he come in today to discuss what he'd called 'your rather dire financial situation.'

And now here was Mrs Lodge whining about the bloody housework!

Inside his pockets, his hands turned into fists. He could feel the pressure building. Stone-faced and angry, he rounded on her. 'That,' he said viciously, 'is *your* problem, Mrs Lodge. In case you hadn't noticed, I have more than enough of my own, so you can either sort it out yourself or . . .'

He clamped his lips together, cutting off whatever he'd been about to say. But his face was white and his eyes glittered dangerously as he took a step toward her, and suddenly she was frightened. 'I'm sorry . . . I'm . . .' she began in a quavering voice as she backed away, but before she could say more, Charles had turned on his heel and left the kitchen.

Mrs Lodge stared after him. She was trembling so hard she had to reach for a chair for support. She sank onto the hard wooden seat, still shaking as the tears spilled down her face.

There were a couple of vans and a small flatbed lorry in the stable yard when Molly drove in, and she could see workmen working with props or poles in the kitchen garden. A sudden gust of wind caught the door as she got out, almost tearing it from her grasp. Strange weather, she thought as she closed it firmly. Only moments ago the sky had been clear and there hadn't been a breath of wind. But then, strange was becoming the norm throughout the world these days. The wind continued to blow as she made her way up the driveway to the side door of the house.

She rang the bell. A few leaves skittered before the wind, another signal perhaps that summer was coming to an end. She waited a few more seconds, then rang the bell again. Still no response. She turned the handle and went inside. After what had happened here last night, the house would be in turmoil, and Mrs Lodge could be anywhere.

Molly walked along the passageway to the kitchen. The smell of paint still lingered, but the hats and coats and boots and shoes were all back in their regular place, as was a wooden bench beneath them. She opened the wash-house door and looked inside. No sign of Mrs Lodge in there. Molly continued on to the kitchen and opened the door.

Mrs Lodge sat at the table, head buried in her hands, crying quietly. 'Mrs Lodge . . .? Molly spoke quietly to avoid startling the woman. 'Whatever is the matter?' She moved swiftly to the housekeeper's side and put her arm around her thin shoulders. 'Tell me what's wrong?'

TWENTY-EIGHT

'They're here,' Elizabeth Etherton said quietly. 'Paget and his sergeant,' she elaborated. 'I suppose that means there will be yet another round of questions.' She moved away from the window to avoid being seen by the detectives as they got out of the car. 'I just hope they don't expect to question Margaret, considering the state she's in. I know Charles said she needed a good night's rest, but I really think he overdid it with the sleeping pills last night. I mean look at her, Steven; she's barely conscious.' Beth walked over to the bed where Margaret Bromley sat hunched over, arms wrapped around her dawn-up knees, head buried in her arms. 'How do you feel now?' she asked softly. 'Can I get you a cup of tea?'

Margaret lifted her head. Her face was pale and bathed in sweat, her eyes were dull, and her hair hung in ragged strands around her face. She'd slept solidly for more than eight hours, but she looked as if she hadn't slept at all. She stared blankly at Beth, then dropped her head again. Beth left the bedside to flop into a chair. Steven Lockwood sat facing her, hunched over, hands clasped in front of him, and elbows on his knees.

'I don't think she even knew who I was just then,' she said wearily. 'I wish Charles . . .' She shrugged, too tired to finish the sentence.

'I know what you mean,' he said tightly. 'I know he believes he's doing it for the best, but I am her doctor. I should have been here last night when Charles rang. Unfortunately, it was after midnight when I got home, so I went straight to bed. I came over as soon as I checked my messages this morning. Not that I've been able to actually *do* anything for her,' he continued wistfully, 'but at least I'm here now, and I think it's time you got some rest yourself. You could use Toni's room.'

But Beth was shaking her head. 'I did get some sleep,' she said. 'Charles was here most of the time.' She smiled wanly, 'Hovering, of course, and checking Margaret's pulse and breathing from time to time even though she was dead to the world. I tried to get him to go and get some sleep himself, but he insisted on staying. What you *can* do, Steven, is make sure that the police don't take Margaret away this morning. I don't see how they can, considering the state she's in, but they may just try, so I'm counting on you, as her doctor, to warn them off.'

Beth pushed herself upright. 'I think I'll make a cup of tea and see if I can get her to drink it,' she said. 'Would you like a cup?'

'Still here, then?' said Paget, stating the obvious as he got out of the car. 'You've had a long night.' He was speaking to Geoff Kirkpatrick, who was stripping off his coveralls. The other two members of the team were doing the same. 'Charlie paying overtime, now, is he?'

Kirkpatrick snorted. 'That'll be the day,' he said. 'No, it's just that we were so close to wrapping it up that it seemed better to stay on and finish it rather than have another shift take over for a couple of hours. We've finished with the room. I did tell Mr Bromley.'

'Any surprises? Any conclusions?'

Kirkpatrick shrugged. 'Assuming that Mr Bromley told me the truth, and it was his wife who stabbed his brother – in self-defence, of course; he made that very clear – we found nothing to suggest an alternative. That's not to say there couldn't be one, of course, but the victim fell where he was stabbed; there were fibres matching Mrs Bromley's dress, as well as bits of skin, under his fingernails, and there were smears of blood on the carpet between the body and the bed to where Mrs Bromley crawled and lost her dinner. Blood types and regurgitated stomach contents will have to be analyzed and matched, of course, as will the fingerprints we found, but I'd say it's pretty straightforward. It will all be in my report.'

He rolled up his coveralls and stuffed them in a bag. 'And

now I'm off to bed,' he said, 'so I'll leave you to it, Chief
Inspector. Good luck.'

A uniformed WPC opened the door as they mounted the
steps, and said, 'Good morning, sir,' to Paget. 'Could I have a
word, sir?'

'Of course, Constable,' he said. 'What's the problem?'

'No problem, sir, it's just that now SOCO's gone, I'm here all
by myself and I'm wondering if you still need me? I was supposed
to be on traffic today. I did call in, but they told me it was up
to you, sir.'

'Is there anything you need to tell me before you go?' he
asked. 'Anything changed? Anyone leave?'

'No one left, sir, but a Dr Lockwood came in just after seven
this morning. He went upstairs to see to Mrs Bromley, and he's
still there as far as I know.'

'Right, then, thank you, Constable,' Paget said. 'Do you need
a lift in?'

The young woman shook her head. 'We've got an unmarked
car patrolling the Clunbridge Road not too far from here,' she
said, 'so I'll call him on my mobile and get him to pick me up.
I'll wait outside for him.'

Paget was about to lead the way upstairs when a door on the
far side of the entrance hall opened, and Charles Bromley
appeared. He crossed the floor and stopped in front of Paget. 'If
you've come to arrest my wife, you're wasting your time,' he
said belligerently. The muscles in his face were set, the lines so
deeply etched they could have been carved in stone. He looked
older, Paget thought. Much older.

'Noted,' Paget told him, 'but we are here to get a statement
from Mrs Bromley, and if she confirms what you told us last
night, then I'm afraid she will be taken into custody and charged.
And we will need you to come down to Hallows End to make
a formal statement as well.'

Charles shook his head. 'Margaret is in no condition to be
questioned,' he said flatly. 'Lockwood is with her; he'll tell you.
As for a statement from me, that will have to wait till another
time. So, if that is all, Chief Inspector, I have to go.' He nodded
in the direction of the open door and scowled. 'It's that damned
east wind,' he said, lowering his voice as if sharing a confidence.

'Gets under the tarp on the roof of the chapel every time. It's done it before, and I can't take any chances, because an east wind quite often brings rain, so I'm going to see what I can do for now, then get the workers back to fix it properly. After that, I have an appointment in town, so whatever you may need from me will have to wait.' With a curt nod, he walked to the door and left the house.

'That went well,' Tregalles observed as he stared after Bromley. 'But I don't get it. He knows why we're here, and he knows his wife is in serious trouble, yet he's worrying about a loose tarp? And then he's off to a meeting in town? I don't understand him at all. Doesn't the man have any feelings for his wife? Or is he just plain bloody clueless?'

'Perhaps he thinks there is not much he can do at this point,' said Paget. 'But you're right, I don't understand him either. However, we're wasting time, so let's go and see if Mrs Bromley and the ever-present Dr Lockwood are any more helpful than her husband.'

It was Lockwood who came to the door when Paget knocked. He stepped into the corridor and closed the door behind him. 'I assume you have come to talk to Mrs Bromley,' he said, 'but I'm afraid I'm going to have to insist that she be left alone. She is in no condition to be questioned. In fact I doubt if she could tell you her own name at the moment. Mr Bromley thought it best to sedate her last night, and she is still recovering. I'm sure you understand.'

'What I understand,' said Paget, 'is that a man was killed in this house last night, killed by Mrs Bromley, according to her husband and Mrs Etherton, and I must talk to her.'

'But it's pointless,' Lockwood persisted. 'Margaret is really not well. In fact, if I had my way, she would be in hospital, and the last thing she needs is someone like you firing questions at her. I mean it's not as if she's going to run away, is it?'

Paget eyed Lockwood narrowly. 'On the other hand, Doctor, now that you mention it, how do I know that Mrs Bromley is even in there unless I see for myself? And we are not in the habit of "firing questions" at anyone in need of medical treatment, so let's take a look, shall we?'

Lockwood hesitated, then stepped aside. 'Very well,' he said. 'Come in and see for yourself.'

Molly Forsythe glanced at the kitchen clock and poured herself and Mrs Lodge another mug of tea from the over-sized Brown Betty teapot. She had intended to talk to Charles Bromley first, to persuade him and then the others to come down to Hallows End to have their formal statements recorded. But after what Mrs Lodge had told her, she'd decided it might be better to wait before tackling the man. Besides, the poor woman needed someone to talk to.

Mrs Lodge sat with wrinkled hands cradled around the mug, drawing comfort from its warmth.

'I'm sure he didn't mean it,' Molly said for perhaps the tenth time. 'With everything that's happened in this house recently, and with his brother being killed last night, and his wife a suspect, Mr Bromley has been under a lot of strain. I'm sure it was nothing personal, Mrs Lodge.'

'Well, it *sounded* personal,' the housekeeper muttered sullenly. 'It was never like this before *she* came,' she added darkly. 'She never liked it here from the start. London was where she wanted to be, and she was always after Mr Charles to sell the place. Mr Charles was born in this house; it's his home, and he promised the old la . . . his grandmother, that he'd look after it. I know, because I was there when she died. He promised her and he's kept his promise, made it his life's work.'

The housekeeper raised red-rimmed eyes to look around the kitchen. 'It's a funny old place, and it's got it's faults,' she said softly, 'but I feel I'm as much a part of it as he is. It's been my home for forty-two years,' she continued. 'Thirty-nine as house-keeper here, so you'd think I'd have earned a bit of respect by now, but the way he looked at me this morning—'

'But there were happier times,' Molly broke in quickly before the housekeeper could get started once again about the unfairness of it all. 'You said yourself that things were different years ago when the first Mrs Bromley was here and Julian was growing up.'

The housekeeper nodded slowly. 'It was,' she said softly. 'Lovely girl, she was. She was an Ashcroft, you know, like her sister, Mrs Etherton was before she married Lionel Etherton. You wouldn't know, though if you saw them. Sisters, I mean. Different as chalk and cheese, but they always got on well, better than you might expect, considering. A bit flighty, Helen was, but nice with it, if you know what I mean. It was a horrible way to die. I shall never forget that day.'

It occurred to Molly that, while Sergeant Ormside had spoken to a number of people about the fire that had taken Helen Bromley's life, she hadn't heard Mrs Lodge's name mentioned at all. 'Tell me about that day,' she prompted. 'I'm told that you were the first to spot the fire.'

'I was,' the housekeeper said, visibly perking up. 'Saw the smoke from my bedroom window just as I'd finished making my bed. I knew it must be coming from the stables, but I couldn't see where exactly, so I ran down downstairs and down the drive and saw the flames. I knew I couldn't do anything about it myself, so I ran back in the house and rang for the fire brigade.'

Mrs Lodge's eyes misted over. 'If I'd known she was in there,' she said huskily, 'I don't know what I could have done, but I didn't, you see. I thought she'd gone off riding, because I'd heard someone go off earlier, and I thought it was her. But it was Mr Paul who'd gone out ahead of her. It wasn't until I came back inside and saw that his boots weren't there that I realized he'd gone out as well. But even then I got it wrong, because I thought they'd gone riding together. We had two maids back then, Millie and Vera, although Vera was on notice because there was a bit of an austerity drive on, and both of them were already up and working in the kitchen. So, with Mr Charles still in London, and Julian in Cambridge, the only one left in the house to tell was Mrs Etherton.'

She shrugged. 'Come to that, I thought she was out as well at first, because her shoes were gone, and I thought she was out on one of her early morning rambles. Loves walking, does Mrs Etherton. Anyway, I remember standing there in the passage wishing there was someone in the house that I could tell. But then I realized that her jacket was still there, and she wouldn't go out without that, so I ran upstairs to tell her what had happened.'

'Did all this come out at the inquest, Mrs Lodge?'

The housekeeper shook her head. 'I suppose so,' she said. 'They took a statement from me, but they said it wasn't necessary for me to be there, so I suppose it did.'

Molly frowned. 'You said something a minute ago about Mrs Etherton and her sister getting on well together, *considering*. Considering what, Mrs Lodge?'

The housekeeper looked at Molly blankly for a moment, then said, 'Oh, I see. Of course you wouldn't know about that, would you? It's just that everyone always thought that Mr Charles would marry Elizabeth Ashcroft, in fact I think they were actually engaged, but something happened and he married her sister, Helen, instead.'

Margaret Bromley could hear him; she knew he was asking her a question, but he seemed so very far away. It was like looking at someone through the wrong end of binoculars. She closed her eyes tightly then opened them again. There, that was a bit better. And she knew who he was, but her tongue wouldn't do what she wanted it to do when she tried to speak.

'Mrs Bromley,' Paget said again, 'do you know who I am?'

'Of course I know who you are,' she said crossly, then realized that he was still looking at her, waiting for an answer. The words were still there inside her head. Nothing had come out. Her mouth wasn't working the way it should. She closed her eyes. Perhaps it was a dream and she'd wake up later and everything would be all right.

Paget drew Lockwood to one side and said, 'A few minutes ago, you told me that Mrs Bromley would be in hospital if you had your way, so what's stopping you? She is your patient, and while I'm no doctor, I think this woman needs help, professional help.'

'It's not quite as simple as all that,' Lockwood said. 'Margaret has made it very clear she does not want to go to hospital, and Charles, who has many more medical degrees than I have, says he will not go against her wishes. My hands are tied.'

'Well, mine aren't,' Paget said, 'so I am arresting Mrs Bromley on suspicion of murder, and since she is quite clearly in need of medical attention, I have no choice but to send her to hospital for a complete examination. Perhaps you would be good enough to call for an ambulance, Dr Lockwood? Once that is done,

Sergeant Tregalles will caution Mrs Bromley, but since we don't know if she is capable of understanding the caution, I want you and Mrs Etherton to witness that she has been cautioned. I will also give you my assurance that Mrs Bromley will not be questioned until I am satisfied that she does understand, and can have legal or other representation with her if she so wishes.'

Steven Lockwood felt as if a weight had been lifted from his shoulders. The thought of Margaret facing a charge of murder was not a pleasant one, but he took comfort in the thought that they would never make it stick, when she had clearly acted in self-defence. And if this was the only way to get to the bottom of what was ailing her, so be it.

The main thing was, she would be out of this environment; away from the manor and the scene of her daughter's violent death . . . and Charles.

It was an uncharitable thought, but one that had been growing for some time. Steven Lockwood had always respected Charles as a noted surgeon and top man in his field, and he regarded him as a friend, but he did not like the way the man kept sedating Margaret every time she had a problem.

'Lowers the stress level,' he'd say. 'There was no point in calling you out, Steven, when all she needs is rest.'

Lockwood sighed inwardly. It was pretty obvious what Charles was doing. He must have guessed that there was more to his relationship with Margaret than that of doctor and patient, and he'd been foolish to think his feelings for Margaret would go unnoticed by Charles. It was true, he was in love with Margaret, and he was almost sure that she was in love with him.

His thoughts were interrupted by Tregalles. 'They want to know if it's an emergency,' the sergeant said, cupping his hand over the phone. 'They're a bit stretched at the moment, and they're asking if we can wait for about an hour?'

Paget looked at Lockwood, who nodded. Paget nodded in turn at Tregalles, and said, 'We can wait.'

There was an audible sigh of relief from Mrs Etherton as Tregalles pocketed his phone. 'In that case,' she said, speaking up for the first time since they'd entered the room, 'I suggest you all leave us alone and let me give Margaret a quick sponge bath to freshen her up before she goes.'

TWENTY-NINE

'Let's go through to the kitchen and see if we can persuade Mrs Lodge to make us a cup of tea,' Lockwood said when they reached the bottom of the stairs. 'I know I could use one. How about you, Chief Inspector?'

'I'll second that,' Tregalles said before Paget could reply. 'In fact I could . . .' He broke off when he saw Molly Forsythe hurrying toward them. She looked worried.

'Something wrong, Forsythe?' Paget asked as she stopped in front of him.

'I'm not sure, sir,' she said, 'but I've just been talking to Mrs Lodge, and some of the things she told me . . .' She glanced at Steven Lockwood, then focussed her attention on Paget. 'If you have a minute, sir . . .?'

Lockwood took the hint. 'I'll go on ahead and get things started,' he said, and was about to set off down the hall when Molly stopped him. 'Please be careful what you say to Mrs Lodge, Doctor,' she said. 'She and Mr Bromley have had words, and she's extremely upset.'

'Right. Thanks for the warning,' Lockwood said. 'I'll be careful.'

'They had words, Forsythe . . .?' said Paget once Lockwood had gone.

'Yes, sir, but it's more than that. It's what she told me about the day of the fire in the stables, and—'

'Then we'd better sit down and hear it,' Paget cut in. He moved down the hall and opened the door to the dining room. 'Now,' he said to Molly once they were seated, 'What did Mrs Lodge tell you?'

'It's a number of little things sir,' Molly said cautiously, already beginning to wonder if she was reading too much into what the housekeeper had said, 'but when you put them all together . . .' She read Paget's expression, and launched into a succinct account of everything the housekeeper had told her, concluding with, 'and

Mrs Lodge is convinced that Mrs Etherton had been out earlier that morning, then pretended that she was still in bed when Mrs Lodge knocked on her door.'

'And this is based entirely on Mrs Lodge's observation of walking shoes that were not in their place that morning?' said Paget.

Put that way, it did sound pretty flimsy, but Molly wasn't prepared to let it go. 'As I said, sir, when Mrs Lodge came back into the house to ring for the fire brigade, she said she was sure that Mrs Etherton must be out on what she called her early morning rambles because Mrs Etherton's walking shoes were gone from the back passageway. But then she realized that Mrs Etherton's jacket was still on the peg, and she knew that Mrs Etherton wouldn't have gone out without it, especially on a cold morning. Then, when she went upstairs, she found Mrs Etherton's door locked, something Mrs Lodge said she'd never done before, and when Mrs Etherton came downstairs, she was wearing her walking shoes, something else Mrs Lodge insists Mrs Etherton had never done before.'

'Has Mrs Lodge mentioned this to anyone before?' Paget asked.

'She says she was surprised and thought it odd at the time, but with everything that went on that day, it went right out of her mind until I asked her about it today.'

Tregalles snorted. 'Come on, Molly, you can't be serious,' he said. 'Are you actually suggesting that Mrs Etherton had something to do with the fire that killed her own sister?'

'Did you know that Mrs Etherton, or Elizabeth Ashcroft, as she was then, was once engaged to Chares Bromley, but he broke it off and married her sister?' Molly countered. 'I think that could have fostered some resentment or even hatred toward her sister.'

'Even so . . .' Tregalles began, but Molly was determined to press on. 'Mrs Lodge also told me that before Helen Bromley died, Mr Bromley had been on what she calls one of his "austerity drives". One gardener had been let go a month or so earlier, and one of the maids was on notice. But thanks to the insurance on Helen's life, as well as on the horse and the stables themselves, life continued on as usual, and the maid didn't have to leave.'

Molly turned to Paget. 'Mrs Etherton told us herself that she's been working closely with Mr Bromley almost ever since she came to the manor, and I came away with the impression that she is almost as keen to keep this place up as he is. And there's one other thing: a friend of Mrs Lodge's, whose daughter works in the bank in Broadminster, told her that Mr Bromley is in financial trouble again, and it's really serious this time. But if Mrs Bromley died, he would inherit a great deal of money – in fact it would be even more now that she inherits her daughter's share.'

Tregalles was shaking his head. 'If that's the case,' he said, 'I'd say you've made a fair case against Charles Bromley. He's the one who needs the money.'

'Except he wasn't here when Helen died,' Molly put in quickly. 'I believe it was established that he was in London at the time, so if someone did set the fire deliberately, it couldn't have been him.'

'Assuming that it wasn't an accident,' Paget began, only to be interrupted by the ringing of his mobile phone.

'Yes, Len,' he said. He remained silent for a while, but his expression suddenly changed. 'Twice . . .?' he said. 'Better give me that again, Len. I want to be sure I have this right.'

Charles Bromley closed his phone and stuck it in his pocket as he entered the house. 'This afternoon,' he muttered in disgust. Damned contractors. Considering what he'd paid them over the years, you'd think they could put themselves out a bit to come and tie down a tarp they hadn't tied down properly in the first place. At least it wasn't raining, but the way the weather had been acting lately, that wasn't much comfort. He looked at his watch. He would have to be going soon, but perhaps he should go upstairs to find out what was happening. Paget's car was still outside, so presumably Margaret was still here as well.

He drew a deep breath and massaged his face with his hands. She would be taken in eventually, of course. Even Lockwood couldn't hold them off forever. He'd do his damndest, though. No one liked to see the woman they loved arrested for murder, and there was no doubt in Charles's mind that Lockwood was in love with Margaret. Now, if it had been him in Margaret's bedroom last night . . .

Charles dismissed the thought. He'd done all he could to delay things by giving Margaret an extra-large dose of Zimovane last night. She was probably feeling like hell right now, but she'd recover. He looked at his watch again. Just the thought of having to go hat in hand to that pipsqueak of a bank manager for yet another extension was enough to raise his blood pressure to a dangerous level. Sadly, there was no other option. Beth kept telling him to hold on, that things would work out all right, but time was running out.

He mounted the stairs and walked down the corridor to Beth's room. He paused. Muffled sounds were coming from inside. He opened the door and stopped, slack-jawed, as he stared in disbelief at the scene before him.

'Don't just stand there, you fool!' Beth hissed. 'Close the door and lock it and come and help me. She's dead weight, and we haven't much time. They've sent for an ambulance, and it could be here at any minute. Help me get her to the window.'

'Beth! What the hell do you think you are doing?' he demanded.

'Oh, for God's sake, Charles, there's no need to look so shocked. You know very well what I'm doing, so get over here and help me. I'm doing this for you, for us, so shut the damned door! Whatever you gave her last night is wearing off and she's trying to fight me.'

Even as she spoke, Margaret began to struggle. Her eyes were open but unfocussed. 'Beth, you're hurting me. Stop it, Beth! Please . . .' Her head slumped forward, and she slid from Beth's grasp.

Panting now, Beth bent to pull Margaret up and wrap her arms around her upper body. 'Well, don't just stand there, help me for God's sake!' she grated. Groaning, she strained to lift Margaret's limp body and drag her across the floor. 'It's got to look like suicide,' she panted, 'so get over here and take her legs!'

'Starkie hasn't completed the autopsy on Paul, but he thought it important to let us know that what he found is not consistent with the information I gave him. He says that when Paul was first stabbed, the scissors penetrated the stomach area and nicked the colon. The wound was serious, and there was a lot of blood, but Paul was still conscious and trying to talk. That was confirmed by

Mrs Bromley and Julian, and in fact Mrs Etherton herself. But what killed him was a second thrust to the heart. He says the scissors were partly withdrawn, then thrust upward into the heart, at which point Paul would have died within seconds.'

Tregalles stared at Paget. 'And Mrs Etherton was the only one near him when he died,' he said softly. 'By God, Molly, you could be right.'

'And if she is, then Mrs Bromley could be in danger now,' said Paget, already up and on the move.

They raced down the hall, Paget leading the way, taking the stairs three at a time. Down the hall to the door.

Locked!

Paget stepped back and booted it. The door jamb splintered and the door crashed back against the wall.

Elizabeth Etherton was at the open window, panting hard, struggling to lift Margaret Bromley's limp body onto the railing. But Margaret's arms were flailing wildly as she tried to free herself, and Charles was trying to catch and pin them down.

'Oh, thank God you've come,' Beth gasped. 'Margaret was going to commit suicide, and we were trying to stop her.'

'Let go of her,' Paget commanded as he and the others crossed the room. 'Now!'

Mrs Etherton released her grip and Margaret slid to the floor. Molly knelt beside her. 'Mrs Bromley, can you hear me?' she asked in a loud, clear voice. 'Mrs Bromley . . .?' Margaret Bromley opened her eyes. 'Beth and Charles,' she whispered hoarsely, 'they were trying to kill me.'

'She doesn't know what she's saying,' Beth said quickly. 'You can see she's barely conscious. She—'

'For Christ's sake, Beth, give it up,' Charles broke in harshly. 'It's over. Finished. Let it go.'

Beth's eyes blazed. 'You pathetic bastard!' she grated. 'You'd turn on me after all I've done for you? You'd have lost *everything* if it hadn't been for me. You were happy enough to take the money when I took care of Helen for you.'

THIRTY

The house was quiet. It was as if a cloak of silence had settled over the manor after Elizabeth Etherton and Charles Bromley were led from the house and taken away in separate cars. The ambulance, followed closely by Steven Lockwood, had taken Margaret Bromley off to hospital, and SOCO had been called in once again.

Grace Lovett and John Rider, a junior colleague, were searching Elizabeth Etherton's room, while two other members of the scenes-of-crime team were searching Charles's room.

Apart from Mrs Lodge, Grace and the rest of the team were the only people in the house. When Molly was sent to tell Julian that his father and his aunt had been arrested, she was told by Mrs Lodge that Julian had left the house for Birmingham.

'I reminded him that we'd all been told not to leave the house after what happened last night,' the housekeeper said, 'but he said he had to be there for rehearsals, and he left.'

That Mrs Etherton was something of a packrat was well established by the time John started on the cupboards in the tiny bathroom, and found a shoebox packed with outdated prescription and non-prescription drugs. 'Is there any point in logging all this stuff?' he asked Grace, 'or should I just put them back?' He picked up a vial at random and peered at the label. 'This one is almost ten years old,' he exclaimed. 'It should have been disposed of years ago.'

Grace picked out a several more and examined them. 'She probably intended to one day, but never got around to it. Some of these are so old.' She frowned. 'Triazolam . . .?' she said on a rising note. 'I thought that was banned in this country years ago.' She squinted at the label as if she couldn't quite believe what she was seeing. 'You think some of the others are old, John. Take a look at the date on this! And there must be twenty or thirty tablets left.'

He tilted his head back to read the label through his bifocals, then whistled softly. 'This woman didn't like to throw anything away, did she? Why were they banned?'

'Too many serious side effects, at least for some people,' Grace told him. 'Headaches, nausea, disorientation, bouts of amnesia . . . In fact,' she continued slowly, 'very much like the symptoms displayed by Mrs Bromley, if I'm not mistaken. I think I'd better give Neil a call.'

Charles Bromley sat slumped in his chair facing Paget and Tregalles across the table. His face was drawn and he looked very much older than he had a week ago. The tape was running and Paget reminded Charles once again that he was under caution, and he was entitled to legal representation if he wished.

'I'm aware of the procedure,' Charles said wearily, 'and I probably know more about the law than our solicitor, so let's get on with it, shall we?'

'Very well. So, tell me, Mr Bromley, when, exactly, did you and Mrs Etherton decide to kill your wife, Margaret? We all heard your sister-in-law confess to killing your first wife.'

Charles shook his head. 'Beth couldn't . . . You misunderstood. You've got it all wrong,' he said. 'I can see how you might think that, but I went up to see how Margaret was before going into town this morning, and it's a good job I did, because Beth was trying to stop Margaret from committing suicide. She was pulling her *away* from the railing, and I went to help her when you came in.'

'*Broke* in,' Paget corrected. 'The door was locked if you remember, sir? Who locked the door?'

Charles eyed him stonily. 'I must have done,' he said. 'Yes, I remember now. I locked it because I didn't want anyone to come in and see Margaret in such a state.'

'So, you opened the door, you saw Mrs Etherton struggling with your wife, but instead of rushing over to help her, you shut the door and locked it, then went over to help. Is that right, sir?'

'Yes, that's right. It only took a couple of seconds, but as I said—'

'I know what you *said*, Mr Bromley,' Paget cut in, 'but if you are going to lie to me I'd prefer you put a little thought into it. Now tell me this: if, as you say, your wife was already at the

window when Mrs Etherton tried to save her, why were there
drag marks across the carpet from the bed to the window? And
while you're thinking about that, would you like to explain what
you meant when you said, "For Christ's sake, give it up, Beth.
It's over. Let it go?" We all heard those words, Mr Bromley, and
we all heard Mrs Etherton's reply. About all that she'd done for
you, including ridding you of your first wife? And she was about
to do it again, wasn't she, Mr Bromley? And you were there to
help her.'

'No! Well . . . All right, yes, perhaps Beth *was* trying to kill
Margaret and make it look like suicide, but I was trying to save
Margaret. I was fighting Beth. You have to believe that.'

'Then why lock the door?' asked Paget once again.

'Sorry to keep you waiting,' Paget said perfunctorily as he and
Tregalles entered the second interview room, 'but we've been
talking to your brother-in-law, or perhaps it would be more
accurate to say he has been talking to us.'

Mrs Etherton remained silent as Paget sat down. Looking at
her across the table, he found it hard to believe that this woman
could be a cold-blooded killer. She looked like someone's aunt,
which of course she was, a benign, middle-aged lady who loved
gardening and gave generously of her spare time travelling around
the countryside collecting things for Oxfam. Hard to believe until
one remembered how the mask had slipped when she had vented
her frustration on Charles earlier in the day.

Tregalles switched on the tape recorder and entered the
required information, then sat down himself while Paget
repeated the caution and advised Mrs Etherton of her right to
legal counsel.

Mrs Etherton brushed his words aside. 'What I would like to
know,' she said acidly, 'is why I've been arrested on suspicion
of murder. Margaret wasn't murdered.'

'If we'd been five minutes later, she would have been,' Tregalles
said caustically.

'We were trying to save her. I should have thought that was
obvious. Margaret's daughter was brutally murdered, then there
was Gwyneth, and having you and your people tramping all over
the place day after day didn't help. And then to be attacked by

Paul, and the stabbing . . . My God, can you blame her for wanting to end it all?'

Paget shook his head. 'I'm afraid you are wasting your breath on that argument,' he said. 'First of all, the door was locked on your instructions, according to Charles Bromley. Secondly, the drag marks on the carpet clearly show that you were dragging Mrs Bromley from the bed to the window. And thirdly, Mrs Bromley herself told us that you and Charles were trying to kill her.'

Mrs Etherton shook her head. 'She didn't know what she was saying, and those marks could have been made when she was trying to drag herself to the window. I was in the bathroom, and when I came out she was on the floor and trying desperately to get to the window. As for the door being locked, I told Charles to do that when he came in because I didn't want anyone else to see her like that. Margaret was my friend. I looked after her—'

'By feeding her Triazolam?' Paget cut in sharply.

She flinched. Elizabeth Etherton recovered in an instant, but too late. Nor could she stop the colour draining from her weathered cheeks, and for the first time, she looked shaken. 'They were found in your cupboard,' Paget told her, 'and the hospital has been notified. In fact, they are testing for Triazolam in Mrs Bromley's system as we speak.'

Mrs Etherton tilted her head and looked away.

'However,' Paget continued, 'as you say, Margaret Bromley is not dead . . . but Paul Bromley is, so let me tell you how he died. According to the pathologist who performed the autopsy, the first wound, admittedly, was serious when it penetrated the stomach and nicked the colon, but Paul would have survived if he'd been taken to hospital in time. But someone pulled the scissors part way out, then redirected them in what the pathologist calls a "savage thrust into the heart", which killed Paul instantly. And you, Mrs Etherton, were the only one near him when that happened.'

Mrs Etherton closed her eyes and sighed heavily. 'That was a mistake,' she said softly. 'I realized that later, but what was done was done. I tried to convince myself that it wouldn't be noticed during the autopsy, but I had the feeling then that things were going wrong.'

Paget and Tregalles exchanged glances, startled by the admission. 'You are under caution, Mrs Etherton,' Paget reminded her, but she just waved a hand as if brushing away a fly.

'I know,' she said wearily, 'and I don't think I care any more. I'm tired of fighting his battles for him. Everything I have ever done has been for Charles, yet now . . .' She lifted her head to look at Paget. 'I should have known it would come to this one day,' she whispered. 'Should have known I would be alone.'

'So why did you kill Paul? Was he blackmailing you?'

'No,' she said with a sigh, 'but I was afraid he might. I couldn't take a chance after I overheard him tell Margaret that he'd withheld information from you about what he'd seen the night Toni was killed. I was afraid I might not get another chance. It wasn't part of the original plan.'

'The original plan?' Paget repeated. 'When *did* you start planning all this, Mrs Etherton?' She smiled. It was the sort of smile one might expect from a child nursing a secret, watchful and guarded.

'Was it before or after you killed your sister?' Paget asked. He eyed her shrewdly. 'I would be inclined to say after. Once you know you can do it . . . Am I right, Mrs Etherton?'

The look she gave him was one of grudging admiration. 'I knew that Helen's money, even with the insurance and everything, wouldn't last more than a few years,' she said, 'so when Bernard Halliday died, I encouraged Charles to marry Margaret. I mean, what better chance would he have of getting his hands on that kind of money? But he needed a push. It never occurred to him until I started to nudge him in the right direction. It wasn't hard. They'd known each other since they were children; Bernard had treated Margaret badly throughout their marriage; Toni was a bitch, and Margaret needed a shoulder to cry on. It only took a little effort on his part.

'Of course, we ran into the same sort of problem we'd had with Helen. No interest in putting money into keeping the manor up, so it was up to me to keep her here, to jolly her along until it was time. We couldn't act too soon, or all the things that Toni had been saying about Charles allowing Bernard to die on the operating table, so he could marry Margaret for her money, would be dredged up again.'

Mrs Etherton's face clouded. 'Toni coming back when she did was a nuisance. It delayed things, and then, when she ran down young Tracy Nash, and was about to run away, I had to act quickly. I must admit, I did have a bit of luck there, but it all worked out in the end. Oh, and speaking of Tracy, I spoke to her doctor yesterday and he says she is doing much better than expected. She still has a long way to go, but she's going to be all right. I was so pleased.'

The church clock in Ashton Prior was striking ten as Paget drove past on his way home, and the echo of its toneless notes were still there inside his head when he turned into the driveway. He stopped in front of the garage door and switched the engine off, too tired to put the car inside.

He got out and stood for a moment to stretch and breathe in the cool night air. The sky was clear and there was a hint of frost in the air. Summer was definitely coming to a close.

Grace was waiting for him inside. She greeted him with a kiss, then stood back and held him at arms' length to look at him. 'You look so tired,' she said, 'and you must be hungry, so come into the kitchen and I'll brew a fresh pot of tea and get you something. What would you like?'

He sat down on one of the kitchen chairs and leaned his head back against the wall. 'Cheese on toast with Branston Pickle,' he said. 'Something with a bit of bite to it. The air is so dry and stuffy in those interview rooms. Tregalles claims they bring it in by the bucketful from bar rooms and swamps to lower a suspect's resistance, and I'm beginning to think there's something to that. So never mind the tea, Grace. I think I'll have a beer instead.'

Grace turned on the toaster oven, then took a beer from the fridge, and poured it into a tall glass. 'Mrs Etherton,' she said with a shake of the head as she handed it to him. 'I still can't believe it. Has she been charged?'

'With Paul's murder, yes, she has. But she talked quite freely about the other murders as well. In fact it became more of an unburdening than an interview. Although, even then, she still wanted to impress us with the way she had planned things down to the last detail. Which reminds me, thanks for letting me know about the tablets you found in her room. That helped enormously.'

Grace held up two wedges of cheese. 'Cheddar or Lancashire?' she asked. He nodded in the direction of the cheddar, and Grace put the other wedge back in the fridge and began grating the Cheddar.

He picked up the glass and drank deeply, then set it aside. 'She told us it was when Margaret Bromley had the mild stroke, or whatever it was, some months ago, that she remembered the symptoms she'd experienced from the side effects of Triazolam many years ago, because they were so very similar. So she decided to use it on Margaret to make it appear that she was losing her mind, and no one would question it when Margaret committed suicide.

'She had just started to do that when Toni Halliday turned up at the manor, and with Margaret so intent on bonding with her daughter, Mrs Etherton didn't have as many opportunities to introduce the drug into her food or drink on a regular basis, which is why the memory lapses were so random and erratic.'

'Did Charles know what she was doing?'

'Mrs Etherton says she didn't tell him because she was afraid of what his reaction might be, so he was just as baffled by the symptoms as was Lockwood. Her exact words were: "Charles didn't always know what was best for him, so I had to make those decisions for him." Unquote.'

Grace put a jar of Branston Pickle on the table, then slid the toast and bubbling cheese onto a plate and set it in front of him. 'But why kill Toni? I'm assuming she did kill Toni?'

Paget scooped a generous portion of pickles onto his plate. 'She did. She said that after Toni had been at the manor for a while, she realized that the girl could be a problem if her mother died. Regardless of the will leaving the bulk of her estate to Charles, Toni would fight him tooth and nail through the courts for more of the money. Charles, already deep in debt, would be swamped with legal bills and Margaret's estate could be tied up for years, and Charles would probably lose everything in the process. So, when Toni decided to make a run for it rather than face the prospect of going to jail after hitting Tracy Nash, it was her bad luck to run into Mrs Etherton on the stairs as she was leaving.

Mrs Etherton grabbed Paul's coat and hat off the peg in the hall to conceal her identity in case anyone should see her, and followed Toni to the barn, where she pretended to try to talk her out of leaving, then picked up the sickle and killed her.'

'And Gwyneth . . .?'

Paget shook his head. 'Of all the choices that poor girl could have made,' he said sorrowfully, 'that had to be the worst. It seems that when Gwyneth met WPC Short and learned that Farnsworth was dead, she realized she was on her own, and could be in a lot of trouble if we found her prints in the barn. She needed to talk to someone who would believe her, someone she could trust for advice, so she went back to the manor and went upstairs and knocked on Mrs Etherton's door.

'Gwyneth told Mrs Etherton everything. She said she'd been waiting for Farnsworth in the back room when Toni entered the barn. Trapped back there, she heard everything but saw nothing until she finally plucked up the courage to come out. Mrs Etherton said Gwyneth told her the voices were too muffled to identify them, but she was afraid that Gwyneth might remember something that would identify her as the killer. So she told Gwyneth she was sure that we'd been concentrating on the immediate area around the crime scene, and probably hadn't had time to look at the back room, then offered to go with her to get rid of any prints she might have left behind.'

'And killed her when they got there,' Grace said huskily. 'I *still* can't believe it. I only spoke to the woman briefly, but I *liked* her. I can't believe I could be so wrong about someone. Killing three people for . . . what?'

'Four,' Paget reminded her. 'You're forgetting her sister.'

'She confessed to that as well?' Grace shuddered. 'That is a horrible way to die. She must have really hated her sister.'

'I don't think feelings entered into it,' Paget said. 'In fact she told us that the two of them got on very well together; but when Charles needed money, and killing her sister was the only way to get it, then that was the way it had to be. I think Mrs Etherton is one of those rare people who are truly amoral.'

Grace didn't look convinced. 'Amoral?' she repeated. 'Is anyone truly amoral, Neil? Or is that just a cover for old-fashioned evil?'

Paget spread his hands. 'I really don't know,' he confessed. 'I do know we spent close to ten hours talking to her today, and the only emotion she showed in all that time was when we were talking about Charles. Although, there was a moment there when I thought I detected a touch of regret over the killing of Gwyneth.'

'So, how involved is Charles Bromley? How much did he know?'

Paget shrugged. 'That may be very hard to prove,' he said. 'I think Charles can be wilfully blind when he wants to be, and I'm not so sure they aren't two of a kind – except Charles doesn't have the stomach for the killing that his sister-in-law has.'

'Speaking of the stomach,' said Grace in an attempt to return to some sort of normal conversation, 'your food is getting cold.'

He pushed the plate aside and picked up his glass. 'Sorry, Grace,' he said. 'I'm afraid I've lost my appetite, but I will finish the beer.'

THIRTY-ONE

Monday, September 19th

No one had said very much during the ride back from court to Charter Lane, but once inside and mounting the stairs, it was Tregalles who voiced the question that was on all their minds. 'I can't say I was surprised to hear Bromley plead not guilty to attempted murder, but I was gobsmacked when Mrs Etherton pleaded not guilty to murder, especially after confessing to everything on tape. At least she didn't get bail. Too bad they gave it to him, but then, he's a Bromley and a magistrate, so what can you expect.'

'Perhaps, after spending the weekend in jail, Mrs Etherton found she wasn't too keen on spending the rest of her life behind bars,' said Paget. He turned to Molly. 'I didn't see Julian in court,' he said. 'You did contact him in Birmingham, didn't you?'

'I did,' she said, 'and he told me that he would come if he could, but if a rehearsal was called for this morning, he wouldn't be able to make it. He said he has twenty-nine lines of dialogue in this play, and there was no way he was going to chance losing the part by not being there.'

'Good to get your priorities straight, I suppose,' Tregalles observed. 'But he'd better buck up his ideas if he hopes to earn a living as an actor, because I don't think he will have a place to call home after the next few weeks.

'I suppose Mrs Etherton *might* get away with it if she pleads insanity,' he continued, but Molly was no longer interested in more speculation on how things would go on from here. Instead, her thoughts were centred on the email she'd received that morning. It was addressed to Reg and Ellen Starkie, but Molly was pleased to see that David was still copying her in. It said: In haste, arriving Heathrow 20:30 Tuesday, Flt CX253. Will drive down Wednesday, but must return to HK by next Monday. Need to work out things with Royal Broadminster, and look into schooling for Lijuan. Tell you more when I get there. Love, David.

'Molly . . .? You still with us?' Tregalles asked.

'Yes, sorry, Sergeant,' she said hastily. 'I was just thinking that I should phone Sergeant Ormside to see if he needs me out there this afternoon. I imagine we'll be spending the next day or two packing up the incident room and bringing everything back in.' She took out her phone, but Paget stopped her. 'My office first,' he said. 'Both of you. The case may be as good as over, but there are still ends to tie up.'

He sounded displeased, and Tregalles and Molly exchanged mystified glances and silent questions behind his back as they followed him in.

Paget moved behind his desk and sat down. One look at his stern features was enough to make Tregalles decide not to sit down unless invited, and Molly took her cue from him and remained standing as well.

'First of all, Tregalles,' Paget said, 'I want you to call DS McLean in Lambeth, and sort out how we are going to handle Conroy now that they've found the car he reported stolen in his own lock-up. But I want it made clear that, while we appreciate their help in finding the car, I want Conroy nailed for his part in all this. He may not have killed the major, but he certainly contributed to his death, and I want to see him pay for that. So, no deals . . . at least from us. What the CPS decides to do when they get it is up to them. OK?'

'Right, boss.' Tregalles turned to leave, but Paget stopped him. 'There's something else, first,' he said as he opened a drawer and took out an envelope. He opened it, and removed a single sheet of A4 paper.

'I received this yesterday afternoon,' he said crisply. 'I think you should read it and give me your comments.' Tregalles reached for the paper, but Paget flicked it away and handed it to Molly.

Her hand shook as she took it, and her eyes blurred as she tried to focus on the fine print. Slowly, her expression changed. She looked up at Paget, who was now on his feet.

'Congratulations, *Sergeant* Forsythe, on a well-deserved promotion,' he said, grinning broadly. 'I'm sure you'll find a copy of this in the post when you get home.' He stuck out his hand.

There were tears in her eyes as she gripped his hand. 'Thank you, sir,' she said huskily. 'Thank you very, very much.' She half turned toward Tregalles, not sure how he might take the news. But he surprised her by putting an arm around her shoulders and planting a kiss on her cheek.'

'Congratulations, Molly,' he said and grinned. 'I've never kissed a sergeant before,' he added with a chuckle. 'Can't wait to tell Audrey, specially if I don't tell her right away who it was.' His manner changed. 'But seriously, Molly, I hope you realize what this means?' Molly braced herself. She never knew what to expect from Tregalles. 'It means,' he said solemnly, 'it's your shout in the pub, tonight, so come prepared.'

There was enough work on his own desk to keep Paget occupied for the next couple of days, but there was just as much waiting upstairs in Alcott's old office, and he couldn't keep leaving it for Fiona to deal with. He looked at the clock, then made for the stairs; he could still get two or three hours in and be home by six . . . or seven at the latest.

'They look worse than they are,' Fiona said as she set out a stack of folders on the desk 'but I can go through them with you if you wish. Most of them just need your signature, but I've put notes on the ones that need your attention.'

'I'll give you a shout if I get into trouble,' he said. 'And thanks, Fiona.' He watched her as she left the office. If he did get the superintendent's job, he couldn't ask for a better secretary.

He settled down to work, but he'd barely started when the phone rang. The duty sergeant was on the line. 'Chief Constable's on his way up, sir,' he said. 'Thought you would like to know.'

Wyckham? Charter Lane was less than a quarter of a mile from New Street, but it could have been fifty miles away, considering the number of times the chief constable had covered the distance between them. It had to have something to do with the Bromley case, but was that a good thing or bad?

Two minutes later, the chief constable appeared in the doorway, and Paget rose to meet him. 'Chief Constable,' he said neutrally as he came out from behind the desk.

Wyckham closed the door. 'Just came by to congratulate you on a successful conclusion to the Bromley case,' he said as he shook Paget's hand. 'A job well done, but I must confess I would never have suspected Beth Etherton. I've known that woman for years. Always rather admired her. Good bridge player, too. Hard to believe. The woman must be demented. But to drag poor old Charles into her schemes . . . Difficult for him, very difficult indeed.' He shook his head sadly, then brightened. 'Still, he was released on bail. No doubt it will all be cleared up in due course.'

'I'm afraid it may be a little more complicated than that, sir,' Paget said cautiously.

'Yes, yes, of course,' Sir Robert agreed. 'Bound to take some time to sort things out. But that's enough of that. I'm really here on a different errand. Shall we sit down?'

He pulled a chair toward him and settled into it with his elbows on the arms, hands steepled beneath his chin. He sat there, frowning as if thinking carefully before he spoke. Paget returned to his own chair and sat down.

'Rather appropriate,' Wyckham said, 'being here in DS Alcott's old office, I mean, since it is the position of detective superintendent I want to talk to you about. I felt I should come to give you the news myself and explain the situation. We had five applicants, although, to be honest, three of them were a waste of time, so it came down to two in the end, both of whom were equally well qualified, and I must say I was very impressed with your record and the way you conducted yourself in the interview. Very impressed indeed.'

'However . . .' Sir Robert paused, and Paget braced himself. The kiss of death. He wasn't going to get it.

'However,' the chief constable said again, 'the decision doesn't rest with me, although you certainly had my vote. It rests with the Local Police Authority, and they feel it is time to redress the balance, to keep up with the times, so to speak, so I'm afraid the vote went to the other candidate. A DCI Pierce from the Thames Valley Police. Fine background. Very similar to your own, in fact. Time with the Met and so forth.'

Paget's heart stood still. *Pierce?* Thames Valley? The Met? He took a deep breath to steady his voice. 'Would that be *Amanda* Pierce by any chance, sir?' he asked.

'Why, yes, that's right. Amanda Pierce. Have you two met? Do you know her?

'Oh, yes, we've met,' said Paget tightly, remembering . . .

Sir Robert got to his feet. 'Well, that's a plus, then, if you two know each other, isn't it?' he said heartily. 'Off to a good start. No, don't bother to see me out. Should know my way by now.'